PRAISE FO

MW01287294

"A raw and unflinching dystopian horror story. Laura Elliott has crafted a deft fever dream and a deeply brilliant meditation on the very real terrors of capitalism, productivity, exploitation and healthcare. Fuelled by nightmares, this book is sure to leave you just as sleepless as me."
Lucy Rose, author of *The Lamb*

"Hugely imaginative, yet meticulous in its detail, this is a disturbingly prescient warning of humankind's greed for power and knowledge at the expense of all else. Haunting and compelling, it is a genuinely plausible apocalyptic tale, and is all the more terrifying for that."
Lucie McKnight Hardy, author of
Water Shall Refuse Them

"Awakened is an utterly compulsive read. Merging the gothic vibes of Frankenstein or Dracula with the chilling horror of a zombie apocalypse and dystopian future, Awakened will keep you up late not just because of it's unputdownable story, but through the questions it poses: what does it mean to be human? When does progress meet a line better not crossed? And is there a way back if it has been? Riveting, insightful and complex, this incredible debut is not to be missed. Just brace yourself for a few sleepless nights…"
Amy Clarkin, author of *Who Watches This Place*

"Tense and timely, Awakened is a deft exploration of a dystopia where capitalistic interests have run rampant. With a well-developed cast of characters and a feeling of creeping dread that becomes a feverish nightmare, this gothic sci-fi tale will keep you awake at night."
MK Hardy, author of *The Needfire*

Laura Elliott

AWAKENED

ANGRY
ROBOT

ANGRY ROBOT
An imprint of Watkins Media Ltd

Unit 11, Shepperton House
89-93 Shepperton Road
London N1 3DF
UK

angryrobotbooks.com
the raven o'er the infected house

An Angry Robot paperback original, 2025

Edited by Simon Spanton Walker and Alan Heal
Cover by Sarah O'Flaherty
Set in Meridien

ISBN 978 1 91599 890 3
Ebook ISBN 978 1 91599 891 0

Printed and bound in the United Kingdom by CPI Group (UK) Ltd, Croydon CR0 4YY

The manufacturer's authorised representative in the EU for product safety is eucomply OÜ - Pärnu mnt 139b-14, 11317 Tallinn, Estonia, hello@eucompliancepartner.com; www.eucompliancepartner.com

9 8 7 6 5 4 3 2 1

MIX
Paper | Supporting responsible forestry
FSC
www.fsc.org
FSC® C013604

For James, who kept me alive

TERATOLOGY (noun): from the Greek *teras*, meaning *monster* or *marvel*

1. The scientific study of human abnormalities
2. Relating to fantastic creatures or monsters in myth

but in the minutes before dawn there is peace in the Tower and this moment is all that there is, with a Traitors' Gate view over the dead city and the river at rush and the ravens, the ravens splitting the fog on dark wings while the two goats bleat in the stable and Thane's lamp is lit, a will-o'-the wisp at Lanthorn which rises through the wet air and grows, grows in my mind to become a beacon of roaring fire and a candle for the dead, the dead who walk and are sleepless and are everywhere and nowhere, and now when the sun rises over London the fog burns away slowly, slowly, and then all at once, raising the curtain on my holy moment and a day that smiles with its teeth

MARCH

2ND MARCH

I've been an insomniac all of my life, but I'm not Sleepless
and I won't become Sleepless, just as long as the chips that
were put into their heads never get put into mine. There's
little chance of that, since I won't put the machinery into my
brain and neither will Edgar and neither will the Professor,
and we're the only three left who could. I don't want to be
Sleepless, but insomnia is a treasured friend and it keeps me
company during the long, dark quiet, during the deepening
hours in which only I'm alive and awake and only Mother
is here as my witness.

Mother, who lies in the spare room across the landing
from mine, who sleeps on a double bed by the window just
like mine, who has eyes that are just like mine and a smile
that is just like mine, though I haven't seen it for a long
time. And perhaps there is something in this doubling that
becomes clear to me only at night, when I walk from my
door to hers and cross the threshold into this room of the
sick, which, like all rooms of the sick, exists outside of time.

Mother's room doesn't alter with the ticking of the clock,
and nor does it respond to the rising and setting of the sun.
It persists apart from these comforting rhythms, a pocket
universe in which the body is the world and the world is the
body, eternal. The streets beyond these walls could burn and

the seas could rise, and she would lie here just as she always does, waiting for me to arrive. Perhaps – an unnerving thought – she doesn't wait for me at all. Perhaps her waiting is a state I've imposed on her, and only I anticipate these nights spent together in peace. But anticipate them I do.

The heavy velvet of the closed curtains. The dust that streaks them like moth tears, and the cardboard wrapped around the walls that I tape and tape in dubious configurations to protect her from the pain of sound. The darkness which has a texture, which grows substance and weight and form the longer I sit there in the chair by the side of her bed. I sit there in the night, and I feel the weight of gravity increase and draw down the darkness like a confectioner spinning sugar sculptures out of the absence of light. I sit there and I think. I think about sleep, and I think that, for once, I ought to try and tell you the truth.

4TH MARCH

We moved into the Tower of London during the frantic summer of 2055. At the time, the city was glutting itself on an excess of industry, and on every street there rang a swarm of tramping footsteps and lowing bodies packed together like cattle for the market. London was in its final bloom, but the impending collapse was hidden by a last long gulp of plenty. Looking back, there was no sense of dread in the air and no subtle suggestion that a disaster was approaching. In those final years, the prevailing emotion was one of exuberance and energy. We let the monster swallow us, and we were happy as we were digested.

Now expelled, that first summer has taken on a peculiar tone in my memory. Nostalgia colours the Tower's walls in gold and the laboratory lights are dazzling, the contrast turned up so high that it hurts to look at too closely. If I close my eyes, I can still see us as we were – hastened, excited, flushed and fat with pride and purpose. A society of ignorants in bliss. Our most generous benefactor was the Anonymous Billionaire, he who had bought the historic site, repurposed it, and settled the Orex Corporation in its bowels.

Our laboratory is still situated on the first floor of the White Tower, in vast and ancient rooms that were once the royal apartments. I arrived there this morning to find

Edgar and Professor Galen already at work. Our three lines of workbenches had been pushed to the walls and the machinery covered in protective sheets. This left only a great open space, save for a single patient bay behind a green medical curtain that drew my gaze like a shroud.

I watched the curtain, and I could almost convince myself that the curtain watched me.

"Courage, dear heart," the Professor said. "All great discoveries are difficult. Let us not cower at the first sign of hardship."

"She can't help it," Edgar told him. "She is a creature of pity." He had dressed himself for the occasion in an embroidered waistcoat, a red cravat, and a bowler hat that Alison had unearthed in the warren of our extant storage. He reminded me less of the Lord he'd once been and more of a praying mantis, thin and wiry and creeping.

Before we could begin, we were interrupted by the febrile whirr of the lift, and Maryam wheeled herself in. She didn't acknowledge us, instead taking up a spot by the door with a pile of knitting in her lap and the air of someone at protest.

"Doctor Bashir. It's good of you to join us after all," the Professor said. "Are you here to bear witness or are you participating today?"

"We're all participating in this, Michael, whether we wanted to or not."

"Does that mean we can count on your assistance?"

Maryam twirled a skein of wool expertly around her wrist and shook her shoulders as though casting off a chill. "I'm here for Thea. The two of you can do whatever you want."

If the Professor was irritated by her dismissal, I wasn't able to tell. He nonetheless affected an air of indifference and asked us if we were ready to start.

The truth, if I'd have been able to tell it to him, was that I was stuck in a peculiar state of anticipation and revulsion. That the thought of the next few hours filled me with primal disgust, which had manifested itself as an intense need simply to get everything over with. I didn't know how to explain that to him, so I merely nodded, and then Edgar clapped his hands together and our patient's shrieking split the air.

I wish now that I could describe the noise they make with any accuracy. I wish it because I am a scientist, and when a thing can be precisely described, it can at least be partially understood. The inability to quantify the sound, the utter failure of analogy, is almost as distressing as the sound itself. The pitch oscillates between ten and fifteen thousand hertz, swooping up and down the frequency scale every five seconds with a stridency that's intensely painful. It clocks in at around 130 decibels, which is about the same level as a thunderclap. Perhaps that's the analogy I'm looking for.

They scream a violent grief like a thunderclap.

But the screaming began – that was the point. The screaming began, and so we put our noise-cancelling headphones on, the Professor handed us all a computer tablet, and he typed on his own the words: *Unto the breach.* The projected screen on the wall behind him relayed the message, and Maryam retaliated with an image of a dog licking its own bollocks, which was impressive because I didn't know the system could send pictures yet.

The screaming continued, and I arranged my desk. I placed the laptop in the centre, then the A4 pad to the right. I had a pencil and two black pens, just in case one ran out, and I put the tablet next to those. Then I helped the Professor put on his surgical gloves and tied his robe more tightly at his waist.

While this was happening, Edgar was setting up the video camera and placing the tripod next to my desk. It struck me that this meant our recordings would be from my perspective, and I didn't know whether that made me feel powerful or afraid. All the while, Maryam knitted and watched us and said nothing.

Is everyone ready? the Professor typed.

Edgar had taken up his position by the curtain. In his bowler hat and waistcoat, he put me in mind of some wild conductor of a cabaret. I drew in a breath and nodded to the Professor, who nodded to Edgar, who looked to Maryam when her needles stopped moving. With a decided flourish, Lord Trevelyan stepped up to the curtain and drew it open. But it didn't feel like a holy moment. It felt like a fall through the veil.

SUBJECT 001:
ASSESSMENT #1

04/03/2063

Subject is a white male, approximately thirty years of age, with dark brown hair shorn to the ears, and unnaturally blue eyes. Subject is malnourished but retains great physical strength. His skin is unblemished and boasts a brittle hardness when palpated.

Skin samples taken at 09:47 revealed nothing unusual when observed under the microscope. However, when the same samples were viewed again at 14:23, subtle changes in mitochondrial replication were observed. By 18:30, the cells had duplicated to such an extent that it was thought safer to dispose of them than to allow them to propagate. The skin cells were incinerated at 19:04 and the Petri dish sterilised.

At first glance, the subject retains an average human appearance. However, subtle differences in muscle mass, bone structure, and dental and nail formation are apparent. The nails of the right hand measure approximately 1.5 inches and display an abnormally formed layer of keratin, giving them increased strength and a sharpened point. The nails of the left hand are the same, except for those on the index and middle fingers, which were snapped off during capture. Despite how recently the injury was obtained, there is already evidence of significant growth. The rate of growth will be monitored as a matter of priority.

The subject is of a standard build for someone of his height and age. However, hypertrophic muscles in the shoulders, back, and arms suggest unusual upper-body strength. Whether the skeleton has evolved to mimic this change will be the focus of future investigations.

The most obvious mutation remains the subject's dentistry. Along with the usual thirty-two adult teeth, subject possesses a second row of smaller teeth protruding from the hard palate behind the gum line. The incisors on this second row are sharper and more prominent, and there is evidence to suggest that they shed and regrow, much like those found in sharks.

Aside from the skin samples taken from the subject's forearms, a mouth swab was also obtained with the aid of an extended dental probe. Three vials of blood were drawn, and a third nail was clipped from the left big toe. Although efforts were made to engage the subject, he didn't respond to attempts at conversation and seemed unable to understand or react to speech.

Subject's reflexes were hyper-reactive and pupils were equal and responsive. Contraction of the pupil when exposed to moderate light, along with pain signs from the subject, suggest a sensitivity to all but the most mild light. This fits with existing knowledge gleaned from previous subject encounters, indicating that they possess increased night vision.

At 16:13, incisions were made into the subject's arms, legs, and stomach. Rate of inflammation and healing will be measured over the coming days. The subject has been held at the Tower for three days and four nights. A review of the security footage from its room confirms what we already suspected.

The subject does not sleep.

8TH MARCH

I used to be afraid of sleep. I don't think that's unusual for children, but the reason for my fear probably was. It wasn't that I had nightmares, or if I did they were only of the garden-variety childish anxieties. It wasn't even that I was afraid of the dark. It was that my mother was plagued by sleep, and I feared the same might one day happen to me.

She'd been a whirlwind of colour in my earliest years. I remember those times as featuring her prominently, amongst all of the usual impressions of texture and sound. A scratchy carpet in front of an open fireplace; thick white bread with banana and sugar between the slices, squashing between my fingers and sticking to the roof of my mouth. But most of all I remember her in the background of it all – the constant movement of some impossible energy in the sparkling edges of my memory.

My earliest recollections are filled with the feeling of being swept away, picked up from carpets and beds and high chairs, and hauled through the air with little warning.

"Come on, little potato. Let's have an adventure."

And then we'd be on the move, from inside to outside, across gardens and over roads, from a beach and into the sea, and always, always moving. When I wrote research applications in my twenties, I invariably wrote that I was adaptable. The truth was, she had made me adaptable.

Refusing her was like trying to refuse the tide. Or perhaps she was the moon and I was the tide, pulled inexorably by her orbit and taken wherever she went. No matter how abrupt the change, I was always secretly grateful for it. What would the ocean be without the tides? Time with her was always better than time without her, and her ability to draw people in was simply a force of nature. Unchangeable. Immutable in the way of the planets. Until, one day, it wasn't.

I don't think there was a defining moment of revelation in my childhood, no point at which I stood outside of myself – outside our little family of two – and realised, *The moon is fading from the sky*. It happened like the fog burning away in the sun – slowly, and then all at once. The house grew quieter, as though silence were a physical thing that had colonised the space. Windows once thrown open to the roar of traffic and passing neighbours suddenly fell shut, and the woman who'd once crackled like a firework and persuaded like the moon took to her bed bit by bit.

They called the illness postviral, which meant a number of different things depending on who you asked. For most people, it simply meant that you'd been sick with something and it was taking too long to get better. For others, it meant that you were crazy, or lazy, or perhaps neither of these things, but at any rate that you weren't really sick. Some doctors thought she'd get better. Some didn't. Some listened to her and ordered blood tests that never found anything. Some wouldn't even go that far.

It came to me in later years that there was little dignity in suffering, but even less in suffering that was doubted. My mother suffered, and she suffered more so because there was a question mark hanging like the sword of Damocles over the legitimacy of her plight. The doubt of doctors was a poison to her efforts to survive. Every appointment became a battleground when it should have been a relief. The effort to become well again was blocked by the very people who were meant to help her. When doctors don't believe you, who else can you turn to for help?

Somewhere along the way, before I knew any better, I developed the idea that sleep was like some terrible magnet, that the more of it you got, the more of it you attracted, until one day you could hardly stand to open your eyes without the compulsion to close them again.

Even as an adult, a researcher in fatiguing illnesses, I was terrified of sleep, and at the same time I was also horrified by tiredness. At every yawn, I wondered, was this going to be it? Was this going to be the day the same kind of illness crept up on me? Under the circumstances, it would have made sense for me to rest more, not less, but our actions aren't always logical. Instead of coveting sleep, I abhorred it. Distrusted and resented it.

When I started university at eighteen, leaving my faded moon of a mother to her four dark walls, I didn't just burn the candle at both ends – I set the wax on fire and stripped out the fuse. If Mother couldn't be the moon anymore then I would be the tide that brought her home.

14TH MARCH

I've always thought of sleep as a form of possession and dreams as a symptom of haunting. Waves of hormones roll through our bodies demanding obedience and unconsciousness, and as we sink beneath their weight our minds replay images and sounds that are beyond our conscious control. In sleep, we might see people long dead, hold conversations with absent friends, walk across landscapes both real and fictional, and wake to find that we never left our beds. Can there be anything more paranormal than that?

I've never slept well, and this morning I woke to find an old spectre standing tall at the foot of my bed. My limbs were locked and my eyes were open, and the woman peered down at me with the kind of focus that no sane person could tolerate. It wasn't the first time sleep paralysis had overcome me, but it had been years since my Grey Lady had visited and I worried over what she might mean.

I understood, of course, that the hallucination was not the power of the mind but one of the brain. It was the fault of hormones and synapses firing out of sync and bringing my dreams to life. But even though I could understand the science, I couldn't influence its effects. In the moment, I was as terrified as a child. My rational voice meant nothing against the flood of adrenaline, the misstep of my neurons, and the faceless phantom that I *knew,* despite all sense and reason, felt me, perceived me, and meant me great harm. She was a shadow of malicious intent, bearing down on me with her dank hair and hooded eyes, and there was nothing I could do.

When the episode had passed, I came to true waking with a sound of strangulation, and heard myself choke out the words, *What do you want from me?* Then I was ashamed, and it was this feeling that lingered within me when I stood on the battlements at dawn.

If any part of this place can be said to be mine, it must be the walkway above Traitors' Gate. Looking south over the Thames, the ragstone battlements are weathered and dark before the sunrise touches them. Beneath the floor, there's the hush of the river as it drains under the bars, following the ancient water path that once bore prisoners inside. Sometimes, the ravens join me, and I find that comforting. If superstition is to be believed, then there's some hope left for all of us just as long as they remain.

I come here most mornings to be alone, straddling the border between night and day and feeling history seep through the stones. It's at this hinterland that I feel myself a part of something. My ego dissolves against the weight of time and the feeble light of dawn, while I watch Alex clear flotsam from the hydro-turbines and track the drifting boats.

It's unusual that I'm disturbed here, but this morning I heard Alison's footsteps before I saw her and knew she was seeking me. She brought me another coffee – a clever way of making sure I couldn't ignore her – then asked me something I wasn't prepared for.

"How do you define yourself?"

I didn't know how to reply.

Alison has always been a mystery to me, even at a distance. Normally, stepping back from a person allows me to get a better read on them – what makes little sense in the micro becomes less opaque in the macro – but it isn't like that with her, although I'd say that we were friends. She's a couple of years younger than I am, but she has a stoic air about her that would seem more natural on someone far older – on a veteran, perhaps, like Thane.

There was something even more inward-facing about her this morning, as though she'd stepped away from the world and was existing a few feet above herself, looking down at us all from on high. She'd come straight from bed, and was still wearing her pink silk bonnet and wrapped in a trench coat that I suspected hid her nightclothes. It isn't unusual for the Professor or me to be seen in our dressing gowns first thing, but with Thane as her boss Alison can hardly afford to appear so dishevelled.

So, what had roused her from her bed so early and with so little of her usual poise, I wondered? Was it the creature we'd locked in the Tower, held in a sterile hospital bay that may as well have been a medieval prison cell? Did she, like me, feel the cloying weight of a thousand words left unspoken, and sense that each of us was still waiting for someone else to break the silence? Did she feel guilt or hope, joy or fear, disgust or admiration? Or did she feel nothing at all? Was that why she was here?

These aren't the kinds of questions you can just ask someone, even if they seek you out at sunrise and hand you a cup of coffee because they don't want to be alone, so I contented myself with asking them inside my head and watching the dawn light play over her face while the fog burned away.

Maryam had once told me she thought Alison had a hard face, like that of a soldier, though she'd only been temping as a porter when the world ended – she isn't real armed forces like Thane. It surprised me, to hear Maryam say it, because I've never thought the same. Perhaps you could get that impression from a distance, if you saw her running drills or standing at the watchtowers looking for signs of life, but up close she isn't like that at all. In fact, in some ways Alison is all softness. Behind the army training Thane puts her through, and the sharpness of her words when tempers become frayed, there's something maddeningly gentle about her. She's isn't nurturing like Maryam or delicate like Miles, but Alison's biggest secret is that she cares.

It matters to her that Maryam gets her seeds and Thane gets to play his game of cards with whoever's available on a Friday night. When Miles was still recovering from his burns and confined for long months to the hospital, it mattered to her that he was in pain, so much so that she'd sit with him through the night even if it wasn't her turn to be there. And clearly, I matter enough to her that she knows how I take my coffee, even though I don't think I've ever told her – black with two sugars, and always in the blue mug with a chip in the rim. I don't think even Maryam knows that.

Perhaps that's what I can't figure out about Alison. Normally I'm better at a distance, but looking at Alison from afar only ensures that you get her wrong. She isn't truthful on the macro level. You have to get closer to see her clearly, and I don't think that's the case for most people. At least, it isn't the case for me.

"People don't always like it when you do that, you know."

Her words startled me. "Sorry, I didn't mean to stare."

"It's okay. It doesn't bother me."

"Really?" It bothered most people. I tried not to let them catch me doing it.

"There are different kinds of staring," she said. "If I thought you were thinking something bad then it would bother me."

"How do you know I'm not?"

She turned away from the river, and even though her face was hard her eyes were laughing at me.

"Are you?" she asked.

"No."

"Well then."

And that was that.

I was still thinking about her first question, about how I defined myself, and whether that was the question she'd really wanted to ask when it would have made more sense for her to be worried about how *she* defined *her*self – if that was really what was worrying her at all. But even though we stood together until the sun was well and truly up, and Alex had finished his daily checks, she didn't ask me again. I hope that standing with me for a while helped her to work something out, even if I couldn't understand what she needed.

18TH MARCH

In 1951, a young Black woman called Henrietta Lacks died of cervical cancer in a "coloured ward" in Johns Hopkins Hospital, Baltimore, USA. Unbeknownst to her, during the course of her treatment her cervix was biopsied and the tissue delivered to the laboratory of a doctor by the name of George Gey. There, analysis of Henrietta's cells would bring about one of the most important breakthroughs in the history of medical research.

Genetically modifying a cell is the basis for creating new life – and improving upon it – but in the 1950s no one had yet found a way to stop transplanted cells from dying before they could be studied. HeLa cells, as they were named, were different. They not only survived their transplant into Gey's culture medium but grew so quickly that they became known as the world's first immortal human cell.

By the time I began my own research, HeLa cells could be found in nearly every genetic research lab in the world. They were instrumental in creating the polio vaccine, researching the effects of radiation, and developing treatments for AIDS. It's no exaggeration to say that without this stolen biopsy millions of people would have died from preventable diseases. But Henrietta never knew that a piece of her body had been taken, and for a long time neither did her family.

I wonder how she would have felt if she'd known that there are more of her cells living on this planet now than there were when she was alive. I wonder what she would think if she'd known just how many of her miraculous cells I've handled, or that they now form the basis of the biomatrix at the heart of every neuralchip. I wonder how she would have felt if she'd known what had been done to her, and the way in which we've made an unholy transubstantiation of her death into life into death. I wonder if her cells might still be the answer, and if they are, whether I've started to ask the right questions yet.

Like all good scientists, I wonder.

20TH MARCH

I suppose we ought to be grateful that the Anonymous Billionaire's pockets were so deep and his ego so grand that he built a self-sustaining community on the site of one of England's oldest landmarks. I thought of him this morning – the man in the 22nd Tower. The man cloistered in self-imposed exile that we still find ourselves compassionate enough to feed.

There was no Alex outside the walls, no draw for my gaze while the fog burnt away. He was on Billionaire Duty, delivering breakfast to our shut-in and clearing away his empty plates.

"Got another note from the loony," he said as he passed me on his way down from the battlements. "Do you think he's mad or just lonely?"

I took the scrap of paper from him and considered the question. "I think he's afraid."

"Of us?"

"Of everything."

Alex's laugh was muffled, the wet mist swallowing sound like a librarian. "He can join the club. He's lucky the rest of us are brave enough to keep him alive."

"I don't think he feels very lucky."

"Do any of us?"

He continued down the stairs, the sound of the cutlery clinking and his half-hearted whistling dampened into silence by the fog. The paper crinkled in my hand when I unfolded it, already wet in the cold spring air.

WHERE IS THE CUSTARD? HOW CAN YOU HAVE RHUBARB WITHOUT CUSTARD?

I don't know why I keep these notes. I should probably throw them away.

22ND MARCH

The subject was returned to our laboratory on a stretcher and placed behind the curtain. This time Dolly was assisting, and I wondered how the Professor had talked her down from righteous indignation to grudging acceptance in the space of only a few weeks. However he'd managed it, she was more than usually competent when we set up the room again.

"Today, we'll be monitoring the rate of healing from the previous examination's exertions," the Professor said, "and if the subject is calmer then we may be able to make use of Edgar's little brainwave too."

I didn't want to know what Edgar's little brainwave was, and for once it seemed as though Dolly and I were in agreement, as she ignored him as well. When a low rumbling sound crept from the patients' bay, her hands began to shake.

It continues to surprise me that Dolly trained as a nurse. While my lack of personal skills prevented me from entering any of the caring medical professions, I've known a lot of doctors and nurses. Some doctors studied medicine because they cared, and the really good ones often burnt out quickly and left the profession altogether. The bad doctors got into medicine for prestige or family pride, and they tended to stick the work out more easily even if their patients wished they hadn't.

Nurses, though, are a different breed to doctors. There have always been those who cared and those who didn't, those who went above and beyond for their patients and those who simply enjoyed their power over someone comparatively helpless. But one thing that all nurses have in common, in my experience, is that they have a vein of steel inside themselves somewhere. It could be a cruel vein or a caring vein, but the strength of it is always there.

Dolly, as far as I've been able to tell, has none of the steel necessary for her chosen profession. This is perhaps because she was still just a student when society crumbled. Given a few more years, she might have found herself horrified by the idealistic choice she'd made fresh out of school. It might be that even now she realised that she'd misjudged the true nature of her personality and yet remained stuck with her choice in a way that felt irrevocable.

Perhaps that's what Alison meant when she asked how I defined myself. If she brings it up again, maybe that's what I'll tell her – that I think my old-world definitions of myself still fit, but that we might have been defining Dolly wrongly all this time. That to think of her as a nurse is fundamentally false, and really she's someone that we don't know, and indeed have never known. The worst thing about this is that I don't think she realises it, or if she does, it's only enough to make her apathetic.

Even with the steady grumbling coming from behind the curtain, even though her body shook with it, Dolly still gave the impression that she didn't care; that her work was just a series of actions she was undertaking until she could get back to the business of living. By that, I mean the business of coaxing the ravens down from the battlements, or allowing Miles to trail after her like a lovesick puppy for most of the live-long day.

Perhaps I'm being unfair. At least without Edgar there, the subject was calm, even when we drew back the curtain and the Professor gestured for Dolly to stand by the instrument tray. This gave me a chance to study it properly for the first time, even though I wasn't sure I wanted to. Regardless of my feelings, my job today was to look – a deceptively simple thing.

The subject had been bound to the bed. Leather straps were wrapped around its chest, the tops of its thighs, and its neck. There were smaller metal restraints at its wrists, ankles, and forearms. It still wore the same ragged clothes we'd found it in, because despite our early attempts at sedation all anaesthesia had been unsuccessful.

Its black jeans hung in tatters from the knees, barely held up by a torn brown belt. Its shirt might once have been white, but now it was a dirty grey-brown, the colour of the Thames at low tide. This, too, was ripped into little more than rags, and against the unnatural smoothness of the subject's skin the sterile incision we'd made in its stomach was vivid and arresting. It reminded me of a caesarean scar.

The incisions on its arm and leg were completely healed, but the caesarean cut was the one Edgar had made, and it must have been deeper than I'd realised. The Professor took swabs from the wound, noting depth and swelling along with any pain response. And all the while the subject growled low in its throat, its eyes roving restlessly around the space. Its muscles strained, but not against its restraints. It put me in mind of a rabbit, flattened to the ground at the approach of a fox. At first I didn't know why this physicality unnerved me, but then the thought came that this trembling was the result of an action that hadn't been completed, that it was priming itself for movement but gave no signal as to what that might be.

Despite the subject's physical agitation, the examination was going well. Dolly handed the Professor the required instruments with a professionalism I'd rarely seen her display. The Professor, delighted by the potential for discovery, hummed to himself while he manoeuvred around the creature, and I fixed my gaze on our nightmare in chains. All was calm, until my spare pen rolled off the desk and clattered to the floor. The sound rang out loud in the quiet.

The subject's head snapped around like a python about to strike, and in that moment I felt electric. Its gaze pinned me, and I knew then that I was the rabbit and it some predator that nature hadn't equipped me to face. I froze like prey, and I swear it noticed me. Not in the primal, snapping sense that it did everyone, the sense of a predator on the hunt. No, there was intelligence behind those eyes. Perhaps even recognition.

"Hold there, Thea," the Professor said. "Hold there."

As if I could have done anything else.

The subject watched me. Sharp blue eyes that looked too deep. It growled, and maybe I imagined it but I thought that the cadence changed. I can't be sure of it now, and I'm trying to be as objective as I can. I hope that comes across.

"What's it doing?"

Its eyes narrowed and I wanted to tell Dolly to shut up.

"Why's it doing that?"

I almost said it out loud – *shut up, shut up, you aren't the one it's watching* – but I couldn't. If I'd spoken, I was certain it would have started screaming, and I couldn't bear the thought of looking into its eyes while it screamed.

"Fascinating," the Professor said. "Look at how it focuses."

"But why is it doing that?" Dolly asked.

"It could be a form of hunting behaviour. Instinctual, you see. Or it could be much less developed than that, like when you hold a brightly coloured rattle in front of a baby's face."

It didn't feel like that to me. There was something present in those eyes, something that catalogued, considered, and toed the line of a decision.

"Keep it there, Thea. Let me see if I can check its eyes."

Caught in the gravity of its attention, I couldn't have moved if the room had set alight. The Professor leant in, holding the ophthalmoscope an arm's length away from the subject's face. Dolly was wittering – *careful, careful, careful*. There was sweat running down my neck, and I felt my spine pull taut as a drumskin and my heart start to pound.

"Fascinating." The Professor leant closer, and I saw the change in its eyes an instant before it happened. The subject's neck snapped forward like a cork popping, its jaw opened so wide that I almost thought it had dislocated. In retrospect, it's difficult to believe the Professor avoided major injury, because the speed was fundamentally inhuman. Perhaps a prey animal's adrenaline can sometimes win the day, but it may have simply been luck.

All of us moved at once. The Professor lurched backwards, Dolly flung her hands over her face as though shielding herself from a horror film, and I launched myself up and knocked my chair to the ground even though I couldn't have reached them in time. The subject's jaws continued to snap open and closed. It didn't seem to be able to stop.

Even when the Professor fell to the floor out of its reach, the subject heaved towards him, its neck elongated at an unnatural angle, tendons straining, jaw vibrating, snarling from between its parted lips. Perhaps I'm letting my imagination run away with me, but I could have sworn it sounded triumphant.

"Professor! Are you okay?" I knelt by his side and helped him to sit. His carefully smoothed hair – always prone to become flyaway in the breeze – was in disarray, giving him the appearance of a truly nutty professor. His spectacles were askew, one of the arms hanging at an angle. He took hold of my elbow with one hand even as he waved me away with the other.

"I'm fine," he insisted. "Don't fuss. Don't fuss now, I said."

Up close, I could hear the gentle wheeze in his chest, see the spider veins that crawled across the bridge of his nose, and note the deep red ring around his lips from his habit of drinking raspberry fruit teas. And then I saw the cut. It was only small, little more than a paper cut, an inch-long slit of red at the tip of his chin.

"Professor," I said. "You're bleeding."

I tried to be calm about it. Certainly, my voice was calm, though a feeling of impending doom was rushing through my blood and I can't be sure my hands weren't shaking when I helped him back to his feet.

"Bleeding?" He sounded as though he were enquiring about the weather, but he paled when he raised his hand to his chin and it came away with a dot of red in the centre of his palm. It looked like a mosquito bite, I thought, and then wondered about malaria, about how a small sting can sometimes be the start of something more serious. About how things in the blood can multiply and swarm, occupying healthy cells and breaking down an organism into feed. I thought that the Professor might have thought of that, too.

"It's lucky we aren't dealing with a parasite." His voice was a little too jovial.

"Yes," I replied. "That's lucky."

My voice was a little too jovial, too.

25TH MARCH

I must continue to remind myself that we aren't dealing with a parasite. Nor are we dealing with a bacterium or a virus. In fact, we know exactly what we're dealing with, even though we don't know exactly how it happened or how to begin to fix it. We're dealing with the Orex Corporation and the company's revolutionary neuralchip. We're trying to turn it off. The problem is how well it was designed – and Edgar, the Professor and I should know, because we're the ones who designed it.

When the Anonymous Billionaire first announced his plan to conquer sleep, few people took him seriously. I was still working at the UCL lab then, keeping strange hours in the university's fatigue centre and attempting to justify my funding. My research had been progressing more slowly than I'd anticipated, and as a result my world was small, focused, and almost entirely nocturnal. I confess the press conference to announce the new grant all but passed me by.

My specialist area at the time was in the brain's glymphatic system. It had first been discovered in the early millennium, and while scientists had made good progress on researching the hormones involved in sleep, as well as the thalamus and its role as a sensory gate, I wasn't so much interested in the *how* of sleep as the *why*. Why would an organism – any organism – evolve to spend a significant portion of its life unaware of its surroundings? The vulnerability of sleep, to my mind, was a major evolutionary flaw. Surely, I thought, it would make more sense not to need it, for the things it accomplished to be achieved during waking, without the need to sink into oblivion?

That thought soon led me to another, perhaps a very simple one, but deceptively so. If every organism on earth had evolved to sleep in some form or another – and we now know that even single-celled amoebas have a limited version of sleep – then sleep itself had to be so necessary for life, that any vulnerability incurred while indulging in it was less risky than going without it. That is, that what was carried out during sleep was not just crucial for health but vital for the very development and continuation of life.

Such a revelation, simple though it was, did nothing to endear sleep to me. Rather, watching my vibrant moon of a mother succumb to it like a curse had left me with a deep and abiding distrust of this need. Because if it went wrong, and the delicate balance of life-giver became time's thief, then it was suddenly an irresistible force to which a person had to submit.

Sleep, those little slices of death, carving out ever-greater chunks of life until precious little of the waking world was left. My colleagues venerated it as a miracle. I treated it with the kind of wary respect one might show to a natural disaster. I didn't trust sleep, but I was fascinated by its stranglehold on our lives.

Still, the idea of ridding the world of sleep hadn't occurred to me. The thought that someone might want to do just that was initially more of a curious eccentricity bandied around our lab after the Anonymous Billionaire outlined his plans.

"Careful, lads, a nap'll cost you!" someone might yell if a colleague came in yawning. Or one of us might chuckle, "Time is money and sleep is loss," never realising that the company's eventual slogan would turn out to be something similar.

The concept adverts always featured some iteration of a woman climbing into bed and settling down with a smile, while on the split-screen at her side, her neighbour was out jogging, tapping judiciously on a laptop, and dancing the night away. By the end of the ad, the sleeping woman was staring, horrified, at her mounting bills, while her waking counterpart bought a house, booked a holiday, or married the love of her life.

Don't let sleep steal your success, ordered the voiceover. *Join the Orex Corporation today.*

It was clever marketing, but back then the whole concept still felt like something out of a sci-fi novel, especially to those of us who worked in the field. If there was one thing I knew to be true of sleep, it was that it was necessary for life. I didn't know for certain why, or what vital process it accomplished that could only be achieved through unconsciousness, but I believed I was getting close to a breakthrough. It seemed that Orex Corp did as well, because one day in the summer of 2052 I received their email:

Dear Doctor Chares,

Cassius Hope would like to meet. Come to the Orex Corporation building this Sunday at 11 a.m. sharp – and don't be late. Cassius hates it when people are late.

Yours in anticipation,

Professor Michael Galen.

I haven't thought about that day in years. It had been hot, London baking in a June heatwave that had made the tube rank with sweat and dust stick to every bit of exposed skin. Michael had met me in the foyer, where I'd been too busy enjoying their aircon to pay much attention to him. Then he'd led me to where Cassius was waiting on the balcony of the penthouse floor.

My first impression of the two of them was that they were a double act straight out of a Robert Louis Stevenson novel, or perhaps an old Pixar film. Michael, his day robe absent in deference to the heat, paraded around the suite in thick navy shorts and flipflops, his bald crown shining with sweat and his budding potbelly peeking out from behind a carelessly buttoned shirt. He was loud and brash, a state that I'd come to learn meant either nerves, frustration, or excitement. Cassius, in abject contrast, was thin and as neat as a pin in his crisp linen suit. He smiled with the air of a sage and hardly spoke a word until Michael had left us alone.

I sometimes wonder how different the world might have been if I'd never shown up that day, nor met with those two men who would divert the course of my life. I think of myself as I'd been then, twenty-five and determined, and I wonder if I could ever have been anything other than hopelessly out of my depth.

As a thought experiment, my reflections are patently useless. Although I can alter this account with words, skimming back and forth across the years on a whim, I can't change reality as it is. The meeting happened, the decision to join them was made, and this is where it led.

so I try to think only of the landscape, where the waterline blurs and meets with the mist and everything is damp and dazzled and shifting like breath, and the skyscrapers are nothing but looming shadows on the far shore where there should be noise and motion but isn't, where there should be life but isn't, and I think of this endless silence in movement and I think of my mother, my mother who is like the statues of this city, who is like the microcosm of this city, who is like the shell of this city and the things that hide inside this city, where every movement is internal and the surface a pretence of calm

APRIL

1ST APRIL

Let's just agree, while we're here together alone, that there's a chance that each of us may be dreaming the other. You have to admit that there's nothing in reality that could prove this theory to be wrong. You are as real to me as my own body, and yet I must be real to you too. Why else would you visit me here, an intrusion of spectral intent, with your grey face and stretched limbs and silhouette sculpted from the dark?

Perhaps I mean instead that you are a spectre of intrusive intent. Certainly, you arrive with a sense of purpose and will that anyone would find difficult to match. I believe you're more than an image. You have personality. You *desire*. You seek something from me beyond the base level of my fear. So while I understand that you belong to my dream, there's no reason to think that I don't belong to yours as well. Couldn't we decide to let each other be?

These are the things I'd like to say to the woman who stands at the foot of my bed. But just as she is a piece of my mind, I am a piece of hers, and she has dreamt me as someone without a voice. In her presence, I am a mouth stitched shut, a body paralysed, a soul screaming silently inside a container of flesh. I am made into thought only, and my thoughts ricochet like moths against the walls of my skull. In truth, I am never more myself, and never less certain of what that self is, than when she follows me out of my sleep.

3RD APRIL

When I was sixteen, Mother and I moved from our seaside bungalow in Hastings to a one-and-a-half-bedroom fourth-floor flat in Deptford. Neither of us had wanted to move, but we'd stopped speaking openly to each other in those years, and before I'd even realised we were considering it, there we suddenly were.

That first day, I remember standing like an avatar of loss in the entrance hall, carrying a box filled with old photographs that was almost too heavy to lift. I'd insisted on bringing it in myself, holding fast to the memories of a life we'd already left behind. Mother struggled out of her wheelchair and began the slow, shuffling walk to the kitchen, where the removal men had left our dining chairs, because the wheelchair didn't fit in the flat.

I hadn't realised it when we'd decided to relocate, if we'd decided it at all. It simply hadn't occurred to me to check. But right then, with our bungalow sitting empty hundreds of miles away and grey light soaking through the flat's grimy windows, and Mother trying her best to smile at this new, decrepit place we'd found ourselves in, I understood that it was a mistake.

We should never have come here. We shouldn't have left the siren song of the waves for the foghorn blare of traffic.

Mother shouldn't have been there, leaning so heavily against the peeling wallpaper that her nails left gouge marks in the woodchip. A fourth-floor flat was no place for someone who couldn't get down the stairs if the lift was out of order. What in God's name were we doing?

As soon as I'd thought it, I realised she had to be thinking the same thing, and that neither of us was going to say anything. It was the first moment in my life I can recall having had an epiphany, a sudden understanding that not only had I been unaware of my own thought processes during this period, let alone hers, but that now the scales had fallen from my eyes, there was nothing I could do about it. The choice had been made. The die had been cast. No matter whether we wept or railed against it or screamed at each other when it all became too much, the house in Hastings was gone, and we were in London instead.

Standing at the top of St Thomas's Tower, my feet planted above Traitors' Gate, I felt that same acceptance of my own short-sightedness, a crystalline understanding of my utter lack of context or power in the face of something inevitable. The fog burnt away as it always did, though more quickly perhaps than usual, as the day was going to be warm.

I'd been thinking about the greenhouses, and wondering whether Maryam would take advantage of the sudden warm snap to plant the leeks and runner beans a touch early, and if the first rows of radishes might be pulled up as early as next week. It had felt like the strangest thing, to have been thinking about thinly sliced radishes, rinsed and damp and laid atop a slice of warm goat's cheese, perhaps with a chilled glass of white wine of the kind I hadn't had in years, when I first saw them.

It's difficult to describe now, this moment of irrevocable change. I had my coffee cupped in my palms, the smell of rosemary from the herb garden drifting on the breeze, the holy moment unfurling around me, and then there they simply were. They were there the way a mountain is there. The way an explosion can blot out the sky. And I was suddenly somewhere else, outside of myself and peering down from a few inches behind my head, staring out of a grimy window in a Deptford flat, wondering how we'd ended up here.

In a state of bewilderment, I catalogued everything in the time it took me to breathe. I assessed myself first. Did I feel in control of my faculties? It was possible, I reasoned, that something in my environment had caused a hallucination. The stress of the last few years was beyond the norm of human experience. The Tower, while refurbished, could still become damp, and there were patches of persistent mould that were no doubt releasing spores into the air. It was also true that I'd been handling tissue and blood samples only recently, prepping gadolinium contrast for the MRI we intended to give the subject just as soon as we were able to sedate it.

Any one of these environmental assaults on my body might have convinced my brain to play tricks and conjure impossible images. Humanity is only rational until the very moment we aren't.

This attempt at self-assessment convinced me that I could reasonably consider myself to be sane. Yes, my heart was racing, but my mind was still calm and on recalling my morning I could identify nothing that might have left me more susceptible than usual to such a trick of the mind.

Similarly, I dismissed at once the notion that I might still be sleeping. There's a quality in the waking world that dreams can't replicate, and that is the sense of linear time.

I remembered waking, washing my face, pulling my hair back, and applying a dab of rose-scented moisturiser to my hands. When I leant forward over my mug, I could still smell the faintest trace of it, a detail that would have been missing if I hadn't been truly awake.

The most likely conclusion, then, was that they were real, but such a thought was as disturbing to my mental defences as if my sanity had been compromised.

The man was a ragged figure, standing with his head lowered to his chest and his face hidden from my eyes. Dirty brown hair, matted and stringy, hid whatever else his posture didn't. A beard that reached nearly to his chest completed the wildness of his appearance, and I felt a senseless rush of anger that he couldn't have looked more like a survivor in a disaster film if he'd dressed himself for the part.

The woman, meanwhile, appeared comparatively well cared for. Her clothes were not the tattered rags of her companion but a flowing red summer dress that swept around her feet in the breeze. She clutched her arms about herself, pulling a thick cardigan to her and leaning into the man's body as though sheltering from my gaze. Her shoulder-length hair was greasy and bedraggled, but while the man gave the appearance of chronic starvation, she, while slim, seemed nourished.

When it became clear to me that they were real, and that there were survivors beyond our walls after all, I was powerless against the rush of emotion that overcame me. I watched them with a hunger that surprised me, and a pride I had no right to feel. Their survival wasn't my success, so why did I feel such a swelling ownership over them? I rushed to the Bell Tower and rang the bell, and as the gates drew open for the first time in years, these strangers walked slowly inside.

* * *

WHO ARE THEY?
WHO ARE THEY?
WHO ARE THEY?

The man and the woman entered the Tower while breakfast was being served in the canteen. An eerie silence hung like a breath of spring over the courtyard as they crossed beneath Byward Tower and breached the curtain wall. I was still standing by the bell, and while our community trickled out from around the keep it was from there that I watched the scene unfold.

The man walked with his shoulders back, as though the Tower green were a runway and he a rising star. The woman bent towards him like a bough in a storm, her shoulders hunched and tilted into his shadow. It was an unconscious bending to his will, I thought, and disliked him even though it was irrational. Alison left the chapel at the eastern side of the compound, and I thought that I saw her smile. It was the first true emotion any of us had displayed outside of blind shock.

Thane, dressed all in black, approached them first, and Alex met him from the other side of the courtyard. I thought for one strange second that this was going to be it, that the moment of our meeting would now become the only moment, with none of us knowing how to proceed. Then, we all started moving at once.

It wasn't an action with purpose. I don't believe any of us actually made the decision to approach them, and yet we drifted towards them like satellites finding a new orbit.

The closer we got, the more their gravity seemed to increase, and the woman began to shrink, curling up on herself and bending closer to her companion.

He, on the other hand, stood straighter, his shoulders pulling back, his eyes still shadowed behind his curtain of dark hair. Up close, his skin was as pale as if he'd never seen the sun, and she was covered in minor scrapes and bruises like those a child might get after playing in the park.

It was Maryam who greeted them first, wheeling across the courtyard so quietly that I didn't notice her until she was right beside me.

"Welcome."

It seemed as good a first word as any.

"Don't be frightened, dear. No one's going to hurt you. Why don't you tell us your name?"

"She doesn't speak."

His voice startled me. I don't know why, now, or what I'd expected in its place – something weak, perhaps. Something whispered with the appropriate solemnity of the moment. I didn't anticipate its dry, rasping quality, as though pebbles were clacking in the cavity of his throat and hardening around his vocal cords.

"Doesn't or can't?" Thane asked.

"Both, I believe. But that may change." The man didn't look at our army captain when he replied. He kept his focus on Maryam, his head tilted towards his companion as though listening for the words she wouldn't say.

"She'll speak when she's ready," Maryam said. "We'll just have to make do with your name for now, young man."

He smiled. "I don't remember my name."

Thane made a sound that suggested disbelief, and Alison shifted beside me.

"So, you don't know your name and she doesn't speak. Next you'll tell us you've only just realised there's been an apocalypse and the rest of the city is dead."

"Not dead. Only dreaming." He brushed his hair away from his face, and everyone leapt back. I confess that the next minute or so is something of a blur in my mind.

I didn't move. I can say that much for certain. In fact, it was remarkably strange. It was as though I'd become a fixed point in space. I simply blinked, and when I looked again no one was where they had been before, except for the man and me. Everyone else was either a few steps further back, except for the woman, who was standing with her arms outstretched between her companion and Alison, who was pointing a gun at his head. Thane was also pointing a gun at his head, while Alex had raised his fists and seemed very confused about what he ought to do next. Maryam had been pulled backwards – by Alison, I thought – and was shuffling to dislodge a rock that had become stuck under one of her wheels.

And the woman… the woman *snarled*. I had never, until that moment, known a human to snarl. The Sleepless snarled – and growled, and screamed – but humans didn't do those things. But the woman did, and I realised that she hadn't been leaning into the man because she was afraid of us but because she was afraid *for him*. She was protecting him from us.

He laid his hands on her shoulders from behind. "Calm yourself," he said. "Their fear is understandable. But their violence isn't excusable."

There was an argument then between Thane and Maryam, but I wasn't paying enough attention to be able to reproduce it here. I only know that it was about whether or not we should shoot the man in the head and whether the woman could stay.

While they argued, Alex lowered his fists and Alison lowered her gun. Maryam stared at the woman, who was still snarling, and I studied the man. He'd turned from Alison when the shouting had started, and his expression was beyond my ability to interpret. Without the barrier of his hair, I could see that his eyes were heterochrome, one a warm, golden hazel, the other the distinctive ice blue of the Sleepless.

Much like the timbre of their screams, it's difficult to describe the colour of their eyes with any accuracy. The only thing I can say is that their eyes are blue the way the night is dark. It's as though they are the First Blue – the blue from which all other hues take their name. Needless to say, it's unmistakable.

Yet there he stood before us – one of the Sleepless, yes, but one who had walked inside our walls and started to speak.

4TH APRIL

Humans are the world's most domesticated animals, and yet we're hopelessly obsessed with wildness. Whether it's the romance and heroism of climbing mountains or the voyeuristic thrill we experience when hearing great stories of survival, humanity still wants to test itself against the elements we've kept at arm's length.

I've been thinking about wildness more and more, about what we mean when we call something wild. The pull towards wildness seems innate to us, even though the way we use the word is as something alien. We seek out wildness to discover something intrinsic to ourselves, yet we fear the wildness because it is unlike us. Both of these things cannot be true. Either we're domesticated beasts who yearn for a return to the wilderness or we're something outside of the cycle of nature, raised above our baser impulses and terrified of anything that reminds us of how ill equipped we are to survive. The only conclusion I can draw from this dichotomy is that it isn't really wildness we seek, but freedom, and it's the freedom of childhood we feel the strongest pull towards, when social conventions and responsibilities didn't hold so much sway over our lives.

True freedom, though, is an abyss. It was the feeling I'd had as a child, paddling out into the frigid ocean and suddenly finding that I'd stepped over the ridge and my feet were flailing over the unfathomable nothingness of the sea. Freedom – true freedom, the wild freedom that people think about when they get nostalgic for hardship – is an absence of the ground beneath your feet. It's the removal of all social ties, the hole in society's safety net, and the betrayal of someone you love. That is why we fear the wilderness, and that is what the Sleepless represent.

SO SAYETH THE ONE TRUE LORD WHO IN HIS ENDLESS MERCY IS THE RECEIVER OF ALL TRULY PENITENT SINNERS

CAST THE DEVILS OUT

6TH APRIL

"I just don't think you should get to decide what the rest of us are okay with."

Thane had called a meeting in the Raven's Nest, the dilapidated pub tucked beneath the shadow of the Bell Tower that was once known as The Keys, in the days when it had still served the Yeomen of the Guard. Dolly was sharing a sofa with Miles, a glass of white wine in her hand and her knees locked together primly.

"I just don't think you should get to decide," she said again. "How could you let him stay here?"

"What would you have done?" Maryam asked.

"I'd have shot him, of course! Why wouldn't you do that? You're putting all of us at risk." She looked to Thane, who closed himself off from her and turned inwards.

"Are you gonna make me into a murderer now, Dolly?" he asked. "You think you have that right?"

"It wouldn't be murder. Not when it's one of them."

"But he isn't one of them, is he?" Alison asked, putting the question to me. "He isn't like them at all."

I was still uncertain on that point, but I didn't want to say so in front of Dolly.

"No one's saying you have to be okay with it," I said instead. "We're saying that you need to let us do what we think is best. No matter what he is, he's important, so he needs to stay here and we all need to pull together to make that happen. Fighting about it gets us nowhere."

"I just don't think you should get to decide that."

Dolly looked around the room, and her gaze settled on Miles, who was thrilled to be noticed at last.

"And I don't think you should talk about everyone pulling together," she went on. "When was the last time you worked with any of us? Locked away in that lab all the time. I don't see why you should get to choose when to put us all in danger."

"Everything we do here is dangerous," I said. "As far as I can see, being locked in the lab all the time is exactly why you should trust me."

"I just don't see why we should let you and the Professor decide. And Miles agrees with me, don't you?"

"What if he really is like them?" Miles asked, obedient to the last. "What happens if this goes wrong?"

"The same thing that happens if we fail," I replied.

"We're safe here now. We shouldn't risk something happening."

"We're trapped here now. If nothing else happens, this is all that's left." I was starting to lose my temper, and since Dolly wouldn't listen to reason, I rose from my seat and held out my hand to Thane. "Captain Selassie, could I have the use of your gun, please?"

The room's silence was weighted. He looked me in the eye and I wondered what he saw in me, but he passed me the gun all the same.

"Thank you."

I crossed the floor to Dolly, and held the weapon out as though I were offering her a gift. "Here you are, Nurse Reed.

There are two survivors in Beauchamp Tower, a man and a woman. If you don't want them here, you know what to do. We'll wait by the bar while you take care of them, shall we?"

Her cheeks pinked and her lips pinched together like those of a child on the verge of a tantrum. I was almost certain she was about to hit me.

"That isn't fair," she said. "I didn't say I wanted to kill them."

"No, you said you wanted one of us to kill them, and I'm showing you why that isn't going to happen. If you want them dead, you can take some responsibility and do it yourself. If you can't, then maybe that's your answer as to whether or not they can stay."

The colour in her face was impressive, and so was the self-control she displayed in not reaching out and slapping me. I almost wished she would, simply to emphasise the reasonable tone of my argument and the hysterical quality of hers. Eventually, I felt I'd made my point well enough, so I returned Thane's gun to him and retook my seat.

"You're all crazy," Dolly spat. "Completely fucking crazy."

I thought that was a little ironic, all things considered, but I'd goaded her enough for one evening so I held my tongue.

"This is an opportunity, Nurse Reed," the Professor said. "After all of this time, we have a glimmer of hope and a chance to make dear Cassius proud."

9TH APRIL

When I first met Doctor Cassius Hope, he was already dying.

He began our meeting on the balcony of the Orex Corporation's skyscraper in Canary Wharf, greeting me with a pink gin martini in a frosted glass and an elaborate afternoon tea. He was tall, thin, with a short afro and a wide smile, and he wore a spotless white linen suit over a pale blue shirt with brown brogues. I felt from the start that I'd stepped onto a film set and no one had bothered to tell me.

Doctor Hope, it turned out – Doctor, not Professor – was something of a wild card in the medical community, owing to the fact that he'd never achieved a research qualification but had been taken under the Anonymous Billionaire's wing from day one. I never did work out how such a man had come to run such a prestigious research centre, never mind one so well privately funded, but his talent was undeniable, both for scientific research and for unearthing more unusual knowledge.

"How is your mother?" he asked while we ate. "Are you close to a cure, do you think?"

I confessed that I didn't think our lab was close to a cure, but that I found it strange he would know about my mother's illness at all.

"We all have our little secrets," he replied. "And the secret you're interested in is that you're much closer to a cure than you think."

Perhaps I should have stood up then and left, taken offence at the oddly long reach of his arm, which had found its way into my private life before we'd ever met. Instead I stayed, and over the course of the long afternoon, while the sun beat down on us and London sweated in the heatwave, Cassius told me everything he knew about the glymphatic system of the brain and how it might be weaponised to cure the most heinous of illnesses. By the time he rang the bell to have dinner delivered to us on the deck, I'd signed a contract to work for the Orex Corporation and he'd called someone at UCL and broken my contract two years before my funding was up.

After that, there was champagne and oysters and a decadent chocolate dessert that made me think I'd never really tasted chocolate before. Then Michael joined us at the table.

"Medication, Cassius," he said.

"How interminably boring."

"Death, my friend, would be far duller."

"And it is this we daily strive against."

I never did manage to work out which one of them spoke so uniquely at first, because I'm certain only one of them did. Over time, these patterns of speech became repackaged and passed back and forth between them like an inside joke, until it became as natural to them as any words ever were. I still hear his voice sometimes in the back of my mind, berating me for not having the answers and goading me into trying again. Some people linger inside us like that, and he has never seemed to fade.

Cassius never made it to the Tower, dying alone in his penthouse before the Anonymous Billionaire moved our operations here. Yet sometimes… sometimes I feel as though this place is Cassius's in the same way it was once the Conqueror's. His influence was wider than his life, wider than his person – wider, even, than mere memory can account for. I can imagine him greeting our survivors, befriending them, and charming them in ways we haven't.

I can imagine that this place is filled with Cassius just as it is filled with William, just as it is filled with Henry, just as it is filled with the executioners and the Krays and the queens and the kings and Sir Isaac Newton, who once ran the Royal Mint. I feel his ghost in this place – that is, his ghost as memory and authority – and I feel that we are readying ourselves to make new ghosts again.

I just don't know what form they might take.

FEMALE SURVIVOR: HEALTH CHECK #1

11/04/2063

Patient is a white female, estimated to be in her late twenties. She has dark auburn hair and was treated for headlice upon arrival. She appeared distressed and was non-verbal, but was able to respond physically to basic requests.

Patient displays systemic myoclonus and mild nystagmus, along with weakness in the extremities. Blood tests revealed deficiencies in vitamins B12, D, and K, as well as calcium, iron, and folate. She was mildly dehydrated. An attempt was made to treat her with IV fluids, but she became aggressive and tore out the line. Bleeding was profuse but well managed, and she received water and hydration salts instead.

Vitamin deficiencies will be treated with a three-month course of supplements, and we suggest regular assessment of her muscle weakness and tremors to ascertain the cause and develop further interventions.

Patient was escorted back to her rooms at 16:15 and left in the care of her companion.

The male survivor refuses to be examined. He is to be kept in quarantine until we can agree on how to proceed.

13TH APRIL

I have a morbid horror of sickness and an enduring fascination with the ways in which a body can transform. All of it is hidden within us, our internal landscape a mystery to ourselves, and yet what secrets might a body keep? How long might a tumour hide itself and grow in peace before we feel its effects? How versatile and how fragile these vessels are, and what an act of hubris it is to try and understand them.

I was in the stable with our two goats, Billie and Gruff, and Billie's body was a marvel. Two months ago she was a slip of a thing, with her delicate legs and soft slim body, and now she'd become a walking vessel for something else. Her four legs were like fragile branches holding the weight of a pendulous fruit, the skin of her stomach stretched and straining like a barrel left too long to ferment. She was restless, butting her soft white muzzle into my palm and bleating, and I pressed my hand to the heat of her flank and felt the ripples move over my skin.

"She's doing well," Maryam said from behind me.

"How can you tell?"

"Some things are the same between human and animal. I didn't spend a lifetime trundling through maternity wards not to know when a pregnancy is progressing."

I removed my hand from Billie's side and climbed over the fence, and Maryam led me across the courtyard to the two great greenhouses between the White Tower and the gates. They were once her rehabilitative project for our patients, and they've continued as her project ever since. She had me planting leek and radish seeds while Miles dug out one of the vegetable patches in anticipation of adding more later in the month.

"How's your patient coping after the Professor's tests?" We'd worked for most of the morning before she broke the quiet, and she emphasised the word *tests* in the same way that someone might say *murder*.

"It's okay," I said. "The wounds were fully healed within a week and there hasn't been another incident since the first."

"Does it help you to pretend he isn't a man?"

I looked over my shoulder to frown at her.

"*It's* okay," she repeated. "*It.*"

I didn't have an answer for her, so I didn't reply. The truth was, it *was* easier for me to think of the subject as an it, something that lacked the very basics of what we would call humanity. But it wasn't a matter of callousness; it was a matter of calm. If we're to reverse what was done to them, we need to run tests. Those tests are, by virtue of the fact we can't sedate the subject, cruel. But if curing billions means being cruel to one creature, then morally we have to continue.

That's what I keep telling myself, and if we have to continue no matter the subject's pain, there's nothing to be gained by me losing my head. Epiphanies don't happen in a panicked mind; revelation is the preserve of the focused, not the guilty. There is a door in my consciousness behind which I've stored my guilt as best as I'm able, and to open it now would ultimately serve no one.

"What makes the subject a monster and not a man?" Maryam asked. Before I met her, I hadn't known it was possible for someone to loom while seated, but her disregard could cut a man down at the knees. "What about the man in Beauchamp?"

"What about him?" I asked.

"Is he a monster or a man?"

That's the question, isn't it? And how are we to answer? The parameters of humanity have stretched. The limits of the human body have changed, and I've had a hand in changing them. When the limits are tested, monstrosity is the result. Monster as something Other, something strange, something not like us but close enough that we see ourselves reflected back.

I don't see myself in the Sleepless. I see my mother instead, just as Maryam must see her children and Thane his wife. Just as Miles must see his parents and Dolly her sisters. What good does it do us to look? What good would it do me to see them in the screams of the subject in the Tower? Must I prove my humanity by destroying my peace? Would our tests be more moral if I wept every night before sleep?

I looked down at Maryam, and for a moment I hated her. She had taken the moral high ground, but when it came to a cure she would still look to me. Is there any fairness in that? Perhaps it's true that there's humanity in it, but not of the kind we should be striving for.

"We're all monstrous," I told her. "All of us."

Maybe she could hear the frustration in my voice, or maybe she'd hoped that I could set her mind at ease. Whatever the reason, she diminished in front of me.

"Yes," she said quietly. "That's what I'm afraid of."

We didn't speak again that day.

14TH APRIL

There are really only two types of monster: the one that can hurt us and the one we don't want to be. The Sleepless are both. They're stronger than the average human, quicker, and far more lethal. They act in concert with their primal drives and not along moral lines. They have no ability to speak, and their reasoning is stunted, or at least focused on the basic survival instincts, the most basic one of all being to feed.

The earliest reports we had of their existence came from the armed forces. Sleepless soldiers had been an aim of the US Army since the early-twentieth century, but it was the Orex Corporation that made it a reality. The soldiers were given their own division, calling themselves the Awakened. The regular army called them the Nightmares, or Mara-class recruits, which has turned out to be prescient if nothing else.

Since our first subjects came from the army, they were the ones we monitored most closely. After the first year we monitored them less closely, and with Orex Corp going global and the programme receiving FDA approval in the US, the outliers that started to have problems never made it to our lab. I'm not even sure I'd heard about them before the disaster was already over, and a lot of good that did us in the end.

According to the information we managed to salvage from the database before it went down, the very first report of a major malfunction came from a corporal stationed at Sandhurst. The neuralchips were designed to go offline periodically, allowing patients to sleep for at least twelve hours a week, a period that had been calculated via a combination of metabolic testing and brainwave monitoring in animal subjects, alongside Edgar's neural network data.

It seems strange to say it now, but the chips weren't intended to eradicate sleep completely. They were simply meant to allow everyone a choice. Initially, we kept the subjects awake for twenty-four hours after insertion, monitoring things like heart rate and respiration and mood changes. After that, we extended their waking hours, allowing them to enjoy three days and nights completely unhindered by sleep.

During those initial tests, the subjects reported feelings of euphoria between thirty-six and forty-eight hours later, with periods of increased focus and wellbeing following. *I feel awake, you know?* we were often told. *Properly awake for the first time in my life.*

Our cognitive tests showed objective boosts to mental reasoning and problem solving during this interval, although any benefit was temporary if the subjects didn't get at least a few hours of sleep after around seventy hours awake.

I wonder, now, what would have happened if we'd thought to keep the chips switched on for longer than the two-week limit we tested. Perhaps it was simply a lack of imagination that prevented us from doing so. After all, sleep was so intrinsic to us, still so inherent to the way we understood life, that it never occurred to us that someone might want to rid themselves of it completely.

The corporal, it seemed, was the first to try and push the limits of the chip, or else he was the first to suffer the ill effects of doing so. Knowing what we know now, the army's medical report is damning evidence of a major flaw in the network. Because we didn't foresee that someone would ignore the guidance of having at least twelve hours of sleep a week, we didn't programme in an override – a way to force the patient to rest before negative symptoms began. This was undoubtedly a mistake.

Court-Martial Interview Transcript
Soldier: Corporal Stuart Bright
Date: 06/07/2059
Interviewing Medical Officer: Captain Andrea Tennyson

AT: Interview commencing at 9:05 a.m. People present: Corporal Stuart Bright, Medical Officer Andrea Tennyson, and Colonel Elijah Brace. How are you feeling this morning, Corporal?

SB: Why does everyone keep asking me that?

AT: Does it bother you?

SB: Yes.

AT: Why does it bother you?

SB: It bothers me because I don't know why I'm here.

Silence lasting approximately seven seconds. Audible on the tape, the colonel coughs.

AT: We had this conversation yesterday, Stuart. Do you remember what we spoke about yesterday?

SB: I wasn't here yesterday. Look, no, don't try that with me.

AT: Try what?

SB: Try to convince me I'm some sort of crazy.

AT: I'm not trying to convince you of anything. I'm simply asking whether you remember the conversation we had yesterday.

SB: We didn't have a conversation yesterday. I wasn't even here yesterday. I don't know why I'm here now. Where's [*Stuart's commanding officer*] Lieutenant De Ritter? Talk to him. He'll tell you I shouldn't be here. Talk to him.

AT: We can't talk to Lieutenant De Ritter right now, Stuart.

SB: Why not?

AT: Because Lieutenant De Ritter is in the hospital. Do you remember that?

Silence lasting approximately five seconds.

AT: Do you remember why he's there?

SB: You're lying.

AT: Why would I lie about that, Stuart?

SB: I don't know, but you are. You're lying to me. Colonel, why are you both lying to me? Why am I here?

AT: The colonel isn't participating in this interview, Stuart. He's only here as a witness.

SB: A witness to what? What is this? What do you want me to say?

AT: I want you to tell me what you remember about yesterday. Can you do that for me, Stuart?

Silence lasting approximately eight seconds.

AT: Stuart?

SB: I don't remember.

AT: You don't remember what happened yesterday.

SB: No.

AT: Okay, how about the day before. Do you remember what happened then?

Silence lasting approximately ten seconds.

AT: Stuart? For the tape, Corporal Bright has folded his arms and refuses to answer the question.

Silence lasting approximately thirty seconds.

AT: Okay, let's try something else. Why don't you tell me the last thing you remember before entering the interview room?

SB: Eating breakfast.

AT: Good. And what did you have for breakfast this morning?

SB: For God's sake, what kind of a question is that? What does it matter what I had for breakfast? Okay, fine. I had a couple of shitty slices of toast with peanut butter, some piss-poor coffee, and a banana that was more bruise than anything.

AT: Was that correct, Colonel?

EB: Yes, ma'am, that was correct.

SB: What the fuck? Why did you just ask him that?

AT: Stuart–

SB: No, I'm serious. Why did you just ask him that? You think I can't remember what I had for breakfast?

AT: Your memory's been patchy the last few weeks. I just wanted to make sure your short-term recall was functioning normally.

SB: This is bullshit. My memory's fine.

AT: Is it?

SB: Yes.

AT: Then why don't you tell me what you remember about yesterday?

SB: No.

AT: No?

SB: That's what I said.

AT: Why?

SB: Because it's a stupid question, that's why.

AT: Okay, how about what happened before breakfast this morning?

SB: I woke up.

AT: So you were sleeping.

SB: Obviously.

AT: Can you remember what you dreamt about?

SB: Seriously? You want to know what I dreamt about?

AT: That's why I asked.

SB: I dreamt about fucking my mum and murdering my dad.

Audible on the tape, Andrea sighs.

AT: I'm not Doctor Freud, Stuart.

SB: No, you're not. And I'm not crazy, so I don't know why I'm here or why you keep asking me these questions.

AT: Humour me.

A crash is audible on the tape. Colonel Brace is heard to release the safety mechanism of his gun.

SB: Is that necessary?

AT: Do you think it's necessary?

SB: No, I'm not a danger to anyone, for God's sake! I just want to know why I'm here.

AT: First, you answer my questions. Then we'll talk about why you're here.

SB: Okay, fine. You want to know what I dreamt about last night?

AT: I want to know what you dreamt about last night.

SB: I dreamt about...

Silence lasting approximately six seconds.

SB: I dreamt there was someone. I mean, I was...

AT: You were what?

SB: Dreaming. I was dreaming. There was... It was dark. I don't... I don't want to talk about this anymore.

AT: Why don't you want to talk about it anymore, Stuart?

SB: Because it's stupid. This whole thing is stupid. Why am I here? You have no right to keep me here.

AT: What's frightened you, Stuart?

SB: Nothing's frightened me. I'm not frightened.

AT: Aren't you?

SB: No, why would I be? Why would I be? They were only dreams.

18TH APRIL

Subject 001 screamed all night. The security footage shows it struggling against its bonds, its head thrown back as though seizing violently. At one point, its jaw dislocates. Although I muted the video, I can well imagine the noise it made.

20TH APRIL

The man asked for a razor today. Something to cut his hair with. The request, via Alison, started an argument in the canteen.

21ST APRIL

Thane reported he heard crying from their tower last night. Alison said it was the woman, but no one went to check on them. Are we a community of cowards?

THE POTATOES ARE ROTTEN AND THE TOWER IS FULL

Pick your own potatoes, then.

23RD APRIL

In 1955, only four years after Henrietta died and her miraculous cells revolutionised medicine forever, there was a disease outbreak at the Royal Free Hospital in London. Between July and November of that year, 292 people – most of them staff – fell ill, and 255 were admitted to the wards as patients, suffering from fever, acute vertigo, nausea and vomiting, and upper respiratory tract infections.

The hospital was shut down as the illness spread, and newspapers ran stories with the headlines "Closed Hospital's Fever Baffles Experts" and "New Virus May Have Caused Outbreak", describing the symptoms as "similar to a form of polio". By the second or third week, patients started to show neurological problems, including extreme pain and dysfunction of the nervous system. The illness would first become known as the Royal Free Disease and a year later as myalgic encephalomyelitis, or ME.

At the heart of this outbreak was a consultant physician in infectious diseases called Melvin Ramsay. I was fourteen when I first saw his photograph, on the back page of his book *Myalgic Encephalomyelitis and Postviral Fatigue States: The Saga of the Royal Free Disease*. The picture was black and white, grainy, and showed a balding older man with thick black glasses, a round face, and a gentle smile. My first thought was how unassuming a person he was for his work to have been so important.

After watching his colleagues collapse into illness over only a few months, Doctor Ramsay was the one who monitored them, tested them, and – importantly – believed them when they didn't start to get better. While some recovered after a period of enforced convalescence, others remained sick for the rest of their lives, and Ramsay's tests proved that their nervous systems had been damaged by a virus they couldn't identify. He would spend the rest of his life researching and writing about the physical reality of postviral illness, but by the time of his death in 1990, few people believed it existed.

I wonder now how often personal belief has influenced testable science. How frequently a misplaced confidence in our own infallible knowledge has hindered our ability to understand. What might my life – or Mother's – have been like if more people had believed in him?

25TH APRIL

Michael once told me that there was no such thing as the scientific mind. This, coming from one of the great scientists of our generation. We were on a pleasure cruise on the Thames at the time, one of the Anonymous Billionaire's team-building exercises disguised as a perk that we had to submit to at least once a year.

The day had been filled with food and alcohol. Ice-breaker challenges between our building's departments were a secondary consideration to the business of proving that we all knew how to have fun. For the first time since I'd joined the Orex Corporation, Cassius hadn't been well enough to join us, and Michael had been drinking in a gentile but no less determined way since lunchtime.

"There is no such thing as the scientific mind," he began.

He was wearing a rumpled navy blazer over an equally rumpled white shirt, and the dark Panama hat he'd arrived wearing was clasped in his hand for emphasis. "Neither, dear Thea, is there a creative mind," he went on. "There is only an endless spectrum of possibilities from which we grasping humans can reach for whatever best pleases us at any given moment."

I, being much less drunk than Michael, felt a great affection for him in that moment. The infectious enthusiasm with which he asserted his position was analogous to the way he approached his work in the lab. Subtlety was anathema to him, tact a dirty word. I admired him for it more than I can say.

"You'll start a riot on deck if the others hear you say that," I told him.

He threw his head back and laughed. The sun reflected off his glasses and he clasped his hat over his heart and laughed loudly enough to cause the people standing nearby to look over in consternation.

"And what do I care of them?" he asked. "No, dear Thea, there are only four people in the Orex Corporation worth knowing, and two of them are sitting here."

It was, I remember, an effort not to blush.

"Cassius," I agreed. "And the fourth?"

"An odd fellow up in cybernetics called Edgar Trevelyan. I'll introduce you later. The point is that defining a mind in such rigid terms is about as nonsensical as defining a hand as creative or otherwise." He tossed the last of his strawberry daiquiri back as though sinking a beer, and then looked at me expectantly – as he sometimes did in those days – when he wanted me to argue an opposing point.

"But surely there's such a thing as aptitude?" I offered obediently, and his eyes lit up in delight.

"Do you think so?" he asked. "Truly?"

It just so happened that I did, but whether or not it was my true position wasn't the point of the exercise. When Michael got a bee in his bonnet about something it was best left to tire itself out or he'd become prickly and morose for weeks. He didn't wait for my reply.

"Certainly not," he continued. "The mistake people make is to treat the mind as something other, something unknowable. An organ beyond the comprehension of others simply because it's where we consider our consciousness to lie. Consider this, instead." He sat back in his chair, calm now that he had a captive audience. "Every person's brain is made up of the same materials. There are neurons and synapses, and everything is washed with CSF. The cerebellum dictates balance and the pituitary mediates hormones, and while there are subtle variations between us all, the commonalities outweigh the differences. What, then, determines our skills and ambitions as individuals?"

He needed no answer in order to continue, so I offered him none.

"It certainly isn't the brain in the physical sense. Now, I know what you'll say, Thea. You'll say that people do have an inbuilt tendency to use different areas of their brain."

I had, in fact, been about to say just that.

"But consider this – that the tendency to use different parts of the brain may not be intrinsic but learned behaviour."

"Nature versus nurture," I said.

"Just so. And let me put it to you more explicitly. The skillset required for scientific research is almost exactly the same skillset required for investigation of any kind – medical, anthropological, in pursuit of the law, or giving chase to new musical melodies. What, then, makes someone a medical researcher and not a violin virtuoso?"

"I don't know," I replied. "Preference?"

"Exactly. It isn't merely aptitude that dictates behaviour, nor is it the brain. It is something far more nebulous, something far less testable. It is early environment, fitness level, health, passions, drives, support, hunger, or lack thereof. Formative moments in a young life. Your mother, for instance. Would you ever have become so driven to unlock the secrets of energy if you hadn't watched her fall prey to a lack of it?"

I frowned, and he offered me an apologetic smile that only partially placated me. As a rule, I didn't like to speak about Mother outside of the flat we still shared – cowardly, perhaps, but the separation of my concern for her from my work was the only way I could exist in the world with any measure of joy.

"So, what do these things tell us?" he asked. "Now, don't mistake me, I'm not arguing for a nihilistic breakdown of reality. Clearly, it isn't the case that anyone can set their mind to anything they want to do. Whether social, intellectual, or physical barriers to success exist is rather empirically obvious, while I have no doubt that, had my parents wished it and retained the money, status, and control over me to will it, I could indeed have become a violin virtuoso. Since I have the full use of my hands and ears, that is."

"But you were never tempted."

"Just so. If I'd dedicated thousands of hours to the cultivation of this skill, no doubt I could have succeeded, ingrained talent or not. However, something would still have been missing. A passion. A joy. The sort of emotion and sentiment that bleeds through a true musician's playing. I could never have replicated it. But is that a function of the brain?"

He was in full flow by then, gesticulating wildly with his hat while he swayed in his seat, listing against the metal barrier that separated the deck from the river.

"No," he declared. "It's a function of something else. Of character. Of preference. At heart, it's a question of *personality*. And that, dear Thea, is why we science-minded individuals, in this society built on knowledge and technology, still cling to the concept of the soul. The unique fingerprint on our hearts that makes us who we are, and not who we can never be. The ghost in the machine."

"Don't take this the wrong way, Michael, but if you're going to start bringing Descartes into this, I'm going to need another drink." I'd hoped to make him smile, to shake him from the strange melancholy that was stealing over him, but he resisted my attempt, and the moment is forever engraved in my memory – as though he himself had left a fingerprint on my eye.

"Perhaps we blame the brain because it would hurt too much to blame the soul," he murmured, so quietly that I was never sure afterwards whether he meant for me to hear it. "Could it be that my soul isn't equal to this task after all? Is there still a way to make dear Cassius proud?"

He stared across the bow of the boat, and I thought him the most achingly tragic figure – an ageing, brilliant man caught in a vacuum of silence, glowing with the death of the day's warm light. If such a thing as a soul truly does exist, I felt mine reach for him then.

AS I WAS WALKING ON THE STAIR I MET A MAN THAT WASN'T THERE

The male survivor has consented to be interviewed. I've volunteered myself for the role, since the Professor's and Edgar's talents are better spent elsewhere.

26TH APRIL

I'm not sure what woke me tonight. I know I'd been sleeping badly, tumbling like a snowflake down the mountainside of my memories. I thought perhaps that I could hear music, but then I wouldn't have remarked on it so strongly when I opened the door. Whatever the reason, I woke in the deep night with a rush of adrenaline and the peculiar sense that something was out of place.

My bedroom was in total darkness, and I lay there with my heart pounding, utterly convinced that someone was there in the room with me, or that they had been only moments before I'd opened my eyes. Eventually, I couldn't convince myself of my safety, and had no choice but to get up and search for the source of my unease.

The flat beyond my room was silent. In slippers and robe I crept across the landing, hesitating at Mother's room before descending the stairs. The thought struck me at the front door that my behaviour was the preserve of children, and once I decided to look outside I could no longer deny that I was behaving irrationally. Nevertheless, my peace of mind is precious to me, and I unlocked our home and peered out into the dark.

I've always considered the night to change the intrinsic quality of a place. Darkness hides the soft edges of things.

Shadows make even benign corners into objects that are sharp and dangerous. Tonight, though, the moon was as bright as a candle overhead, a pale silver luminescence that turned the White Tower into a fortress of ice.

I stood there alone in the springtime cold, and a fathomless, soaring sensation held me in its grip. Familiarity breeds complacency, and living within the Tower's walls these last few years it's become commonplace to see the white stone burnished in the sun. But there under the moon, in a monochrome landscape of cold beauty, the Conqueror's palace possessed an eldritch quality that could almost have convinced me to believe in magic.

The sensation was multiplied by the melody that caught on the breeze. For a moment, I had a sense of prescience, of a glaring circularity between my thoughts and the music on the wind. It felt like a glimpse of something important, a personal revelation that drifted from my grasp as quickly as I reached for it. Recalling it now, I believe that the sense of connection, of witnessing something greater than myself, occurred because of my preoccupation before bed.

I'd settled into sleep thinking about Michael that day on the boat. I'd imagined a scenario, an alternate timeline in which he'd taken up the violin, feeding a musician's passion rather than a scientist's. How different might the world have been? It was a shock, I suppose, to have been so recently thinking about performances and violins and then to hear one swelling across the green.

The song was a sorrowful thing, filled with aching minor notes and shivering vibratos. I followed it into the courtyard, half believing in something Fae hiding behind the corners of the buildings or creeping malevolently across the battlements. A light was on in the window of

Beauchamp Tower, and the glow drew me towards it and across the damp grass.

I stood in front of our two glasshouses, and I saw that it wasn't the only light in the dark. Beyond the iceberg beauty of the White Tower, the window at the top of the 22nd Tower was open and lit, and the song crept beneath the glass and danced its way towards me. The Anonymous Billionaire was playing and I wondered about him again.

What do any of us really know of the man? That he was rich and now he is not. That he funded our research and now he hides from it all. That his passion project was the catalyst for the collapse of society, but that his safe haven is perhaps the last bastion of humanity in the country. And now, I suppose, that he plays the violin. Does that mean he has the soul of a musician and not that of a businessman? Is it any more reasonable to consider a soul particularly creative or scientific or kind, than it is to consider a mind in that way?

I decided then that although I didn't know him, I didn't need to either. It was enough for me then – it is enough for me now – to be able to stand beneath the spectre of the moon, in the shadow of William's palace of ice, and listen to sounds that I'd thought were long lost. The melody pulled deep, tugging at my lips until I had no choice but to curve them in a melancholy smile. Nostalgia came upon me, first as an unfurling sensation and then as an urge to cry.

Perhaps I might have done had movement over Raleigh's Walk not drawn my gaze. I shrank back into the shadows, and above me, strolling the battlements over Wakefield, the woman who should have been in Beauchamp stumbled and swayed against the sky. She was still wearing her red dress, yet in the moon's glow it appeared like bloody velvet, and the silver light on her skin made me feel as though she were the true Fae creature here. Her hair, too, caught the peculiar light, and although I knew it to be auburn it looked as dark as ink.

Her appearance was so striking that it didn't immediately occur to me that there was anything wrong with her being out of the Tower and strolling across the battlements. In fact, her mannerisms unnerved me before the simple fact of her being there. Her feet drifted across the stone as though she were about to dance, but as her body shifted to sway to the violin she jerked violently backwards and wrung her hands together.

The movement put me in mind of an automaton, or a puppet swung back and forth at the whim of some unseen hand. She seemed for a moment to be falling. Just as she'd bent towards the man, now she leant towards the music, forgetting herself until something pulled her upright, and I imagined that the expression on her shadowed face was one of fear, of anxiety.

Guilt arrived as a cold feeling, the colour of the moon-drenched Tower. In the face of her distress, my own life seemed small, my hopes and worries insignificant, my preoccupation with my own concerns a supreme act of selfishness. I was ashamed to have abandoned her in Beauchamp, to have forgotten her in favour of her companion. I saw clearly then that I should have visited and reached out to her somehow, tried to become a friend.

No sooner had the thought occurred – and also, I think, the conviction that I ought to approach – than a second body moved against the stars. It was Alison, and despite my decision to befriend the woman, I didn't stop her, although I believed then that Thane's subordinate was about to cause a scene and escort her back to her bed.

She didn't. In the uncanny light, the two silhouettes turned to each other, as slow and steady as a waltz. They considered one another, and from my vantage point on the ground the violin felt like a soundtrack to their meeting, its performance a serenade. I had that sensation again of being clasped within a bubble of time, of there being one drawn-out moment in life alone and this the centre of it.

The two figures turned at some unspoken signal and looked together over the city. Though they stood a metre apart, their position seemed intimate. Alison had one hand resting at her hip, and I realised only once I'd returned to bed that she must have been holding her gun. The tension in the other woman's movements drained through the ground, her myoclonus diminishing, her twitches and jerks settling, until she stood in perfect stillness against the horizon, the very picture of calm.

I don't know how long we stood there for. We stayed until the violin drifted into silence and the sound of the rushing Thames and the chill, searching wind took its place. Then, I saw the woman shiver, and in that too-perfect silence Alison turned and led her away. She followed at her back like a child, and only after I'd heard the sound of their footsteps on the stone fade away and the doorway to Wakefield open and close again did I stir from my hiding place and retrace my steps back home.

The night had unsettled me, and at the same time it had induced in me a strange sense of peace. I turned at my doorway and looked back, and the feeling of the Tower as a place of safety, a structure of hope, clung to the edges of my thoughts. I thought for a second that I saw someone else returning home, but I couldn't say for sure who it was or even if they were there at all.

In bed later, struggling to sleep, I returned to the moment again. It seemed to me that a performance had been played out between the walls, that what I'd witnessed had been a considered, stylised thing – a staging that was meant to be seen. It's a fool's notion, of course, but I can't quite excise it from my mind. If the performance was staged, who was the intended audience?

Ridiculous though it may seem, I have the unsettling feeling that, far from being the unseen watcher, I was in fact observed. At the border between waking and sleep, I had the strangest vision of seeing the night from the perspective of the top of the White Tower. From that vantage point, I watched the silhouette of the Anonymous Billionaire drawing his bow across the strings. I felt the ache of his loneliness and somehow still despised him for it. My eyes were sharp – clearer than before – and when I turned my back on him and looked towards the Thames, the woman's dress seemed like the brightest red in the world when set against the black of the sky. I saw her as a creature made of wounds, of broken skin still bleeding, as though the red of her dress was naught but blood. Then, like a scaffold, I saw Alison as something bright and sturdy, the supporting wall of a crumbling house keeping the darkness at bay.

I knew then that I would be forced to see myself, and the unsettling insights this perspective afforded me triggered nothing but terror. Even though I knew it to be futile, I fought against the movement forward, close enough to the edge of the roof that I could peer over and find my hiding place in the cloister of the wall. Still, of course, I looked.

I saw myself from above. A small, curious creature poised on the edge of action. I understood then that this was what I was and had always been: the match at the point of striking, the clouds just before a storm. Beneath me, my body dispersed and changed, until I became the crest of a wave always reaching for the shore but never falling, never tumbling. Forever waiting for one more push to break against the beach. I was suspended action, a rock in the great flowing river of the world, and around me the tides of life surged and changed.

I wanted to linger in this revelation with almost the same desperation that I wanted to look away, but as is usually the case in dreams, I had no choice in the matter. It was with a wrenching relief that I turned from myself – and my attention was caught by the secret attendant lingering beyond the greenhouses. I knew at once that it was Edgar, but my assessment of him was so beyond my previous knowledge of his character that I believed for a moment I'd gone mad.

I've always thought of Edgar as something sly and creeping, like a reptile. A creature that stirs in the grass but feels no compulsion to act or to take. But this man was an absence. He was a thing made of greed and want and desire, and a heat that might burn the whole world to ash if allowed to spread unchecked. The sight disturbed me, and it loosened something inside me as well. I wanted to hurt him and I wanted to flee. That duality of emotion paralysed me, and sank within me like groundwater leaching through bedrock. I felt like I'd been poisoned.

28TH APRIL

I've always felt disconnected from my environment, as though I were a tiger placed in a bird cage or a sparrow trying to swim. Desire, for me, is a desire for the Other Self – the fictitious version of myself that lives only in my head – but also for the environment that might allow that person to be expressed.

The Tower is a lesson in perspective. When I left my home this morning, I was unsettled yet unusually calm. Our lives have been changed by being here, but I suspect that our characters persist, and when I joined Edgar and the Professor in the lab I felt myself to be part of a cause that was far greater than myself.

We'd progressed to the next stage of testing, with all of the problems it entailed.

"You want to scan the subject?" I asked when I arrived. "And you've found a way to do that without sedation?"

"Sleep isn't the only stillness. Unconsciousness isn't necessary for calm." Edgar mumbled the words, his back turned to me and his hands busy on a surgical tray.

"You're going to drug him," I realised. "A neuromuscular blocking agent instead of sedation."

"Paralysis of the body not silence of the mind."

"Are you sure that will work? What if they're just as resistant to paralysing agents as they are to sedatives?"

"That's why we're going to ready a selection of inhibitors," Michael said. He was almost fizzing with excitement. "Edgar has calculated the estimated metabolic increase in the subject's cells and adjusted the dose accordingly. The tricky bit will be keeping it alive if it doesn't take. Tell me, Thea, have you ever performed an intubation?"

I had, once, on a woman on a respiratory ward during my hospital rotation. She'd been an elderly, bird-boned creature with metastatic lung cancer and bright eyes, and she'd looked at me so steadily as she'd slipped into semi-consciousness that I'd had the unnerving thought that there was a young woman staring out at me from within her ageing skin.

I told the Professor that I had, and once Dolly arrived we followed him down to the lower floors. The temperature dropped as we descended and the stone walls stole the heat from the air. It had been a long time since I'd visited this area. Edgar or the Professor usually brought the subject to the first floor when we observed him, and the former dungeons and torture chambers have always seemed to me to have retained an air of disquiet.

We met Alex in the radiology suite, in the viewing room behind the thick pane of glass and lead. He was standing with his hands stuffed into the pockets of his jeans like a young boy grown too big too quickly. When he saw me, he tipped his chin just slightly and smiled in a way that struck me as both too exuberant and too honest for the situation we'd found ourselves in. We were all of us ignoring the door along the corridor that led to the holding cell beyond.

"You're certain the wiring is sound?" the Professor asked him.

"I told you, Mike," Alex replied, and I could see the Professor bristling behind his smile. "It wasn't ever an issue with the wiring. The problem is the amount of energy the machine's going to swallow from the generator."

"And has that problem been solved?"

"You know as well as I do that you're ignoring it. Do you want me to tell you it'll be fine?" Alex has a faint West Country burr to his r's which endears him to me, and just then his accent curled around the consonants, as though his frustration were seeking a home in the sounds. "It'll probably be fine, but don't power it down without me. And if you're planning on using it again, we're going to have to set up some kind of energy well to pick up the slack or we'll be relying on gas lamps before you know it."

The Professor seemed content with this and gestured for Edgar to pass by him down the corridor.

Standing there with Alex and Dolly while the Professor busied himself with the computers, I don't know why I was suddenly uncomfortable. I've never much cared what Dolly thinks, and I believe the feeling is mutual, and Alex and I are probably considered quite close by now. Still, there was a definite heavying of the atmosphere when Edgar left, a shuffling, teeth-aching tension that made me not want to look at either of them. Instead, I stared at the ground.

Down the corridor, a door opened and closed. The Professor tapped on the keyboard and Dolly clicked her nails against the camera's plastic casing. I followed a crack in the floor with my eyes until it disappeared behind the skirting board, and I wondered whether the original flooring was hidden beneath these tiles and if there were still bloodstains there as well.

Alex cleared his throat as the door to the holding cell opened and closed again. I looked up when the trolley's wheels – one loose and clicking – echoed through the cavern, and that steady growl raised the hairs on the back of my neck. Alex shuffled his feet and his eyes met mine. They were wide and scared, and I found then that I could smile at him after all. It seemed to make him feel better.

"Right then," he said to no one, as though ending a conversation. "If you have any problems with the machine, send someone up to get me."

He nodded to Dolly, and then surprised me by touching his fingers to my arm as he passed.

"I'll be in the engine room later if you want some company," he said.

It was kind of him to offer. I didn't tell him so, but I'm sure he knew it anyway.

Time seemed to misbehave after that. It's rare these days that I live in the continuous present. History has a way of crowding in on me, both my own and everyone else's, but this afternoon I was inside my body and operating from within it in a way that felt visceral and empowering.

It seemed like the simplest thing in the world to take a step outside of reality and convince myself that this creature was merely a patient, and our actions so common as to have become a part of our routine. I felt nothing when Edgar strapped its head to the stretcher. My hands didn't shake when I injected the first ampule of succinylcholine, nor when I added the second after the first failed to take.

The subject's fingers were lax when I slipped the pulse oximeter onto them. The routine placement of the electrodes on its chest and the slow, listless beeping of the heart monitor was both disturbing and reassuring. In a human, we would have said he had dangerous bradycardia, and Dolly had to mute the alarms that kept going off to urge us to bring its heart rate up.

After that, it was routine. Dolly lowered the stretcher so the subject was lying flat. The Professor took Edgar's place by an array of needles and ampules that caught the fluorescent lights, while Edgar moved into the viewing room to manage the MRI. I no longer experienced the subject as a whole organism, but as a detached set of body parts that might have made up something greater but whose nature was beyond my ability to fathom. A chin, tipped back. The coldness of the metal laryngoscope through my latex gloves. A gargling in the back of an open throat, and the dark pink trail of vocal cords swallowing into darkness. A push. A slip. Resistance in the flesh. Then a sudden release as the plastic tube pushed down and into the lungs.

I don't think any of us spoke. The Professor injected something more – two somethings – to make sure the paralysis held, and then there came the hiss and rush of the ventilator, loud in the quiet room. I was vaguely aware of Dolly flitting about the space, her hand glued to the camera to capture the images.

It was only when we'd transferred the toneless body to the scanner, and arranged the tubes and wires to allow it entry into the machine, and scurried back like children behind the glass, that I felt my vision pull back like a viewfinder to see the whole of it again. It was unsettling to see the subject that way, shirtless and still, its chest, rippled with knots of wiry muscle, expanding as the air was forced into its lungs like a bellows.

I sat in the chair Edgar wasn't using, my eyeline just

higher than the monitors, and stared at the body in the tube. The way its chest moved was violent, as though even with the paralysis the subject was fighting the machine. I imagined that it was painful – the plastic in its throat, the great gust and pull of the ventilator, even the contrast dye we'd run through its veins. The movement of its chest was hypnotic. It reminded me of Lamaze classes, of the preparation of a body for pain, the brace and clench and sink of it.

I'm sure that the Professor and Edgar were talking during this time, and I have a vague memory of excited chatter when the first images came through, but I couldn't say for certain what was said. During the hour or so we waited, I let myself drift, and in my mind's eye I saw the past overlay the present. I saw the bright, shifting centres of the subject's mind alongside the brutal crack and draw of the torturer's rack. I felt then as though a grisly cord stretched between us and the past, as though we were a single point on a continuum of curiosity and pain. This clinical, removed peek into the subject's skull coexisted alongside the snap and splinter of the bones in a torture victim's fingers.

Were they not the same impulse? We may have sanitised the action, but both were meant to reveal secrets by breaking through the barriers of the body. Really, I have no excuse for it. At least today we weren't committing cruelty for cruelty's sake, but on the other hand there was no way for the subject to make us stop. It couldn't give us what we wanted or turn the King's Ransom to save itself. We will continue to explore the intimate places of its body until we find what we need for a cure. The subject has no agency. We are the agents of its disillusionment, and we too believe we are called to a higher purpose.

I wondered if Cromwell had felt the same.

* * *

Afterwards, I went to see Alex. It was perhaps his smile in the face of our crimes that had left me with an unusual yearning for company, but I think more than that it was the brush of his fingers against my arm. A very human kindness, to touch so gently. Things like that seem to matter more these days when so little of humanity remains.

The room he calls the engine room is in the basement on the eastern side of the keep. The wooden staircase leads down to the old storage area, which is now a workshop that Alex has taken possession of. Inside there's the generator, a great rumbling monster of a thing that keeps everything running. The basement is large and sweltering in the summer, but in the winter wind or the springtime chill it's a warm and comforting place.

Alex was waiting for me, which I suppose means he knows me better than I think. Even I wasn't sure I'd visit him, but he was certain enough to have made two mugs of tea, and when I got there mine was being kept warm on the generator's casing. He smiled when I walked in, and again I found that I couldn't return it. It didn't matter. My place on the worn green armchair was empty, and Alex was busy at his worktable, and the tea was sitting next to a small silver key on a chain that I picked up and replaced around my neck. He didn't mention it, for which I was grateful, and neither did I.

The decision to create a contingency hadn't come about through any moral debate on my part. Whether or not my actions were fair to the rest of the survivors was meaningless, given the simple fact that an escape route was necessary – if not for me, then for Mother, who was unable to arrange one herself. I'd heard Alex speak about the boats he'd tied to new moorings often enough to know that some of them still ran well. It had taken only a little nudge from me to persuade him to equip one with supplies in case the worst should happen.

It isn't in my nature to rely on other people, but I have no reason to step outside these walls, and it's been relatively easy for him to slip onboard the boat with the supplies I've stolen for us. If he feels any guilt over our actions, he hasn't confided in me about it, and I see no reason to ask just as long as the task gets done. Perhaps that too is cowardly, but we must all choose which battles we fight.

I took my mug, my key, and my place, folded my legs beneath myself, and watched him work. We all have our little peculiarities. Alex's obsession with the boats that drift down the Thames is a more understandable one than most. The hydro-turbines are our only source of power. The unchecked passage of the boats threatens them constantly. Alex and Thane work hard to tow in the ones that drift too close, but we're all aware that an overnight storm could be the thing that sinks us. Consequently, Alex is building a net that he plans to unfurl beyond the turbines to snare the boats and debris that rush around our source of power. In the time before, this would have been a minor undertaking for some construction company or other, but these days such an unlikely scheme is almost on a par with our own.

Even if he could take one of the abandoned boats out safely beyond the turbines, even if he could secure his stakes in the half-ring beneath the current, even if he could brave the water to dive deep enough to drill in the hooks and survive to come up for air, one man attempting to wrangle that much net while the roar of the Thames fights against him feels like nothing more than a death wish.

But after all, why shouldn't he try? It isn't as though our attempt to find a cure is any less of a pipe dream. Really, this Tower is filled with impossible dreams – to cure a world afflicted by death, to build a net big enough to keep us safe, to grow enough food that by the time our vast stores run out we will have no more need of them. To save the world.

I thought of this sort of optimism while I watched him and drank my tea. Such a thing must only be the preserve of humanity, mustn't it? We're the only creatures who have a concept of time passing, which means that we're the only ones who know that the future can always be worse than the present. To live with this knowledge and not to despair is a burden too great to fortify ourselves against.

But Alex's net keeps growing, just like Maryam's plants. It started as a single square and now it's piled in a mass behind him and taking up great swathes of space. Every day he settles down here next to the humming generator, the smell of varnish and rope all around him, and he works with his hands until there's more of it. And at the end of each day, he can say, *Look, I made this. Before I sat down, this wasn't here, and now it is, because of me*. There's something hopeful about that. Even if it's never used, he will still have made it. Something will exist because of him that didn't exist before.

I wanted to ask him, who taught him to tie knots like this? Why go into maintenance at the Tower when he could have been on a boat, tying nets to catch fish and not enclosed by all of these walls? When did he realise he was the only one here who could do this? Did he miss the person who taught him to weave? What did he think about while he worked, down here alone for all of the long days? And did he know that we – that I – care that he's here? That watching him from the battlements is usually the highlight of my day?

Of course, I didn't say anything. You can't really, can you? But I do wonder. I wonder if we all have these thoughts – if even Dolly, with her false vocation and accidental survival, thinks about the rest of us here.

I think, perhaps, that all of this might have its own purpose, even if it isn't so grand as saving the world. Just as long as Alex keeps weaving his net, there's hope for another sunrise, and maybe that's all we need to remember for now if we want to go on as we are.

but I resent these thoughts and so I push them out into the fog where they might burn, and they circle back like the ravens coming home to roost and cawing in the peace, in this fragile peace that I seek and seek and never seem to find, finding instead the clawing of my own feeble thoughts, feeble mind, feeble soul, which must by now be as black as wing and as bloody as carrion beak, and yet perhaps I am being cruel, cruel to myself and cruel to the torn flesh of the dead things that feed on the earth and birth, birth the soil and the plants and the rot and sing bright and clear with the promise of new growth

MAY

1ST MAY

People used to believe that washing your face in the first May dew would bring you good health and a bright complexion for the rest of the year. Moving to London didn't quite rid me of the natural superstitions you pick up by the sea. At the battlements this morning, I brushed my hands through the herb garden and cupped my face with my palms. I don't think the ritual will gift me with better health or glowing skin, but there's something special about it anyway.

The dew was cold, refreshing in the way that sea swimming in winter is refreshing: a short, sharp shock to wake you up and put you back into your body again. I stood there, watching the fog – thinner now that summer was on its way – and I thought about what it means to live inside a body and not just in our minds.

Humans are strange. We make these rituals and build them into our lives as though compelled to find meaning in each little thing. We're eager, always, to remind ourselves that we're present, that we exist tangibly in the world, perceived and recognised by other people like us. And yet so much of what we consider to be *us* happens beyond the borders of our bodies.

I've spent a lifetime attempting to exist as something other than the vessel I inhabit. The body, after all, is untrustworthy. We all live with the awareness that we're housed inside a perishable flesh sack that will one day rot away from us, leaving us with nowhere to go. What else but that knowledge could ever drive us to imagine so vividly a life after death, a ghost in the machine that might exist long after our bodies are gone? Humanity isn't good at anticipating or accepting our own non-existence. How can we be?

I've never known the world except through the living receptacle of my body. The sky is blue only because my eyes tell me so. Snow is cold only because I can touch it with my hands and feel the chill spread through my nerves. Sadness and fear are biochemical reactions that churn through my brain and excite hormones that make me feel bad. What would the world look or feel like without the body to interpret it? Would we even recognise it, or ourselves, if we were removed from this casing once and for all?

I don't believe that we would, and yet the thought horrifies me. What precarious lives we all lead, trapped here inside ourselves, forever reaching into the world for something that might make meaning, forever trying to move beyond what we are into something that will make us whole. The city beyond us is emptier and fuller than it's ever been, but it's as closed to me as the road that ran parallel to our home when I was a child. Forbidden without a chaperone. Dangerous, though we don't know how to make it less so.

But I don't feel as though I'm stagnating here, and that's a revelation I didn't expect. I find, today, that I want to speak to Mother with a fierceness that chokes me. I want to tell her that I had it wrong, that my understanding of her was limited by the functioning of my body, which watched hers slowly fade into entropy. Perhaps I can admit it here, that I often wondered in the years when she could still speak why she never asked me to help her die.

The best thing about her particular illness was that it was unlikely to kill her. The worst thing was that it wouldn't allow her an end. She slipped from the world so slowly and soundlessly that, after a while, it seemed as though only I was left to remember that she'd ever lived in it at all.

I used to look at photos of her from before the virus – a tall woman with thick chestnut hair, a pointed face, a bright smile. She favoured wide trousers, cinched at the waist, and crop tops that made her seem even taller than she was. There's motion in all of the photos I kept. No falsely posed smiles or self-conscious tilts of the head. She is alive, lively, laughing at someone off-camera. Dancing in the kitchen. Standing at the top of Mount Snowdon, surrounded by fog that obscures the view she came for, her arms open and her hands disappearing into the mist while sunlight pours onto the droplets on her face. It's a moment so bright that it horrifies me.

People will tell you that moments last forever, but they're wrong. There is only ever the present, only ever experienced at the whims of the body. These moments haunted her until she simply stopped thinking of them, until the woman on Mount Snowdon and the woman in the bed were as distant from one another as an adult is from the child they once were. The illness took light from her. It left her perpetually in the dark with the curtains drawn, an eye mask over her face and noise-cancelling headphones clamped to her ears. In the end, all she had left was herself.

I've always thought this to be the worst fate in the world, to be trapped inside a body so pained that all there could ever be was the pain. No one to distract you. No music to send you somewhere else. No new stories except for the ones you could recite inside your thoughts while knowing that more were being made around you every day, beyond your reach, as far from your reach as the moon. Further than that, even, because at least other people can look outside and see the moon shining down. She doesn't even have that.

But she never asked to die. I thought, for a long time, that this was a state she maintained purely out of hope for a better tomorrow. I believed that such stagnation could only ever be torture, that it allowed for nothing else inside of it. But now I think that no matter how small the world a human inhabits is, they are at heart still human.

I have the full use of my body, it's true, but I still feel myself to be worthy of life whether I lay that body down to rest or whether I stand on the battlements and look for something more. The ghost in the machine – if there is a ghost at all – doesn't distinguish between a day spent sleeping and a day of action. I am compelled to make meaning as we all are, but I can do that just as well with my eyes closed and my thoughts flying beyond me as I can standing beneath an open window and listening to a violin play.

What has always looked like mere stagnation to me, an endless living death, was not so endless as to be meaningless. I knew it before now, I think, but I didn't fully understand. The days when the curtains could be opened meant more to her than the days when I stepped onto a train to travel somewhere new. The nights when she could sit up and speak were more precious for them being rare. And when she lies there in the dark, day after endless day, she isn't simply waiting to move again. She thinks. She dreams. She remembers what it was to be well and she persists inside what it is to be sick.

I want to tell her that I feel I appreciate her a little more, now that the walls have closed in around us. She suffered. She still suffers horribly and I want to save her, but she isn't made of suffering alone. She's made of what we're all made of: a ghost trapped in a machine, looking for more than we can see. We are not mere stardust decaying across time, we are thought and hope and our own inner dreams, and I think I'm beginning to understand.

3RD MAY

There's a room in the basement of the White Tower that was once used for pre-insertion assessments. It's three doors down from the radiology suite, which is six doors away from Subject 001's holding cell. The space is something like a police interview room. The walls are cold grey stone, except for one which holds a two-way mirror. It contains a desk and two chairs, and a ticking clock like a bullseye on the wall. There are cameras in the ceiling and one behind the mirror. There was also a third camera positioned behind my right shoulder when I sat down today, its red light blinking at the empty chair across from me.

I was nervous, but I didn't want to give Edgar, watching from the other side of the mirror, the satisfaction of appearing to be. I had a pad and two pens and I arranged them on the desk. It was exactly 9:30 a.m. when the door opened and Thane delivered the male survivor to me in handcuffs, his wrists bound over his stomach.

This was the first time I'd laid eyes on him since he and his companion had arrived, and I was surprised to find that he was terribly ordinary. No longer caked in dirt and grime, he stood tall with a military bearing. His hair and beard were still long since we'd refused him the use of a razor, but now clean, the colour was a deep chestnut brown with a hint of red at the tips. His eyes were still heterochrome and just as piercing. His face had filled out in the intervening month, but whatever starvation he'd suffered had hollowed out the space beneath his cheekbones, giving him a regal yet cadaverous look it's difficult to describe. He was dressed in black jeans, and a loose denim shirt that sat too tightly at his shoulders and chest while billowing over his hips. This was my first confirmation that he possessed the same altered muscle composition as the Sleepless.

"You're waiting for something," I said. "What are you waiting for?"

"To be told to stand or invited to sit." No longer rasping with disuse, his voice was deep and rich, with a smooth RP accent that held a hint of something eastern European at the edges.

"Sit," I offered. "Please."

He moved to the other chair with an economy of grace, fluid and self-contained, and I picked up my pen and looked down the list of questions I'd prepared. In his presence, they seemed primitive and scrabbling, a useless analytical tool meant for someone too unlike the man in front of me.

"How are you feeling today?" I asked him. That question wasn't on my list, but it seemed important regardless.

"I'm a little cold."

"The heating isn't very good down here."

"No, I expect it wouldn't be."

I've never been good at small talk, and in this situation it seemed even more absurd than usual.

"As you know," I went on, "you've been brought here as a patient of the Orex Corporation's Tower Division, with a view to establishing your general health and how you and your companion arrived here. I have a duty to inform you that all of these conversations will be recorded. However, should you feel uncomfortable at any point, you have the right to request a halt to the proceedings and the interview will be terminated until another time. Do you have any questions before we begin?"

"I don't believe so. But if I think of anything, I'll be sure to let you know."

I considered my questions again.

"Am I right in thinking that you haven't told anyone your name?"

"Few have spoken with me since we arrived here, but if they had, I would have told them the same thing I told you that day. I don't remember my name."

"If you can't remember your name, what would you like to be called?"

"I have no preference. If it would help you to have a way to refer to me I will try to think of something before we meet again."

Already, this posed a problem. It's difficult to proceed with a conversation or study without having some sign or symbol to refer to the person being studied with.

"I'll mark the patient name as absent for now," I said, "but at some point we'll have to pick something."

"Very well. In the meantime, would you object very strongly to telling me your name?"

It surprised me to find that I did, but there seemed to be no reason to deny him so I offered it anyway. My reply seemed to delight him.

"Thea," he repeated. "A name that means, if memory serves, a gift of God. Although it can also be a reference to the Greek goddess Theia, who was also called Euryphaessa, known as the wide-shining and one of the twelve Titans in ancient myth." He steepled his fingers together over his chin, the first overt movement he'd made since taking his seat. "It can also be a shortened version of any number of names – Althea, for instance, which may be related to *althos*, or healing. That, perhaps, would be particularly apt for one attempting to cure this calamity. Or maybe you're a Theodora, or a Dorothea? Dorothea, who is also God's gift. Or perhaps you're rarer still. Chares is from the Greek, so perhaps your mother christened you Pasithea, to ensure that you always knew grace?"

I find, in my memory, that he drew all of the air in the room.

"My father was Greek, but I never knew him," I told him. "As far as I know, I'm only Thea."

"Well then, Only Thea, I'm pleased to know you. It's good to be able to put a name to a face, isn't it?"

I was disconcerted by the path the conversation had taken. There was even, I thought, something faintly mocking in the way he emphasised his knowledge of my name while withholding his own from me. I felt put upon, destabilised in a way that was difficult to challenge or codify.

"We seem to have got off topic," I said. "If you can't tell me your name, do you remember how old you are?"

"I'm afraid I have little memory of myself before this began. Perhaps it will return to me, but until then we must both remain in the dark."

Here I must declare a potential failure of my perception. Scientific observation relies on objectivity, or at the very least trust in the senses of the observer. It seemed as though the lights dimmed while he spoke, yet I see on the tape that they didn't.

"Let's start with what you do know, then. What's the first thing you remember, as far back as you can go?"

"I remember waking."

"Waking where?"

He blinked, long and slow, like a man emerging from sleep. "I woke in the dark and knew that something was wrong. There were blankets beneath me. They were wrapped around my legs."

"Were you at home? Somewhere safe?"

His silence stretched. He appeared to be thinking.

"No, I wasn't somewhere safe," he said. "The blankets were wrapped around my legs and I was in the dark. I felt that something had gone wrong. I felt that I'd been forced awake. Called, perhaps, by some strangeness in the air."

"And apart from the darkness, what else did you notice? Did you know where you were?"

"I had no memory. I lay there for a long time, trying to remember myself. Trying to recall why I might have been lying in the dark with the blankets around my legs."

"You weren't successful?"

He clasped his hands together on the desk. "No."

We held each other's gaze. His manner is a fascinating thing. It's beyond the norm of human interaction that a man should be so still, or hold himself with such focus without appearing to tire. His face was smooth, devoid of any expression, and something about it was false.

"What happened next?" I asked.

"What do you mean?"

"You can't have lain there in the dark forever or you'd still be there. What happened when you decided to get up? What did you see? Can you describe the room?"

"The room was in darkness. I do not recall it."

"What do you recall?"

"It was dark, and I felt as though something was wrong. The silence was terrible."

"In what way?"

"I don't know, but I felt that it was terrible all the same."

"You were afraid."

He paused then, and nodded, and for the first time I thought there was something very human behind his eyes.

"Yes, I was very afraid. I was afraid that I was alone, and that the silence wasn't just in the room with me but everywhere in all of the world. I was afraid that if I did get up and explore, I would never find anything else apart from myself, still searching."

"But you did get up and search in the end?"

"Yes. I was hungry, and thirsty. It was hot, and the blankets scratched my skin. I wanted to know where I was, to know if I might recognise it or recognise myself."

"And did you?"

"Not at first. I walked outside. The sun was like a dragon's breath. It burnt my skin."

"Are you sensitive to the sun?"

This was something we'd observed in the Sleepless. They preferred the dark. In the early months, when they were still active in the streets, the night was filled with the clamour of their movement. We watched them from the battlements while they streaked through the city like panthers. During daylight hours they confined themselves to the shadows, but in the first year we knew they were only waiting for a way inside.

"That depends," he said.

"On what?"

"On what you're comparing me to. Compared to most humans, I'm sensitive to the sun. Compared to an angler fish, I'm almost impervious to daylight."

He was making a joke, and that was perhaps the strangest I'd felt all day. I found it difficult to hold his gaze.

"Let's assume, for ease of understanding, that if I ask a comparative question it's related to other humans, shall we?"

"Of course."

When I looked up again his face was closed to me, as though the attempt at humour had never been made. I felt as though I'd failed some sort of test.

"I would like to return to my rooms now," he said. "Am I allowed a razor?"

"Will you let us test you?"

"No."

"Then you have your answer, don't you?"

7TH MAY

Postviral patients are some of the sickest in the world. Thirty years ago, when Mother first fell ill, it was estimated that around twenty-five per cent were housebound or bedbound and seventy-five per cent unable to work. Quality-of-life scores consistently placed them below the level of patients with congestive heart failure, multiple sclerosis, and other degenerative conditions, and yet the only prescribed treatments were graded exercise and cognitive behavioural therapy.

For a postviral patient, exercise is like pouring oil over a forest fire and watching the landscape burn, and by the time I reached secondary school Mother's internal landscape had become a silent conflagration. At the very severe end of the spectrum, the body shuts down its most basic functions – the mechanisms that process and maintain cellular energy collapse until even light, sound, and touch become too agonising to bear.

Before the failure of our digital systems, I used to scroll through images of severe patients online and see Mother in every one. They all had the same brittle appearance, like a pane of glass that was about to crack. All of the pictures were taken in darkened bedrooms, the people lying like corpses on the bed, noise-cancelling headphones over their ears and sleep masks over their eyes. Often, my attention would be drawn away from them to what little comforts were in view: a vase filled with white flowers; a strip of dust-speckled sunlight glowing through the curtains revealing a phone or a notebook, or some bright scrap of fabric for comfort or familiarity; a worn blanket or teddy bear; side tables stacked with medication; or sometimes an IV or feeding tube coiling like a vine from under the bedcovers. Still worse were the ones featuring photographs of the patient in better days, hiking through forests or smiling at bars, surrounded by the people they loved.

This was a torture of the modern day, but while the pictures tormented me, they also made me feel less alone. The habit I've acquired of sitting by Mother's bed in the night began back then, when she first drifted to the most dangerous end of the scale. No longer able to speak or listen, she would lie there in the dark in agony, unable even to cry out at the pain.

I was convinced that one day I would go to sleep in the room next door only to wake and discover she'd died in the night. Perhaps this was when my insomnia began, staking silent vigils at her side with my hand wrapped around her wrist and my fingers pressed to her pulse, fluttering like the wings of a hummingbird against me, her breaths a grated wheezing, exhausting even to listen to. I would watch her chest struggle to rise and fall, her jaw draw tight and lips become parted, and I'd fight against the urge to sleep, half-believing that the only thing that kept her tethered to this world was my witness to her trials.

When the gap around the curtains became grey with the onset of a new day, I'd finally leave her to ready myself for school. In the morning light, I'd sit in the bath, the water near scalding and steam rising in great plumes towards the mould on the ceiling. Then I'd slip down beneath the water until it covered my head, and scream and scream and scream where no one could hear me, a useless catharsis in the epicentre of disaster, before sitting in the classroom again.

12TH MAY

Memory is the seat of personality, a fragile and tenuous thing that chains our present to our past and allows us to anticipate a future. It's housed in the deeper, more instinctive parts of our brain, areas that light up and assault us with sensations, images, and emotions in response to something so subtle as scent. We are all of us victims of our own recollections and servants to what they make of us.

The stories we tell are collective repositories of remembering. They remind us of who we were, who we might be, and who we hope never to be. What, then, does it say about us that there are certain tales we've carried into this new world? Dracula. Troy. They shape our fears as much as they give us the language to describe them. And yet how many stories have been lost? What wisdom have we already forgotten that we may never discover again? What of himself does our missing link not know, and how much of him can we trust while we also live in this space of forgetting?

Sleep is crucial to the consolidation of memory. During slow-wave sleep – the deepest and most restorative phase of unconsciousness – our brains replenish the connections between neurons which allow us to process and store memories of the previous day. Without sleep, we are cut adrift on a plane of forgetfulness, unable to recall not only what we've experienced but also that there's something we've forgotten. Our lives become opaque, a mysterious past we know we've lived but whose shape we can never quite discern. Sleep is the thread that binds us to memory, and with it, secures us to ourselves.

It's clear to me that the destabilisation of personality was one of the earliest symptoms that should have shown us the fatal flaw in the neuralchip. I've spent the evening reviewing the transcript from my talk with our survivor alongside the interview between Corporal Bright and Captain Tennyson. They share certain similarities, but what strikes me most, now that I'm able to approach them analytically, is how they differ.

Corporal Bright is in distress during his interview. The symptoms of amnesia – his growing knowledge of his own forgetfulness – suggest to him the potential for a terrible reality he can't recall. The presence of a medical officer and a guard only make him more paranoid. He knows where he is and who he is, but the details of how he came to be there elude him. As a result, he's combative, frightened, and hostile to questioning.

He's also a being of questions. He seeks answers compulsively, as we all do in times of uncertainty. Not content, and perhaps not even able to answer Captain Tennyson's questions, he invents more of his own. *Why am I here? Why are you asking me this? What's happened?* Endlessly: *Why, what, how, where?* Humanity can't bear uncertainty – it's where we feel most on the edge – and yet our survivor maintains his position on the threshold of chaos with an almost offensive level of calm.

I'd say that he was ambivalent about his memories, but the very thought he might be aggravates me. How can someone be ambivalent about the loss of their self? How can he be brought to the Tower of London in chains and ask only for a razor and my name? Surely he ought to be in distress. He ought to rail against the fates that have brought him to us. He should demand that we, as doctors, fix him. He should implore us to treat him with all of the science and care available to us. Yet he does none of this. Why?

I see three possible conclusions here. The first, and the most simple, is that he's lying. As an explanation for ambivalence, this is the one I find the least offensive and also the most likely. As a scientist, someone who has compulsively sought answers throughout my life, I find the idea that someone could lose both their self and the world and simply not wonder about it intolerably maddening. If he were lying, I could at least reconcile his behaviour with something that makes sense to me.

The second possibility is that alongside amnesia he's also suffered some other, more mysterious form of brain damage. Before the advent of the neuralchip, sleep deprivation was known to cause personality changes and mood disturbances. Research linked long-term lack of sleep to illnesses ranging from Alzheimer's to diabetes and schizophrenia. Short-term sleep deprivation was responsible for a number of cognitive deficits, and more crucially the sufferer was unable to recognise that their performance had worsened.

If short-term sleeplessness can cause mood and behaviour changes alongside intellectual deficits, then ambivalence may be a symptom in itself. If this is true, it could prove useful in attempting to isolate where the damage occurred. Disorders of adrenaline can cause lethargy and low mood, and damage to the amygdala could explain this kind of accelerated apathy. It may be visible on a brain scan – if he ever consents to being scanned.

Thirdly, and perhaps most unlikely, is that he isn't lying and nor is he brain damaged. Instead, some form of trauma has created his lack of care. I say this is unlikely because while depression can numb the mood, this sort of hollowness is more likely to occur during active trauma or far after the event. In the timeline as I see it, our survivor has potentially lived through a number of traumatic experiences, but we are neither in the middle of the catastrophe nor so far beyond it that it could be called retrospective. Moreover, he isn't apathetic to everything.

In many ways, he's interested, but about the wrong things. He is, I think, interested in me, although now, with the benefit of hindsight, I suspect that his interest is a veil he's hiding behind – that is, it isn't true interest but merely a way of controlling the conversation. A clutch for balance and power in a space where he could be said to have neither.

Additionally, he seems to care for his fellow survivor's well-being far more than he cares for his own. It's this factor that I intend to exploit during our next interview. While he may find it easy to obfuscate about his own life, I suspect that he'll find it less so when she's brought into the conversation.

HE WASN'T THERE AGAIN TODAY

15TH MAY

The interview room was just as cold when I returned. I'd worn a jumper under my lab coat, but the stone walls trap damp and a wet chill is difficult to shake. Thane delivered the survivor to me, bound as before, and as before he waited for me to offer him a seat.

"I wanted to go back to the subject of your name and your companion's name," I said.

"You wish to know whether either of us have recalled our memories or our speech."

"Have you?"

"No."

I'd expected this but was still frustrated.

"It unsettles you not to have a way to refer to me. To us," he said. "Why?"

I'd thought to redirect him, but then I recalled how quickly he'd ended our interview after I'd ignored his attempt at a joke. Perhaps by drawing such a hard border between us, and standing too firmly at the boundary between clinician and patient, I was harming our ability to communicate. I did him the courtesy of thinking about his question before answering.

"It's an issue of categorisation, I think. In science, all new discoveries are named. The lack of a name implies a lack of discovery, which in turn implies a lack of understanding. We discover, we name, we attempt to understand. Without a name, it's difficult to proceed."

"And for a person and not a science project?"

I paused, considering. "A name is often the first thing we learn about someone. It tells us something about them, socially if not intrinsically. Their class, or their parents' class. Their culture or language, perhaps. On a more personal level, it allows us to build a relationship around them, which isn't so dissimilar to scientific discovery. We meet someone, we learn their name, and as we build a picture of who they are and how they relate to us, we attach certain knowledge to that name."

"A name has power," he said. "It's a method of control."

"I'm not sure I'd put it that way."

"How would you put it?"

I twirled the pen between my fingers – a thinking habit I'd acquired from Mother. "I'd say that a name is a method of understanding and an offer of connection. We give someone our name and we're inviting them to know us, to connect with us and see what happens next. An offer of a name is an offer of a relationship, in whatever form that may be. Will we be friends? Acquaintances? Will we never see each other again? No one knows, but it all begins with a name."

He seemed pleased by this, and thoughtful in a way that felt like progress.

"Perhaps you're right," he said. "In which case, I'm particularly sorry that I can't offer you my name, Thea Chares."

He studied me in silence for a long moment.

"They call her Helen, you know."

The statement seemed to come out of nowhere, yet he looked at me as though I should have been keeping pace.

"Your companion's name is Helen? Has she spoken, then?"

"No, she hasn't spoken, but that's what they call her."

"Who's they?"

He tilted his head, reminding me of a bird contemplating an interloper from on high. "I'm afraid they haven't told me their names. The man who brings me here, and the one who turns the lights off at night."

Thane and Alex.

"Do you know why they call her Helen?" he asked. "If you do, please tell me. I would very much like to know." For the first time that session, I looked down at my notepad, my glasses slipping down my nose. He tilted his head again. "Does the question make you uncomfortable?"

"No." I twirled my pen again. "I hadn't heard that they'd given her a nickname, but my guess would be that they call her Helen for the same reason they call the Tower Troy."

"Ah." He leant back in his chair, the first time I'd seen him do something so commonplace, and I had the impression he was pleased. "Helen of Troy. Yes, I can see why that would fit. She is on some level a daughter of the night."

"How do you mean?"

"She arrived here with me. Arguably, you understand that the Sleepless are creatures of the night. And you suspect, I know, that I'm one of them."

"Aren't you?"

"How would I know?"

I let my face show my scepticism, and with a sharp flash of teeth his mouth opened in a grin. The effect was startling. Until that moment, I hadn't realised that the blank expression had been camouflage, or rather, I hadn't considered what it was camouflage for. The answer, I discovered, was Otherness. When he smiled – truly smiled – with teeth bright and on display, there was no mistaking him for anything other than something eldritch and abominable. I felt that I'd been cornered.

"Do you know what they call me? And don't lie. I will know if you lie."

"Yes, I know what they call you."

"But you don't approve."

"What makes you say that?"

"A number of things." There was a loose thread from my jumper, dark green against the table top, and he pressed the tip of his finger to it and drew it back towards him. "You were annoyed to hear the name Helen, knowing what it meant, but you didn't try to obfuscate. The nickname visibly surprised you, but my own doesn't. Therefore, the only reason you might not wish me to know it is that you believe it may be insulting, and so you disapprove. Does it worry you that I might be offended?"

"It doesn't worry me."

"But you would spare my feelings if you could?"

I wondered, then, just how many feelings this man had, and whether they were so unlike my own that it would be impossible for me to understand them. Out loud, I said, "Why not spare pain if you can?"

"Why not, indeed? Regardless, I would like to know. If it would make you feel better, I absolve you of any guilt should I find myself distressed."

In truth, I was less worried about his reaction than I was embarrassed by having to admit that the others thought him vampiric. But it suited me for him to believe that my primary concern was for his welfare, so I didn't correct him. "They call you a few things," I told him. "The Count is the most popular."

He wove the thread between the fingers of his left hand, no longer looking at me. "And the others?"

"Would you like a list?"

"Perhaps. Don't parents usually prepare a list of names before deciding on one?"

For the second time that session, he'd surprised me. "You're intending to pick a name?"

"I may. And isn't it usually the case that a name is chosen after being selected by other people first?"

"I suppose, but children don't often get a say in their given names."

"Even so, I'd like to hear whether any more have been attached to me. As you've already demonstrated, names have power, even if they aren't intended to control."

This was, I realised, the very first thing he'd asked for that I could give him. It put me in a position of power. "If I tell you, will you answer my questions?"

"You offer an exchange?"

I nodded.

"Then we have an agreement."

"All right then. The Count, Vlad the Impaler, Vladimir, Dracula, Dantès, Drac, and I believe sometimes Adam. Does that help?"

He watched me. "Many of those are self-explanatory, if a little obvious," he said.

"But?"

"I find myself perplexed by two of them – Dantès and Adam. Why those in particular? Do you know?"

"Dantès because the Count of Monte Cristo was called Edmond Dantès."

He inclined his head. "And Adam is Biblical, perhaps? The first of my kind, like the first man?"

"Yes and no. Adam was Edgar's suggestion, and I think it was more to do with the Adam of Victor's labours."

"The child of Frankenstein? Charming."

"Are you offended?"

One of his hands flexed against the table. "Why should I be offended? It isn't the child who's the monster in the story."

"But you still might not want to choose it as a name."

"Perhaps not. What would you choose, if you were me?"

Once again, he'd surprised me. The act of naming is intimate. It suggests a deep level of care for the one being named, and perhaps a certain level of ownership by the one doing the naming. Parents name their children. Owners name their pets. Scientists occasionally get to name our own discoveries. I didn't want the responsibility of claiming either ownership or care of him, but he'd offered it to me anyway.

"I think it's a choice you have to make for yourself," I said. "Are you so sure you won't remember your name?"

"I don't believe so. Besides, after all that's happened, perhaps my old name won't fit. Maybe one of these new names would suit me better."

"Like the Impaler?" I couldn't keep the sarcasm from my voice, and as before my answer was that unnerving grin.

"It would make a statement," he pointed out.

"But is it the kind of statement you'd want to make?"

He considered this and began to toy with the thread again. "Perhaps not. But since we last spoke, the absence of my name has begun to bother me more than it did before."

Here, then, was a glimmer of progress. Far from the insistent apathy that had characterised our first conversation, he now seemed to have some small care for himself as an autonomous creature.

"How do you feel about it now?" I asked. "And how does that differ from how you felt before?"

He was quiet for a long time. Long enough that I began to notice the ticking of the clock and the bright flash of red reflected in the mirror.

"May I stand?" he asked at last.

"Are you uncomfortable?"

"No, I'm not uncomfortable. I only wish to look." He tilted his head towards the mirror.

"Do you have a mirror in your rooms?" I asked.

"No. I believe it was thought safer not to allow us access to sharp objects."

Thane's influence, probably, but not something I disapproved of.

"Then please." I gestured for him to rise, and he did, moving to face his reflection. I avoided my own in this room, since I was aware both of the camera recording behind the glass and Edgar watching the interview unfold. I didn't want to find myself in the position of looking into my own face, while on a level beyond my perception, I was really looking into his. Still, I was fascinated by the idea that our survivor hadn't seen himself yet, and what revelations he might uncover when he did.

He stepped forwards two paces, methodical and controlled, and then stopped with his back turned towards me. His reflected image was preternaturally still, and he gave the impression of a king awaiting an execution. If I'd hoped for a sudden flash of insight, or to watch the play of great emotion over his face when he met himself for the first time, I was to be disappointed. The blank mask, entirely neutral, didn't waver, although his eyes tracked across his features, focusing on his eyes and mouth and eventually performing a cursory glance of his torso.

"You asked how I felt about my name and whether that differed from how I felt before," he said. His eyes met mine in the mirror, and I nodded to his reflection to continue. "Before, when I was alone or when it was merely my companion and I, the lack of a reference point didn't concern me. Don't you, for instance, think in the first person?"

"I imagine that everyone does, for the most part," I said.

"And haven't you ever experienced it as a shock when someone uses your full name and you're reminded that 'I' only exists in your head, and that everyone else sees you as Thea, although you don't think of yourself that way?"

In truth, I hadn't given it much thought, but I nodded anyway.

"But didn't your companion want to know your name?" I asked him. "Or you hers?"

"Why should she? She doesn't speak, and as far as I was concerned we were the only two people who might converse if given the chance. I was perfectly content to think of myself as 'I', my companion as 'she', and the two of us together as 'we'."

"But you aren't content anymore?"

His gaze, which until now had held mine, turned to his reflection again. "As you've said, a name not only categorises a person to themselves but also in relation to others. We offer our names as a way of connecting with other people. When it was just myself and Helen, as your people call her, it didn't matter because for different reasons neither of us could communicate our names."

"And now?"

A frown line appeared between his eyes, and he lifted his bound hands and ran a hesitant finger along it. "Now,

I find it odd not to know the names of the people around me. After you gave me your name, it was easier for me to think about you afterwards. I didn't need to think of you as an image, or attach some mannerism or behaviour to you, or even recall an interaction we'd shared to be able to bring you to mind. I simply thought the word *Thea*, and there you were."

"And that makes things easier for you?"

"In some ways. I find it comforting."

He stood there in silence for some moments longer, and then, with a slow release of breath, he turned and resumed his seat.

"Thank you for that," he said. "It's a strange thing, not to have an image for one's self."

"And do you feel better for having one?" What I really wanted to ask was whether he had an opinion about himself. Had he, before he looked into the mirror, had a conception of how he appeared, and if so, had that changed? Was he more or less attractive than his own mind had anticipated? If he'd pictured himself before, had his mental image now altered to match the reality, or was he in some way split? Put simply, I was less interested in how he felt than in what he thought, but I didn't believe he would respond to these questions, so I didn't ask them.

"I feel less abstract," he answered. "More of a person than a concept."

"You feel more of a connection to yourself."

"No. I feel as though I understand other people better, now that I know how they see me."

"In what sense?"

He looked up again, pinning me with such concentrated eye contact that heat crawled down my neck. "Your reactions to my appearance were a surprise to me. Until that moment, I'd assumed Helen's nerves were for herself. It hadn't occurred to me that I might be in danger."

"You didn't realise you might be a threat?" I found this hard to believe.

"I knew I wasn't a threat because I knew my intentions in coming here."

"And what were they?"

"I wanted to get help for Helen."

Here, then, was an opening.

"I wanted to talk about her today," I said, and watched carefully for his reaction. But something about him, the part that I was beginning to recognise as a feeling being, was once again hidden behind his neutral facade.

"You don't want to return to our previous conversation?" he asked.

"I do, but not today. It seemed to distress you."

"I wasn't distressed." He spoke too quickly – the first lie I could be certain was a lie.

"Even so, I wanted to talk about your companion today. You arrived here together but she wasn't present in your earliest memories."

"She wasn't."

"So, how did you meet?"

He didn't answer.

"She wasn't there when you woke, and it doesn't seem as though she'd be capable of taking care of herself for very long alone. So at some point between you waking and arriving here, you must have come across her. How did that happen?"

The clock on the wall ticked. The red recording light blinked.

"Did she welcome you? Was she afraid? If you can't tell me how you met, maybe you can tell me where?"

Again, he didn't reply. I waited. I felt that I was on more stable ground than I had been in our previous interview. Before, he'd been an enigma, a creature entirely closed to me, denying every impulse that I would consider human. Today, he'd at least expressed an interest in learning his name and in seeing himself through our eyes.

"I'll remind you that earlier you agreed to answer my questions today," I said.

His fingers stilled for a moment and then resumed their weaving of the thread. "To what end?"

"Sorry?"

"To what end do you ask these questions? What do you hope to achieve by them?"

"I should think that was obvious," I said. "We ask questions in expectation of receiving an answer."

"And what then?" he asked. "When you have my answers, what do you intend to do with them? Do you ask merely to have a record? Do you seek some more personal truth for your own satisfaction? Do you wish to know more about the world beyond these walls? Or are you hoping that my answers may have value medically, in discerning whatever it is you think that I am?" He tilted his head, in that bird-like way of his, and watched me. "What is the purpose of these interviews?"

I didn't answer, curious to see where he might take this line of thought to uninterrupted.

"If your questioning was merely for some medical benefit then my history wouldn't interest you. Likewise, you would learn more about Helen by submitting her to testing than by asking me about her. And yet here you sit for a second time, your curiosity trained upon me." He mimicked my position then, folding his hands against the table, his focus on me never wavering. "So, I'd like to know. What do you hope to achieve, other than my answers? What purpose have they to you?"

The truth, of course, was that I wanted his cooperation. I wanted him to understand that he was important to our research and to consent to further tests. To achieve this, I needed him to trust me, but the fact was that I was curious about him as well. He was a mystery, and one I intended to solve.

I tilted my head, mimicking his own gesture, and saw a flash of something in his eyes that was gone before I could parse it.

"Obtaining a detailed patient history is a cornerstone of all medical care," I replied. "No matter the illness or condition, a doctor must always begin with their patient."

"But that surely assumes I'm sick?"

"Of course you're sick."

"Am I?"

The question brought me up short, because it hadn't occurred to me to ask it. The Sleepless were sick. It was an inalienable truth. They'd succumbed to whatever flaw was contained in the neural network, taking leave of their personalities, behaviour, and sense. They descended upon the world like locusts, abandoning speech and thought, and none of them were able to sleep.

This man, however, was none of those things. He showed no signs of being a rapacious monster. Although he clearly survived on a primarily carnivorous diet, he'd made no move to harm us. He retained his speech and his reason, if not his memories. And while his movements and manner were disturbing, in the sense that they skewed both too close and not close enough to recognisable humanity, his impulse control seemed as strong as anyone else's. Why, then, had my mind categorised him as sick? Perhaps it was only his strangeness I was seeing and not illness at all. But then, how were we to classify him?

"You don't believe you're sick?" I asked.

"I don't."

"Then what do you believe you are?"

"Different," he replied. "Divergent, if you'd like. An anomaly, if that would satisfy your scientific need."

"And do you want a cure?" It seemed incredible to me that I hadn't thought to ask until now, and yet, as I stared into the smooth mask of his face, I realised that he was no more committed to my intentions than I was to his. He didn't behave as a patient ought to because he didn't see himself as a patient – a truth so simple it had eluded me.

"For myself? I'm ambivalent. What could a cure offer me that my current reality doesn't?"

"Is your reality so comfortable that you wouldn't wish to change it?"

"Is yours?"

I managed to keep the frustration from my voice. "We're talking about you. Aren't there things this change has brought about in you that you'd want to change back?"

"Such as?"

"The ability to sit in the sun and rest after a long day?"

He did me the courtesy of at least contemplating this, or at the very least he gave the appearance of contemplation, which may be the same thing. "I miss the sun," he admitted, "although I'm not sure I remember it well. But there are other things I've gained as well. I'm stronger than you, faster than you, and I require less sustenance than you. While you may see these changes as a sickness, isn't it possible that I'm better protected against disease than you?"

An intriguing and horrifying thought in one.

"You're suggesting that your increased rate of healing may be of evolutionary benefit?"

"I'm suggesting that it may be of benefit to *me*, regardless of whether you see it as a benefit to humanity."

It was on the tip of my tongue to tell him that whatever he was now, it wasn't human. Until then, I'd been categorising him as a person suffering from some malady, something to be analysed, understood, and cured. But if he didn't see himself as sick, was it even possible to see him as human at all?

These questions were too large for us to address. I had the feeling, again, that I'd been steered into a conversational diversion, backed into a semantic corner so that he might avoid speaking of subjects that made him uncomfortable. The skill with which he was able to redirect my train of thought angered and unsettled me.

"An interesting observation," I said. "But perhaps we can get back on topic. How or where did you meet your companion?"

"I'm still not certain of what benefit that question is to you."

I allowed myself a small smile. "Does it matter? Humour me. Let's say I'm satisfying my own curiosity and nothing else."

"And are you?"

"In part."

He smiled then, not the unsettling grin of too-sharp teeth and eldritch manner, but a subtle quirk at the corner of his mouth. A twist of humanity on display. "Very well. I met Helen on the outskirts of south London, wandering the banks of the Thames."

"And what was she doing?"

"I told you. Wandering."

"Besides that. What was her manner? Was she alone? Agitated? Did she seem in distress?"

"She was eating a dead rat at the time."

My pen grew still in my hand. "A dead rat."

"Certainly."

"Your companion was eating a dead rat."

His head tilted, his expression impassive. "Do you imagine that food is so plentiful beyond these walls that a person would reject any that crosses their path?"

I hadn't considered it, but now my thoughts were consumed by it. Against my will, I saw her crouching in stinking mud, her hands tight around the rodent as she brought it to her lips. Worse still was that I couldn't stop my own sense memories from conjuring a synaesthetic experience. For a moment, I could smell the salt and shit, feel damp, reeking hair in my mouth, and the bitter, repulsive flood of blood onto my tongue when my teeth bit down on the flesh.

"Are you all right, Thea?" His voice seemed very far away. "You've suddenly gone quite pale."

When I came back to myself, he was leaning forwards in his seat, and there was true concern in his eyes – or, at the very least, an emotion that looked like concern, but could have been no more true than had I declared my love for him. The thought of his play-acting made me furious, and I became aware that I was little more than a toy with which he was entertaining himself. A diversion to pass the time.

"I'm quite all right, thank you."

"Are you sure? Perhaps you should ask the man with the gun to bring you some water?"

"There's no need for that." I gathered my papers and stood. "That concludes our interview for the day. Our captain will see you out."

He sat back in his chair. "Can I have a razor?"

"Will you let us test you?"

We both knew the answer was no.

16TH MAY

The human mind is one of the most adaptable evolutions in history. It took us from the animal to the self-aware, capable of perceiving of ourselves as individuals, understanding the intricacies of the world, and analysing the passage of time. It's also a fragile thing, housed within a body that responds to even the slightest shock with a cascade of hormones, triggering biochemical changes beyond our conscious control.

I have never slept well. Sleep is an interloper, a thief, a mysterious void we fall into and give up our bodies for lost. Sleep is nourisher and commander, the seat of health and creativity, and also the irresistible force to which we must all surrender. Someone who sleeps well may never give much thought to the process we put ourselves through every twelve to eighteen hours, but if sleep is invisible to those who have it, then it's an astounding force to those of us who struggle to find and keep it.

Sleep comes for me with a rush of hormones whether I like it or not. These aren't just soporific but stress-inducing, in the medical rather than the psychiatric sense. The suprachiasmatic nucleus tells the brain that there's a repeating cycle of night and day via the hormone melatonin. This is the signal system for our circadian rhythms, but there is also another, more unforgiving chemical: adenosine.

For a long time, my research focused on this hormone above all others, for one very simple reason. From the moment a person wakes, at every minute of every day, the concentration of adenosine builds up in the brain, turning down the volume on wake-promoting areas and turning up the dial on sleep-promoting regions. The combined effect of this process increases sleep pressure. No matter how strong a person's will, eventually adenosine will ensure they long for sleep like an addict.

It's a particularly cruel quirk of the human mind, then, that it can work against such biological stress and resist the combined pull of sleep time and pressure. The last few nights, I have slept barely. In the darkness behind my closed eyes, I see strange shadows, creatures with too-long limbs sloping across my field of vision. Flashing red and green lights float in the space between sleep and wakefulness, coalescing into waves, a river. A rodent.

In the moments I do find sleep, my dreams are bright, vivid things, but curiously mundane. I see myself walking along the beach by our old home. My feet are bare, and the sand is so viscerally real, the dreamscape so well constructed, that I can feel it crunching between my toes. The world is peaceful. It's a warm summer's day. The sea is lapping like an animal's tongue at the shore. I hear seagulls – although I can't see them – as well as the laughter of children and the conversations of their parents. All seems well with the world.

Then it strikes me that I'm alone. That on a day like this there should be crowds jostling for space. Towels fighting for the best sun spot. I look around, and I realise that I can hear the world but I can't see it. I hear the laughter and the shouting, but there's no one here but me. A deep dream logic begins to infiltrate my mind, along with the knowledge that I'm sleeping.

With this realisation comes an almost irresistible urge to find my mother. She's here somewhere, trapped in the dreamscape. If I could find her, I could bring her back and rescue her from wherever fate has taken her.

The noise grows louder. The sea starts to roar. The sound of the gulls becomes a squall, and I feel air whip past my face as though their wings are no more than an inch away.

The laughter changes, becomes mocking, and I start to hurry. Ahead, there's only the long stretch of sand, waves crashing, a pier so far away that it's little more than a blister on the horizon. I know, somehow, that Mother will be at the rock pools, but they never seem to get any closer. I break into a run, and all around me there's movement in the sand – waves kicked up as though ghosts are running across it, depressions where towels ought to be, and impressions of footprints that have no owners.

I must find my mother. I think I hear snatches of her crying on the wind, but the sea and the gulls are screaming. The sky darkens, clouds roll in over the ocean, and my hair sticks to my face as the first fat drops of rain begin to fall. The ghostly beachgoers start to shout and squeal, and I feel them moving around me, running back to the shore. The beach tilts and sways, scatters of sand kicked up by hundreds of invisible feet, and I realise that I won't reach her. Instead, I'll be trampled by all of the ghosts I can't see, who also can't see me.

When I wake, I'm standing by the bedroom door, and my Grey Lady is perched like a carrion animal at the foot of my bed. Her hair is a tangled mess dripping over her face, her hands claw-like and biting into my bedsheets. I sense her intent, and it is to consume me. Paralysed, I stare into the pits where her eyes ought to be, and I feel my body give up, disintegrate, and seep like an oil spill through the floor.

When I came back to myself I was collapsed in the doorway of my bedroom, my legs aching and chest heaving as though I really had been running. The Grey Lady was gone, but there was a sense of general disorder to my room – objects moved just slightly out of their rightful place – that suggested I'd been sleepwalking.

It disturbed me to find that my body had been walking around without my permission, and that I'd been little more than an automaton careering around the room. It was still dark outside, and I roused myself in a twilight state and went to prepare Mother's breakfast. The kitchen tiles were cold beneath my feet, and by the time I'd carried the tray back upstairs I was shivering and out of sorts.

Mother was quiet when I entered, the air in her room stale and the darkness so thick it felt like wading through treacle. I felt… What did I feel? I felt that we'd been possessed – me by a dream-maker who had taken control of my body, and she by some force that had stripped her of all sovereignty of hers.

"I'm sorry," I whispered while she ate, but I wasn't sure what I was apologising for. For not being good enough, perhaps. For not having the answers. For understanding that she would be crying if she could, just like the voice in my dreams, and for knowing that I was selfish enough to be grateful that I couldn't hear it.

22ND MAY

To listen is the very least that a doctor owes to their patient, but sometimes we listen for the wrong things.

When I look back at the history of medicine, collecting past moments like breadcrumbs in the hope they'll make sense of today, the silence of the patients rings out as loudly as a clarion call tolling to an empty civilisation. I think of Henrietta's stolen cells, revolutionising medicine forever while she remained a footnote in the story, and the scores of women in Charcot's photographs of madness whose names no one can recall.

In the history of postviral illness, the first major wall of silence was built in the 1970s by two eminent psychiatrists, Colin McEvedy and Bill Beard.

In 1969, fourteen years after the Royal Free Hospital outbreak, thirteen years after the medical journal *The Lancet* first named the condition myalgic encephalomyelitis, McEvedy and Beard wrote to Doctor Ramsay. They wanted his permission to view the records of the nurses involved in the 1955 event, as part of their work at the Department of Psychological Medicine in Middlesex Hospital. Seeing no reason to refuse, Ramsay agreed.

On 3 January 1970, the four-page report entitled "Royal Free Epidemic of 1955: A Reconsideration" was published in the *British Medical Journal* and its findings spread through the profession. In direct opposition to Ramsay's tests, which showed glandular swelling, severe infections of the pharynx, and damage to the nervous system, McEvedy and Beard viewed the outbreak as a simple case of mass hysteria, their primary reason for this being that most of the patient group, as nurses in the 1950s, were women.

The two psychiatrists made this claim without ever having examined a patient of the Royal Free Hospital.

I WISH I WISH HE'D GO AWAY

25TH MAY

Helen, if that's what we're to call her, is a peculiar creature. She drifts around the compound like some strange wanderer, mute and captured within her own mind. She joined us in the canteen today and sat at one of the tables alone, hunched and leaning forwards as though expecting a blow.

"What's she doing here?" Dolly's voice carried and Helen's back turned rigid.

"She's here for the same reason you are," Maryam replied. "To eat."

Helen made no move to indicate that she'd heard her. She held her fork strangely, clenched in her fist like a child still learning to use cutlery. She trembled, the food wavering as she ducked her head closer to the plate to guide it into her mouth. I must admit to experiencing an undercurrent of revulsion, the sense-memory of her biting into the flesh of the rat enough to fill my mouth with water and the metallic tang of blood.

Alison, too, watched her closely. Her gun was on the table nearby, a warning and a threat, although Helen made no move to acknowledge it as either. She ate silently, with unerring focus, her whole attention on the path of the fork to her lips and the considered chewing and swallowing that seemed as though it took her great effort to regulate. Only when she'd finished did she look up and around the room, and in the moment our eyes met I felt a needle of terror shoot through me, similar to the one my Grey Lady evoked in the night.

Her face didn't change. Her pale green eyes looked into me as though I were someone she'd never seen before. It seemed as though she was trying to come to a decision about who I was, and that she'd failed. When Alison appeared at her side, she didn't look up; she merely got to her feet, with that same subtle twitching I'd observed in her before, and allowed herself to be escorted from the room.

"She shouldn't be allowed to eat in here with the rest of us," Dolly said as the doors swung shut behind her. "If Edgar and the Professor want to study people then that's their problem, but none of us agreed to it, did we?"

"Helen isn't being studied," I replied. "She's a survivor, and she has as much right to be here as you do."

"Maybe you should be studying her, though," Dolly countered. "Did you ever think about that? It's weird, the way she shuffles around the place."

"In what way?" Maryam asked. I hadn't expected her to speak, and it appeared that neither had Dolly.

"Did you see her holding her fork? She's like some savage from the wilds. And what about all of that shaking and teeth gnashing? She's mad. She's probably dangerous."

"So, because she doesn't move through the world in the same way you do, she's wrong?"

"Of course she's wrong! Anyone with eyes can see she isn't right. You only have to look at her."

"And at me?"

The room grew very silent and still.

"You aren't dangerous," Dolly said. "And you can't tell me that you wouldn't choose to get out of that thing if you could."

Miles sucked in a breath through his teeth and looked away.

"Would it surprise you very much to learn that I wouldn't, beta?"

"Of course you would. Wouldn't you like to be able to get to all of the places you can't reach?"

"Of course," said Maryam. "But why should I have to change to do that? There's nothing wrong with me as I am. It isn't my fault the world is filled with stairs."

Dolly stood, tossing her hair over her shoulder and fixing Miles with a pointed look until he got to his feet as well. "Then maybe you're as mad as she is," she said. "You can stay broken if you want, but you shouldn't expect everyone else to be okay with it. Come on, Miles. We have work to do."

He hesitated, which is the best thing I can say for him here. Dolly marched to the door and disappeared with poise and conviction, and he whispered a guilty apology and followed her outside.

Maryam seemed far older in the moments after they'd left.

"She didn't mean it," I said. "You know what Dolly's like."

Her smile was sad and small. "Sadly, I think she did."

There was little more I could say, and I've never been very good at providing comfort, so I simply sat with her while she finished her food, frustrated that Dolly's notion of what was right was the same as what was normal. Although it isn't, in truth, entirely her fault.

Normality has acquired two meanings that are so closely entwined they can hardly be separated from one another. To be normal isn't just to be average, but what's normal must also be *right*. I reject, and have always rejected, this feeble thought. Humanity is drawn to the novel, the new. Rid ourselves of difference and we rid ourselves of humanity. I think in many ways that's why I struggle to see the Sleepless as human. They are all of them one and the same, and I find that sameness appalling.

30TH MAY

When I was very young, perhaps five or six, we visited a petting zoo during late spring. Mother was going through a better period then. She wasn't able to work full time, but she could spend most days out of bed, doing a little painting and walking on the beach. I'd never been to a farm before. The thick, brine tang of the seaside was the only thing I'd known. By comparison, the dusky musk of dung and straw and animal sweat was the most intense sensory experience I'd ever had.

I was astounded by it. The bleating of the sheep calling for their lambs, the whuff and whiffle of the horses, and the velvet softness of their noses against my fingers. I remember I was wearing red wellington boots and a puffy purple coat, bundled up against the unseasonal chill, but I refused to wear my gloves. I wanted to be able to touch everything – to hold the food pellets in my palm and feel the strange thrill of trembling noses pressed against me, snuffling for the food and somehow resisting the urge, which I felt sure they must have had, to bite.

It was, and still is, a day drenched in technicolour in my memories. Mother laughing with the farmworkers, the smell of the animals, the horses and chickens that clattered around me, and the cardboard tub of ice cream when we left. But it was the kids and the lambs that made it magical.

The youngest animals were only a few weeks old, their bleating high-pitched and concerned, and their little trotters clip-clopping across the pavement pens. Maybe because it was mid-week and quiet, or maybe because Mother had befriended one of the farmhands, we were allowed into the pen while they were being fed. Mother took hold of a soft white lamb, with legs too long for its body and a surprising strength when it suckled at the bottle.

One of the workers settled a tiny kid in my arms, a late birth that he called the runt of the herd. It was delicate and a deep auburn colour, with patches of white on its chest and around the bottom of its ears. It made a panicked whining noise when I tipped it onto its back, holding it the way I'd seen adults cradle human babies before. The man showed me how to hold the bottle to its muzzle, and after a few false starts it began to suckle.

I was awed by this soft little creature. It lay there in my arms, humming against the bottle, its hoofs waving in the air and its body warm on my knee. When the milk was gone, it bleated, and I ran my fingers over its head and touched the strange thickness of its feet, and it grew tired and fell asleep with its muzzle tucked under my chin. I sat there in a state of wonder, hardly daring to move, a sense of pride and an odd maternal instinct running through me at the knowledge that this fragile thing trusted me to keep it safe.

Such maternal feelings have never come so easily to me where human children are concerned. I want them to be safe and happy in a rather abstract sense, but I've never really understood them, even when I was one myself. I was a child who preferred the company of adults and found something horrifying about the yelling and screaming of others my age. The gentleness of animals, on the other hand, has always appealed to me.

Needless to say, I cried when I was told we couldn't take the kid home. He'd been so safe and warm on my knee, and now they wanted to put him back in the pen, with its cold stone floor and all of the bigger kids to push him around. He'd have been safer in our garden, I kept telling Mother. I wouldn't let anything hurt him and I'd make sure he got enough food and that he wouldn't be lonely. When we left without him, I felt something akin to heartbreak, and for weeks afterwards I dreamt about him freezing to death. We didn't visit the farm again.

The next time I encountered a goat in the flesh, it was here on my first day in the Tower. I'd been reading patient transcripts all morning, assessing suitability for the insertion of the chip. At lunchtime, the Professor walked me across the green, and there was the therapeutic petting zoo I'd heard so much about with three bleating goats pressed against the fence.

Today, when we reached the barn the first thing that hit me was the smell. It was the same farmyard musk from my childhood, laced with the thick tang of blood. It was a deep, cloying scent that reminded me, perversely, of starting puberty, of the way the sanitary pads smelled after too long between changes when a teacher wouldn't let you leave class.

In a wide pen, Billie was in labour, her white speckled nose slick with sweat and her legs braced and clenching. She made a deep lowing sound through her mouth, not all that dissimilar to that made by a human in the throes of birth. Her eyes were wide and unfocused, her entire attention bent to the task of making life.

Alex stepped over the fence and unlocked the gate for Maryam to follow, and I hesitated at the threshold while she cradled the goat's head in her lap.

"Don't just stand there, girl," she said. "Get the harness on and let's see what we're dealing with."

With Alex's help, I secured the lead around Billie's face and lashed it to the side of the pen, until she couldn't move more than a metre or so in any direction. The poor creature panicked, a very human scream coming from her mouth, and I felt it a cruel thing we had to do when she seemed so driven to pace circles around the enclosure.

I slipped on the pair of surgical gloves Alex handed to me and gritted my teeth against the stench. The straw was wet beneath me, the goat's waters slick and slimy on the floor, and I lamented the state of my jeans as it soaked through to my skin. I'd never taken a maternity rotation during medical school – the whole process of bringing life into the world filled me with primordial horror – but Maryam's voice was soothing as she talked me through stabilising Billie and easing my way inside.

I placed my hand flat on her warm right flank, just in front of her udders, and felt a small protrusion when I pressed down, a thin ridge that might have been a hoof shifting inside her stomach. Billie pawed at the ground, struggling against the harness and backing into me, until my nose was filled with the scent of animal and straw and the birth fluids beneath my knees. Her flesh was hot and slick, and when I pressed down the muscles contracted as though trying to suck me inside. The gulping pink mouth of her made me nervous, a gaping wet thing that seemed to want to consume more than expel.

"What am I looking for?" I asked.

"If everything's going well, you should feel the hooves, but you might find a nose instead."

"Is that a good thing?"

"No."

I pushed my fingers in further, and Billie pulsed and clenched around me. The pungent smell of the farmyard and birth made me want to gag, and not for the first time I thought about how cruelly designed mammals were for this task.

"Well? How does it feel?"

"It feels like I've got my fingers up a goat's arse, Alex. I'm just hoping that something in here isn't going to bite me."

Alex grinned, and I felt a bit better when I pushed deeper inside. My fingers brushed over something fibrous and slick, and beyond it a soft curve and the unmistakable smoothness of a nose.

"I can feel the head. That isn't what we want, is it?"

Maryam's sigh was resigned. "No, it isn't." She drew a hand over her eyes and I waited with my fingers still inside Billie to be told what to do next. "Okay," she said. "Let's try something new."

It took me and Alex both – along with Alison, who had arrived to help – to hold Billie steady and rearrange the unborn kid inside her. A vet could probably have done it more easily, but without the internet to ask for guidance we were working on a combination of Maryam's maternity knowledge, my medical training, and Alex's brute strength. The process seemed like it hurt her.

Alex and I both reached inside while Billie bleated and strained, and Alison clamped her arms around her legs to stop her from kicking us in the face. Meanwhile, Maryam called out directions and cradled Billie's head on her lap, attempting to calm her even though she had two hands seeking entry and a kid seeking exit, which I thought would be enough to panic any living creature.

In the end, I delved deep, holding the birth canal open while Alex reached inside and found a path beneath the kid's nose to its neck. His arm brushed mine inside the tunnel, both of us sweating, our faces pressed close as we panted through our mouths. I felt his arm slip against mine like a sea serpent, rolling inside the womb. Eventually, with a deep grunt and a breath of air that fogged up my glasses, he succeeded in pushing the kid far enough back that we were able to reach its legs, folded like a concertina beneath it.

"Gently now," Maryam cautioned. "The baby will need its limbs."

Working between us, hands brushing inside Billie's womb, we each unfolded a spindly leg. The sensation was disconcerting. There was at once a coiled strength in the limbs, already pushing back against us and fighting the manipulation, while at the same time I was all too aware that one wrong move – a twist at the wrong angle – might snap a bone or tear the muscles before it had even arrived.

We managed it eventually, and pulled our arms out with a deep sucking sound and twin sighs of relief. We were red-faced and sweaty. Alex's honey-coloured hair was sticking to his forehead in damp tendrils and his upper lip shone with perspiration. I took off my glasses and cleaned them one-handed with my shirt, and when I put them back on again everyone was smiling. Billie settled down soon after, and the tips of two small hooves began to peek out of her, straining to live.

It felt like a victory at last.

31ST MAY

Nature is cruel, so the saying goes, but I think I'd amend that to nature is unpredictable, and it doesn't answer to us. By the time darkness fell this evening, Billie still hadn't calved. The hoofs protrude from her like two great pincers, as though she's carrying a crab inside her womb. They click against each other while she strains, and through my open window I can hear her labouring still. In the past, humans read portents into such things.

I used to think it ridiculous, that superstition could supersede science in a society so advanced. Centuries of amorphous *hysteria* bleeding out and clotting around the passage of truth. Now that we're so removed from stability, however, I think I can see how curses and omens were once such a feature of life. Humanity is primed to look for meaning, and we're uncomfortable with precarity to an obscene degree. The whole of human history has been about the creation of certainty, and that worship of certainty and self-determination has led us further away from it.

In the old world, society championed personal choice. If only you worked harder, you could have things like food and housing. If only you ate well, you were protected against mortality. If only you did x, y was sure to follow.

But the scope of cause and effect has always been wider than the individual. What did hard work matter when the neuralchips were introduced?

Technology was meant to ensure that we had an easier life. Instead, all it did was make certain that we'd always have to work harder for less. Sure, you worked a twelve-hour shift, but on a minimum wage that wouldn't cover your bills. Why should it? You could always work more. Get a neuralchip. Abandon sleep. Work twenty-four hours and then you'll have enough to eat. Sure, you ate well and did everything "right", but the air's poisoned and your genetics are uncertain, and so cancer got you anyway. It seems so clear to me now that we can't game a system individually. We can't predict nature when it's constantly in flux.

Human greed has always outstripped human needs. Our nature is to push beyond, ignore all portents, and cast aside advice because "it couldn't happen to me". That's what led us here, and now I find that I understand the need to look for signs more than I ever did before. Precarity breeds a desire for certainty.

I want to be able to say that Billie's difficult birth is pre-ordained, that it comes not from the chaos of nature and luck but was passed down from on high to teach us something, and to warn us of more to come. I want to believe that if we fail here, it is out of my hands, that a difficult birth couldn't start a downward spiral because of something so untameable as chance. If we lose her and then Gruff later, if we can't make cheese and milk, if it limits our diet and a bad winter kills Maryam's plants, if our stores run out and we're ended by something so common as hunger, then I want to believe that I have the power to alter this *now*, or that someone else made it happen instead. I don't want to fail here simply due to bad luck. I want what we do to matter, even if it's part of some cosmic will.

The truth, I suppose, is that what we do as individuals matters both more and less than we believe. Without us, the world would never have had the neuralchip, but in a different society perhaps the neuralchips could have been something good. They were a cure for so many illnesses, and they could have left us freer than ever to relax, to create, to connect to one another without the threat of poverty looming over our heads. But we didn't build them in that kind of world. We released them into a world that was greedy, where more was always better and competition more vital than community.

The evidence was there, if we'd bothered to look. We should have known that greed would outstrip good, that individual selfishness, the desire to be better than everyone else, would succeed where we had failed. How far back does it go? Would we ever have been able to stop it? Would it have taken a rewrite of human nature, or merely a rewriting of our laws? Is Billie's struggle our fault or nature's?

Questions like these will drive anyone mad. All I know for certain is that nature is unpredictable, but humans, perhaps, could always have been predicted.

We just ignored the signs.

and in this place I will admit that what grows in us and around us and through us isn't always glorious or good, and when the holy moment comes I don't feel purified but instead forsaken by a god, a god that I don't believe in but still curse with every breath, and if He is listening then I hope He feels guilt for what His absence has made of us, for what His abandonment has done to us, for what His indifference has grown in us, which is the darkness between stars and the moment of falling and the conviction that we are broken because we cannot ever be perfect

JUNE

1ST JUNE

"You are unhappy today."

The Tower baked in the churn, but underground the damp stone walls retained their chill. It was a relief to be away from Billie's struggles and out of the oppressive heat.

"Can you consider why I might be?" I asked.

"Are you testing my empathy or my reason?"

"Does it insult you that I might be testing the limits of both?"

"No, it doesn't insult me. It disappoints me."

"Why?"

"You're asking why I'm disappointed that you might treat me as less than human?"

I rearranged my papers. They'd become little more than a crutch, a barrier between him and me, but I had no desire to get rid of them. "The question of your humanity is one of the reasons for these interviews," I said.

"You seek to establish what makes a human, human."

"I'm trying to establish the differences that have occurred in you since the neuralchip was implanted."

"And whether or not I'm a new species." His tone was accusatory.

"I'm more interested in whether or not you have anything to tell us about the Sleepless. Taxonomy is less important to me than a cure."

"For them or for me?"

We were back to his usual diversion. Personal feelings obscured by questions of philosophy.

"Those are issues for another time. You said I seemed unhappy today."

"I said you *were* unhappy today."

"Can you tell me how you drew that conclusion?" I very particularly didn't ask him whether or not he cared.

"It seemed logical," he said. "Your goat is in distress. The expectation of a new life is being replaced by the fear of two deaths. The people here are nervous, waiting for a resolution."

"A rational analysis, then. And a reasonable interpretation."

His mouth ticked – an almost-smile. "You also have dark rings under your eyes from a sleepless night. In our previous interviews, you've never worn make-up, yet today you've tried to hide your fatigue beneath a layer of cosmetics. You fiddle with your pen more when you're uncomfortable, and you have yet to put it down today although we've barely begun." He met my gaze. "And you sound sad." He tapped at his temple. "In here."

I didn't know how to respond. I was aware that his powers of observation were impressive, but the sheer volume of what he'd recognised about me was unsettling.

"What do you mean, I sound sad in here? How does sad sound?"

"It's listless. Like water becalmed ahead of an approaching storm."

"And you say you can hear this?"

He looked up at the ceiling. "Perhaps hear isn't the right word. Perhaps *feel* would be better."

"You feel that I'm sad today."

He lowered his eyes to mine. "Isn't that what empathy is?"

We watched each other. So far, all that my conversations with him had proved was that he was clever, able to lead me away from the subject at hand and into more complex questions of nature and morality. But it wasn't morality I was concerned with. I needed to establish a medical authority, a body of knowledge that would lead us to new areas of investigation. It was maddening to find myself so misdirected.

"Do you sleep?"

My question seemed to catch him off-guard. "What do you think?"

"I think there must be a vital divergence between your assimilation of the neuralchip and every other person's. Given that sleeplessness is the first symptom, it's logical to suppose you might not share it."

"Sleeplessness is the cause."

"I'm sorry?"

"You said that sleeplessness was the symptom. It isn't. Sleeplessness is the cause and what happens next are the symptoms."

"You're right. In that case, why aren't you exhibiting the same symptoms. Do you sleep?"

He didn't answer. My instinct was to grow angry with him, to remind him that he'd agreed to these interviews, and that his meandering was hurting not just us and the people we were trying to help but him as well. Instead, I waited.

"How is the animal?" he asked eventually. "Does she suffer, do you think?"

"Yes, I think she suffers."

"And does that distress you? Do you suffer alongside her, even now while you sit here and speak with me? Or since she's out of sight and sound, does something inside of you settle as though she's no longer real?"

I twirled my pen, thinking. I'd learnt by now that he could usually tell when I wasn't giving his questions due consideration, and that this behaviour irritated him almost as much as his irritated me.

"I'm still worried about her," I replied. "I'm worried that when we're done here, I'll go back upstairs and find that she and the kid have died."

"But?"

"I'm not as distressed as I was having to listen to her all night. Down here, my focus is on you and this conversation, which doesn't leave as much room for worry."

"Your empathy is lessened by distance."

"I wouldn't say that," I replied. "I'd say that no one can maintain their attention on a crisis indefinitely. If Billie was alone, without help, I'd struggle to sit here talking to you, but since I know there are people with her and my presence isn't needed to make a difference, I'm able to tuck my worry away."

"And if you imagine her labours, do you feel the same distress as though you were still listening to her?"

I shifted beneath his scrutiny.

"Forgive me," he said. "I only ask because I'm curious about the limits of your imagination. My description of meeting Helen caused you visible discomfort. You were able to enter her reality so quickly that I was surprised to find you able to ignore your animal's situation today."

As though at his behest, my mouth flooded with saliva, a bitter tang of phantom blood sitting heavy against my teeth. He watched me intently and could hardly have failed to notice that I swallowed, or that my tongue ran around the back of my teeth like a cloth. "Your story about Helen surprised me. I hadn't expected you to say it."

"So, without being able to brace yourself against the situation, sensations arrived unbidden?"

"You could say that."

He tilted his head. "You are very unusual."

"Strong words coming from the nameless survivor of a new species of human."

Something remarkable happened then: he laughed. And it was startling, the way the action changed everything about him. For a brief moment he was no longer calm and closed off, a marble statue pretending at flesh. His eyes shut, his head drew back, and a very human flush of blood rushed to his cheeks. When he opened his eyes again, they were sparking, bright and pleased and almost as surprised as I was.

He settled back into his seat, no longer quite so composed, and he looked indolent all of a sudden, as though a completely different person to the one I'd spent the last month getting to know had taken his usual place.

"I concede the point," he said. "Ask me, then."

I had to make a concerted effort to clear my head. "Ask you what?"

"Whatever it is you wanted to ask me."

I felt like we'd come to some kind of an accord, as though I were being offered a temporary truce in a battle I'd hardly realised I was fighting. For a moment I was at sea. Part of me wanted to push him on his history, while another wanted to learn more about how he and Helen had met and what their relationship had been like before they'd arrived here.

I wanted to know if he knew why she didn't speak, and I wanted to understand what the world looked like outside the Tower's walls. I wanted to know if he slept, and if he knew why or why not that might be. I wanted to know if his new body felt strange to him and whether he'd taken his temperature recently. And I wanted to know what he thought – about himself, about us, about whatever help he'd intended to get for Helen.

But the peculiar effect of our time together had left me with an acute horror of failure, a wariness in conversation that was akin to wading through a minefield. One wrong question and I was certain I'd lose his cooperation.

"Helen and you," I began. "Were you together for a long time before you came here?"

"No more than a month."

"That isn't very long."

"It isn't."

"You said you wanted to find her help. What made you come here? Did you know we were here? Did you think we might be able to help her?"

His fingers drummed on the table top. "Those are difficult questions to answer."

I waited.

"I'd known that there were people in the Tower for some time, but I was wary of approaching alone."

"You said the last time we spoke that you didn't know you'd be perceived as a threat. What made you wary?"

"Fear of death and injury aren't the only fears. While I was alone in the world, the Sleepless didn't attack me, so I was perfectly safe. I feared containment, to find myself no longer free to leave. It wasn't such an unreasonable fear, was it?" His tone held a subtle challenge, but one tinged with an odd sort of amusement. I had the feeling that I'd entertained him, and in return he was willing to indulge me.

"Maybe not, but your freedom was a safety concern."

"It still is, I believe, or else why would my hands still be bound and my door still locked at night?"

This gave me pause. At the last meeting, we'd agreed that both he and Helen would no longer be locked in. He would still require an escort, true, but he'd be able to call a guard if he wanted to leave.

"Ah," he said. "You didn't know. I had wondered. Thank you for confirming it."

I was surprised to find myself indignant on his behalf. As a group, we'd agreed that he'd have a certain degree of freedom in return for his cooperation. Now I found that we hadn't kept our end of the bargain, so was it any wonder he was combative?

"I'll see what I can do about that," I said. "You should have had your doors unlocked last month."

"It's of no matter, but I appreciate you looking into it." He leant back again, his gaze on the ceiling. "Now, where were we? Ah yes, my decision to bring Helen to the Tower. It seemed clear to me that she couldn't continue in her condition alone for much longer."

"You felt she was vulnerable on her own."

"I felt that she was vulnerable even with me. She needed somewhere secure, somewhere she wasn't constantly looking over her shoulder for danger. Somewhere like here."

"But you didn't have to come with her. If you were worried about confinement, you could have accompanied her to the gates and left before we ever saw you."

He inclined his head. "I could, but Helen persuaded me that I ought to meet with you. She thought I might learn something from the experience."

"Helen doesn't speak."

"That's correct."

"Yet she persuaded you to come here and learn from us?"

A small smile bled across his lips. "There are more ways to communicate than speech."

While this was true, I felt that it wasn't the full story. I made a note on my papers and his eyes followed the movement. I resisted the urge to hide my words from him.

"You said the Sleepless don't attack you," I said. "Is that because you're careful to remain out of their way, or is there some other reason?"

He drew in a deliberate breath, and his eyes darted around the room before coming to rest on the mirror. The red recording light still flashed, drawing my awareness, and he watched it with a cool expression before his attention focused on his reflection.

"Tell me, Thea Chares, what do you see?"

Within the mirror, we looked at each other. The room seemed sparse. The only colour came from the bright spot of red blinking behind my shoulder. The humming LED bulbs leached what was left, washing everything in too-sharp white that contrasted starkly with the stone. Against its darkness, the two of us were picked out like spotlights. My hair, in reality a dull medium brown, seemed so light as to be white at the tips, disappearing into a blind spot above my head while the rest was swallowed by the walls.

By contrast, my white lab coat was a point of absence, a static sort of image that gave the impression I was flickering.

The expression on my face was lost behind my glasses, and the paleness of my hands was overshadowed by the black pen between my fingers. Across the desk from me, it appeared as though my own personal inversion sat, calmly watching me make my assessment.

While my hair, tied back and away from my face, left the edges of my self unstable, his wild growth curled around his head, almost cradling the stark whiteness of his skin. His hazel eye was a spot of golden colour in an otherwise blank face, and the blue was so striking it seemed like its own light source. Whereas my lab coat made me into something unstable, his dark jumper camouflaged him against the wall, a shadow sitting in a chair. We were opposites, as though crafted to be so – him imposing, even while reclined, and me somehow small next to the bulk of him, my back self-consciously straight. It was a disturbing image, but nonetheless fascinating. Had someone taken a photo of us in that moment and presented it to me for analysis, I'd have said I could draw only one conclusion.

"We aren't the same."

He watched my mouth move, and I watched his tick up into that half-smile that was becoming so familiar.

"There are undeniable differences between us," he amended. "Perhaps all the more obvious for our similarities."

He moved his chair, deliberately turning his back on us and angling his face to mine. I mirrored him, fighting the uncomfortable sensation that neither of our reflections had turned, and if I were to look back I'd find my own face staring back at me still.

"What do you think the Sleepless see when they look at me? What do you think their senses tell them?"

"They recognise you as one of them. So it's true that they don't attack their own."

This had been a topic of debate during the first year. At that time, it wasn't unusual to see groupings of them beyond the walls. The few that had turned while here and escaped – or been forced – out of the gates retained some knowledge that there was life inside, and enough self-will to stalk along the path around us. But so much was new to us then, and horror makes a mind slow. The survival drive dominates rationality in all things.

We didn't consider studying them during those months. Instead, we watched them like a sailor watches the clouds or a hare considers a fox. We were less interested in their behaviour than in whether or not they would find a way in. Only towards the end of that first year, when something changed in them – a listlessness that caused them to drift further away from our keep – did it occur to any of us to try to analyse what we'd seen.

Retrospective analysis, unfortunately, is hopelessly flawed. The memory is selective, manipulated by time and hamstrung by other people's interpretations. Dolly and Alex maintained that they were mindless, acting instinctually in response to sound or movement on our walls. Alison and Thane believed that some were more aware than others, leaders in a pack that directed their assaults on the city. Maryam, of course, never saw them after they'd escaped, with no lifts up to the battlements so no way for her to observe.

Whatever Edgar thought of them, he kept it to himself, but he watched them perhaps more than any of us. It wasn't uncommon for me to arrive at St Thomas's Tower to watch the sunrise and to find him already sitting further down the battlements, his legs folded beneath him and his sunken eyes bright. The Professor felt them to be akin to animals, possessing awareness, certainly, and a strong instinctual drive, but he didn't believe they retained the higher levels of cognition seen in humans.

As for myself, it was cowardly, perhaps, but I tried not to think too much about how they felt or thought. Empathy is a powerful barrier to scientific endeavour. How can one have empathy for an animal yet subject it to tests that make it suffer, even if the end goal is a cure for some terrible disease? Similarly, how could I maintain a hold on my work if my thoughts were filled with who those people had been?

Whether or not they were more animal than human didn't matter to me, because both possibilities were too terrible to contemplate. If they'd regressed to the animal, all that they once were had been lost. And if they did still retain cognition, if they remembered on some level who they were, that would have been just another kind of horror. To know yourself yet to descend into savagery. To have killed the people you love and to live like an animal while deep within some part of you still screamed. It's the creation of a hell on earth, and one I still struggle to face.

One thing we did agree on was that fighting between them was rare. It was also difficult to identify whether it happened at all. There would sometimes be scuffles nearby, terrible growls and awful screeching, the Sleepless crouching and clawing like lions on the hunt. We watched these events with morbid curiosity, until it became clear that they weren't attacks on each other but on some unsuspecting human who'd attempted to reach us and been summarily taken by the pride.

This new knowledge, then, that our missing link was left alone by them, suggested the Sleepless weren't simply mindless, and perhaps not even merely animal. Animals, after all, fight for territory. Humans, even, are very good at killing our own. And if this drive isn't seen in the Sleepless, what does that say about who or what they are?

"You seem troubled," he said.

I blinked myself back to the room.

"Does it trouble you that the Sleepless recognise a kinship with me?"

"It concerns me that they distinguish you as someone not to be harmed. In times of starvation, even an animal will eat its own kind."

"Even a human will, as well."

A repulsive thought, but one I had to concede.

"Do you feel a kinship with them?" I asked.

"I feel a responsibility towards them. We aren't so dissimilar."

"Aren't you? You sit here speaking to me, reasoning through your choices. You expressed care for Helen and made a plan to bring her to us. These aren't behaviours found in the Sleepless. These things aren't in their nature."

"Are you so sure that you understand their nature? Or mine, for that matter?"

I sat a little straighter in my chair. "How would you characterise their nature, then?"

"I'd say that there's no single nature that can be applied across all of them. They're as dissimilar as you and I, or perhaps as humanity itself."

He leant forward, then, and I had the sense that I was being brought into a confidence at last.

"You make the same mistake so many people have made. You speak of human nature as though it's one single thing, and so you're unable to see the breadth of nature in another. Is what is natural the same as what is good? Is divergence from a norm unnatural, or is that an easy shorthand you use in order to explain your revulsion?"

His face was too close yet I couldn't pull away.

"Tell me, Doctor Chares, where do you draw the line between unnatural science and nature's monstrosity? How far would you step over it to survive?"

Where does the difference between nature and science lie? The question continues to trouble me, and I think the answer must be that nature doesn't decide. Nature grows at its own whims, creating and destroying and changing without thought for a reason why. It imposes no limits on itself except for those that exist in its form. Yet if science is the manipulation of nature, we must question its application every time. No matter how monstrously the natural world may march, there's a moral choice at play every time we decide to intervene.

We intervened today, in the oppressive heat of the late afternoon, crowded around Billie's pen. Her endless bleating had grown weak, and in the spotlight of the sun an argument raged with Maryam and Miles on one side and the Professor and Edgar on the other. The question at hand was whether or not we ought to attempt a caesarean, and in truth I could see both sides. On the one hand, none of us were vets and the risks to Billie and the child were great. On the other, it seemed unlikely she'd deliver without help and her energy was nearly spent.

We anaesthetised her in the pen and moved her to the laboratory, the Professor's appeal to the severity of her suffering swaying even Miles in the end. Once there, Miles left us alone to our work and four of us crowded around the surgical table, Billie's body a quivering mass between us. She looked almost dead already, her neck limp and drooping at an odd angle, her eyes rolled back in her head, and her tongue lolling from behind her square teeth. Even unconscious, her body strained. Muscles trembled, rippling from her jaw to her feet, as though she contained a river that was trying to burst its banks.

Maryam inserted the breathing tube down her throat, and Edgar swept his hat from his head and made a circuit of the room to close the windows, which had the effect of sealing us in as well as keeping everything else out. I could no longer hear the ravens cawing, nor the rush of the Thames. All that was left was heat and the awareness that we were attempting to control something wild.

Michael made the first incision. It's difficult to describe the tension in the air, but for a while at least the four of us shared a common cause. I felt the oneness of us when he slit through her abdomen, the blood welling like lava through the fissure of her skin. The room quickly filled with the stink of blood and of our own pungent bodies sweating in the heat.

Billie opened for us like a rotten flower, her skin peeling back and the placenta pulsing under layers of pink flesh. Then, beneath it, there was the twisting mass of her kid ready to be born. Water gushed out of her and stained the pale fur when Michael punctured the sac, and then Edgar and I worked to pull the kid out while Michael stood back and observed.

The placenta was slippery. It was like trying to hold onto ice, though it radiated a feverish and disconcerting warmth. The kid kicked, a bleating noise rising in the room, and only when I'd peeled the amniotic sac away and it had struggled to stand did we understand why it had almost failed to be born. It was a twin, unsuccessfully separated from itself, something that previous generations would have called a monster birth, and although we've moved on since then, it was difficult to say that there wasn't something monstrous about him.

"Thea, don't just stand there," Maryam chastised me. "See to it that he breathes."

"Which one?"

It was a glib thing to say, but what I was really asking was, *Are we going to let it live*?

"Don't be a smart arse," she replied. "We can debate the issue later but only if the kid survives."

I could see the logic in this even if I didn't want the responsibility. The animal was flailing against the tiles, blood and fluid dripping off it in streams while its two heads bleated as one. I took it into my arms and its heads rolled towards me and then away again, pulling in separate directions. I thought briefly of the hydra, of the many-headed monsters in so many myths, and of Medusa's head of snakes.

The kid continued to bleat, first one head and then the other, as though they were performing a call and answer with each other. One mouth was already making suckling motions, its lips puckering, searching for its mother's teat. I gave it the edge of my palm, allowing the grasping wetness of its lips against my skin while I ran my free hand down its side.

Apart from the second head, it seemed to be fine. Its legs were strong, although they trembled with the shock of being born. Its white fur was slick with amniotic fluid but it rippled with chaotic breaths. I placed my palm flat on its flank, wondering which head was drawing air into its singular set of lungs – and then came the thought that while the two shared one body, perhaps there was more beneath the surface. Maybe an ocean of organs jostled for space within the cage of its ribs.

The suckling head became distressed, realising that its efforts to draw milk were in vain, and the second responded by attempting to search elsewhere. The muscles between their necks strained, pulling in separate directions, and I was convinced for an inexplicable moment that they'd tear each other apart. I placed my hands on the outside of each head, drawing them back together, and in the quiet darkness of my thoughts I wondered what this monstrosity might mean.

2ND JUNE

My animal instinct to recoil wasn't replicated in the animal. Billie woke in the pen and searched at once for her kid. A small group of us watched, breath bated, as she touched her nose to each of them and began to lick them clean. I confess that her easy acceptance startled me. I'd expected her to refuse to nurse it, to take one look at the strange thing she'd borne and do what animals do to weaker members of the herd.

I'd expected her to drive it out.

6TH JUNE

During the summer, the Tower feels more like a prison than it does at any other time. The stone walls radiate heat, pushing it inwards, turning the compound into a tropical bell jar with little hope of reprieve. On days like this, a lethargy overcomes us, all conversation labouring under a pall of sweat. The Tower itself is plucked out of place, a structure of winter that has no place in the sun.

This afternoon, the scent of Maryam's flowers was cloying, the pollen almost as thick in the air as the heat haze that shimmered from the flagstones. Even the ravens were torpid, ignoring Dolly's attempts to coax them down from the battlements with pieces of bloodied meat. I was listless, for once directionless, and I couldn't suppress a sudden flinch when I came across our survivor sheltering in the shadow of the chapel.

"My apologies," he said. "It wasn't my intention to startle you."

"You didn't startle me."

"Then why is your heart racing?" He waited for a response to his question, and I felt that I'd been coerced into giving it.

"You can hear our heartbeats."

"I can hear yours at present, although it's fading. Would you walk with me?"

"Why?"

"It's been a long time since I was able to take a walk unbound, and I'd appreciate the company."

I saw then that the handcuffs I was so used to seeing on his wrists had been removed. I had a sudden urge to look around for help – wondering, perhaps, if Thane had lost sight of his charge and I was being lured somewhere alone. The survivor tipped his chin towards Lanthorn, where Alison was standing with her rifle balanced over the edge.

"You need not worry for your safety," he said. "I am still in their sights."

He began to walk then, graceful and sedate, his hands crossed at the small of his back as though he were some ancient noble taking the air. There seemed to be no harm in following, and truthfully I was curious to see him outside of the sterile environment of the interview room.

We fell into step together, keeping to the shadows close to the walls, me on the outside and him almost brushing the stone. He seemed taller than usual, although perhaps I was simply used to approaching him while he was sitting. I had to tip my chin up to see him as we came upon the greenhouses, where Maryam and Miles were tending to the vegetables. He watched them with a benign expression.

"I wonder if you wouldn't mind telling me a little more about the people here?" he asked.

"That depends on what you'd like to know. Some things aren't mine to share."

"Would starting with their names be acceptable to you, or is that information classified?"

I tilted my head to look at him. "I don't know. Yours certainly seems to be."

His lips twitched, almost a smile, and he inclined his head as we stepped apart for a moment to avoid one of Maryam's planters. "I concede the point, but would it assuage your sense of fairness if I were to tell you that I'd decided on a name?"

"You've named yourself?"

"I have chosen from the list of names provided for me."

"And which name have you chosen?"

We circled the greenhouses, coming to a stop at the corner of Queen's House. He turned to me and held out his hand, and I stared at it as though it had teeth.

"Is this not how introductions are usually made?" he asked.

His hand was still waiting for me to take, and I realised he was offering a bargain. If I shook his hand, I would get his name. If I ignored it, he wouldn't tell me. I sighed, knowing that he'd won already. Curiosity wouldn't allow me to delay. I took it, surprised by the gentleness of his grip and the heat of his skin, and he smiled.

"My name is Vladimir. It's very nice to meet you."

Before I could respond, Alison charged around the corner with her rifle primed. It was only then that I realised we were standing in a blind spot, and we couldn't be seen from the towers.

7TH JUNE

There is power in a name and manipulation in how one might influence our perceptions. Advertisers have always known this, pouring millions into the cultivation of their brands in the hope of making many millions more. Perhaps the Anonymous Billionaire knew this too when he withheld his name from the records, signing his emails only as AD – shorthand for the Anonymous Donor.

The renaming of myalgic encephalomyelitis first occurred in 1988, following an outbreak of a chronic flu-like illness in Incline Village, Lake Tahoe, years earlier. With a number of patients remaining sick during those years, the US Centers for Disease Control coined the term chronic fatigue syndrome to describe their symptoms, and this use spread around the world.

I've always hated the name *chronic fatigue syndrome* for its total manipulation of perception. *Myalgic encephalomyelitis* described the intense pain of its sufferers, and recognised Ramsay's discovery of brain inflammation at the onset of illness in a number of his patients. These patients, like my mother, weren't simply fatigued; they were incapacitated by the most basic exertion.

As the illness progressed, Mother could no longer read or write and would stumble over her words, pointing helplessly at the curtains and intoning *bedcovers off, bedcovers off,* when she couldn't remember what they were called or how to ask for them to be closed.

The name the CDC chose made it seem as though these patients were simply a little more tired than the average person – lazy shirkers who needed to get up and get on and get over it.

After that, it wasn't long before the psychiatrists got hold of them again.

8TH JUNE

The atmosphere in the Raven's Nest was subdued this evening, and I hadn't wanted to attend. Something about the heat and the kid, and Vladimir's expression when Alison had held him at gunpoint, had left me chasing answers to questions I could hardly form before they slipped away.

There was something in his manner that had unnerved me, an inability to anticipate his actions or understand his mind that gnawed at my thoughts while I waited for the meeting to begin. Even the most stoic of humans will broadcast their intentions from time to time – a flicker of emotion in the eyes, a bead of sweat at the temple, an unconscious twitch of the fingers when caught out in a lie. Vladimir displays nothing of the kind, and I turned this thought over while Michael thanked everyone for their help with Billie and called the meeting to order.

"The kid isn't what we'd expected, but he seems to be doing well," he said. "And if he continues to feed then I see no reason why he shouldn't make it to adulthood."

There was an uneasy silence that was eventually broken by Thane.

"And then what? What happens in a couple of years when we have an animal with an extra mouth to feed and no reason to think it'll provide for us?"

I made an effort to focus on the room.

"What do you suggest instead, Captain?" Maryam asked.

"You know what I suggest, and I know you disagree."

"We can't just kill him," Dolly cut in. "He's just a baby. He isn't hurting anyone."

I wanted to say that I thought her outrage was strange, contradictory perhaps to her comments about Helen and Maryam. Was it a misplaced maternal instinct that made her stand up to Thane, or was there some difference for her between animal and human sickness? An innocence, perhaps, that she saw in the kid yet perceived as a threat among us?

"Does anyone else feel this way?" the Professor asked us all.

There was silence, and a general looking away, before Alex raised his hand and Alison mirrored him.

"Perhaps, then, we ought to put it to a vote."

I thought that Dolly might effervesce in her anger. "You can't be serious!" she said. "You're talking about murdering an innocent creature."

"We're talking about keeping the other animals alive," Alex corrected. "I spend more time with them than anyone, save for maybe Miles, and I'm the one who feeds them every day. Look around you, Dolly. Do you see a convenient field they can graze in?"

"But we knew there was going to be a baby," she argued. "The fact he's different doesn't change anything."

"On the contrary, it changes everything." Edgar, for all his faults, has an innate gift for commanding attention without ever having to raise his voice. He sat by Michael's side, calmly sketching in his book, and he didn't even have to look up to have all of us turn and listen. "A healthy male could breed and a healthy female could be made to give milk. New blood makes new life, so that when the old ones die the new will be there to replace them."

He blinked and put down his pencil.

"There won't be any milk from this animal, and breeding him might be a mistake."

"You couldn't have bred him anyway," Dolly shot back. "The only female goat is his mother." She sat down and Edgar tipped his head to the Professor.

"Is that true, maestro?"

"In an ideal world, dear Dolly, I would agree with you," Michael said. "But we aren't living in an ideal world. While an incestuous coupling isn't without its problems, for the purposes of a continued food source it's perhaps the lesser of two evils, and in this Edgar does have a point. Cruel though it may seem, the Tower does have to think about our survival long term."

Dolly slammed her glass down onto the table with so much force that the wine leapt out of the top. "If survival is all that matters then why stop there? Why not breed us all out if we need to continue the line? Maryam's too old so she's out, but me, Thea, and Alison are all fertile. Which one of the men do you want us to spread our legs for?"

"Dolly." The rebuke came quick and sharp from Maryam's mouth. "Now you're being hysterical."

"Am I? You heard what he said, and with that thing they're keeping in the Tower and those freaks in Beauchamp, you can't tell me that ethics is at the front of their minds. I can't believe you're even considering this. If we start picking off weaker members of the pack just because they're inconvenient, what next?"

The thought hung in the air like smog, and it made me want to shake her. The words were out of my mouth before I could stop them.

"And what have you done to help, Dolly? You swan about this place, playing with the ravens and primping and preening yourself when nobody cares, and all you do is complain. You want the world back. You want to go out for dinner. You want to go dancing and go on holiday and you want, you want, you *want*. But what exactly are you doing to help us get it?"

The simplicity of my anger was a relief. I was a clock wound too tightly, chasing down the seconds until vulnerability set in. In those sweet moments between release and exposure, I berated her for her frivolity, her uselessness, and her unwillingness to make the choices that the rest of us – that *I* – had been forced to make.

"You can sit on your high horse if you like," I told her. "But the moral high ground is only in your head."

There was a deathly silence when I'd finished. Unlike with Vladimir, there was no ticking of the clock for me to focus on. No blinking red light to distract my attention. Only a raw feeling, as though I'd been flayed and peeled open like Billie.

"I hope you don't expect me to feel sorry for you," Dolly said, "when this, all of it, is your fault. You did this. You and the Professor and Edgar, and the Anonymous Donor hiding like a coward in his tower."

She stood, cold fury in the beam of her eyes.

"So take that to your moral high ground and hang yourself with it, because if it were up to me, none of you would get a choice about anything."

The door didn't slam behind her, it closed with a soft thud

and locked her words inside. I felt them in the air, slipping down my throat when I breathed to settle like sediment in my lungs. A truth wide enough to choke myself on.

A GLACIER KNOCKS IN THE CUPBOARD

9TH JUNE

I don't remember leaving the Nest last night, but I remember the silence. The space in which no one stood up to speak in our defence and we were left alone. I found myself sometime later in an armchair in Edgar's living room, with the Professor pushing a glass into my hand. I sipped it obediently, coughing when the whiskey burnt down my throat and heat sparked up my nose. I felt unworthy of it. Michael had two bottles of whiskey in the beginning and he rationed them carefully, ever mindful of the last mouthful waiting at the bottom.

"Desperate times call for desperate measures," he said when I pointed this out to him. "Besides, there's no one left in this world that I would rather share my precious things with."

I laughed, but it came out like a sob, mortification coasting swiftly in its wake as he passed me a clean white handkerchief.

"Was she right?" I asked them. "Was it our fault? Is that what they all think of us?" Unspoken in my question: was that what they all thought of *me*? I looked to Michael, forever my North Star, and I wanted him to reassure me.

"She's angry," he said. "Out of everyone, you know that Dolly's had the hardest time adjusting."

"She's a maladaptive creature," Edgar murmured, "plucked out of the ecosystem that sustained her. She doesn't have the talent for adaptation that other creatures develop. Do you know what happens to a caterpillar that can't be reborn?"

I shook my head.

"It eats itself and dies."

He seemed delighted by this, and Michael reprimanded him with a soft click of his tongue.

"Not everyone can thrive in the places they find themselves in," he said. "Dolly wants to go back to a time when everything was simple, forgetting perhaps that life has never been simple. It suits her to have someone to blame."

I felt the rightness of his words, and at the same time I found them inadequate. "But is she wrong?" I asked.

"She's only partly right. She's right to say that, of those of us left, we three had the greatest hand in the technology's development. But she forgets that everyone here was instrumental and, dare I say it, committed to the work before it went wrong." His hand rose, pouring another shot of whiskey into my glass, and I thought of how old the skin of his fingers looked, translucent and paper-thin in the light of the flames.

"Where would we have been without Alex tending the machines? Without Maryam to rehabilitate the patients? Even Dolly, nursing those before and after surgery, had a hand in what we did here. Don't you remember, Thea, the excitement that took us in those years? The optimism?"

"People clamoured for our work," Edgar said. "People begged to be allowed to come here, for work and for help."

"Just so," Michael agreed. "Can't you recall the excitement? The patients, once dying, now returned to health? The weeping relatives, the relief and happiness that touched us all when another person left here, hale and hearty again?"

"We were proud," I said, remembering with a shock. "We were proud to be helping people who'd had no hope."

"Exactly. And it wasn't only we three who felt that. The applications we had to work here, the people who never had a chance to join us but desperately wanted to be part of it." He coughed, the sound rattling, and then fixed me with a kind look, fond like a father. Familiar. "Never forget that we didn't begin this with thoughts of disaster and doom. We worked here with Cassius – dear Cassius – to push the borders of medical science–"

"And break the limits of technology."

"–so that we might cure people of disease and give them more from life than nature had decided they should have. Does that make us monsters?"

I realised then that this was a discussion Edgar and the Professor had had before, and I felt foolish and naive for never having given it such thought. Their words had the tone of a well-rehearsed argument, picked over, established, and discarded all too frequently. I felt something inside of me settle, eased by the way their words evoked the truth in my memories. I'd forgotten how this had begun – not as a lone bastion of humanity on a scorched and dismal wasteland, but as a shelter, a beacon of science and hope that the world had flocked to like pilgrims.

"We were trying to help people," I said. The words felt strange in my mouth, coming with the taste of revelation when they should have been known to me already.

"We *did* help people," Michael corrected. "And perhaps if we're given the chance, we may yet help them again. Don't let Dolly's childish anger make you forget what we really do here. Not now we might finally have some hope."

I let his certainty cradle me, as I had so many times before. For all that we might rage at the world, one thing has always been clear to me, and that is that the Professor is one of the most remarkable minds to have lived. If I trusted nothing else in this world, I knew I could trust in him.

12TH JUNE

I first met Edgar Trevelyan on a cold Thursday in 2054. It would be another year before we moved our operations to the Tower, and in the Orex Corporation's skyscraper, which we called Hope Towers, every faculty had their own floor. Cybernetics was higher up the physical realm than neurobiology, and on that day Michael swept me into the sleek lift and brought me to the place he described as Edgar the Gentleman's lair.

My first impression of the floor he dominated was that it was technological chaos. Rows of metal tables ran in parallel lines, and interspersed between them were great feats of robotics that looked like something from a film set. Huge metal arms picked up and replaced shards of glowing tech behind thick panes of glass. Vast computer monitors took up two walls, riddled with equations and computer code that was so dense as to be unreadable to me. And in the centre, like a metal tree growing through the heart of the laboratory, an enormous Faraday cage bracketed an equally enormous computer, its lights blinking in a series of pulses that reminded me of the path of brainwaves during sleep. A neurological mimicry.

Edgar brought to mind a caricature of a gentleman. His pinstriped suit trousers were pressed and creaseless under a crisp white shirt and waistcoat worn without a jacket. A red cravat hid his rather thin neck, and he had a white rose boutonniere that had to have been picked that morning. He slid from the dais his desk was perched on, putting down a chunk of whirring metal and wiping his oil-stained fingers on a rag.

"You must be dear Thea," he said, sweeping my hand to his mouth and pressing a dry kiss to my knuckles. "I've heard such a lot about you."

So began a day that made me feel intensely ignorant, and inspired me with renewed belief in the work being done at the Orex Corporation.

In essence, Edgar told me, the mistake his contemporaries had made was to think of the brain as something mechanical. The metaphor of the brain as a computer was useful for a time, he believed, but it had become limiting once technology had advanced well enough to collect data on our own neural processes. The problem, as he saw it, was that as long as computers operated on a binary logic system, they could never progress far enough to be able to replicate the processes of the brain.

"A neuron isn't a binary switch," he told me. "You can't simply turn it on and off and expect to create a result. Instead, neurons respond in an analogue sense. They alter their activity in response to stimulation far more sensitively than a yes or no question can replicate."

The idea that had risen from this thought was simple enough, as most brilliant discoveries are, but the fact that Edgar was able to put it into action was what made him remarkable. If, he reasoned, thinking of a brain like a computer limited the scope of our understanding of the brain, then couldn't the reverse also be true? That thinking of a computer like a brain, instead of a binary system, might expand the capabilities of what a computer could do?

He was speaking, of course, of designing for emergence.

"We see it often in deep-learning programs," Edgar explained. "At their root, the way they behave can't be explained by those of us who designed them. Essentially, they develop emergent properties that should be beyond the scope of their code."

"You're describing artificial intelligence," I said. "Machines developing consciousness."

He'd smiled, then, thin and thoughtful. "Yes and no. AI focuses on repeating the abilities of the brain, but it doesn't yet seek to create what it feels like to be an actual, living consciousness. AI is mimicry, not creation, and even that isn't as advanced as people think."

"So you want to make it more advanced?"

"I don't want to create consciousness, but I think there's more we can explore in this area."

This exploration involved the prototype for a new neuralchip. It was a diminutive metal thing, its surface smooth with conductive alloys, and when Edgar zoomed in on the detail I was able to pick out engravings around a central container no bigger than a pinprick. The longer I looked, the more they reminded me of a simple neuronal network when observed under a microscope.

"The reasoning is fairly simple," Edgar said. "That we combine a computer's binary code with a separate, woven program that allows for ambiguity. The binary system would still run at the centre, but outside of that supporting structure we're working on creating branches – extracts of code that, for want of a better word, react to influence by the human mind once inserted. Put simply, the neuralchips will run the way they were designed to, but they will also respond to the signals of the brain they're implanted into, learning how to assimilate with their host."

"You're recreating a neuronal network inside a computer chip so that it's indistinguishable from the brain?"

"No," he replied with that huffing laugh through his nose. "It won't be indistinguishable but sympathetic. Eventually, the idea is that, rather than being an extra piece of hardware alien to the body, the chip will be assimilated into the neural network of the host brains and become just another part of the mind."

"You're building a piece of technology that can grow." The thought fascinated me almost as much as it repulsed me. It was something on a small scale, yes, but it was the proposal of a true fusion of man and machine.

Of course, there was a greater part to cybernetics' role in the creation of the neuralchip, and that was the ability to turn it on and off. The chip was never meant to be active indefinitely; it had to be controllable by its host. In this, Edgar's genius proved once again to be a deciding factor in its success. Inside the chip, in that small, covered area within the neuronal computer code, was a transmitter which enabled connection to a personal network, linked to a phone or computer. The interface allowed its user to control the chip, not as a binary on and off switch but as a gradual turning down of influence. This network was a closed line – it ran from the biotech to the phone and back again – but the records of every neuralchip were stored on a server at the Tower. And while I've been working with Vladimir, Edgar has been trying to find a way to access the neural network of our imprisoned subject.

"Think of it this way, Thea," he said last night, perched in an armchair. "If we could access the personal networks of every member of the Sleepless, we could use those networks to turn the chips off." He would, in essence, be reverse engineering the failsafe mechanism that should have been installed all along, a system override that would stop the chip from performing its most basic function. An off switch. A solution.

A cure.

15TH JUNE

The city looked like a painting this morning, solidified in the motionless air. The skyscrapers reflected the light, winking in code across the river. The boats drifted so lazily they might have been suffering from ennui. I felt a great kinship with it – the silent buildings, the empty roads, the maddening sheet of purest blue slicked across the sky like a doorway.

The city's strangeness and silence were familiar to me, but for the first time in my memory the silence didn't feel like an absence. I didn't believe any longer that it was a benign and static thing, waiting patiently to be filled by our noise again. I felt that it had accepted its fate and turned inwards, closing its borders and waiting for us to move on. I wanted to resist this change. A certainty rose within me that one day we would come back into the city and conquer its silence whether it wanted us to or not.

"It is beautiful like this, don't you think?" I had felt Vladimir approach and heard his steps scuff on the stairs. "You watch it as though you have an expectation of life within it. Is your watch a benevolent one, or do you look at it and imagine all of the ways its people might harm you if you look away?"

"Who says I'm watching for anything?" I asked him. "I might just be enjoying the view."

"You might, but you watch it with an attention that's pointed. It has purpose. I'm merely wondering what that purpose is."

Behind us, Thane was standing guard in the Bell Tower, the light from his scope reflecting on the wall in front of me.

"There's no purpose," I replied. "I come up here to be alone at the start of the day."

"Then I've interrupted you."

"You wouldn't be the first. Is there something you wanted?"

"Would the pleasure of your company not be want enough?"

It was a mark of how far our relationship had progressed that I felt comfortable enough to scoff rather than horrified by the implication. "While you do seem to seek me out more than anyone else," I said, "I doubt you'd have climbed all the way up here with a rifle at your back simply to speak about the view."

I noticed that the skin of his cheeks was beginning to turn pink, and he'd folded his arms to tuck his hands away from the light. "You're burning," I told him.

"Does that trouble you?"

"I should think it would trouble you."

The flush across his cheekbones was deepening, a line of blistered red slipping down the bridge of his nose like a teardrop. I had the sudden urge to reach out and touch it, to place my hand over his skin and shield him from the heat of the sun.

"It's of no consequence. It will be healed soon."

Still, it made me uncomfortable, to be standing there enjoying the warmth while he burnt beneath it.

"I'm done here anyway," I said. "What did you want to speak about?" We descended the stairs.

"You haven't scheduled another interview between us this week," he said.

"I have other work to do."

"On your other subject?" We stepped into the shadows, the pink of his skin hidden in the gloom.

"The Professor wants another set of eyes on the test results. I said I'd help."

"And do you feel as though you're close to a breakthrough?"

"I feel like we're closer than we've ever been."

He afforded me that rare half-smile, his eyes dancing with repressed humour. "That's a very devious answer, Doctor Chares. You're careful with how you speak to me."

"No more careful than you are with me."

He inclined his head, conceding the point. "Regardless, I'd hoped to ask you for a favour."

I didn't answer, merely waited for him to tell me what had struck him as so important that he'd brave the sunlight to ask.

"You know, of course, that my purpose in coming here was to seek help for Helen. The transition here hasn't been easy for her, as I'm sure you realise. It seems that she's found some comfort with your animals, although some of your number are uncomfortable with the association."

We'd started to walk by then and had reached the goat pen, where Billie and her unfortunate kid were resting.

"I'd appreciate it if you might speak in her defence," he said, "if the topic should come up in conversation."

In the midst of the straw and dirt, Helen sat in a soft white summer dress, cradling the kid in her arms. It was a strange image, and again that morning I felt as though I'd fallen into a painting. Her red hair tumbled over her bare shoulders and the white-brown fur of the goat brushed over her skin.

The scene looked almost like a Renaissance portrait, one of the Virgin Mary cradling the infant Jesus to her chest and caught in a beam of sunlight. Except, of course, that instead of the perfect son of God in her arms, the two-headed goat slept peacefully against her. It was as though Dalí had painted a religious image and we had wandered inside.

"I don't see any reason she shouldn't be here, but I also don't see why you think anyone would listen to me," I said.

"You're a doctor here. It was my understanding that the medical division held sway in this place. Was I wrong?"

I thought about the meeting and Dolly's bitter anger at us all. About the silence that had followed her exit. The fact that no one had made a move to challenge her.

"We make decisions together," I said. "In medical matters, I probably hold some sway."

"And is this not a medical matter?"

Helen must have heard us speaking, but she behaved as though we weren't there. Smiling down at the sleeping kid, her fingers tracing one of its muzzles, she hummed a familiar nursery rhyme beneath her breath.

"I suppose it could be made one, if you think she's traumatised enough to need rehabilitation."

"Don't you?" He was leaning on the fence, a deceptively casual posture, and I was lulled into a sense of security by it.

"I do. I'll speak to Maryam about it. Rehab's more her area than mine."

"As I said, I would very much appreciate it."

The reflected light from Thane's rifle blinked in the corner of my vision.

"I will take up no more of your time."

18TH JUNE

Sleep announces itself differently for everyone. Some people welcome it, slipping easily into the solace of a restful night. Some seek escape in it. Others distrust it. Some see creative value in it. Still more dread it, when it doesn't arrive as it ought to and throws everything else into disarray.

Sleep disorders were once some of the most common illnesses known to humanity. Insomnia, which turns every fall of darkness into a nightly battle. Hypersomnia, where days and hours are swallowed in blankness and the world shut out behind the force of closed eyelids. Narcolepsy, in which the bridge between sensory gates fails, summoning sleep as sudden unconsciousness against all will and sense and need.

And in the midst of it all, fatigue, the modern affliction that seems so easily described but contains so many different meanings we rarely stop to examine. I knew, from a young age, that the words we used to describe tiredness were wrong. Just as for pain, where the same word could be used for a papercut as for an amputation, *fatigue* covered all manner of sins. It might mean a week of poor sleep to some, an encroaching mental weariness to others. It could be used by sportspeople, great athletes who ascribed their post-workout tiredness the same weight as that of an illness sufferer whose body was shutting down.

Still, there were greater problems. Fatigue in a cancer patient, who may regain their energy once treatments are completed, is not the same as the fatigue of someone suffering from a chronic illness which never truly ends.

And then, insidious and unacknowledged, postviral fatigue, ME, long Covid – all had the same problem. They were not simply fatigue; they were a metabolic fault, whereby energy was not only inaccessible but unable to be sustained on a cellular level. They caused the kind of fatigue that left Mother lying there, day after day, her heart beating out a tachycardic rhythm because every available ounce of energy had been diverted to maintain basic bodily functions.

They called that *fatigue* and it sounded wrong. Weak in my ears. Inadequate in the way that a firework is to a nuclear bomb. Sleep, then, I thought. The answer to her problems must be found there, in the glymphatic system that cleaned the brain every night and was somehow no longer good enough. But how deep might it go? What area of rest had gone so wrong, and how were we to identify it? We would look, I decided, in the first instance to brainwaves.

There are two main stages of sleep: REM sleep, in which we dream, and NREM sleep, in which we don't. These stages of sleep engage in a push-and-pull battle throughout the night, cycling between each other around every ninety minutes, beginning first with NREM. These things I learnt at the very start of my career, but the beauty of sleep as seen through brainwaves had eluded me until I worked with the Professor.

When I first joined the Orex Corporation, Michael was conducting a study on the benefits of deep-brain stimulation during sleep, particularly in Alzheimer's patients early in their diagnosis. We shared a floor back then, and at the start of the study, when the participants were readying themselves for their second night of stimulated sleep, he called me into his office to analyse the data.

He ushered me in and brought up the MRI scans alongside the brainwave visuals. We sat together in front of his array of monitors and studied them.

"You see, Thea, how the REM brainwaves and the waking brainwaves are the same?"

"Of course."

"Now, observe the NREM waves. See how they pitch and fall like a tide drawing in over the shore? Indulge me, just for a moment, and try to tap a beat."

"How can I?" I asked. "There isn't any sound."

He grinned, exuberant. "Ah, but there is. Dear Edgar lent me the tech and we converted the subjects' brainwaves into sound only this morning. Would you like to hear?"

It was a rhetorical question – he'd already turned the volume up and hit Play. The beat of the REM waves was erratic, a discordant, asynchronous sound that followed no measure and repeated no rhythm. The activity was chaotic and grating to listen to.

"Do you know why it sounds so bizarre?" he asked.

"Because different parts of the waking brain process different pieces of information at different moments in time," I told him. "Even though our waking thoughts are more logical than our dreaming mind, across the brain they have no electrical consistency."

"Very good. Now, the NREM waves."

Here, then, was where the conversion into sound became useful. In deep slow-wave sleep, the up-and-down tempo of the wave activity decelerates dramatically, becoming ten times slower than the frenetic activity of the brainwaves produced while awake or dreaming.

More than this, though, the slow waves of NREM are far more synchronous and reliable than those of waking or REM. Converted into sound, the slow-wave sleep of the subjects filled the room with a steady, pulsing drumbeat. It reminded me of a heartbeat, of echo-location skimming over the sea floor. It was meditative and calming, a tidal ebb and flow of sound.

Then, in the midst of this repetitiveness, there came another, more discordant noise. A sudden trill overlaid the waves, like a bird singing in the garden of sleep.

"A sleep spindle," Michael said.

We let the wave wash over us, the meditative beat interrupted by the discordant purr of the brainwave surge, the spindle meant to protect a sleeper from becoming aware of external noise.

"Now," he went on, after some time had passed. "Observe the brain scan as well."

The pattern of the brainwaves was replaced by a bright MRI image, and the beat continued. Alongside the sound, we could watch the brain light up, a wash of white light that began within the frontal lobe, just above the eyes, and swept back in a single uninterrupted wave, drenching the whole of the brain in light until it disappeared at the brainstem – only to begin again from the front and push back.

"At the advent of sleep research," Michael told me, "it was assumed that the slower waves of NREM reflected a brain that was idle, compared to the more frantic REM patterns they observed."

"But they were wrong," I continued for him. "NREM is where the brain works the hardest."

"Exactly. This, dear Thea, is one of the most epic displays of neural collaboration that we know of. Through an astonishing act of self-organisation, all of these thousands of brain cells have decided to unite and sing at the same time."

His enthusiasm was infectious, and in that moment it was easy to see why so many of my fellow sleep researchers waxed lyrical about the beauty of the sleeping mind.

During wakefulness, the brain fires chaotically. Different neural networks light up and respond to both internal and external stimuli, but rarely do the neurons at the front of the brain have any connection to the ones elsewhere. During NREM sleep, the waves function as a long-wave radio, opening up communication possibilities between disparate regions of the brain, allowing them to collaboratively send and receive their repositories of stored experience. If wakefulness is dominated by reception of information, NREM is characterised by reflection; the brain assimilates the day's experiences and washes away the details that it decides are unimportant.

It was here that our research was focused, in the slow waves of sleep, where the brain is more connected than it ever is at other times. Michael's theory – or I should, perhaps, say Cassius's theory – was that if you could stimulate a brain to require less of such sleep by boosting its existing capacity, you could cut down the hours needed for unconsciousness. Essentially, by making the brain's sleep process more efficient, you could ignore quantity of sleep in favour of upping the quality.

What we don't understand about the Sleepless is how their brainwaves function now they're perpetually awake. It was this the Professor wanted me to consult on today.

The laboratory had been set up in advance, and when we entered the subject was half-reclined on the bed, straps tying it in place. It was disturbingly still, atonic under the pressure of the nerve blocks, and would have looked almost as though it were sleeping if it hadn't been for the blue of its eyes. The camera was set up by the foot of the bed, taking in the length of its body and focusing on its face.

It was strange to be in the laboratory with it again. Before, it had been a creature to be feared, snapping and growling with a coiled strength in its muscles that trembled to attack, the only one of its kind we'd managed to trap and our only hope of uncovering the secrets of these monsters we'd unleashed. Then, its blue eyes had been the mark of a predator, of something speechless, sleepless, and perhaps even soulless.

I didn't feel that way about it today. Perhaps it was the result of spending so much time with Vladimir, but I'd become so used to seeing a sharp intelligence in the blue gaze that I couldn't help but search for it again. I expected the subject to, at any moment, open its mouth and question me.

Can you tell me why this is happening?

Do you believe you'll find what you're looking for?

Is this worth it? Am I not as alive as you?

It was disconcerting to hear Vladimir's voice inside my head, and I almost believed in telepathy, that he was the filter through which Subject 001 was able to speak. Restrained so thoroughly, it was easier to treat it as something helpless rather than as a threat to our lives.

Did it still possess sentience? Did it understand the conversations that passed between Michael and I? Or was this the gaze of an animal, aware that it was unsafe but unable to articulate why? I wondered if it had a concept of rescue. Was it aware that we were its only path to escape? Did it wait for one of us to have a crisis of conscience, to release it and apologise for what we'd done? Was its look towards me pleading, or did I imagine it? Was I superimposing human emotions onto something that no longer felt them, or was I ignoring its humanity in order to assuage my guilt about the way it had been treated? There was no way of knowing, but when we attached the electrodes to its face I had the impulse to reassure it that this wouldn't hurt, in the same way a vet might soothe a frightened animal.

There now, I wanted to say. *This will be okay. Nothing will hurt you today.*

I knew enough to understand that empathy in this situation was useless, and even detrimental to the greater good we were trying to achieve. The history of humanity is the history of suffering, and this event a mere drop in the vast ocean of cruelty that preceded it. It's curious, though, that such knowledge doesn't absolve us. If absolution is what we seek, we'd be better off praying for understanding.

Michael's soft exhalation of surprise broke me from these thoughts, and I joined him at the sleep monitor. Together, we watched the oscillating patterns of brainwaves track like caterpillars across the screen, and I felt the shifting of a new paradigm take hold.

Impossible, I thought but didn't say. And yet there it was.

The subject was awake – undeniably and unequivocally awake. The monitors confirmed as much. But its brainwaves weren't the discordant march of waking or the drumbeat of REM. These were the waves of slow-wave sleep, beating back and forth across the screen with no sleep spindles to touch them. By all that our machines could discern, this creature languished in the very deepest recesses of sleep. It should have been catatonic. It should have been so far beyond consciousness that its eyes wouldn't open and its muscles wouldn't move.

The absence of the sleep spindle, however, suggested something different. There was no pulse to keep it protected from external stimuli. It was sleeping while awake. Except that couldn't be right. It may be more accurate to say that it was awake but that its brain moved through the deep, restorative waves of an endless sleep. There was no border here. No burst of brain activity to keep it from consciousness and no dampening of external sound. The subject had entered an entirely new pattern of consciousness, neither asleep nor awake but something wholly Other.

19TH JUNE

Belief is a peculiar thing. It encompasses both science and faith, both superstition and the proof of fact. I argue, for instance, that I believe in science, but science isn't a static thing. Science is mutable. It twists and turns, uncovering new discoveries and shifting paradigms, sometimes multiple times within a generation. To say that I believe in science is therefore to say that I believe in change, that truth may mean something different today than it will tomorrow. It was a fact that every living organism required sleep to exist, until it wasn't any longer. Now, I find that sleep is something the Sleepless have altered to mean something entirely new again.

More than this, I've reviewed the subject's brain scans, analysed the damage to the thalamus and basal ganglia, seen the atrophy of the cingulate cortex, and made my best conclusions – the first, that the neuralchip's insinuation into the brain is prolific, and the second, that turning off the chips may not be enough. We need a way to counteract the loss of neuronal mass at the thalamus, which appears ragged like motheaten clothes.

This, then, is to be my role, to create a new cell matrix that will undo the damage once the machinery is shut down. I can't pretend it isn't daunting, but I must believe it's possible. So much that seems impossible has already occurred, so why not this as well?

Yesterday, I would have said that sleep is the state of unconsciousness. That it is mediated by certain hormones, driven by electrical signals rushing down the neural pathways, and visible as a track on a brainwave monitor. I know that a sleeping person looks decidedly different to a dead person, and different again to one merely pretending at sleep. The subject resists that belief, rejects and dispels it like wind over the sea. Like the fog burning away in the sun to reveal a whole new landscape beyond.

22ND JUNE

"Do you believe in God?"

We were back in the interview room between the cold walls, watching each other again.

"I believe in the gaps," I replied.

Vladimir's mouth ticked up at the corner, and he leant away from the table with one arm slung carelessly over the back of his chair. "So, you will allow God a space in your philosophy, just until science marches on?"

"I personally don't pray to a creator," I said, "but I see no reason why a scientist should spend their life disparaging the possibility that there's more than we can observe."

"That's another devious answer, Doctor Chares."

"Your questions are no less tricky."

He hummed and drummed his fingers on the table top, a slow, deliberate movement that seemed calculated to draw my eye. The tips were stained with something black – charcoal, from his recent habit of sketching in one of Edgar's spare books, I thought.

"What happens when there are no more gaps left to be filled?" he asked.

"What do you mean?"

"The problem with forcing God into the gaps is that every

year His home grows smaller. Every new discovery pushes Him to the edge. Every moment of enlightenment is an incursion upon His allotted space."

"I don't see it like that."

"Don't you?" I had the feeling he was amused. "How do you see it, then?"

I wasn't sure how to answer.

"You offer up the gaps as though it's a benevolent gesture," he said, "but the prison God has found there shrinks all the time. What happens when there's nowhere left for Him to go? Does He vanish into obscurity? Another hypothesis disproven by humanity's quest for truth?"

I thought for a moment. "I think you over-estimate our ability to learn everything. No matter how advanced our technology or how evolved our minds, there will always be things we don't understand, phenomena and processes we can't explain."

"And you hope that God lives there, in the inexplicable."

"I don't hope for anything," I told him. "I only say that we can't prove that something doesn't."

"Does that comfort you? Or are you disturbed by the notion that something could exist that you'll never have any knowledge of in this life?"

I looked away, my gaze drifting to the ticking clock while I organised my thoughts. The truth was that I was tired and hadn't slept at all well, waking from dreams in which Edgar walked the battlements holding a brain in his hands while the Professor applauded from the top of Beauchamp and declared him a genius for the ages. I felt that Vladimir was testing me again, but my powers of observation were compromised by fatigue.

"I suppose I find it disturbing," I decided. "I spend my

life looking for answers, and it's a little depressing to realise there will always be some things I'll never know."

"And a little frightening at the present time, I assume."

"How do you mean?" I asked.

He sat forwards in his seat.

"God, as you say, is an unknowable variable. He cannot be fully disproven by logic just as long as gaps remain in your knowledge. You readily admit that there will always be gaps in what humanity can learn, so doesn't it concern you that the largest gap might be found here?"

"You're asking if I think we'll find answers to the Sleepless."

"I'm asking if you're prepared for the possibility they're inexplicable."

"You," I corrected him, and he tilted his head in question. "You said *they* could be inexplicable, but aren't you one of them? It would have been more accurate for you to say *we*."

"Would it indeed? In that case, Thea Chares, what do you believe? Am I inexplicable?" His mouth twitched. "Does God live here after all?"

BE EVER WATCHFUL FOR YOUR ADVERSARY THE DEVIL PROWLS AROUND LIKE A ROARING LION SEEKING SOMEONE TO DEVOUR

30TH JUNE

The sky was as leaden as a gunship this afternoon. Clouds of sharp metal frothed over the city, swaddling the tops of the skyscrapers in grey. I wandered the courtyard, squalls of warm wind lifting stray hairs from my face and tugging at my lab coat. I felt restless, untethered. A storm was on the horizon, the end of the June heatwave approaching in butter-thick air and burgeoning thunder.

My head pounded and a migraine was brewing behind my eyes, giving colours a sharp edge and sounds an even sharper spike. The courtyard was unusually deserted, and I winced when the door to the engine room swung shut in the wind. Alex was waiting for me. Over the wide expanse of space we watched each other, until he gestured me towards him with a hopeful expression and disappeared inside.

I stood for a long moment in the turbulent air, the atmosphere pressing down about my temples and bringing a pulse to the base of my skull. He'd given me the opportunity to ignore him, to go back to my home and hide if I wished. With the drumbeat in my head and every colour too bright, I almost did, but I had the feeling that if I refused a conversation now we'd simply never speak about what had happened at the meeting, and it would fester like an open wound.

Feeling somewhat condemned, I crossed the courtyard and opened the door, and was immediately hit by a blast of hot air, the chemical smell of the varnish, and the humming purr of the generator. There was a cup of tea waiting for me on the warm metal, and I curled up in my usual chair while Alex worked on his net. The silence was uncomfortable, broken by the scrape of the ropes on his worktable and the trundle of the machine. I felt exposed, like being brought before a teacher at school and waiting for the punishment to be delivered.

I wondered what Alex – perhaps my closest friend here beyond the Professor – felt about everything. Did he agree with Dolly? Did he blame me, too? The thought made me nauseous, and then panicked, and then, very suddenly, angry. Had I been judged all this time and never known it? Would he take the opportunity to insult me now that Dolly had paved the way? I put my half-finished tea down on the generator and confronted him, and the way he froze, possum-like, was all the confirmation I needed.

I grew agitated, and recited his side of the conversation for him while he watched me and said nothing.

"Let's see, shall we? You're sorry about the meeting, but while you think that Dolly shouldn't have handled it that way, you can't really disagree with what she said. You know, just like everyone else, that what happened was our fault. That without us, the Sleepless wouldn't exist and the world would still be alive."

I hadn't actually said the words out loud before, although I'd grappled with them internally, and I was shocked by my own capacity for horror. He tried to interrupt but I waved him away, believing that if I allowed him to agree with me, to confirm what I already knew to be true, I might simply burn up inside the hearth of my own disgust.

"And of course you're right," I continued. "It is our fault. It wouldn't have happened without us. But if you think for one second that Dolly can judge me – judge *us* – when we're doing everything we can to change it, then I don't know how you could ever have called yourself my friend."

I couldn't look at him. There were tears pressing behind my eyes and I drew my hands up over my face, determined that I wasn't going to break in front of him. He was across the room before I could take note that he was moving, and I realised I'd backed myself into a corner only when he closed in on me.

"Thea."

He crowded himself around me, and I thought of how cruel that was, not to give me a chance to leave and save my dignity.

"What?" I snapped. "What more could you possibly need to say?" I pushed at his chest and he stumbled backwards. "You want to say that we're not friends, is that it? That you were just being polite. That you didn't want it to be awkward. That it's the end of the world so we may as well all pull together and–"

"Thea, will you shut up for one blessed second?" Then his palm was on my cheek, and his face was so close that I could feel his breath on my lips and smell the mint of toothpaste in the hot air between us. I stilled, something like panic making me cold and confused.

"I don't want to be your friend," he said very quietly.

Then, he kissed me.

I confess that I've had little experience with kissing. A few drunken nights with men and women in bars, always leaving before they invited me home with them, or suggested they'd like to come home with me. Sloppy and wet and, in retrospect, revolting. A boyfriend in my teens who liked to bite more than I thought was normal, so that I always tasted blood after another endless make-out session. A woman in the cybernetics lab who was gentle and soft, and probably dead now even so.

Alex's kiss surprised me. Or, I should better say, it stunned me so deeply that I stopped feeling anything at all. For a long moment my mind was a blissful blank. My anger was gone. Shame was simply a word I'd heard but had never once felt. I couldn't hear the humming of the generator or smell the varnish. I had no concept of my body's existence beyond the press of his lips and the intense heat of his palm against my cheek. When he pulled away, all I could do was blink.

He blushed, brown eyes scanning my face, and I wondered what he saw there. How I would look if I were able to assume his perspective and see myself staring back. I had no idea what my expression was telling him, but his hand stayed on my cheek.

"Sorry," he said, soft as a breath. "I've been wanting to do that for a while. I should have said something at the meeting. I should have stood up for you, told Dolly to go to hell, and made sure you knew that everyone doesn't blame you. That I don't blame you."

He was very serious, his gaze holding mine and his palm still hot on my cheek.

"I don't think this is your fault, Thea. I don't think any of this is your fault."

Language came back to me then, like a match struck against flint. I became aware that my hands were on his chest and my fingers tangled in his t-shirt, holding him in place.

"What do you think?"

He hesitated.

"I think you're wonderful."

I think I kissed him, then. At any rate, in the next moment we were kissing, and this time it wasn't gentle. I was backed into the corner and my fingers were on his chest and pulling him closer, and his hand moved to the back of my neck while the other held tight at my hip. He pushed me back into the wall, and I felt his leg slip between mine while our tongues met. My heart was pounding, the heat of him like a furnace, like a generator pressed to my front that filled me with a strange nervous energy that was almost – but not quite – desire.

I don't know how long we kissed for, hands grasping inexpertly at each other and faces flushed in the heat of the room and everything there was between us. I know that we stopped when the door opened at the top of the stairs. We broke apart, breathing heavily, and I thought that I'd never seen someone look as real to me as he did then, his hair mussed and sticking up at odd angles, his lips kiss-swollen and cheeks red, and a delirious, honest smile on his gentle face, as though I were a great gift he'd been granted. I almost judged him for it.

The moment shattered when Dolly arrived. Her face twisted with scorn, and I felt both a desperate desire to hide and also an unbearable smugness. I wanted to rub her face in it.

"Oh, God," she spluttered. "*Really?*"

I didn't stay to find out what was said. I simply straightened my clothes, walked out of the room with my head held high, and closed the door behind me as I left.

and it is the gap, the terrible gap between asking for help and being refused, the space in which hope raises its delicate head to the sun and pleads for warmth and understanding, and the night comes crashing down about its ears and it is cold and unforgiving, and somewhere there is a child forever watching her mother lying prone on the bed, forever crying because she doesn't understand why the room is so dark, and the stillness, the appalling stillness is so heavy and so thick that it could choke them both, and when it chokes them there will be no one who hears them or tries to come to their rescue

JULY

1ST JULY

The storm broke over London at 2:43 a.m. I'd been drifting on the borders of sleep, nose filled with the scent of burning and limbs fizzing with formless anxiety. The first rolls of thunder were distant, like the sound of a party on the other side of the city, and my migraine was in full force. Each crash was more painful than the last, and when the first flash of lightning lit up the sky the resulting blindness was like a strip of magnesium catching fire in my retina.

My body felt very real to me. It thrummed with pain and my surroundings bellowed to match it, as though I and the world were of one mind. I knew, almost a full minute before the thunder settled above us, that the atmosphere was ready to break. Curled up on my side, able to do little more than clutch the blanket around me and wait, I laughed when the cloudburst rained down and the storm shattered overhead.

The sound was terrific, amplified by my ailing body until it became a drumbeat on the roof, a tidal wave of water and noise, and then it seemed as though I'd heard it before. Déjà vu took me, cradled me in an inexplicable reality, and the sound of the storm was the sound of brainwaves, the rain the discordant pitter-patter of REM, and the thunder the rolling slow waves that scattered dreams to the wind.

I had the oddest notion that I was listening to the Earth's great mind, or else to the dreaming mind of a god, and I was startled, then, to hear screams. I didn't move at first, half-convinced that it was merely a hallucination. But the shouting continued, first a woman's voice and then a man's. There was a drunkenness about me, and I felt myself wholly compromised and thoroughly inspired.

I raised myself from the bed and slipped my feet into my shoes. The stairs beneath me were mountains, swaying at my every step, lightning and shadow playing with the sparkles at the edge of my vision and blind spots sloping through the hall. When I flung my front door open, the air hit me like a needle to the skin, and I laughed aloud, giddy and Other and so beyond myself that I felt I was imagining the world anew with each second that skimmed by.

By the time I'd crossed the green, I was windswept and drenched, my canvas shoes squelching and slipping, the sodden laces whipping around my ankles, and there were human-shaped shadows flitting along the wet paths of torch beams. Perhaps I ought to have returned home and taken shelter, but in that moment I could think of nothing I'd less like to do. It's difficult to explain now – difficult always, I think, to explain an altered state of body and mind to someone who hasn't experienced it – but I felt as though I was soaring.

The pain was fierce, breath-taking even, and I took leave of myself and passed out of time, a passive observer of stop-motion snapshots that resisted a linear narrative. The roof of the goat pen tore away. Helen cradled the two-headed kid. An army of shades roved around me and the sleeping God dreamt of destruction. There was shouting, and Alex, and Alison pushing Helen to the ground. And then a dull and sudden pressure against my shoulder as I was knocked from my feet.

There was no pain when the debris hit me. My capacity for feeling such a thing was far outstripped by the agony in my head. The clouds raced above me, and I felt the rain run down my throat and up my nose. Everything was spinning, and the earth churned wet and soft beneath me. I felt that I would sink, that I'd already left the world and was simply waiting to be forgotten. And then I was being hauled up, hot hands on my arms and Alex's face above me and the crackle of static on an ancient television set dappling Vladimir's face.

"You," I said.

"Me." The lightning arced across the sky and his eyes burned.

I slipped from time again and became aware that I was inside the chapel, alone and in the dark. The stone walls buried the sound of the storm, and the only light came from a burning candelabrum by the pulpit and white streaks of lightning through the stained-glass windows. I walked the aisle, feeling that the chapel had become another world so different from its nature during the day.

In truth, I've rarely set foot inside the place. I've never felt the need to pray to a god. Nevertheless, chapels, churches, and temples have always struck me as places that harbour memory. History is in their stones. Echoes of voices long silenced, raised in worship or despair, are stitched into their very fabric.

We humans made worship, and from that worship we made a place for history to contain itself. I felt that I was creating history as I lit the candles and placed them around the room. Perhaps I was myself at worship, but if so who or what I was worshipping was a mystery to me. The act was meditative, almost holy, although that's a difficult word to credit without the belief to sustain it, and I still felt myself to be operating inside something that was like a dream.

I stood by the altar, staring up at the windows and the memorials, and I felt history stretch and warp around me. Then I sensed something new. Whether it was a prickling down the back of my neck, a sense of premonition, or merely a bout of paranoia that turned out to be true, I can hardly say. All I can say for sure is that I became certain, between one heartbeat and the next, that I was being watched – and when I turned, I saw it was true.

Like a bride awaiting a ceremony, Subject 001, unbound and aware, watched me from the other end of the aisle. We stared at each other, and I felt the moment pull taut and begin to strain. Here we were, suspended in a moment of glass, and it would take only one of us to throw the stone that would begin whatever came next. I didn't scream. There was no point.

The lightning flashed, and its eyes were sapphires in the death mask of its face. I thought of Alex and the engine room, and the way he placed my tea on the generator to keep it warm. I thought of the Professor and our work and I wondered, if I died, would he have any chance of saving them? I thought of Mother, and felt guilty and ashamed and wanted to apologise to her before the end. And then a particularly loud crash of thunder sounded and the first wayward pebble crashed through the glass.

Subject 001 screamed. The sound was a thunderclap and the storm was inside and I reacted without thinking, flinging myself sideways and diving across the floor. I realised, as I flew through the air, that I'd never had cause to use my body like this. I'd read about it in books, or watched on film screens as people leapt for their lives, but the practicality of such a thing was something I'd never thought about before.

My body wasn't used to leaping and I had no time to consider how I'd land. I fell hard, snapping my little finger as I reached out to brace myself against the floor, and the whole kinetic motion of my body was flung forward. My chin hit the stone, hard enough to rattle the inside of my skull, and I gasped at the shattering pain. But adrenaline is a saviour hormone.

I didn't think. There was no plotting or deliberation. I simply rolled upon impact and found myself beneath the benches. The creature screamed, a soul-shaking sound, and landed in the space I'd been. He splayed himself over the ground, his jaw dislocated and his arms and legs extended, bent at elbow and knee. Had I still been lying where I'd fallen, we'd have looked as though we were about to make love.

Precise and methodical, he lowered himself to the bloodmark my chin had left behind, and inhaled. It was sensual – almost intimate – and all the more frightening for the perversion.

Adrenaline kicked in for a second time and I rolled again, graceless and helpless, and found myself two more benches away. I spared a brief thought that they were drilled into the stone, and that flipping them would be difficult even for a creature of such strength, but when I looked again all hope shrivelled up and fled.

Subject 001 pursued, crouched on hands and knees, serpentine and relentless. I crawled deeper into the rows and made for the doors, with a vague idea that beneath the seats I might be able to stay far enough ahead of him to reach the wall, and at that point it would be down to luck as to whether or not I made it outside. Lightning lit up the room, auras pulsed in my vision, and he made not a sound behind me until I reached the final bench and felt his hand close around my ankle. I did scream then, twisting onto my back and kicking with all of my might, but it was useless.

The strength in him was terrific, and while I writhed and lashed out, a hurricane of screaming and fight, his grip never wavered. His hand crept up my calf, red jewels of blood bursting beneath the passage of his claws. In the midst of my terror, it embarrassed me that I was begging, hands outstretched and clinging onto the bench above me while I tried to pull myself away. But my pleading was useless. Who can plead with a lion for mercy? He moved inexorably, almost teasingly. First, his hand grasped my knee while with his other he pinned my still-flailing leg to the ground and moved up my body until his chest was pressed flush to the top of my thighs.

All thought abandoned me. He laid his hand over my stomach, pressing just hard enough that my breath left me and my screams turned into a guttural choking. Up close, I could see the saliva collecting in pools at the base of his gums. The two rows of teeth opened wide in a snarl, and there was an inescapable flash of intelligence – of humanity – in his eyes.

In a final grab for life, I forced myself to fall limp. The movement jostled him. His hold on me slipped, and I kicked out with such frantic force that both my head and his slammed into the bench above us. Fireworks burst behind my eyes, a splitting pain reigned supreme, and then the chapel doors blew open in a wave of stormwater and thunder and the creature's weight was gone.

Warm hands grabbed mine and pulled me free. The grip closed around my broken finger and I shouted, dimly aware that it was Alex who was pulling me up and back and struggling to lift me to my feet. At the edge of my perception, Thane and Alison moved inside with their rifles drawn, beams of red light tracking across the chapel from their sights. I realised in the moment the doors swung shut that they'd come here for me, and in doing so they'd risked their own lives.

The lightning. The lasers. The guttering candle flames and the migraine aura. All of them seemed gentle and distant, the darkness a canvas for their lightshow, and in a flash of electricity Vladimir approached, his eyes intent on me. Alex tightened his hold on my waist as he drew to stand by us, his finger held over his lips.

"You must let me take her," he said.

"Like hell I do."

"Do you think that you can protect her? Her blood is like a siren. If the creature isn't already driven mad by it, he will be soon. Can you stand against him?"

"I think that between the two of us I'm the least likely to want to tear her apart."

Vladimir's face contorted in a sneer, and the disdain in it was electrifying. "If I'd wanted to tear her apart, I would have done so already. Do not let your misplaced hero complex cost Thea her life."

"I'm standing right here, you know," I said.

The room exploded in gunfire.

Vladimir pulled me from Alex's arms, lifting me easily from the floor and leaping backwards. We landed in an alcove on the other side of the room, and I felt for a second that we were flying. I had the barest glimpse of a candelabrum falling to the floor and spilling its flames like an upturned cup, before he forced my back to the wall and twisted to bracket me with his arms.

Blades of red light cut across my vision and my ears rang. Beneath Vladimir's arms, I saw a shadow leap from the wooden beams, dust bursting in the air as bullets missed their mark. Everyone was shouting, and when I drew my gaze away and looked into Vladimir's face, my chest collapsed inwards with useless panic. The look in his eyes... I can hardly describe it now. The way the shadows pooled in the hollows of his cheekbones, the pressed line of his lips, and the dilation of his pupils that in any other situation I would have called desire, but which looked more like hunger.

My breath caught, pinned beneath the monster I knew and pursued by the one I didn't. The moment seemed frozen in time, the commotion in the rest of the room drifting while we stared at each other. I felt a primal and visceral fear. My face flushed. My palms sweated. The pounding in my head was intense, and the way he looked at me, as though charmed like a snake, felt both dangerous and powerful.

The moment was broken by an explosion of stone over our heads. The subject descended from above us, arms outstretched and mouth opened wide, and I didn't have time to cry out a warning before it landed hard against Vladimir's back. The force of the collision was astounding, creating a sound like a boulder meeting the earth. The only thing that stopped me from being crushed was the strength of Vladimir's arms as he held himself back while his legs buckled, and then a terrible light entered his eyes and he flipped them both away from me.

The movement was almost too fast to follow. One moment they were upon me, and in the next Vladimir had thrown Subject 001 across the room and leapt like a devil after him. Gunshots rang out, more of the ancient stone rained down, and amidst all the shouting I found myself frozen, watching two monsters pursue each other like an ouroboros.

There was little to distinguish them from one another besides the length of their shadows. They bled through the darkness like paint in water, illuminated in strobe flashes of lightning and the light from the rifle's lasers until, with a crash of splintering wood, Vladimir cried out and fell through one of the beams.

It seemed to happen in slow motion. Bullets exploded around the subject, he leapt from the ceiling, and I saw the whites of his eyes as he fell towards me. I thought his face would be the last thing I ever saw: bright blue eyes wide and wild, teeth bared and throat howling, his arms extended towards me. And then I blinked and Vladimir was between us, and the subject sank its teeth into his neck as they collided with the pillar beside me.

The impact knocked me sideways and I slid to the floor, while Vladimir clasped the subject to him in a strange and terrible embrace, and the creature's jaw clamped down at the juncture between his neck and shoulder.

"Help him."

It took me a while to realise that the words were coming from me.

"Someone help him."

I staggered forwards, my legs like water and the pounding in my head torturous, but Vladimir held his hand out to stay me and the whole of the room fell still. In the beam of Alex's torch, we watched them, the subject sucking on Vladimir's neck while he supported it with one arm around its waist and the other pressed to the back of its head.

"A moment," he murmured. "A moment and it will be over."

It was a strangely beautiful moment, a perversion of an embrace, and as I slid to the floor and the pounding of my head finally drew me under, the last thing I saw was Vladimir lowering Subject 001 to the stone and keeling over sideways beside him.

2ND JULY

My dreams were torrid, vivid, confused things. I dreamt that I was kneeling by a riverbank, the taste of dirt and blood on my tongue, while long fingernails picked fetid fur from between the gaps in my teeth. I dreamt that I was on top of the Shard, hunger coiling tight in my belly, contemplating a bright-blue bird that flew just out of my reach. I dreamt of a fire burning in the greenhouses and Maryam's screams became my mother's, and I looked up and saw her falling to the earth as though the clouds had spat her out and she was lost, ejected from the heavens for her crime.

I wanted to say, *No, the crime is mine. You must take her. Keep her safe.* But I was not myself. I was merely a scrap of dirt on a wall, watching and witnessing but unable to influence anything.

I dreamt that there was blood in the chapel, and it slipped beneath the flagstones and watered the bodies in the crypts, and they opened their mouths and drank and drank until their eyes glowed blue and they screamed.

I dreamt of Cassius, as he was and as he became, and in the turmoil of those dreams I was ashamed.

3RD JULY

2054 was the last year that Cassius would see. I'd been avoiding him and his slide towards death, but Michael had made frequent trips to the top of the penthouse and something in his manner had convinced me that it wouldn't be long. I took the lift up to his rooms, where once he'd served me afternoon tea and changed the course of my life. Then, the airy living area had been wide and open, bright with the sun that had streamed in cylinders through the windows. That time – the final time – it had seemed more like a holiday home abandoned over winter.

Cassius was confined to his bedroom, propped up on a parliament of pillows atop the four-poster bed. He reminded me of a living corpse, his skin stretched tight across sharp cheekbones and his hair shaved close to his scalp. Even in sickness he was elegant, although smaller, as though time had reversed and was leading him back to childhood, until one day he'd lose so much of himself that he'd return to a foetal state again.

"Does my appearance shock you, Thea?" His eyes were closed when I entered, and the thin rasp of his voice startled me.

"I didn't realise you were awake."

"Am I?" he asked.

"Don't you know?" I sank into the chair at his side and he turned his nodding head towards me.

"Reality has never seemed so much like a nightmare, and nightmares so much like dreams."

"If I promise I'm not a figment of your imagination, will you answer something for me?"

I took the more obvious jerk of his head to be a nod of agreement.

"Are you in a great deal of pain?"

"An interesting question." He sighed, long and slow, and the stretched expression of his face fell into weariness. "I have asked so many patients that before and thought it to be a simple question. I even…" At this point, he wheezed out a laugh that reminded me of something tubercular. "I even believed that I could tell how much pain a person was in simply by looking at them. Arrogance, thy name is medicine."

"I don't think it's arrogant to believe in our ability to assess our patients," I said. "Pain tends to present in a few predictable ways."

"Does it, though, Doctor Chares? Tell me, how much pain do you believe me to be in?"

I looked at him for a long time, and tried to recall my days as a clinician before research carried me away. Despite what I'd said, pain assessment is difficult when the patient isn't showing obvious distress. Cassius was calm. He was lucid enough to hold a conversation with me. I noted the IV running into his arm delivering slow-release morphine. His heart rate was elevated, but at the end of life this was only to be expected. Clearly, he was incapable of standing unsupported, but with the loss of muscle that was less about pain than capacity.

"I'd say that you were in a reasonable amount of pain, but that it was well controlled."

"And on the pain scale? Where would you place me?"

"Between six and seven, maybe. Closer to six."

He smiled, his eyelids drooping, and his lips pulled back from his teeth to reveal pale white gums that were bloodied around the edges. "I would have assessed myself the same way, were I you. We are too often taught that extreme pain comes with certain non-negotiable features."

My heart sank. "You're going to tell me that my assessment is wrong."

He coughed again, a wet sea of fluid crackling like popping candy in his lungs. "Wrong? You're so far beyond the remit of correct that it's almost ironic."

His eyes had a wild, fevered look about them, and I wondered how long it had been since he'd had a new audience. Someone who wasn't Michael to sit with him day after endless day.

"The problem with the pain scale and an outside perspective is that it presupposes a starting level of zero pain, or of nearly no pain," he said. "From that starting point, we then assume that anyone who'd suddenly found themselves at a pain level of nine would be screaming. But what happens when the starting point is a six or a seven? What would be the point in screaming? Where does tolerance diminish and animal instinct kick in?"

"Where would you place yourself, then?"

"Oh, dear Thea, I am comfortably at a nine. Lift me into a standing position and I'm certain I would scream if I could."

The glazed look in his eyes told me that he was at least partially sedated, and I wondered how often we'd assumed that sedation meant a lack of pain rather than an inability to respond to it.

"Is there anything I can do?" I asked.

"Do? No. There's nothing anyone can do." He sighed, wistful and strangely beatific. "That's what poor Michael can't seem to accept. He thinks there must be a solution to every problem. If there is an effect then there must be a cause, and if there is a cause he seems to take it as a personal affront that there's no action he might take to alter it."

"Causal links can be broken," I argued.

"But not without the proper technology."

"Are you so sure we don't have it?"

The skin around his lips was dry and cracked, a bright red rose bleeding through the waxy pallor of his skin. "You are Michael's student indeed," he murmured. "All life must end. These bodies we live in are nothing if not perishable. Are you so certain that you'd want to find a cure for humanity?"

I woke from my memories in the hospital night, and I wondered if Cassius had known then. Had he understood what the neuralchip was? It seemed impossible that he could have had such prescience and said nothing. But then, we live in the realm of the impossible. It's impossible for a living organism not to sleep, not to age, not to die. It's impossible for a monster to leap through a chapel, and even more impossible for another to stand in its path.

It felt impossible that I should wake in the moon-drenched darkness, alone in the hospital and still with my mind so compromised. A concussion. I remembered Maryam saying so in the space between sleeping and waking, but I couldn't be certain she hadn't been a hallucination as well.

I crept from my bed, uncertain as to why I was creeping. Illness, like childhood, carries with it the sense of being rebellious purely by making a choice. I chose to leave my bed for reasons that are still unclear to me, and in the room next door I found them, Vladimir and Helen, awake.

I was ushered into a seat like a secret, she startled by my appearance and he seeming to have expected it, and there I sat while he calmed her, promising that I didn't mean them harm. She softened, and I had the feeling that I was being searched for some quality she deemed important. I wanted to say something comforting, but what was there to say to someone who didn't speak? She was an enigma. I had no frame of reference for her, for what would calm and what would frighten. I didn't know her history beyond how Vladimir had found her. It struck me that I felt more comfortable with him than with her, as with Helen there was no common language to bind us.

Eventually, she came to stand in front of me, peering down into my face as though I were a specimen in a lab and she the scientist observing me. Slowly, she reached out and touched the tip of her finger to my forehead, and I nodded even though I had no idea of her question. But it seemed to be the correct response, for she retracted her hand and raised the same fingertip to her temple, staring at me as if willing me to understand.

"She's asking if you think of her," Vladimir said. "Do you think of her in the same way you would think of another person?"

"I think of you often," I told her. "I worry that you're hurt."

She sucked her bottom lip backwards into her mouth and began to chew on it. I wanted to reach out and stop her – there were scabs and blood lines over her lips and angry red marks that looked sore and liable to split. After a moment she raised a hand to her chest, holding it flat on her heart, and then crossed the room to Vladimir. He gave her a gentle smile I'd never seen before as she placed her palm on his chest and then looked for my reaction.

"I think of him, too," I said.

She crossed back to me, bringing her finger to my temple and then pointing at my chest.

"Yes, I care. I won't let anything happen to you."

She subsided, relieved of some silent burden, and tapped my hand in a motherly gesture that left an unsettled emotion behind. She looked between the two of us once more, and at a subtle nod from Vladimir, beamed widely and opened the door. She didn't linger on the threshold, and when it closed again behind her I found that she'd left us in a quiet space – the peace of night and a single lamp, the softness of shadows in the corners of the room, and the intimacy of unbroken silence.

"She's very protective of you," I observed, voice soft in deference to the night.

"She feels that she owes me her life."

"The two of us have that in common."

Fragile silence like a moth wing, and the awareness that we'd entered into something private between us, a bond that neither had foreseen.

"He bit you. The subject bit you." I found myself by his bedside, reaching for the loose collar of his shirt before I'd consciously realised it. He allowed me to undo the few buttons at the neck and pull the fabric away. Beneath it, there was a white square of bandage taped at the space between his collarbone and shoulder. My fingers hesitated above it.

"Go ahead," he said. "It will likely be healed soon anyway."

Beneath the dressing, the bite mark was livid and arresting. It looked like a wound already a week healed, but it was clear that the subject's jaws had nearly torn a chunk of flesh from his body.

"It's healing well," I said.

"Yes."

"Why did you do it?" I raised my eyes to his, my fingertips still trailing the edge of the mark.

"You're asking why I saved you?"

I nodded. His gaze pinned me, and I realised we'd rarely been so close. Usually, there was a table between us and eyes watching through a mirror. Now, there was no such barrier, but the abhorrent energy in my body wasn't fear.

"Is it not usual to protect a friend?" he asked.

"Are we friends?"

It was the wrong thing to say. His expression closed off, as though a shutter had been drawn over his soul. "I suspect that question is an answer. Friendship is an agreement that's entered into from two sides. Clearly, our relationship is one-sided." He made to pull away, reaching to close the shirt I'd unbuttoned, and I stopped him before I could think better of it. He stilled, face turned away, and I stared at our joined hands as though they belonged to someone else.

"I didn't mean that," I said.

"What did you mean?"

"Only that our relationship is a strange one. Friendship occurs between two equal parties. It's difficult to say that there's ever been equality between us."

He considered this, his hand tightening almost imperceptibly on mine and drawing it down to rest over his knees. "So you do not deny an emotional connection. You merely debate the name that should be applied."

"Something like that," I replied. My fingers felt weak beneath his touch, brittle as bird bones caught in a snare.

"Then you have your answer. I did not want to see you torn to shreds, although sometimes I think that I should."

The statement should have angered me, but I found myself agreeing with him. I often felt that he shouldn't exist, and was that really so much worse?

"I'm grateful that you didn't," I said.

At that he smiled, and with a delicateness I would have thought him incapable of he lowered his head and brushed a kiss to my knuckles. "As am I."

In the quiet, both of us heard my breath catch.

"You are very unusual." His voice was as gentle as his touch, and I slipped my hand cautiously from his and stepped away.

"You've said that before," I said, "although you never explained in what way."

His gaze tracked me as I backed away, and I realised I was trembling when I lowered myself into the chair.

"I suppose I didn't. Would you like me to enlighten you?"

Neither of us had looked away from the other. I nodded.

"Very well, then. You are focused upon your work to the point of fanaticism, yet you do not possess the unbridled passion of the fanatic. You are analytical, but not so lost in analysis that you're able to ignore emotion."

He raised himself to his feet, slow and measured, and my hands gripped the wooden arms of my chair as though they might protect me.

"You seek to understand me, yet you hold yourself behind walls I cannot breach. You have performed miracles upon humanity, yet you remain refreshingly human."

He took a steady step towards me, and I realised I was being pursued.

"You care for the people here, yet you don't see yourself as one of them."

Another step, and I could have sworn the lights flickered.

"You've been afraid since I've known you, yet you haven't lost yourself to that fear. You pursue knowledge with a fervour that could almost be termed a sickness, yet you don't seem to know what to do with it once it is in your possession."

A final step, and I had to tip my head back to hold his gaze.

"Your companions see you as cold and aloof, yet I have experienced warmth from you, although you've tried to smother it."

He knelt in front of me, and I stared down the length of my body and fought not to blink.

"But above all other things that make you strange, Thea Chares, is that you are a liar."

He reached out, tracing a fingertip over the bones of my hands, and it seemed as though I might suffocate while still breathing.

"You are a liar," he repeated, "in pursuit of the truth. And I don't believe you are even aware of it."

My breath rasped in the desert of my throat, and it seemed a miracle that I might still be able to speak. "What do you think I've lied about?" I asked.

His hand stilled on top of mine. "Oh, Thea. You've lied about everything."

4TH JULY

I cannot bear to write down my thoughts of Vladimir, and so I must choose another topic, one which is safer but no less difficult to relate.

Subject 001 is dead. I left the hospital to this discovery, the Professor's hand guiding me down into the cellars, into the cold and dark, where the subject rested under a white sheet. He seemed just like any other dead person, blank and lifeless and not at all as though he were sleeping.

He'd been cleaned, and there was no blood around his mouth, no clue that in the final moments of his life he'd sunk his teeth into Vladimir's flesh hard enough to rend muscle from bone.

I looked at him for a long time, at his face and the peace in it, and I could find no hint of the monster that had leered at me while his claws tore holes in my leg. He seemed so average, so *normal*. And this, I discovered, was the operative word.

Michael drew the sheet down to expose him in all of his normality. The marble hardness of his chest was gone, and where there had been no hint of blemishes in life, a small surgical scar at the point a doctor might remove an appendix was a pale white mark over his abdomen.

He was devastatingly skinny, the thick mass of muscle in

his shoulders wasted almost to nothing, and his legs were those of a bird's, damaged and weak.

The subject was human again.

5TH JULY

Every civilisation has its rituals around death. The washing of the body. The laying out or the shrouding. The post-mortem surgery and application of cosmetics to return the mask of life to an animal long gone. Or else the turning of the mirrors and the black dress to mark grief and prevent forgetting. The evidence that lives were touched by the person who's passed on. Even the smallest collection of humans will mark a death in some way – a burial, a burning. A vivisection.

The subject was disintegrating before our eyes. No matter how cold the room, it was as though the rot had set in well before death and his decomposition accelerated at a frightening pace. The Professor and Edgar moved him into the surgical suite, and we put on our gowns and masks, slid on gloves, and arranged scalpels. Maryam sat in the room, her knitting needles click-clacking, and I wondered if she was here for me again or if she simply couldn't keep away.

The smell of putrefaction was thick in the syrupy summer, and by the time the Professor had made the first cut we were already sweating. Before long, he, Edgar and I were covered in gore. Streaked with it. Yellow fluid and black blood and lines of bile that stank with the horror of what we were doing. The monstrousness of the act was undeniable, and when I looked at Maryam her face was pallid. Dishes of dead organs sat around us like morbid constellations, and the rancid scent seeped through my mask to catch in the back of my throat. I thought of it as something like a spore and all of us infected.

The final thing we did was drain the blood, decanting what was left into great tubs hanging from the end of the bed that brimmed with dark liquid.

"Take what we can," Edgar had advised. "It's doubtful that we'll get another opportunity like this."

And so we eviscerated him. His tendons we stripped from his bones, coiling them like white snakes inside boxes found for the purpose. His muscles we sliced thin like steak, soaking them in bromide and preserving the smallest slivers under microslides. His bones we washed clean, and some we snapped to tease out the marrow and lay it under our scopes. Edgar scooped out his eyes, brown and no longer a Sleepless blue, and pickled them in a jar.

Eventually, I took an instrument to his teeth, prying out the back row, which was already rotting away from the hard palate of his mouth. It was brutal and sickening, and there was an ardour inside us that I didn't recognise. It felt good to tear him apart, to see the monster destroyed beneath our hands and packaged away tidily where he might yet do some good.

The Professor and Edgar stood opposite me when it was done, across the table where once there had been a human being and now there was only a partially shredded skull, a gaping chest cavity devoid of all organs, and thick black blood dripping onto the floor. The spark of madness was in their eyes, and beneath their gore-streaked masks they were beaming, delirious and triumphant.

I'm ashamed to say that I was, too. Soft flesh clung to my gloves, sweat stuck my hair to my forehead, and the smell of death was a symphony in the silence of the room.

I looked at us and I felt joy, and in that joy I was horrified.

The aftermath was something far worse. After the triumph, the comedown set in – reality, a brutal thing that doesn't vanish simply because we look away.

I peeled away my surgical gown and threw my ruined gloves into the toxic-waste bin, then stripped off my mask. His fluids had darkened the space where my lips had been as though I'd been chewing on something dying. The blood had stained the surgical tape on my broken finger and seeped up my wrists, giving me the appearance of black handcuffs around my arms. It had darkened the edge of my shirt and spattered my face and neck. I had to wipe it away with a cloth and pull thick clots from the ends of my hair.

I stayed at the sinks for a long time, long after Edgar and the Professor had left and Maryam had sought sanctuary elsewhere, and I thought of the monster pursuing me through the chapel, and then of the decomposing human who had made it to the cellars.

Who had he been before he was a monster? It was a thought I hadn't allowed myself while he was alive, but now that he'd been pulled apart I let myself imagine it. Had he grown up in London, or had he moved here for work, or followed someone who had? Did he live in a shared house, renting a dilapidated room for over half of his monthly salary, or did he have family who could have him to stay? Did he have a favourite bar, a best friend, a partner? What did he dream about when his work was dull and fancy carried him away? Had he ever imagined he would end his days as a monster on a slab while doctors who were sworn to care for him tore him apart?

I cried then, quiet tears for Subject 001, whose name no one left alive now remembered, and the life he might have lived had the world been different. And tears for us, too, the survivors wrist-deep in blood, dripping with the world's endless death, this sublime act of a dying earth.

We can't turn back time or put a stop to entropy. I can't return and choose not to join the Orex Corporation, no matter how much I may want to. But really, was it ever a choice? To have walked into that penthouse and faced Cassius's innate charisma and gigantic resources and knowledge, to have had my eyes opened to new possibilities, and to have turned away? I would have had to have been a wholly different person, one whose mother wasn't sick and who had fallen into the study of sleep by accident, with no real passion or drive. My dreams would have had to have been those of stability and a comfortable nine-to-five, work that could be put down at the end of the day and left in favour of the business of life elsewhere.

It's impossible. There was never a scenario in which I – that is, myself as I am – could have refused the opportunity to discover what we did. What use is there, then, in berating myself for the crime of being me? Sometimes our choices bring us to ruin, but the scope of those choices is so much smaller than we believe.

My tears ebbed eventually, and the self-pitying display remained private. I re-taped my finger, the dull ache grounding, and pulled on a fresh lab coat to hide the bloodstains on my shirt. Then I tucked the afternoon away in a little space in my mind, where I put all of the things that won't help us to achieve our aims.

I'd hoped to slip away unnoticed, to take my pounding head and sickened heart to bed and sleep until the next few days were nothing more than a memory, growing ever more distant through time. But people were worried for me, and Alex was waiting in the courtyard, his expression tentative and hopeful.

"You shouldn't be back at work so soon," he said.

"What else should I do instead?"

We looked at each other, and I wondered when I'd first stopped seeing his face. For so long, he was simply Alex. I needed no further investigation to inform myself of who he was. Alex with the generator. Alex with the net. Alex who stands with his hands on his hips and watches the boats drift away. What else should I have looked for in him? What else did I feel I should be looking for now? Attraction, perhaps, whether from him or me. Did I feel it? And, more importantly, did I deserve to feel it with the blood still drying on my clothes?

"You could have come to see me," he said. "I was worried about you."

It occurred to me to ask him why, but I restrained myself at the last moment. His expression was guileless, open in a way that I found almost offensive, uncomfortable to look at. He wore his affection so plainly on his face, it felt as though I were seeing him naked.

"You didn't need to worry about me," I said. "I'm fine."

"Don't be daft."

He laughed, and it felt like a strange thing for him to do because I hadn't been joking.

"I'm not. I really am fine."

"Thea," he said, very slowly. "A few nights ago you had a migraine so bad you were delirious, and then a monster nearly killed you."

"I know that."

His hands came to rest on my shoulders, bearing me down to the ground. "If you know that, then how can you say you're fine?" His eyes flickered around my face, and I thought that he was waiting for me to burst into tears and cry on his shoulder. I wondered if I ought to try and do it even though I didn't feel like crying anymore. That's what people want, isn't it? The ones who care about you want an opportunity to comfort you. But I'd already done my crying, and not for myself but for the monster. I didn't have it in me to force a tear now they'd been shed.

"I don't know," I replied. "I just am."

The frown lines in his forehead deepened, and I realised I was disappointing him, or at least spoiling whatever plan he'd had for this conversation before I'd joined in and ruined it.

"You can't be fine," he said. "No one would be fine after that."

The discussion was going to become circular if I corrected him again, so I simply shrugged – or tried to; it was difficult with his hands in the way.

"You must still be in shock." The doubtful expression on his face disappeared and he looked almost relieved. "It's okay, you know. I'll be here whenever you're ready."

It was a kind thing to say, and his hands rubbing the tops of my arms were also kind, in an objective kind of way, but my skin was crawling at the contact, at the tall, sweet, sympathetic heat of him leaning so close that I felt crowded and overwhelmed.

Would he be sympathetic if he knew how I'd enjoyed tearing the subject's body apart? Would he blame my behaviour on trauma and close his ears to the way my blood had sung when I'd snapped the teeth out of its mouth? I stared into Alex's open, affectionate face, and I thought, *You are in love with a person who doesn't exist. A sweet, delicate reflection of the complex heart of me. I'm an invention of longing in your eyes, and maybe I want to believe in her too, but I know she isn't real.* Perhaps we all imagine our lovers to be something other than they are, but I knew then that I didn't want to be an imagined idol to anyone.

I wanted to exist.

O CLEANSE YOUR HANDS WITH WATER ALTHOUGH THE BASIN BLEEDS RED

8TH JULY

"I've brought you something," I said.

Vladimir was standing, unbound once again, and I laid out the instruments Edgar had given me and sat at the table to observe him. He stared down at my feeble offering and then slid his attention back to me.

"I am to be offered a reward, then. Does that mean I'm human after all?"

"It means that I'm grateful, for whatever that's worth."

He looked back to the shaving set, his hands clasped behind his back and his manner impossible to read.

"Do you feel better now?" he asked.

"It would be difficult to feel any worse."

He made no response, his attention fixed on a high point of the wall somewhere behind my head.

"The subject was human," I pressed.

"He always was."

"You know what I mean."

"You mean that, at the point of death, the man in the Tower took on the usual features of humanity that you recognise as being human in your limited taxonomic system."

I rubbed my fingers over my forehead and closed my eyes against a headache. "Yes, Vladimir, that's exactly what I mean. Could you be a little less existential and combative today?"

He made no sound when he moved, but the whisper of air and the dull thud of the chair told me he'd returned to sitting. "Why?"

"How about politeness?"

"Manners are a peculiar thing to be concerned about in a situation like this."

"What situation is that?"

We held each other's gaze.

"The equilibrium between us has changed," he said. "The benevolent razor aside, you've been sent here to ask me something."

There was no point in asking how he knew. A leap of logic. An easy guess.

"Did you know it would happen? Did you know the subject would escape?"

He released a long breath through his nose and settled back in his chair to observe me. "That depends on what you might call knowledge. Had I, by acute observation and the recognition of patterns, been able to discern the march of inevitability where your subject's bindings were concerned, at least well enough to come to a prediction about future danger? Yes. Did I know, beyond a shadow of a doubt when the storm began, that it would be the night your sorry prisoner broke free? No. Although had you paid as much attention to him as you do to others in this Tower, you may very well have drawn the same conclusions I did."

"And what were your conclusions?"

"That it's more common to bite the hand that feeds you when that hand is tying a chain around your neck."

I mimicked his position, hands folded, my papers forgotten in front of me. "And is that what you'd like to do,

Vladimir? Do you fantasise about the strength in your limbs being put to better use? Do your teeth ache to find a place in our necks?"

He stared back at me, pupils dilated. "Is that what you'd like to hear, Doctor Chares? Does it unsettle you that my nature might be so easily contained by little more than my own will?"

"Not at all," I replied. "In fact, I'd find that very human indeed."

His lips quirked, but his amusement didn't reach his eyes. "Humans are famously bad at resisting their baser impulses. But then, they are made in God's image."

"You believe that God has a problem with impulse control?"

"Undoubtedly. We are never insured against acts of God."

"Like the storm. If the storm is an act of God, whatever came next can't be blamed on anyone here."

"Precisely," he said.

"But it wasn't God who released the subject."

He cocked his head. "Can you be so sure?"

There was an energy in the room, something heavy like a thunderclap not spent, sitting in the space between us.

"You know the Professor isn't going to be satisfied with that," I said.

"Nor are you."

"I'm getting used to it."

"Am I so unsatisfying, Doctor Chares, that you would abandon your attempts to reach into the heart of me?"

I looked away. "They think it was you," I said.

"I who released your prisoner?"

"You who changed him when he died."

"Ah."

We looked at each other.

"They're going to ask for samples of your blood, you know."

"And you know I will not give it."

"You should."

"Why?"

I swallowed, and his eyes tracked down the length of my throat and then back up to my face. "Because I don't want to have to make you."

A CONVERSATION
WITH MARYAM

We met by chance in the chapel. I'd hoped to exorcise the memories of mine and Vladimir's blood being spilt there, but I'd found little peace inside the holy walls by the time she found me. She'd followed me inside, intent on checking me for signs of concussion, although I'd been avoiding her care.

She had the temerity to apologise to me. To apologise for sitting like a conscience in the corner of the laboratory and for sitting in judgement of me. I confess here that her sincerity sickened me. That a person so unutterably good – so without a cold edge or impulse to cruelty – would apologise to me and mean it felt like an injustice greater than any we'd perpetrated here.

"You have nothing to be sorry for, Maryam," I said.

Then, language failed me. I wanted to tell her that we needed her, that the conscience she held within her she held for us all, keeping it safe for a time when we'd need it again. But I didn't know how to articulate that, or how I might impress upon Maryam her own inherent value – her abiding value to *me*, although I might sometimes begrudge her for it.

I felt that she understood me anyway, and understood what I meant when I asked her how she'd joined the Orex

Corporation in the first place. Her lips curved. She gestured me down to sit on one of the benches, and reached beneath her jumper to draw out a plain silver ring on a chain around her neck.

This was my husband's wedding ring, she told me. He was a stern man, stoic, but kind beneath all of that conditioning. We met in the hospital gardens when he was working as a landscape gardener and I was struggling through medical school. I used to say that I fell in love with him for his roses, but it went much deeper than that.

After we married, Tariq slipped his wedding ring onto a chain and placed it around my neck. *This*, he said, *is my promise to you. Only you can choose to keep it.*

I was surprised to find myself loved, she admitted. As a child, I'd always been made to feel like a burden for needing more than other children my age. More support, more equipment. More care. But Tariq loved me, and that was the end of the sentence. He didn't love me in spite of my chair, and he didn't love me *anyway*.

Before him, I'd always thought that love was a give and take, that each took something and each gave something, and it was a good love if you both came out about equal in the end. At the same time, I was convinced that I'd always have to give more to be worthy of someone else's love, but he changed that for me completely.

With Tariq, I realised I'd been wrong. Our love wasn't a push and pull but a circle between us that looped back on itself and grew. There was no tally, no sense of something given to one that was removed from the other and so had to be repaid. Whatever we gave, we gave each other freely, and neither of us felt we were losing anything in the bargain. This ring, it was a promise to love me in my entirety, without judgement or caveat, and it was a promise he kept right to the end.

"What happened to him?" I asked.

"He was older than me by ten years, and he died of a heart attack between the roses in our garden, and I couldn't bring him back."

I told her I was sorry, and I was embarrassed by my emotion and by my witness to hers.

Don't be, she said. We had a good life together, and when he died I realised something important. The love we had for each other didn't just disappear because he was no longer here. Without him, I discovered that I had all of this love and all of this tenderness and nowhere for it to go. Our children were grown and didn't need me day-to-day anymore, and there I was with all of this useless love and all of my need still to care.

I was near retirement by then, and too old to go traipsing through maternity wards as I had been, but I'd worked in rehab before and I knew the good it did some of my patients to see me here as I am, imperfect but happy, and to know that even if they didn't achieve a full recovery, a good life was still possible. So I joined the Orex Corporation because I was old and grieving and content all in one, and not quite ready to stop caring yet.

There was an indescribable peace in the wake of her story, as though the chapel had been designed just to hear it. Peace, and my own appalling curiosity, which I didn't stifle in time.

"Do you miss your children?" I asked softly, and a splintering, unholy pain gathered in the lines of her face.

"I can't allow myself to think of them. If I do, there will be no will to life left within me, and I need that will now.

I feel as though I have to continue here, to make something, to grow something, no matter how imperfect it might be. In the face of so much destruction, I remember what Tariq used to say, that there is nothing so hopeful as a garden. I intend to live whatever is left of my life that way. For him, and for the memory of our children as well."

I knew then that the conversation was at an end, and I didn't complain when she pulled an ophthalmoscope from her pocket and began to check me for signs of concussion. It occurred to me that I'd been guilty of seeing Maryam as someone too easily content, someone whom loss didn't touch just as long as she still had a job to do. I understood then that it wasn't the case at all. It wasn't that loss didn't touch her, or that she wasn't wounded by it; it was simply that she was better at losing things than most of us are. She already knew that she had the strength to survive disaster. She'd survived it before she'd ever arrived here.

I must have fidgeted while she was assessing me because she let out a throaty chuckle and tapped me on the knee. "You aren't a very good patient, are you?"

"An impatient patient, maybe."

"To a doctor, every patient is an impatient one," she said. "And to a patient, all doctors lack urgency."

"What happens when you're both a doctor and a patient?"

"No one is ever both at the same time."

She shone a light into my eyes, and when she removed it again coloured spots danced in my vision.

"Weren't you?" I asked.

She shook her head. "I've always been a patient first. That's why your Professor and I have never seen eye to eye. If you see someone only as something to be fixed, you stop seeing them as a person, and I'm a disappointment to him."

"Why do you think that is?"

"Because I refuse to be fixed to his satisfaction."

I didn't know if that was true, but then Maryam has never seemed broken to me.

15TH JULY

First, do no harm. This is the guiding principle in medicine, yet I lost my faith in this comforting lie when I was still only a child. Mother's illness had waxed and waned for years by then, roving from bedbound horror to the delirious freedom of gentle walks on the beach. I was already attuned to the ebb and flow of her unhealth, the tendency of her body to fall out of the orbit of the hale and into the freefall of the sick.

One remarkable plummet happened only a few days after my eleventh birthday, when a period of improvement was cut short by a sudden tremor, worse on her left side. I remember watching her hand twitch and shake while she ate, and observing the dragging of her foot as she walked down our hallway and tried to pretend she was okay. Looking back, I don't know why I was brought to the appointment with her, but whatever the reason, this was the first time I'd been present for one of her visits to the doctor.

To my eyes, he was simply an adult of indeterminate age, as all adults are when you're eleven. In my memory he was a man of about forty, with light brown hair and bright blue eyes and a disturbing tendency not to blink. He listened to Mother recount her symptoms with a surface air of interest that struck me as false, and when she held out her limbs to show him how they spasmed, he hummed and looked at his computer.

We sat there in silence while he read, and I felt Mother's hope fade out of her with every second that elapsed. Eventually, he leant forward with his hands clasped on the desk and pinned her with that unblinking gaze.

"You've been to see us a lot over the last few years," he said. "Have you considered that you might be anxious?"

I still don't know how to describe Mother's manner in that moment. She didn't move a muscle, nor did her expression alter, yet something internal shifted within her like the scrape of a tectonic plate.

"The shaking is mostly one-sided," she said.

"Perhaps it's only partial anxiety, then." He made a dismissive gesture with his hand and Mother's voice remained perfectly calm.

"You're saying that my left side is more anxious about the world than my right?"

He sat up straighter in his chair and his attention grew cold. "If you're going to become aggressive, Mrs Chares, I will have to ask you to leave."

It was my first introduction, embryonic, into a knowledge I was too young to articulate – that a patient's sanity could conveniently end at the same point a doctor's medical knowledge ran out. I hated him more than I'd ever hated anyone before.

We didn't get any help that day.

18TH JULY

Perhaps it isn't surprising that I'm uncomfortable with my role as a doctor, but what's more surprising to me is how at ease others are with that power. I met with Edgar and the Professor this evening to tell them that Vladimir wouldn't allow us to take his blood. I was disturbed by their reaction.

"He must agree, Thea," Michael said. "Something about him changed our subject, and whatever that something is it must be studied."

"I don't have any power over him. I can't force him to help us."

"One man, a wall against hope," Edgar murmured. "One man can't stand in the way of our progress, maestro."

"Indeed he cannot. I'm afraid that if he won't offer willingly, we will have to take it by force."

I swallowed. "We can't just ignore what he wants. This isn't like the subject. Vladimir can reason, communicate. He has agency."

"It isn't an ideal situation," the Professor allowed. "But you must understand that one man can't stand in the way of a cure. He is someone with agency, yes, but he's also a miracle. How can it be ethical to put his life above the lives of so many others?"

"Persuasion is a kind of force," Edgar said, "yet we use it all the time."

"That's different. The use of reason isn't the same as the use of violence."

"Reason can be violent. Just ask anyone who's had their reason manipulated."

"Regardless," Michael interrupted, "we must have his blood. Reason, morality, and good sense demand it." He placed his hand on my forearm. "I'm relying on you, dear heart. Don't let us down."

20TH JULY

I've been trying hard not to think too much about the storm, or about how Subject 001 escaped, but the problem didn't go away just because I didn't want to look at it. At the meeting in the Nest, Alex confessed that the camera by the subject's room hadn't come back online after the power returned to the Tower. A loose thread wrapped around the wiring had short-circuited the system.

"I knew it!" Dolly crowed. "*He* must have let it out."

"He saved us," I argued. I felt a bristling inside me, hackles rising, although a small voice wondered why I felt the need to defend him. "If Vladimir hadn't been in the chapel, who knows what would have happened."

"He shouldn't be here," Miles piped up. "You should make him leave."

They were all looking at me, except for the Professor, who had one hand raised to his eyes as though trying to soothe a headache.

"We need him," I said. "He's our only hope for a cure."

"You don't get it, do you?" Dolly asked. "Look at us. Look at where we are. There isn't going to *be* a cure. There's just *this*. Just us, locked away here, wondering if the rest of the world still goes on."

"That's enough, Dol," Alex said. "You don't know that

for sure. They invented it, right? If anyone has a chance of finding a cure, it's them."

"And until then, what are the rest of us meant to do?" Dolly shot back. "While they're keeping monsters in the Tower, the rest of us just have to sit here and pretend like it's all okay? Like the world isn't over and our lives completely pointless?"

"You could do something useful," I replied. "Something better than poisoning yourself with nostalgia and stringing Miles along just to have something to do." It was an unkind thing to say, cruel in the context of a crowd. Miles flushed a furious shade of red and Maryam shot me a disappointed look from her spot by the empty hearth.

"You're one to talk," Dolly replied. "How is that any different to what you're doing with Alex?"

I didn't have time to be embarrassed. Alex slammed the palm of his hand against the table top and locked eyes with Dolly, and the intensity of some personal argument conducted silently between them was such that no one even bothered to look at me. After long seconds, her jaw ticked and she slumped back in her chair, conceding defeat.

"I think we need to let them try," Alison said at last. "A few months ago, we were sure we were alone in this city, maybe even in the world. We were giving up, all of us, and you know it. Then Helen and…" She stumbled over the name. "… Vladimir arrived, and everything changed. I don't know about you, but I'm glad they're here. Not because it isn't terrifying, or dangerous, but because it was worse before. Hopeless."

She raised her head and looked me in the eye. "Life used to be full of little dangers. Full of choices we had to make every day. This might be harder, but I've missed having a choice. I've missed having hope. Haven't you?"

A CONVERSATION
WITH ALISON

It was after the meeting in the Nest and we were sitting on Raleigh's Walk, where the Queen's erstwhile favourite had once paced like a tiger in a too-small cage, waiting to see if he was condemned. The night was overcast, a crescent moon hanging like a Christmas decoration above a cotton-wool sea. She began by asking me if I believed in fate, and I had to tell her that I believed in causality. In every choice we'd ever made piled up on top of one another like the ill-fitting pieces of a puzzle.

"Personal responsibility, then," she said. "The individual as king."

"Not necessarily," I replied. "We all have choices, but we make so many every day. Things that are inconsequential at the time can become important later on, and other people's choices affect us too."

The night had the flavour of a confessional, and when Alison asked me to elaborate I found myself speaking of my mother.

One day, I told her, Mother decided to go to a party. She wasn't going to go at first. I was still young and hadn't been sleeping well, and she was exhausted, but the babysitter had been booked and she hadn't seen her best friend for months, and so she went. She drank a little. She had a good time. The next day she had a sore throat but put it down to a mild hangover. A few days later she had a fever and took some time off work. Two months later she was still sick. She could barely walk to the end of the road. She grew dizzy when she stood up and her heart raced even while sitting at her desk.

A friend at the party had been getting over a bout of flu when they showed up, I told her. They were feeling better but were clearly still infectious. Most people there didn't get sick, but a few of them did. By two months in, only Mother hadn't recovered, and that was the last party she ever attended. The next thirty years were spent either housebound or bedbound, trailing between doctors, starting part-time jobs from home and then having to quit because she couldn't manage them. Applying for disability benefits and being denied. Going to court, winning for a few years, and then repeating the process all over again.

If she hadn't gone to the party that night, I asked Alison, would she have got sick? Was it an accident waiting to happen, something in her genetics that had made her susceptible? If so, would she have had another year, another ten or more, before it happened if she hadn't encountered the flu on that particular night, when she was tired and run down from being a new single mum? It disturbs me now, but that one simple choice changed the course of her life.

And still, it wasn't only her choice. Her friend who arrived sick made the same choice that evening. When she was pregnant, she chose to keep me rather than abort. She worked herself ragged for money to support me, but was that in itself a free choice? Would she have had to work so hard if the welfare system could have offered her more? In that case, then, it was a political choice, and so entirely out of her hands.

More than that – and I was aware, as I was speaking, that my voice had taken on the tone of the outraged and the powerless – the fact that there was no treatment for her condition was a choice. Postviral illnesses were well-known by the time she got sick, from the outbreak at the Royal Free Hospital in 1955, to Lake Tahoe in the eighties, to Covid four decades later.

Here, Alison interrupted me. "But they thought it was mental illness, and so no one bothered to research it."

I smiled at her, a little bitterly, and shook my head. "Plenty of people knew it was physical. Ramsay in the fifties knew it. They were treating postviral patients with immune therapies with some success in the eighties. Then a group of very well-respected psychiatrists decided it was psychosomatic, and suddenly all the funding went to them. No more biomedical research studies. More forgotten lives. More deaths. More suicides. No help. So, whose choice was it for Mother to stay sick? How did she end up having her life changed? It wasn't fate. It wasn't God. But it wasn't simply personal choice, either. It was something bigger than that. The whole interconnected organism of society."

After the fact, coming late to my epiphany as we all do, I wanted to tell her that what she called Fate I called a mycelial system, that our society was akin to a living organism like a mushroom, passing impulses back and forth along lines invisible to the naked eye. A choice made by someone you never met five decades earlier might be the reason your life changes when you least expect it. And isn't that all that Fate is, really? A series of events that make their ending seem inevitable in retrospect?

I wonder if it's that much more frightening to believe in the cosmic chance of the universe or the operations of a human neuronal system. Both are out of our hands.

Later, I returned to Mother in the dark, Mother in the bed, Mother in the nightmare that simply wouldn't end. I returned to her and I felt like a supplicant begging forgiveness from an unwilling sacrifice. If only her sacrifice had meaning.

I didn't tell her about my conversation with Alison. I didn't tell her about the monster in the chapel, or Vladimir, or that after I'd spoken with Maryam I'd started to dream about her husband hanging wreaths of roses around the Tower that made the walls bleed. Instead, I sat there in the dark with her, in the silence, until I fell asleep in my chair. I didn't dream, sinking softly into a longed-for oblivion, until I opened my eyes to the sight of my Grey Lady waiting in Mother's bed.

This hallucination was different to the ones I'd known before. The Grey Lady was solid, palpable in a way that set my bones alight with terror. She crouched on Mother's chest, and she was something fungal. Pustules of grey-and-white mushrooms bloomed over her skin, growing even as I stared and tried to scream – but couldn't. She bled out an ecosystem of fungi, the spores burrowing into Mother and the blankets and the bed.

The smell that came from her was dank, rotten, and in the midst of my horror I realised that I'd never hallucinated her scent before. Then came the histrionic belief that she was becoming more real the more I dreamt her, and that soon she would slip out into reality and replace me, staking her own silent vigil by Mother in the night.

I fought to move, internally and uselessly, and the Grey Lady turned her face to the ceiling and sank back into Mother's body as though she belonged there. They rested there together, two souls inside one body, and I thought to myself, *This room has become a deathbed after all.*

24TH JULY

There are old taboos against vivisection. The consecration of a dead human's body as something more important than roadkill. Many cultures believe you can't enter the afterlife if your body isn't intact, although I've always thought that people who suffered violent deaths should be particularly frustrated with that rule. Subject 001 was gone, and in its place there were tags on containers, scribbled notes on freezer bags, and an overabundance of fluids in macabre jars on the shelves.

It was still early in the morning when I sat by the blood cleaner, watching the plasma separate out, when the click of the door opening reached my ears. I looked up, expecting to see Michael, and instead came face to face with Vladimir.

His appearance startled me. Gone was the beard and the hair that dropped to the small of his back. Instead there was a sharp jawline, clean-shaven and uncommonly smooth. Chestnut hair feathered around his shoulders in a way that felt too average to suit him, while the camouflage of a disaster survivor was gone. Without it he was indescribably Other. My first fearful instinct was to tell him to leave, but there was a quality to his entrance that suggested I'd be ignored.

"So," he said, very softly. "This is what became of the man I saved."

"You didn't save him. He died."

"There are worse things than death."

I agreed with him silently, and he strolled between the samples with the air of a man at judgement.

"Has his death meant something to you? Have you found your answers in the decaying parts of his body?"

The hum of the blood cleaner was the only sound and I looked down at the filter, red and black with clots. "Not yet," I said, "but it's still early. There are a lot of samples still to go through."

"A life's worth of samples. An embodied charter of potential." He pressed his eye to a microscope, and when he looked up again I felt as though I were being studied. "There's a new light in you today, Doctor Chares. A devilish heat behind your eyes."

He took hold of my wrist, and I let him raise my gloved hand towards him, streaks of Subject 001's blood stark at the fingers.

"Is this who you are, Thea, when only God is watching?"

"There's no such thing as God. No one's watching."

"I am."

My wrist was hot where he held it, and I disengaged his fingers as though disarming a bomb. "You're no god, Vladimir."

"To you, I may as well be." He drew out another stool and sat opposite me, our knees almost touching.

"That depends on how you define a god," I said. "If greater strength is all that defines one then a lion is a god. An elephant, even."

His lips curved. "I cannot claim to be an elephant, therefore I cannot claim to be a god?"

"You don't look much like Ganesh to me."

His smile grew and then fell from his face just as quickly. "You had the meeting recently. Did you discuss me?"

"We discussed a lot of things."

"And what were your conclusions?"

"That we needed your blood, and that you ought to be convinced to give it to us."

"You say *we* because it's easier to hide in a crowd, but you are a liar, Thea Chares."

Our gazes held like magnets.

"Tell me what you want," I said, "in return for your cooperation."

"You propose another bargain."

"Yes."

"And you'll give me anything?"

"Within reason."

"Then I want you to tell me the truth. Tell me why you want my blood, truly. Tell me about your mother. She matters a great deal to you."

"She isn't up for discussion."

"With me, you mean."

I looked back at him and understood why he'd asked. "You were listening. When Alison and I were talking."

He smiled. "*And down by a brimming river I heard two lovers speak.* If you are to discuss such things along the battlements from an open window, you can't be surprised when they're overheard."

"Alison and I aren't lovers."

"No, but it was a lovers' talk nonetheless. A sharing of selves beneath the light of the moon."

I scoffed. "Are you a poet now?"

"No, but I can appreciate poetry when I find it."

"Why would my mother be important to you?"

"She isn't, but she's important to you. I see her wrapped around the core of you. Your heart is consumed by her like a serpent. A worm."

"That isn't what she is."

"What is she?"

I chewed on my lip, flushed and furious. "If I tell you about her, will you let me examine you?"

"Within reason."

I felt the trap he'd spun for me close tight around my legs. What else could I do but agree?

CAN YOU PULL IN LEVIATHAN WITH A FISHHOOK OR TIE DOWN ITS TONGUE WITH A ROPE? CAN YOU PUT A CORD THROUGH ITS NOSE OR PIERCE ITS JAW WITH A HOOK? WILL IT KEEP BEGGING YOU FOR MERCY?

26TH JULY

The end of the world happened on a Wednesday. I remember the day of the collapse in flashes as though I witnessed it through a strobe. There had been pockets of violence around the world by then. The previous weeks had featured news reports of unprovoked attacks featuring strange biting patterns, and insomnia as a prevalent complaint.

Separately, we at the Orex Corp had received emails and phone calls from the government and the army, quietly confirming that those affected all had neuralchips implanted. We'd begun to examine the patients in our care more closely, but nothing in our investigations had revealed a problem. That morning, however, Edgar had presented us with data regarding odd electrical activity in some of the chips and evidence that the neural network was being overloaded.

Later in the afternoon, I was down in the lab alone, and we'd heard that the prime minister would be answering a question about the Orex Corporation during Prime Minister's Questions. There was a small TV mounted on the wall, and I was half-listening as the Leader of the Opposition asked a question about our oversight and the over-extension of technology into ordinary people's lives.

While I was reviewing the most recent blood tests for one of our long-term patients, a wave of shouting, different from the usual public schoolboy jeers, erupted from the Commons. I looked up just in time to see the chancellor of the exchequer stand from her position behind the prime minister and sink her teeth into his neck.

There was an outcry. Outrage, terror, disbelief. And then it started happening all across the floor. MPs stood, stiffened, convulsed briefly, and turned on their fellows. The feed cut out, but not before the BBC voiceover had said, "The prime minister is dead. It looks as though the prime minister is dead." I sat there for long seconds, the bloods forgotten in my hand, and I thought, *Something new is coming.* I wanted to turn to someone and ask them if they'd seen what I'd seen. Instead, I took out my phone and scrolled through social media.

The top results were already coming in. Attack in the Commons, uncertain of cause, more details imminent. Then more reports, more attacks, health services overwhelmed. I remember one message, from a student I followed at UCL who was doing some interesting work on adenosine and its role in sleep: *They've all gone mad. I can't get through to the police. People are killing everyone inside. We're locked in Lab 2. Someone help us.*

I wonder, now, how long it was before she died. At the time it simply felt surreal, as though I'd fallen into a zombie film and no one had thought to tell me.

I went upstairs, horror still a distant thing in my mind. I'm not sure I was even numb, merely operating in the world I knew without realising I'd entered a different one, and so my reactions were all wrong.

Aboveground, the Tower was frenetic. People were

shouting. I remember I'd intended to show the Professor the news on my phone, but everyone seemed to know what was happening already.

There was blood on the ground in the courtyard, and I watched a patient – an elderly woman who'd been suffering from ALS before the neuralchip – leap from one of the Towers like a comet, her floral skirt and cardigan flapping in the breeze, and career into one of our porters. I saw his body crumple and knew instantly that his spine had shattered. It was as though he'd been run over by a truck, not by a nice little old lady who preferred Jammie Dodgers to Bourbons and always took two sugars in her tea.

After that, it's all very patchy.

I ran home and made sure Mother was safe, locking her in to keep her from the worst of the violence. Then I fled outside and helped Maryam corral those who didn't possess a chip into the canteen and bar the doors, but I couldn't stay inside. I went out and watched from the battlements. Thane and Alison had closed the gates and we seemed to be safe, but the whole of London was burning.

Cars were overturned outside the walls. Boats drifted on the Thames. Thane and Alison fired on the monsters as they attempted to reach us. I have a vague memory of a car driving straight at us over the concourse – the way it flipped and caught fire. How the Sleepless descended on it, and then Miles's screams for help, trapped in the back seat. Thane went out after him, Alison firing from on high, and we opened the gates just long enough for him to be hauled to safety, badly burned but alive. His parents in the front of the car didn't make it.

Having a patient to treat helped us in the days that followed. Miles's injuries gave us something to focus on while we waited for news. There were surgeries to prep for, and antibiotics to administer, and a traumatised teenager whose grief felt so much more real than our own.

Later, over the following weeks, there were brief flurries of activity from outside. Crackles on the radio. Posts online from people still trapped across the country. Then, there was nothing.

The world fell to silence and we were alone.

CONVERSATION
WITH ALISON #2

Recounting Mother's life has made me vulnerable, but I sensed there was more that Alison wanted to say. When she finally spoke, her voice had the quality of the night, dark and deep and from somewhere so personal and secret I was almost embarrassed to hear it.

I could never settle before the world was like this, she told me. Mum used to say it was because all of our family came from somewhere else, every generation displaced, and so we kept wandering to find somewhere that felt like home. I never really bought into all of that. I just thought it was because I was easily bored and there was always something better around the corner.

At school it was whatever was going on in the playground, then the parties at the weekend, then a new job or an online course. Finally it was university, just because I thought it might hold my attention for longer. I've had over fifty jobs in twenty years of working. I've done everything from tour guiding to cleaning to curating a museum, and none of them felt right, not in Scotland or France, Birmingham or London. And then the world ended and we all got stuck here.

During the first few months, I thought for sure I'd go mad. I'd never stayed in one place for so long, not since I was a kid, and waking up every morning and seeing these walls and knowing there was nothing outside of them, nowhere to run away from or to, nothing new in all of the world that I'd be able to find... It was my worst nightmare, to be so alone with myself and to have to listen to my voice, endlessly talking inside my own head. The same walls. The same people. No hope.

This Tower has always been a prison, whether for a Conqueror who imprisoned himself or the real prisoners that came later, and that was how I felt – trapped and stripped of liberty. But being here has forced something out of me as well. I realised, in that first year, that I didn't know what the core of myself was outside of movement, of people, of activity. I didn't know how to be still. I didn't have anything to dedicate myself to like you did with your research or Maryam did with her plants.

"But you have now?" I asked, and I was curious. Genuinely, passionately curious. I realised that I was meeting Alison for the first time, Alison as someone separate from my own ideas about the way she was. Alison as a person and not an invention inside my head.

I have, she told me. These last few months, I realised that I don't need to be in motion for the world to mean something. The world isn't waiting for me to take it. It exists independently from me. The world simply is, and there's no bucket list, no checklist counting down in my head of how many places I need to live or how many people I need to meet to consider this a worthwhile life. Life itself is worthwhile.

She smiled.

Getting trapped here, I thought I was never going to see the world, and I thought that meant my life was pointless. But I realised recently that I am seeing the world, that the world comes to us whether we go looking for it or not. The sun rises every morning and it rises over everything, and we're a part of that everything, no matter where we are or who we're with. I don't think I'd have figured that out without these walls around me.

Being made to stop, to look at myself and try and figure out what I was without every external thing influencing me – I think it could only have happened like this. I'm not saying I'm happy, or that I don't miss the world or see the horror in all of this, but for the first time in my life I think I finally feel content. Does that make me crazy?

I told her that it didn't, and I meant it. How can you even measure crazy in a world like this? If anything, Alison sounded saner to me in that moment than anyone I'd ever met. She needed no obsession to carry her through the days. She didn't have the guilt of her own complicity making her too scared to sit and examine herself truthfully. She was simply content in the world as it was, at peace in her self-ness in a way that few people ever are.

That, I think, is something to be truly envied.

28TH JULY

Vladimir and I met in the laboratory, as we'd agreed. He reminded me of our bargain – that there would be no recordings and I wouldn't be able to take any samples until he was satisfied with my answers. He asked me whether he ought to take the bed, and it disturbed me to see him in Subject 001's place.

I started with the basic assessments, using an otoscope to look into his ears and then asking him to open his mouth. He complied, his gaze never leaving my face, and I had to suppress a shudder as I shone the light inside, a depressor over the wet muscle of his tongue.

His teeth were perfect. Absurdly, abnormally perfect – no stains and no discolorations. Perfect, that is, except for that second row, jagged and so much sharper than any human's teeth ought to be. The closer I peered, the more they looked exactly like the teeth of a shark, the incisors sculpted to needle-thin points hidden by the more average appearance of the ones in front.

"Do they shed?" I asked when I'd retracted my hand from the predator's jaws.

"What do you think?"

"I think our subject's teeth showed signs of shedding, but yours seem not to. There's no swelling around the gums and no evidence of new growth behind them."

"I suspect if I bit more often, they'd behave more like your former subject's. Since I'm not in the habit of sinking my teeth into anything more difficult to pierce than your own cooked meals, I haven't been able to verify this."

"Not even before you came to us?"

He cocked his head. "You ask me if I were a killer before I came here?"

"Yes."

"I've killed no more people than you have, Doctor Chares."

I looked away.

"Am I to be permitted to ask a question before you take my temperature?"

"If you like." I waited, noting down the details of his peculiar dentistry and avoiding his eyes.

"How old were you when your mother became sick?"

"I was three when she first caught the flu, six or seven when her illness became severe. But it fluctuated a lot in the beginning."

"And did you understand what was happening to her, young as you were? Or did you resent her for not being the kind of mother you wanted her to be?"

I opened my mouth to reply and he held up his hand.

"Careful. You promised to answer my questions truthfully. Remember, I shall know if you lie."

I lowered my gaze to the clipboard. The truth was that I avoided thinking about Mother, and at the same time her reality impacted every decision I made. It was an uneasy disconnect between conscious and subconscious thought, and one I took great pains to maintain.

"I suppose a little of both," I answered at last. "I understood that she was sick and that she wasn't shrinking our world because she wanted to, but there was a part of me that resented her for not getting better anyway, or for not trying hard enough."

"You blamed her for her illness."

"No, I blamed the doctors more than her, I think. Doctors are meant to make people better. When I was younger, I didn't understand why every time she went to see them, she came home crying and even sicker than she was before. I wanted her to *make* them help her, and I felt resentment that she didn't."

"You were disturbed by your mother's lack of power. The first realisation by the child that the parent is not all powerful."

"Something like that," I agreed. "Open your mouth."

It's more accurate to use a thermometer in the ear, but I was unnerved by the conversation and, quite frankly, I wanted to give myself a moment's peace. I'm sure Vladimir realised this, for although he complied without question there was a twinkle of amusement in his eyes when he placed the probe beneath his tongue and closed his mouth around it.

"While you're doing that, I'm going to put the pulse-ox on your finger. It will register heart rate and blood oxygen level."

He, of course, couldn't reply, but he lifted his index finger from his knee, and when I clipped the instrument on he raised an eyebrow as though challenging me to call him non-compliant.

We sat in silence for a long minute, until the thermometer began to beep a frantic, staccato beat, and he opened his mouth to allow me to remove it.

"Do you not find this work intimate, Doctor Chares? The trust a patient must put into their doctor's hands, and the closeness they must cultivate in order to examine, is beyond the bounds of normal human interaction, yes?"

The thermometer read 110°F.

"It's more intimate than office work," I said. "Less intimate than gynaecology."

He smiled. The pulse-ox had his heart rate at fifty yet was unable to detect his oxygen level. I unclipped it from his finger to show him. "Is that because you have no oxygen in your body or too much for the sensor to pick up?" I asked.

"Logic would dictate the latter, unless you're concerned that I lack a heart."

"Let's test that theory, shall we?"

I held up the stethoscope and instructed him to remove his shirt, and it was here that he hesitated.

"Are you shy?" I asked.

"No, but if you'd like to listen to my heart then you owe me another answer. When did you first fall in love with Professor Galen?"

The question shocked me so deeply that I merely blinked at him, the stethoscope still in my hand. "You think I'm in love with Michael?"

"You misunderstand. I don't mean that you had an affair."

"Good, because we haven't."

"Nor do I mean romantic love, necessarily. But do not try to stand there and say to me now that you haven't spent the last few years loving him. You agreed not to lie, remember?"

I couldn't meet his eyes. I felt exposed, as though the most intimate parts of me had been laid on display to the one person in the world I'd never wanted to know. I think for a moment I truly hated Vladimir then, and there was a small voice in my head that whispered, *Why bother with this bargaining? Why not take the easy route and compel him to obey?* Instead, I drew a deep breath and sat down in a chair by the bed.

Throughout these long minutes of self-reflection Vladimir continued to watch me, and when he spoke I convinced myself that there was true concern in his voice.

"Forgive me, I was certain you knew. Is this yet another thing you've hidden from yourself?"

It was on the tip of my tongue to tell him that his perception was skewed, his views of me no more true than anyone else's, and perhaps he was simply playing at invention rather than uncovering truth. But he had established himself as a bargaining chip, coercing me with the promise of access to his body and blood. I knew with certainty that, should I argue with him now, all hope of cooperative study would be lost.

"I suppose that depends," I answered. "Admiration and esteem aren't the same as love."

"But they can be the ingredients for it. Don't we admire our lovers before we adore them? Attraction is at least a cousin of admiration."

"Then I suppose the answer to your question is that I don't really know," I said eventually. "I admired his intellect, his drive, almost from the very first, although in our earliest meetings his mind was overshadowed by Cassius's." I frowned. "I would guess that any love I feel for him began when Cassius was dying."

"Why was that?" He was watching me steadily, his eyes unblinking.

"He was upset. Cassius and the Professor, it's difficult to explain, but I often thought of them as two halves of the same person rather than as individuals in their own right. To imagine Michael without Cassius was to introduce myself to a whole new kind of grief. One I didn't want either of them to suffer."

"You discovered your love for him in his vulnerability," Vladimir replied, his gaze growing distant. "Yes, that does seem to fit."

"Why do you say that?"

"Why shouldn't I? Your life so far has been ruled by it. Your mother's sickness made her vulnerable, and you responded to that vulnerability with an all-consuming desire to fix it, one that led you to medicine, to research, and finally to ruin."

The thought unsettled me and I regained my feet, the better to meet him eye to eye.

"I don't think it was that simple," I said. "Will you let me listen to your heart now?"

"One final thing. You said that you saw Cassius and Professor Galen as two halves of the same person, until Doctor Hope began to slip away."

I nodded.

"Did you love him too? Of the two of them, which did you feel the greatest emotion for?"

I considered the question for the first time, and felt a sensation akin to peeling a scab from a healing wound.

"I suppose I loved them both," I said, "but I cared more for Michael. I think a part of me was angry at Cassius for leaving Michael alone."

"You resented him for his sickness," Vladimir observed. "Much as you once resented your mother for hers."

"Cassius and Michael weren't my fathers."

"No, but they were the closest thing you had."

The conversation was maddening. I felt like I'd been stripped bare, a feeling compounded by the fact that I had no way of discerning whether there was any truth to these revelations, or whether Vladimir, like Alex, was seeing a version of me that didn't exist.

"Will you let me examine you now?" I asked.

His expression closed off. "Very well, but you must remember that you asked for this. If I were you, I would preserve my ignorance as a comfort."

I didn't have time to ponder the nature of this sentence. In slow, deliberate movements, Vladimir raised his fingers to his collar and began to unbutton his shirt. He was right, I realised in the moment his skin was revealed – this was intimate, and I had no guard against it.

Only when I heard the fabric slip from his shoulders and observed, out of the corner of my eye, him folding the shirt and placing it on the bed, did I turn around and raise the stethoscope to his chest. And here, in this mundane pursuit, did I approach the first light of revelation.

"What happened to you?" I asked him.

His skin was like marble, smooth and intolerably perfect, save for the litany of scars that decorated him like branding marks. The stethoscope fell from my hand, and instead my fingers brushed against an oval imperfection at the top of his chest. The skin there was raised, pale white – paler even than the rest of his skin – and ragged at the edges.

A bite mark.

Once I'd found the first, the others assaulted me one by one, down the sides of his ribcage, along the muscle of his biceps, livid as shark bites across his powerful forearms. And the most recent one, still healing over with a sickly purple hue – the one from Subject 001.

"You said the Sleepless didn't attack you." I had both of my hands on him by then, tracing the thick knots of scar tissue, and my voice came out as an accusation.

"They did not, but that doesn't mean I didn't allow them to bite."

My hands shook. I was furious, incensed that he'd allow himself to be injured and dismayed to think he'd been harmed. Then I thought of how the subject had become human before death. Not at the moment of his expiration, but before.

I looked up at Vladimir, both hands braced on his chest, and I saw something other than the monsters that prowled the world. I understood, for the first time, that he was something different.

"What are you?" I whispered.

Rooms can be held suspended, moments frozen, given more weight and form in their silence than any memory ever has. I felt that then, a moment of crystallisation before the bitter plummet over the cliff-face of discovery.

"Isn't that what you're hoping to discover?"

We were standing too close, my fingernails digging into his ravaged skin. I couldn't move away.

"Why won't you let us take your blood? What do you think we'll find there?"

He raised one of his hands to cover mine, pressed over his heart. "Oh, Thea, I don't know if you'll find anything at all." His lips curved. "But that doesn't mean there's nothing to find."

Later, after he'd left, I drew back the curtain at the base of the Great Stair and turned off the camera recording behind it. Perhaps now I am truly condemned.

and somewhere there lies a mother heavy with the weight of sickness who cannot get up to comfort her child because the doctor who is a god because he is absent just like a god says there is nothing wrong, and he will always be right even when he is wrong, even while in the black room in the silent room in the choking room someone is dying for his beliefs, and the child will not understand even though there is something within her that feels this choking and hears this belief and there will be a splintering in her mind when she watches the rest of the world, the world that carries on and says there is no time for rest

AUGUST

1ST AUGUST

There's no single definition of madness. No definition yet agreed upon that might confirm the loss of a mind. Yet I believe I can say with some certainty that madness isn't a single state – one entered into that can never be returned from – but a process whose steps we might walk back and forth throughout a life, never knowing how close we've come to the ledge until we've thrown ourselves off. When, then, did I first step so close to the precipice?

Surely, this sense of falling didn't happen in a single moment. There must have been signs that I was drawing closer to the brink, signals I missed as I pulled away from a stable life into one that's tossed by the illogical. So, I must ask myself the question: when did self-destruction begin to appeal to me? And when I find the answer, I must be honest about the truth of it.

Every scientist knows that the universe is gradually descending into disorder. The scales of justice tilt that way only so long as people are willing to fight for it, but the process of entropy has only chaos as its end. Seen in a wider context, then, perhaps my behaviour merely follows the rules of nature. No matter my propensity to seek knowledge for its own ends, to impose order and structure upon the paths of nature and medicine, it must seem from a God's-eye view that this grasping at certainty is only a fiction, an illusion of stability as comforting as a fairy tale spoken into the dark.

That is how I perceive the world today, as something watched over by a god. I feel that I'm seeing from His perspective, and in taking His perspective I perceive myself as a dust mote caught in the light of a sunbeam. How can dust have agency when it's swept up by the howling wind? What can dust accomplish, except to be noticed by something greater than itself? I feel, inexplicably, as though I've been noticed, and in that noticing I wish to disappear.

HELEN X:
EXAMINATION #2

05/08/2063

The patient is a white female. She was brought to the White Tower's laboratory by security officer Alison Jagne at around 13:30, where, upon further examination, she was discovered to be pregnant. Based on the date of her arrival at the Tower and an extensive medical examination, I judged her to be somewhere in the third trimester with a due date around October or early November.

The patient was visibly distressed and I was unable to perform amniocentesis to check for foetal anomalies. The ultrasound scan was unclear, although I determined that it was unlikely she was carrying more than one child. The possibility of abortion was discussed and rejected despite medical concerns.

The patient's status remains confidential at Alison's request.

WHO CAN PENETRATE ITS DOUBLE COAT OF ARMOUR? WHO DARES OPEN THE DOORS OF ITS MOUTH, RINGED ABOUT WITH FEARSOME TEETH?

8TH AUGUST

There's no knowing what kind of child Helen carries. Conceived beyond the walls and brought inside, this Trojan horse can't be broken open yet. Still, I wonder what might be ready to spring from her. Whatever it is has been secreted here already, and now we can only await the consequences. Alison may have sworn me to secrecy, but there's one person I'm certain must have known. One who has called me a liar and yet has kept this secret from me.

10TH AUGUST

Beauchamp Tower has a single spiral staircase curling up through its centre, leading to an ancient oak door. I knew the walls of the chamber beyond still bore graffiti made by the centuries of prisoners who'd been held there: flowers carved into the stone by a supporter of Lady Jane Grey, religious extracts painstakingly etched by the disgraced Earl of Arundel – all imprisoned and all condemned. I wondered if Vladimir had signed his name there.

The door was open when I arrived, as though he'd been expecting me, and soft piano music drifted from a vinyl player by the sunken window. I hesitated, aware that out of every place in the compound, this one was more his than mine.

"Do you plan on maintaining your position on the threshold, Doctor Chares, or will you be crossing through the door?"

His voice startled me and I took an involuntary step backwards, and found my foot hanging over open air. I cried out, hands grasping for purchase as I fell, and then a strong hand shot out and I was hauled inside while the door slammed shut behind me.

"Must you have so little awareness of your surroundings? You walk up the stairs, yet the moment they're behind you they cease to exist."

He let me go with a disgusted sound and flung himself into an armchair in a manner I might have called petulant. The display of emotion startled me, and I could do little more than stare at him while my adrenaline level settled again. He looked at me for a long moment and then gestured around himself, his movements strangely open in this place he'd made a home.

"You're here now," he said. "You may as well look your fill while you recover your powers of speech."

I found that insulting, and no less so because it was accurate. The place they lived was remarkably cosy for a prison, I thought. There were tapestries spread across the floor, dark bookcases, and two armchairs – one of which Vladimir occupied – set in front of a cold hearth. The vinyl player sat on a sideboard near a sofa, and a coffee table bore a few books and Vladimir's sketchbook on top of it.

"It's nice," I said.

"Just as long as you don't mind sleeping next door to a monster, you mean?"

I took my seat in the spare armchair. "You knew, didn't you?"

"I know many things, Thea. You'll have to be more specific."

"You knew Helen was pregnant. That's why you brought her here. It wasn't just to save her from the Sleepless. It was to save her and her child."

He didn't answer.

"How could you have known all the way back then that she was pregnant? It must have happened only weeks before you met her, if that."

His face remained impassive and a terrible thought struck me, one which he must have seen pass behind my eyes.

"You've thought of something, Doctor Chares. Ask it."

I hesitated. "Is it your child?"

"No."

My shoulders sank back into the chair. Some crisis had been averted in my heart, but I didn't understand how or why.

"It mattered to you," Vladimir observed. "Whether or not her child was mine."

"It was either yours, or by one of the Sleepless, or another survivor who didn't make it," I said. "On balance, it would be safer if it were another survivor."

"For her or for you?"

"For her. If it were one of the Sleepless, we have no way of knowing what the child will be. And it isn't as though she could have consented."

That thought, which hadn't occurred to me until I'd spoken it, made me go cold, and I felt a swelling ball of nausea rush up from my stomach to settle at the base of my throat.

"God," I choked. "We've been concentrating on their feeding, on how they kill. But if that's not all they do, if they... if they..."

"Thea."

Vladimir's voice sounded distant. I felt like my mind had drifted away from my body, unable to see what was in front of me nor hear what was in the room. Instead, I felt Subject 001's hand on my calf and saw two blue eyes, brighter than the sky, bluer than the ocean, and darker than the void bearing down on me. My chest burned, my breath stuttered, and then a sharp jolt through my legs startled me as I slid from the chair and onto the floor. I realised then that I'd closed my eyes, but I couldn't remember where I was or why I would do such a thing. There was a hand cradling the back of my head, a thumb brushing rhythmically down my neck, and this struck me as odd enough that I finally came back to myself.

Vladimir was looming over me, a furrow between his brows, and one palm was pressed over my heart while the other, I realised, had prevented my head from striking the floorboards.

"Breathe," he said.

It was on the tip of my tongue to tell him that I was breathing, thank you very much, but when I opened my mouth all that came out was a rasping, ragged breath that made the edges of my vision dim as though someone had turned down the light on a gas flame. The frown line between his eyes deepened.

"Berate me later. For now, only breathe."

The retreat of my panic was like water coming off the boil, slipping down to a simmer. I imagined the particles of myself cooling from a frantic bounce to a steady wave. Vladimir's hand crept up from my chest, skimming the hollow of my throat until his fingers rested at my pulse point. I felt trapped, enclosed, and for the first time I could remember, very, very safe.

We stared at each other, and my wayward heart began to settle beneath his fingers and the strange, steady gaze that monitored me. I didn't want to move from his embrace, and that thought frightened me more than the fact of my capture by a creature so well designed to destroy me.

"Come. You cannot stay on the floor all afternoon."

I wasn't certain my legs would hold me, but I needn't have worried. He swept me up without the slightest appearance of effort and deposited me back into the chair. There he stayed, kneeling at my feet, and I wondered what I must seem to him. Fragile. Hysterical. Human. Unable to imagine the horrors of the world even while I'm mired within them.

"Your reactions are a mystery to me," he murmured. "So many horrors you've seen. So much pain by your hands and the hands of the people you call friends. And yet the thought of Helen's plight has always moved you to paroxysms of panic and grief."

He cocked his head, studying me, and I watched him in return. His peculiar eyes no longer unnerved me, and where his face had once seemed to be a blank and monstrous mask, I could see now expressed there a depth of feeling that I was incapable of dismissing as mirroring.

"She's blameless in what happened to her," I said. "And what happened to her is an abomination."

"And you hold yourself responsible."

It wasn't an accusation. There seemed to be no value judgement hiding behind his words, yet they struck me nonetheless.

"You feel regret for her suffering," he said. "Would you then have preferred it if her child had been mine?"

"Yes." The word emerged as a reflex.

"You are a liar, Thea Chares."

How I hated him then. How the monstrous mask of his face repulsed me, in the simple fact that I wasn't repulsed. Anger, frustration, and shame because I couldn't lie and have it be believed, could not express where his strangeness came from, could not articulate why it so attracted me. I reached out, fingertips trailing along his forehead, beneath his hair. A shiver in my hands when I wanted to wind it around my fingers and pull until it hurt, and the flex of his hand on my knee as though he'd heard the errant desire slip behind my eyes.

I resisted the temptation, my fingers skimming down his temple, along his too-sharp cheekbones to the bridge of his nose. He remained completely motionless, adopting a stillness no human could replicate. I positioned my finger between his eyes, and I thought of a red laser on a gun and the final pull of the trigger. His face didn't move, and yet I could tell with certainty that he was laughing, delighted, behind this false aspect. I ran my fingers lower, over the line of his nose, fallen, falling down, until my thumb traced the curve of his lip. I knew only then what I was going to do, my body and mind at opposite ends on the spectrum of intent.

I brought my face to his, and I kissed him. I kissed him, and he kissed me, and I don't know why it happened.

13TH AUGUST

There has long been a tendency in intellectual thought to view logic and emotion as occupying opposite ends of a spectrum, as opposing forces that cancel each other out, with one positioned as more worthy than the other. But while it's true that emotion isn't always rational, that doesn't negate the fact that it's valuable. Fear, a protective emotion, is an innate instinct to guard your own life. Passion and enthusiasm are valuable when they result in joy or dedication to a skill or way of life. Sadness is a rational response to hurt, and grief – grief is the most rational emotion of all, although it can lead us to ruin.

What does it say about me, then, that desire and fear are so closely aligned? Admiration – I will not say, love – breeds in me a desire to consume what I admire. Is it rational to want to absorb the thing we aspire to, which may also be the thing that we fear? It seems to me that desire and fear are the same emotion, one a force that attracts and one a force that repels.

There is a French psychiatric term I've always been drawn to: *l'appel du vide*, or the call of the void. It refers to the human impulse towards oblivion, the disintegration of the self. It's the prickle we experience, the temptation, when peering down from a cliff face or watching for the oncoming train. The little voice, self-harming, that whispers, *You could jump*.

For me, this instinct has never been towards death, and I would hedge this description with a caveat. *L'appel du vide* is not the desire to be obliterated but the desire to both take and cede total control. In amongst the monotony of the day-to-day, so many decisions we make aren't within our conscious control. I don't decide to be pleasant to other people; I don't decide to work even when I don't want to; I am forced to by society, and my impulses are so trained in this way that I barely notice my own conditioning.

Until, that is, the train rushes through the tunnel, or the void opens up atop the cliff, and I realise I've been operating on autopilot and my decisions are not my own.

But this… This is not a conditioned response. Nothing in my life teaches me that to jump would keep me safe. It is a desire for chaos, a desire to see: *what would happen if…?* And of course, the rational mind knows what will happen and the rational mind pulls us back. But the emotional mind rebels, knowing that this feeling, at least, will remain forever out of our reach.

I feel that I have stepped into the void, stepped over the edge of the cliff, and instead of falling like I ought to, now I hang suspended. Beneath me there is chaos, an area of life I've never invited into me, and yet it appeals to me and I desire it and I am afraid. I am afraid because it is irrational, and still the thought of ignoring it makes me want to batter myself against the Tower's walls. I am playing with fire. I do not understand. And yet, for once, this lack of understanding doesn't make me seethe.

It's almost liberating, not to desire understanding. To desire, instead, ignorance and chaos. The oblivion of ignorance is as tempting as the apple from the serpent's tree. Unfortunate, then, that I've allowed myself a taste when all might yet be snatched away. In my search for the void I've begun to separate myself, to unpick the subtle threads that have always bound me to my work and, consequently, to the Professor. We are diverging, and in that divergence, too, there is the potential for harm.

AND I SAW A BEAST RISING OUT OF THE SEA HAVING TEN HORNS AND SEVEN HEADS. AND ON ITS HORNS WERE TEN DIADEMS. AND ON ITS HEADS WERE BLASPHEMOUS NAMES. AND THE DRAGON GAVE IT HIS POWER AND HIS THRONE AND GREAT AND TERRIBLE AUTHORITY.

25TH AUGUST

Some mistakes, like neuralchips, marriages, and medical research take years to show their teeth. Others barely leave us with time to draw breath before they're snapping at our heels. My manipulation of Vladimir has grown tendrils, and the hidden camera by which I betrayed his trust has also harmed another. The Tower knows of Helen's pregnancy, and Edgar is the vector of that knowledge.

"They had a right to know," he told Alison in the darkness outside the Raven's Nest.

"No, Edgar. They really didn't."

Amidst the argument between us, it was Thane's reaction that concerned me. Ever calm and stoic, there was a bubbling fury beneath his skin, and when he rounded on Alison in the shadow of the White Tower I felt something between us crack.

"We have no idea what kind of creature she's carrying!" he shouted. "If it's like one of those monsters, what then?"

It was a question I hadn't allowed myself to ask out loud, and now it was out there for everyone to hear.

A CONVERSATION
WITH THANE

After the argument I followed him into the bar and we toasted to insanity, and in the warm night this was what he told me.

I was a twin once, he said. We were identical, born five minutes apart, and me the older one. His name was Drew. We grew up together, and later it turned out that we didn't have so much in common as we had done living on the estate. I was the bad kid, you know? The one who couldn't get on too well in school, while Drew was great at all that stuff. He aced his exams and went off to the local uni. Me? I joined the army.

I felt so grown up. I was good at it, you see. The exercise. The discipline. The handling of the weapons. I idolised the superior officers and wanted just a little bit of that respect, that awe, that control. But for all the army says it'll do for you, it takes as well. You get discipline, and you get purpose, and you get your brothers and sisters in arms, and in return you sign a little piece of paper that says they get to send you away to die. It isn't an equal exchange, and it gets to you. *They* get to you. Inside your head, I mean.

You stay on the barracks and you're isolated just like that. You spend all your time with this core group of people, bonding, team building, competing, and it's drilled into you that you are the good guys. These are the good guys, and you've got to protect them. They'll protect you, too, but you've got to protect them, and their lives are in your hands just like yours is in theirs. It's like a cult, except no one calls it that, because the country always needs more kids to go and sign their lives away for a little sense of power and the respect they can't find anywhere else.

"I always thought you loved the army," I said. "You've always seemed so proud."

"I do love the army. It made me what I am. And because of that I hate it, too."

It's difficult, he said, when you get leave, to be around civilians again. Their lives seem so easy. So uncontrolled. So meaningless by comparison to the constant reinforcement you get inside the barracks that you're special. You're doing something. You stand apart.

I came back to town a few years after I joined. I'd been on two tours of service by then, and lost a good friend, and seen things I still don't think any person should have to see. Drew was doing postgrad, something to do with literature, and when I stood with him back on the estate, I realised we weren't identical anymore. We were two Black boys, you know? Two outsiders, big lads, conspicuous. But while I'd grown harder, more severe, thicker muscle and a shaved head and every inch the kid who'd signed his life away at sixteen, he'd got smaller and somehow more noticeable.

He was wearing this ridiculous poncey blazer, and a thin pink scarf round his neck, and these glasses that I never found out if he needed or if they were just a fashion statement. He still had friends in town, and we went down to the local pub, and he introduced me to all of these arty types, with dyed hair and weird names who drank IPAs and talked about things like colonialism and nationalism as though they were the same thing.

It was awkward for everyone, but the more they talked and the more I drank, the more pissed off I got – with the apologetic glances when someone talked about national pride, with these in-depth discussions about borders and histories and the violence of the state. And Drew got quieter and quieter, and I knew then that he was embarrassed by me. Disappointed in me.

There I was, risking my life, warped and turned into this person who had respect and a purpose, who'd stared down the barrel of a gun so that – as I believed – I could keep people like these little shits safe to drink and discuss my life like it was an abstract morality question. And here they were looking down on me for it with Drew sitting there, pressed between them, saying nothing in my defence.

I dunno how it happened, but someone made a comment, some dig about working for the enemy, and I lost it. I stood up, right there in the middle of the pub, and I told them that they were only able to sit there and chat shit and read their books in peace because of people like me, risking our lives and breaking our bodies for them, and with more courage in our little fingers than they had in their whole damn skeletons.

Then, of course, Drew got up, and he's apologising for them and telling me I'm out of order, that I just don't understand these issues like they do, because I hadn't read the books or done the studies. And I'm there yelling at him that I might not have read about this stuff but unlike them I lived it every day, and maybe if he'd been more of a man he'd understand it the way I did too.

Then Drew, he just starts crying. He just starts crying, and this guy, one of his friends whose name I've forgotten now but I remember had the greenest eyes I'd ever seen, puts his arms around him and kisses his cheek, and I... I was disgusted. I'd always thought I was fine with homosexuals, you know? But seeing him, my little brother – *myself* – standing there, looking down on me while being kissed by this stranger who thought I was some big dumb killing machine, snapped something in me. I walked out and I left.

We were all pretty drunk by then, though, emotions running high, everything a big melodrama and no perspective left. Drew came chasing into the street after me, still crying, still with his boyfriend trailing behind and trying to pull him away, and he's there asking me if we aren't still brothers and don't I still love him, because he loves me? And I turned around, in the middle of the high street, rain coming down and people everywhere, and I called him a fag, and I told him to call me when he'd decided if I was good enough for him to hang out with.

When I walked away, I heard these security guards on the door to one of the clubs laughing and repeating it to them: *fags, ponces, cissies*. One of them shoved his boyfriend, and Drew stood there between them and told them to get fucked, and he... he looked back to me for help. He looked back to me for help, and I said to him, *I'm just the muscle, remember? Maybe you should use some of those big words you learnt in your books to figure it out*. And then I left.

I got a call from Mum the next day. Drew and his boyfriend were both in hospital. The kid with the green eyes was gonna be fine, but Drew had put himself between them and taken the brunt of the beating. He was in a coma. He stayed that way for three weeks, and while I was back on the barracks, training sixteen-year-old kids in how to earn respect, Mum turned off the life support. And that was that. I wasn't a twin no more.

I came back for the funeral, of course. Stood there in my uniform, surrounded by a few army buddies who'd got leave to come with me, and all of Drew's arty friends were there, dressed up like goths in mourning, telling stories about him I'd never heard before. About his gentleness and his kindness, and his bravery. The green-eyed boy was there, still with his arm in a cast, and he sobbed like the world was ending and wouldn't look at me. And I couldn't cry. I saw the way my brothers, the ones the army had made for me, looked at that kid, and I couldn't cry. Couldn't appear so weak.

I kept on coming back to it though over the next few years. Rising up the ranks and thinking, thinking about what bravery is. Because it isn't just going into warzones and doing what you're told. It was Drew, my little brother. Not a big man with a gun or the backing of a unit, just a young guy who liked books putting himself between those security guards and his boyfriend, wearing his stupid pink little scarf. Even later, I realised it was his boyfriend, too, who was brave enough to cry when crying was the right thing to do. Even with the army-brute brother who'd called him a fag standing there in his uniform, watching.

I got out of the army a few years later. Couldn't convince myself we were always the good guys. Started to understand what Drew had said, that making things right at home could be a quiet act as well as a declaration of war. So I quit, and I came back home to our little shithole town, and I took up a position as a security guard at one of those clubs on the high street, and I promised myself that I'd make that street safer for people like my brother, even if I had to stand up to the guys on the door to do it.

The army made me into someone strong. Made me big. Made me dangerous. Took me out of my place in the world and dropped me into somewhere new. But I brought myself back, and I made myself into someone who would protect people, on my terms and not on anyone else's. But now... now the whole world's gone and died on us, and it seems like we might be the only people left.

Who am I if I can't protect us from those things outside the walls?

Thane left after that, and I hadn't known what to say. What was there to say in the face of such guilt? How could I absolve him for abandoning his brother? How could I condemn him for what he'd done after? How is his crime any different to mine? I was drunk by then, coffee liqueur like a fur in my mouth and everything softened and blurry.

The world was the sky and I was a cloud, and I felt unmoored and transparent. All of the feeble atoms of myself splitting apart, drawing away into fog, and here I was, here at the end of the world, making mistakes too big to speak of. I wanted to be solid. Safe.

I stepped into the dark and I felt the light from Beauchamp all over me, its spectre watching from the windows. Alex had left the door to the engine room open and I dissolved through it, overflowing down the stairs and into the bleak darkness, and I planted my lips on his.

He met me, nervous, willing, and warm, and he tasted of man and rope on my tongue. I thought of him as an anchor, and he did weigh me down. He brought me down so hard and so fast that I wondered if he wasn't the void after all. I went down onto my knees and I took him out of his jeans, hard and wanting. Simple, in how simple it was to arouse him. The simplicity of being wanted. Skin to skin, mouth to cock, bitter and alive.

He didn't try to stop me. In fact, he encouraged me with his hands in my hair, tugging and moaning, a man feasting even though it was my mouth that was full. Full, and yet emptied of something important, because it wasn't his face I saw behind my closed eyes, shut against the reality of what I was doing. It wasn't his hands I imagined in my hair. And I didn't think of him once while he took the pleasure I gave him.

I thought of a young student bleeding in a gutter, and of Alison with boots made of stone standing on the Tower's walls. And I thought of a monster with two heads growing inside Helen's body. And I thought of Vladimir, cold and hard and gentle, a predator that made me want to be prey. And when Alex came, burning salty and unpleasant in my throat and spilling down my chin, I drew back, and I was empty save for a tolling thought.

What has become of us, and what new thing is inside me now?

because if there is enough time for rest then there is not enough time for work and if there is not enough time for work then there is not enough time for money and if there is not enough time for money then there is not enough money for food and if there is not enough money for food then there is not enough life to rest, and so life will end because there is no time to rest, but she won't understand the truth until she is standing in the burning fog and there will be a serpent rising from the water and baring its fangs at the lament of the moon

SEPTEMBER

1ST SEPTEMBER

It's funny, Mother, what the body and mind can do. What the bodymind combined together can compel us to do. There can be a terrible logic in cruelty, and logically I know I've been cruel. I've known of Alex's feelings for me, played on them as though they were unimportant. I've given him my mouth to use and in so doing I've used him, too. Used, because I don't feel for him what I think he feels for me. For the version of me that doesn't exist but who lives in his head and heart as a figure more real than I am.

Oh, Mother, he thinks I am good and kind and clever. He thinks I am truthful and I'm not. He thinks we will run away together and live – how? Live in the mythical Eden, perhaps. The wilderness where our cups will runneth over and we will be beyond these walls and the monsters within them.

Within. Outside. It seems to me to be the same thing. His hope is a fiction, as is my image in his eyes, but how cruel to shatter it like this. How unconscionable to dangle hope and heat when nothing else feels real, and then to take it away. How bitterly I realise that he didn't expect it, which is to say that he expected better from me. And is any more proof needed that the version of me he cares for is a fiction than that? He thinks I am better than I am.

You were quiet today, Mother. You ate little and you watched me, and I thought somehow that you knew. I confess – here, I confess – that I hated you. I have often hated you for not being better than you are. For making this of me. For setting me on a path I couldn't turn from, even when we crossed into the realms of the impossible and kept on pushing with no thought for how badly things could break.

How could I stop, Mother, when you still needed me? How could I ever break away from you when I was all that stood between your life and your death? How is it that I can hate you and love you still? And how can I contain all the hate I have for this world and bear my love for it as well? I hate you, and I hate myself, and I loathe the people within these walls.

And yet to save them is the only absolution, to cure you the greatest revenge. But revenge against whom? Perhaps against God and Fate and circumstance and medicine. Against the myths of life and health and sickness and death. Revenge, perhaps, against the ending of death, which is the ending of life. Revenge against myself for using Alex to elicit jealousy from a monster, and for being too cowardly to look and see whether or not I've succeeded.

Well, Mother, it is another day, so what shall I do with my body and mind? I shall tell you: I will go on, and it will hurt, and I will go on even though I don't know how I keep on going on.

3RD SEPTEMBER

This morning dawned cold and blue and bright, with a screaming from the stables. A screaming.

The kid – two kids, monster child – has died, and there are two mothers heartbroken and screaming. From the green, their voices sound the same. Perhaps grief has a language common to all animals, so really it doesn't matter which of them feels it most deeply. There's little for us to do against it. No words to soothe the hurt. I passed by the stables, drawn to tragedy as we all are, and there was Helen cradling the dead thing and wailing with her eyes raised to the sky.

A few paces away, Billie's neck was tipped back and her soft white muzzle bleating, and they made a chorus together, a lament as powerful as any Greek tragedy. I knew, then, where I would find Vladimir, and in knowing it I realised that I'd understood something about him at last.

I left the scene of tragedy and went into the White Tower, down the stairs and into the cold interview room, where of course he was waiting for me. Funny, the way he pretends. How he stations himself within a setting where I should hold all of the power, but in choosing it for himself he takes that power from me.

"The kid is dead," I said.

"I know."

"Helen's distressed."

"I know that, too."

He was sketching, loose and regal, and didn't look up when I took my seat.

"Shouldn't you go to her?" I asked.

"She has Alison."

"I know."

His hand stilled. "Do you, indeed? And what else do you understand today that you didn't understand yesterday?"

"I know that I don't understand you. The more I know of you, the less I understand."

"Do I not reward further study?"

"Do I?"

He looked up and I regretted the question. He looked at me – *saw* me – and in seeing me, I felt that he grew stronger while I diminished before him.

"What is studying but an unravelling?" he asked. "Haven't you spent your life bent to the task of pulling at the threads of things? Tell me, what happens to the thing being studied when finally you understand?"

"It becomes something new. It's made more real."

"Or it falls apart."

I didn't know if I was falling apart beneath his attention. I *did* believe that he couldn't fall apart. No matter how long I stared, seeking truth and insight in the blasphemy of his face, he would remain as he was, unknowable, and offensively the same.

"You build rules for yourself, Thea. You create them and you follow them, and in this way you believe you'll be safe. But the strength of your belief doesn't create truth. How does it feel to have broken your own rules? Do you feel safe now?"

"I've never felt safe." It was the truth, and I saw that he knew it.

"You have contained yourself, and now you've broken that container. Do you not feel it? Now that you've stepped outside into reality, doesn't the world feel different? Don't the people?"

I felt that he was leading me towards revelation, but I couldn't see the shape he wanted me to find. "What do you think I should have noticed?" I asked.

"They are unravelling." He leant across the table, his face too close and yet not close enough. "This community. This world. The collective endeavour you've created at the very end of all things, it has been an illusion and it is coming to an end. What will you do when the scales fall from your eyes?"

I didn't know what he was referring to. I didn't want to know what he was referring to, but still I asked. "What do you see here, Vladimir? What do you see that I don't?"

"I see movement. Decisions being made that will alter the Tower's course. And I see you."

"I know." Another truth. They were slipping from me like snowmelt, and that was more dangerous than anything I'd done yet. "What do you see in me?"

"I see a liar in desperate search for the truth. And I see the serpent beneath your skin, wrapped around your heart like a strangling vine at the very core of you."

"My mother."

He inclined his head, his face so close that I felt his breath on my lips. "Can you not unpick her, Thea Chares? Uncoil her from the heart of you so that you might be free?"

The thought was impossible. "I can't free myself from her."

"Can she free herself from you?"

I shook my head, because of course she can't. There's no separation to be found for either of us. We are bound, and have been since the moment she fell ill. Perhaps some people might look upon mothers and daughters as being bound from birth, but it's easier to cut an umbilical cord than an obligation. She once held my life within her, and ever since I've felt the responsibility for her life on my shoulders. If she is my mother then I am her saviour, and we have both failed in our roles. We are linked by our failure, held close, inseparable, like rings of DNA wrapped around one another that will fall apart if separated. A lovers' knot.

Perhaps Vladimir is right. Perhaps we are unravelling. The more I try to hold fast to my purpose, and the closer we seem to its achievement, the more I am tempted by sabotage. To love and hate my mother is no surprise; to love and hate myself also; but to behave in the way I am, and to see the same strange deviations from our routines occur in the others too, is enough to send a chill through the soul.

Even the Professor, forever my North Star, has changed in the last few months. Or perhaps he's been changing for longer and I've merely not noticed. There is a purpose about him now that hasn't been there since before Cassius died, and the change in me comes through in his reflection. Where once his enthusiasm would infect my own, drawing us to greater pursuits, now I find that it makes me hesitate. I am nervous. Afraid. Can it be that I no longer trust him?

If that is the case, how can I trust myself?

THEY WORSHIPPED THE DRAGON FOR HE HAD GIVEN AUTHORITY TO THE BEAST, AND THEY WORSHIPPED THE BEAST SAYING, WHO IS LIKE THE BEAST AND WHO CAN FIGHT AGAINST IT?

5TH SEPTEMBER

I am trying hard to be good, to be kind, to be clever. I am trying to find calm in my routine, and yet the very air seems determined to thwart me. What is it about September that makes a person long to lose their mind? Is it merely its false pretence of summer? The knowledge that it may contain the last true sun until February breaks?

I once read about the lemon trees that bloom themselves to death. They recognise that their end is drawing near, and instead of drifting away and dying quietly they produce an overabundance of fruit, buckling the boughs of the dying tree, creating such bright bursts of colour that a person might believe in the inevitability of plenty. It is a lie of immortality, overabundance before the act of death. An illusion of health that hides the end of everything.

September has always felt like that to me, the wind cool enough for you to notice the oncoming chill but the sun so bright you might easily ignore it. The death of so many summer flowers while there's a second revival of others. The days are still long, the birds still busy building and shoring themselves up against the oncoming winter, yet the dark season approaches nevertheless.

Childhood is contained here, the memory of school and of conkers falling to the ground, of the frenetic new beginning that comes at the end of warmth. I feel it here in the Tower, too – a sense of things gearing up, poised to embark on some new adventure. The days feel portentous. I stand, often now, watching not just the river but the streets to the north. The empty Tube stations and the rubbish-strewn civilisation made of ghosts, just as you are a ghost. Perhaps I am waiting for you to appear out of the blue September sky, just as Vladimir and Helen did in April.

April, September – they are the same month after all.

Another new beginning came today, and I met with Edgar and the Professor in Edgar's laboratory on the top floor of the White Tower, within the dimly lit rooms.

"I've hacked into the computer system," Edgar said. "We can see them all."

On a screen across the farthest wall, the neural network bloomed like a flower. Pink pinpricks of light fluttered across a map of London, lit up like a constellation of stars. It was the Sleepless, I realised. All of them. I could see the pulse of them, the ebb and the flow, and the wireless connection that linked the hub to each neuralchip expanding like a spider's web. The lines grew, bubbling in shades of pink and red like silken veins, and I understood something at last.

The chips were no longer transmitting to our server as they ought to. They were transmitting to each other. An electronic hivemind, a symbiosis with the human brain that had created a mycelial network. An ecosystem. A single human mind joined in perpetuity by technology.

"That was why they malfunctioned at the same time," I said. "It didn't matter who followed the rules and who didn't. One single person could affect them all."

"A perfect connection," Edgar agreed, his eyes shining in

the glow of the screens. "A true society, each one linked mind to mind, sharing their consequences together."

"Perhaps even sharing one mind," the Professor added.

The implications were staggering, yet also intensely hopeful. If Edgar can access the network he might be able to rewrite the code and submit a reset action to the chips.

If we can close the sensory gate, we can take them all offline.

7TH SEPTEMBER

Helen is silent. She hasn't moved from the stable, and she and Billie keep a lonely watch over the dead kid. It's fascinating to witness the proliferation of concern, how it multiplies with her condition. There's never a moment when she isn't watched over, although she seems not to notice. If it isn't Alison, then Maryam is sitting nearby, observing from the greenhouses. If not Maryam, then Miles and Dolly have taken to bringing her food. Even Thane has quietly left water by her side or attempted to take her back to Beauchamp.

She grieves surrounded by offerings, and of course Vladimir is never too far away. It's perhaps more concerning that I'm never too far away from him. The engine room door has been left open yet I don't descend the stairs. I stand at the top of St Thomas's Tower yet I don't watch Alex tending to the turbines. Instead, I stare out at the farthest shore and pretend that I don't feel someone's eyes watching at my back.

It's a chain of pretence, pretending at uncaring. I find Helen's inability to pretend refreshing, in as much as it deviates from my own personality. She feels no need to hide her emotions. Perhaps she can't. She is honest because she knows no other way to be, and so there can be no subterfuge or manipulation. Every human must respond to that in some way.

Even I, preferring distance at all times, have found myself drawn to her. Not during the day, when everyone can see, but at night when insomnia strikes I've taken to joining her there. We don't speak. No doubt she would make an excellent confessor, but I am no penitent and she no priest. Instead, I lean on the stable fence and I bear witness to her grief as though observing a play.

She is beautiful inside it. Even Billie is moved. Our goat rests her head on Helen's knee and there is a strange comfort in that. The kid, however, must be disposed of soon. It's benefited from the chill in the air, but it's starting to decompose. Flies are gathering. We cannot afford an outbreak of sickness merely because no one had the heart to burn its body with Helen still holding vigil.

8TH SEPTEMBER

Another night in Helen's company, and I was perturbed to hear footsteps approaching and knew without looking that it was Alex. Funny, how proximity to a person can provide you with a sixth sense about how they move, the scuff of their feet becoming familiar, even if you aren't consciously aware of it. He approached me in the dark September cold and leant his elbows on the gate.

"Do you think we can do it?" he asked. "Raise a child in a world like this?"

Helen was sleeping, or appeared to be. She was curled around herself, her head tilted against a corner of the stable, one arm resting on the prominent curve of her stomach.

"We?"

"You know what I mean. Do you think she'll be able to raise it alone?"

"She's already a mother. She's been a mother since she first arrived here. The only difference is we know it now."

"But she isn't…" He cast around for the right word, and I knew what he meant but wanted him to be forced to say it. Not capable. Not *normal*. An unfit parent before the child was even born.

"We'll all end up having to help," he said. "She won't be able to manage on her own."

It was true, yet the undercurrent of disdain in his voice didn't make me want to agree.

"It takes a village," I said, and felt him become frustrated.

"I only meant that it will change things. A child makes everyone vulnerable."

"It also gives people hope."

The truth was, I knew what Alex meant. Part of me even agreed with him. Even if Helen's child is human, healthy, and the most docile baby ever to have been born, its fragility will pose a problem. It will change the way we organise the work. The risks we're willing to take. It shatters routine and brings forth the void. In a way, we will all become its parents, and that's a responsibility few of us are equipped for.

Still, I didn't like his implication that Helen wasn't enough. That because she was so truthful, so without guile or manipulation, she wasn't up to the task of love. It seemed to me that she may be the most natural mother here. Certainly more natural than I am.

"Maybe you're right," he said. "But that's not all it'll give."

We lapsed into silence, and I felt the ghost of the words he wanted to say buzzing about my ears like pollen. The pressure to break the quiet rose in me like a sneeze, but I resisted.

"You haven't come to see me, since."

The silent ending of that sentence was funny. *Since you had my cock in your mouth.*

"No."

I meant no in the sense of yes, you're right, and also no, I don't want to talk about this, and no, you're wrong about me, and no, I don't know how to fix it either, and no, I'm not worth it. A small word for so many meanings.

"Is that my fault?" he asked. "Was I too rough? It's been a while, and I wasn't sure–"

His words were so ridiculous, so far from the reality of the situation, that I was mortified. I grabbed his forearm before he could make it worse, before he could start apologising to me for the choices I'd made.

"No."

And this time no meant of course you weren't, and no, it wasn't your fault, and no, just because I sucked you off that doesn't mean it was about you, and no, I know that doesn't make any sense, and also God no, please don't apologise to me for the things that I've done. He stopped talking, and his eyes were fixed on my fingers clamped around his arm.

"No?"

And this time, I knew, no meant, really? And, are you sure? And, does that mean...? No meant hope and can we do it again? And of course I had to say no, but didn't. Instead I said, "I'm sorry."

Alex's brow furrowed, a strip of shadow where his eyes should have been, and he stared so hard at where my hand rested against him that I didn't feel able to move away. Very slowly, like watching a disaster unfold, he placed his fingers on top of mine and grew still. A smell came from him. The scent of coffee, and rope, and the ubiquitous varnish that hung around the engine room, and I thought that if I were smart, I would find that attractive, that these things that comforted me, this man who so simply wanted me, would be enough.

"I wish you wouldn't apologise," he said. "You don't have to know everything right now, do you?"

And I thought, *Oh Alex, how little you really know me.* Because of course I do. Of course I must know. Of course I should have known and did know but lied to myself anyway.

He sighed, and smiled with an easiness I envied. "I know you don't find people easy, but you must know how I feel about you, Thea." His gaze flickered to the chain at my neck, and I felt that it was choking me. "I know you feel something for me. You must, mustn't you?"

How could I tell him that the thing I felt for him, the two principal things that I felt for him, were guilt and pity for the rose-tinted glasses he wore and his complete misapprehension of our relationship and the person I really was?

His fingers trailed upwards until they brushed the chain over my chest, skimming down to rest between my breasts, where the key hung, waiting. It was our little secret, and I suddenly realised that it seemed to Alex my promise to him, although I hadn't intended it that way. I felt my heart beating against his fingers and stepped back just enough to dislodge him from my skin.

"We shouldn't do this," I said.

"Why not?"

And how could I tell him the truth? That he was in love with a woman who didn't exist, and that the real Thea, standing here in front of him brimming with guilt and yet somehow not enough self-recrimination or self-hatred, wasn't suited to him. How could I tell him that, in fact, I had lost my mind, and even while we stood there in the dark, Helen sleeping peacefully in the pen, I could feel an invisible set of eyes on us both and it was they that were making my heart beat faster?

Under Vladimir's gaze, I wanted to lean into Alex and press my lips to his, but not for his benefit. I wanted to provoke the monster waiting in the shadows, to compel him to act. To say what he meant. To offer me truth and honesty even though I wasn't offering him the same. But there must be some impulse within me that still cares for Alex, because although I came close, and although he leant in and kissed my cheek, soft and sweet, and it would have been so easy to turn my head and catch his lips with mine, I didn't. And I could tell he was disappointed.

Instead, he told me he would wait for me to work things out, and he caught the key against his fingers again, and I thought, *Yes, he is looking for Eden. But he will not find it in me.*

9TH SEPTEMBER

Vladimir took the dead kid from Helen and I was there to witness it. The night was dark, the wind cold, and both mothers bleated at his intrusion into their grief. She fought him, wailing, and the sound was spectral in the air.

"It is time to let the child go," he said. "The creature is gone, Helen."

She screamed then, and in a blink of impossible speed Vladimir snatched the kid from her clutches and held her at arm's length. Helen's face twisted, an almost feral expression contorting her features, and she sank her teeth into his arm.

I cried out, my gaze drawn to the circle of red blood, the sucking point at which Helen's teeth had pierced his flesh. Vladimir closed his eyes, pained but calm, and I saw then that she was drinking from him, her tongue slick with blood, the viscous fluid dripping like raindrops down her chin. My mouth flooded with sympathetic saliva, nausea rising as I tasted phantom metal and felt it run hot down the back of my throat.

Jealousy rose within me then, a feeling of ownership over him that shouldn't have found purchase in the tearing of his body. I was protective and territorial, and then numb with the light of revelation.

"You saved her," I whispered.

"You knew that already."

Yes, I had, but not like this. "How many died?"

His expression creased in pain. "Too many. In forty-seven attempts, she was my only success."

She was quiet now, and with a gentle pressure from his fingers against her temple, she released him and sat back, mouth ringed by a circle of blood and her gaze drunk and distant.

"Was she a success?" The sight of her was more horrifying to me than anything I'd seen yet, and I wondered how we could dare to call this a cure.

"She is healing." Blood dripped from his arm and I went to stem it, only to be stopped by the same gentle pressure of his fingers he'd used on Helen. "Leave it. It will heal soon."

But I couldn't. The sight of it repulsed me. I dug in my pockets and found the Professor's handkerchief, from that night so many months ago when Dolly had challenged us all. I pulled it out and pressed it to the wound. The heat of his lifeblood met my chilled fingers, and I stared down at the stain and felt his eyes on me.

"I must take her back to our rooms," he said.

I nodded, lingering, uncertain of why I wanted to cry. He pulled away, and with no visible effort, hoisted Helen into his arms. We left the stable in silence. Billie curled up in a corner and watched us accusingly while Vladimir turned to face me.

"You're searching for truth, Thea," he said, "so allow me to give you one. You have no great talent for cruelty."

I watched him leave, straight-backed and elegant in the encroaching night, and I understood that cruelty didn't need to be a talent to exist. I can shy away from cruelty and still be the cause of it. My very existence is proof.

15TH SEPTEMBER

Mother's recovery is still my ultimate aim. I might cloak my desire in hope for the Sleepless, but she is the root of all things. Vladimir has saved one life in forty-seven, which is one more than we have but still not enough. And now, now that I know, I cannot ignore the fact that we need his blood.

Today, I met with the Professor and Edgar in Edgar's lab, the curtains drawn and the scattered petals of light blinking along the wall. They were buoyant, ebullient, and I held the secret I knew behind my teeth until it choked me.

"We've been able to isolate the signals by geographic area," the Professor said.

"Does that help us?" I asked.

"A chain reaction," Edgar replied. "Concentric circles in a mushroom cloud."

"We may be able to detach our influence by geography," the Professor clarified. "Focus on the chips of those within a ten-mile radius, say, and test a reset."

"That's... brilliant."

"There are also greater pursuits still to come. We may find that switching the chips off returns these people to themselves, but your biomatrix may give us another route."

"What do you mean?"

"A cure, dear Thea, just like we always talked about. To keep the chips while curing the madness."

"You want to leave the chips in? But why?"

"Evolution," Edgar said. "We are evolving."

"Think about it, Thea," said the Professor. "The Sleepless are monstrous because they've forgotten themselves, but if we could remind them, if your matrix could curtail the more violent effects of the chips, think of what we could accomplish! A world without sickness, one where our lives were extended. Imagine the things humanity might do!"

"That isn't our aim." The words were out before I could stop them. "We need to cure them, Michael, not change them. The neural network has to be shut down."

"And if they die?" Edgar asked. "Would it not be better for them to live?"

"Of course it would, but you can't implement a biological cure at a distance."

"Which is why geography is so important," the Professor said. "If Edgar here can hack the network and gain full control, we'd be able to bring them inside the walls without fear, one by one."

"Two by two," Edgar chuckled. "Observe."

He swept his fingers across the tablet in his hands, and the map on the mounted screen zoomed in, shrank, until it was a bird's-eye view of the Tower. With a thrill of terror, I saw the single light blinking within our walls and knew with certainty that I was lost.

"Vladimir," the Professor said. "Do you see, Thea? We can track your friend."

"More than that," Edgar added. "If I were able to hack the network, I could use it to control him. A living consciousness." There was a light in his eyes that disturbed me, and I could hardly bear to look at either of them.

"You can't believe that to be a good thing," I implored the Professor. "Control of another person's mind on that scale... It's horrifying."

"Of course it is," he agreed, too easily. "But in terms of administering a cure, it's of great benefit. With the proper tools, Edgar will be able to bring the Sleepless to our doors, and allow us to fix them once and for all."

YOU CRUSHED THE HEADS OF LEVIATHAN. YOU GAVE HIM AS FOOD FOR THE CREATURES OF THE WILDERNESS, AND THE CREATURES OF THE WILDERNESS KNEW DEATH.

18TH SEPTEMBER

There is too much in our world that is wicked, too many things that have gone wrong, and yet the sight of the single chip persists in my mind.

I found Vladimir at twilight at the top of Raleigh's Walk, and knew him by the plume of smoke that curled into the air like fingers. I wasn't shocked to learn that he had a vice.

It felt fitting that I should find him there. A man caged but still prepossessed, deprived of the expression of his nature and yet staking a claim to whatever of himself was left.

I climbed the stairs, the rest of the courtyard silent and still, the Thames softly flowing and the city still dead. And there he was, sitting propped against the battlements, one leg extended in front of him and the other bent at the knee. The first thing I noticed was the coldness of his beauty in indolence, and the second was the glazed look in his eyes and the appallingly sweet scent that bloomed from his mouth. A pipe dangled from between his elegant fingers, and I blanched and went down onto my knees.

"Opium?" My voice was a hiss.

He smiled and dipped his head. "Your friend grows a great number of poppies. It wasn't difficult for me to liberate some seeds from her stores."

I gaped at him, and felt that he enjoyed my discomfort immensely.

"Do not look so shocked, Doctor Chares. The seeds of the poppy have been used since the advent of humanity to enable people to better see their dreams."

I noticed only then that the hand not holding the pipe was in motion. His sketchbook was propped up against the stone, and he was drawing without looking at the paper, his hand moving smoothly across the page while his vision was fixed on a point in the distance somewhere over my left shoulder.

"What do you see?" I asked him.

"Longing," he replied. "And loneliness."

His eyelids flickered and he drew on the pipe again, this time leaning back with his eyes half-closed and his hand still moving. I hesitated, then stepped over his legs and settled myself with my back to the river, peering over to look at what he was creating.

The lines were confident, striking, and the page crowded with various people bent to peculiar tasks. A man with lost eyes stared down at a puddle choked with dirt, a single leaf floating in the centre. A woman had her fingers pressed to a tree where a poster had once been stapled, the ruins of it now torn and illegible. An old man sat in an abandoned shopping cart that was too small to carry him, his legs and arms contorted to fit, while above his head a pigeon watched from the branches of a skeletal tree.

"This is what you dream of?"

"These aren't my dreams." His speech was slightly slurred. "They are theirs."

His head lolled onto his shoulder and his hand slipped from the book, drawing a dark charcoal line through the man's yearning face. I plucked it out of his reach and he didn't stir again, though I felt he was straddling the borders of sleep and hadn't quite fallen into it yet.

My hands shook when I opened the book, and on the pages there were hundreds of these portraits. Some were set here in the city while others grew to life amidst abandoned fields and rolling hills, northern city tower blocks, and coastal views. I tried to see them as nothing more than inventions, creations of imagination only, but I couldn't. They were portraits in the truest sense, seen and reproduced, not pictured in the mind's eye.

"You're dreaming of the Sleepless. Does that mean they're dreaming too?"

I didn't expect an answer, semi-comatose as he seemed, but when he spoke he gave no suggestion that it was an effort for him to hear me.

"Their life is one long dream. They simply cannot rest."

"How are you dreaming with them?"

He didn't answer.

"Let me see your eyes."

He drew in a breath and tilted his head towards me. "You're welcome to look."

It seemed he could aid me no more than that, so with some trepidation I leant over and pulled his eyelids open. His eyes rolled slightly, but when they finally focused, I was able to see that the hazel one had a small pinprick pupil while the blue was almost swallowed by the dilation at its centre.

"What do you see right now?" I asked.

His gaze struggled to focus on mine, and this close I could smell the sweet smoke of the opium drifting from his mouth. "I see you, frightened and determined. And I see others, caught in a web of your making."

I removed my thumbs from his eyelids and let them fall closed.

"By all rights, I should hate you Doctor Chares," he said. "You, and everyone else who stole sleep from the world."

"But you don't, do you?"

"No more than you hate me."

I settled back against the wall to watch him. His blue eye rolled beneath his lid, yet he seemed as calm and relaxed as any man at leisure, except for the furrow of concentration between his brows.

"Why is that, do you think?" I asked.

"You are not so easily categorised. Others, they decide their own realities, create their justifications, excuses, myths. You are steeped in reality, drawn in too many directions by its myriad contradictions. You omit, but you do not invent."

"You're saying that I show the appropriate guilt?"

He let out a sharp breath through his nose. "No guilt could be appropriate for what you've done. But guilt is meaningless without restitution."

He opened his eyes with what appeared to be great effort.

"I see the possibility for restitution within you, but first you must be able to unpick the serpent around your heart."

"You speak of guilt and restitution as though they're the inevitable parts of me," I said. "What are the inevitable things inside you?"

His eyes fell closed again. "Me?" he murmured, as if to himself. "There's nothing inevitable about me anymore. You have seen to that."

I stared at him – this man, this creature – and felt fury at the knowledge that I could place him in no category. Vladimir: a false name, satiric in his own choice, a creation myth as a marker of personhood. Sleepless and yet sleeping. Human and yet monster, dangerous yet enticing. He is nothing that I can explain, he should not exist, and yet there he sat, high and drifting in an opium haze. I hardly dared turn my head from him, certain that he was in fact a dream, and should I blink or let my eyes trace the paths of the Tower, I would turn back and find him to have vanished.

Still, I knew that were I to reach out and lay my hand on his I would find his skin hard and solid beneath mine. What can science do in the case of such an anomaly?

"Edgar thinks he might be able to tap into the neural network," I said. "He believes he'll be able to bring the Sleepless here for treatment."

Vladimir's silence had stretched for so long that I wasn't sure he was awake, but at my words his eyelids fluttered. "And what do you think of Lord Trevelyan's plan?"

"I think we need some way to administer a treatment, but I don't think this is the way to do it."

"And have you shared your concerns with the Professor?"

"Yes."

He opened his eyes. "What did he say?"

I didn't answer, and when it became clear that I wasn't going to his eyelids fell shut again.

"It's a difficult idea to contemplate, for one who clings to control as you do," he said. "What is it that you most fear?"

"Helplessness," I answered at once. "What do you most fear?"

He smiled. "Haste, and the monstrous march of industry."

22ND SEPTEMBER

How do you heal in a world in which you aren't allowed to rest? Humanity gains knowledge as the years go by, but it loses it as well. Arrogance becomes self-harm, progress the path of destruction. Our bodies are not so evolved as to be able to forgo the need for rest. It used to be common knowledge that to recover from an illness a person would require a period of convalescence, and then, when it became clear that there was no money in convalescence, it was swept out of history again.

Life is a chronic condition for which the treatment is sleep. To deny ourselves sleep is to render ourselves sick, and exhaustion is a tool of control. Keep a population exhausted and you keep them compliant. Keep an individual exhausted and you strip them of their humanity.

The monstrous march of industry and the destruction of rest. They are the very same thing.

26TH SEPTEMBER

I don't remember falling asleep last night, but this morning I opened my eyes and found myself on the battlements at Raleigh's Walk as though still searching for Vladimir. I came to waking as though rising through water, and my mind recalled that in my dreams I'd been chasing something – a person, a cure. An idea? Even as a scientist, sleepwalking feels somehow paranormal, as though I had become the ghost walking the Tower's walls, possessed.

It was still early, pre-dawn – fog-choked, cold, and otherworldly. The sky was a bruise, gathered and cradled by smoke, and there was so much fog that when I observed the river I could hardly tell where it ended and the sky began. The thought came to me that I'd entered a liminal place, poised on the cusp of my own sleeping mind, the breaking of the dawn, and the line between land and air. Where ought I to draw my own lines in such a state?

I stood there for a long time, chilled and shivering, and I felt myself futile and small. This life seemed unimportant. What are our lives worth, really, to the clouds and the oceans that pass us by?

Eventually, some movement in my peripheral vision made me look towards Tower Hill to the west. The buildings there seemed like behemoths, waiting behind a veil of mist, the sun scudding behind them watery and eerie. Then came a thrill of fright.

There were Sleepless gathering in the protective shadow of the skyscrapers. They moved erratically, huddled close together, and yet they put me in mind of a pride of lions stalking prey from the trees. I counted them more than once, the wet air making their shadows expand and lengthen, so that when the clouds moved over the sun there was little way of distinguishing shadow from substance.

Seven, I decided at last, although I could tell little more than that. Footsteps on the stairs in Byward Tower alerted me to the presence of someone else already awake, and I knew with certainty that it was Edgar. He emerged into the mist like the lord he'd once been, and in his hands there was a computer tablet bearing a strange control panel I'd never seen before.

"Morning dawns on our success," he said. "Your dreams have followed you into waking."

There was nothing particularly lascivious in the way he looked me up and down, his eyes roving over my nightdress and the purple cold of my legs. Still, I felt my skin crawl and wished I'd had a gown to pull closer about my shoulders. "It was you, then," I said.

"The theory's been tested. The result is a positive one."

"We don't have a cure to give them."

"Not yet, but we will, with the help of your friend."

Despite the depth of my cold, a bolt of frightening heat leapt through me. "What do you mean?"

"Only that it was good of him to indulge himself so recently. His cooperation has been invaluable."

I thought I saw the void waiting in his thin-lipped smile, but I didn't give it a second glance. I left the battlements in a daze, as though I sleepwalked still. I crossed the green with its dew-soaked grass casting rainbow patterns beneath my feet, then approached the door to the White Tower, and then I was running, my limbs clumsy with cold as I entered the lab.

The door crashed open in my wake, and there I fell frozen, presented with a tableau that made my very soul rebel.

"Ah, dear Thea," the Professor greeted me. "I see that Edgar found you after all."

A thousand words crowded my throat and died on the back of my tongue. Vladimir was strapped to the bed, belts and chains at his forehead, his throat, his chest, his legs. He was shirtless and his limbs were spread-eagled, the better to grant access to the tubes that were siphoning his blood out into bags.

At the foot of the bed, there was an icebox filled with more bloodbags than I thought it possible for someone to donate and still live, and his face was a mask of stone when his eyes met mine across the room.

"What are you doing?" I was almost embarrassed by the shriek in my voice. I hurried to him, and I was shivering as I searched his face for signs of pain.

"Research, dear Thea. Your matrix is falling behind."

Whatever Vladimir saw in me, his expression changed. "Ah," he said, so quietly I was certain the Professor didn't hear. "You didn't know, then."

"Of course I didn't know! How could you think I would do this to you?"

"You did it to your other subject."

"That was different."

"Why?"

A question like a blade, and I felt myself wounded by it. I slid the needles from him, cutting off the flow with a firm pressure over the gauze and stilling the trickle of blood into the placental sacks.

"Do not fret. He was in no danger."

Vladimir's blood now safely contained inside his body, I whirled to face the Professor. "You've nearly drained him dry! None of us consented to this."

"His blood replenishes at a remarkable rate, and it was for a worthy aim. I suspect you know this better than anyone, Thea, for having been the one to examine him."

My eyes flickered over the bite marks that covered him, their grey edges deep in the fluorescent light. "It doesn't matter what I know," I argued. "He hadn't consented."

The Professor's brow furrowed, and he shook his head at me wonderingly. "Neither had our first subject, but we took what we needed from him anyway."

I wanted to say again that it was different, but I was running out of reasons to see it that way.

Behind me, I sensed Vladimir watching, and with a final disgusted look at my mentor and friend I turned and began the process of unbinding him.

"Are you sure that's wise, my dear?" the Professor asked.

Vladimir's eyes were intent on my face, and I ignored the impulse to slow or to stop. "He isn't a monster."

"Aren't I?" His voice was low, dangerous.

"I don't think so," I said.

"Then how terrible a sight this must be."

My hands shook, because it *was* a terrible sight, and I couldn't reconcile that with how we'd torn the subject's body to shreds and delighted as we did it. My own hypocrisy disgusted me, and I knew he was aware of it.

I'd thought that, once free, he would get up and leave this place – perhaps even the Tower altogether – but when his restraints were finally gone he merely lifted himself into a more comfortable position. The sight of how he struggled enraged me.

"You can barely sit up on your own."

"So it would seem."

"Fear not," Michael said. "I requested that Edgar bring some food for our patient after he'd tested his theory. Did it work, do you know?" He'd turned to face me and I couldn't meet his eyes.

"It worked."

"Wonderful! We are so close, Thea. So close to the next stage. With Vladimir's blood, there's no telling what we could do."

I rounded on him, anger replacing shame and all of my blood heating.

"You had no right to take it from him! It was *his*. It belonged to him. It wasn't ours to take." Behind me, I heard Edgar return.

"Come now, you're better than this. Haven't you, more than anyone, fought for a way to make everything right? You know as well as I do that one man's comfort can't stand in the way of our success."

I felt that I'd entered a mirror world, one where everything I'd previously taken to be true was reversed and made strange in the negative aspect of my ignorance. There I stood, cold and dishevelled in my nightgown, my feet bare on the tiled floor. Opposite me, more put together than I'd ever known him, was the Professor, forever my guiding light and the greatest mind I'd known, eccentric and slovenly but ultimately kind and brilliant. Except that now, none of that seemed true.

Gone was the affected day robe, the rumpled shirts and slippers, and the flyaway hair. Instead, he wore patent leather shoes polished to an abhorrent shine, pressed shirt and trousers, and a stark white lab coat. There was no trace of warmth in his eyes, only a feverish greed and excitement that turned my stomach and set my teeth on edge. Where was the man I'd known? What had happened to him? And, more than that, what had happened to me?

The centre of myself seemed to have shifted, the building blocks of my personality scattered. I believed it was me who had to be in the wrong. How could I, woken from dreams, standing in the laboratory in my nightdress in front of this confident and accomplished man, ever be in the right? But then I thought that I must know some things about myself and others to be true. I must always believe that draining someone of their vital fluids against their will must be wrong. But – a more frightening realisation – if I'd always known that, what excuse had I for what we'd done to Subject 001? Only the same one the Professor was using now.

I felt sick, and he watched me with a pitying, disappointed expression that still had the power to shame me.

"Your empathy is commendable, but don't let it cloud your judgement," he said. "Do you see, Thea? The patient is well fed and cared for, and his blood will help us to make life from death."

The words very nearly placated me, and I turned to ascertain the truth of them, only for nausea to rise like a firework through my stomach. Edgar had, indeed, brought food to his patient, but just what he'd brought him was an aberration in itself.

Placed on the table, wheeled over Vladimir's lap, was a white paper plate piled high with raw meat. The chunks of what I thought to be beef still dripped with blood, and seemed to be partially frozen and at least somewhat rotten.

Edgar had done him the courtesy of bringing him cutlery with which to eat his monstrous meal, and there he sat in the hospital bed, face drained of colour, body drained of blood, and he ate like the most polite member of society. Methodically, almost primly, he cut through the bloody offering, slicing it into small chunks and inserting it into his mouth. With every stomach-turning bite, his gaze never wavered from Edgar's, and Edgar smiled right back at him.

My stomach rolled so violently that I almost retched where I stood, and yet I was transfixed. He ate slowly, the fork raised to his mouth, the bloody morsels disappearing to be chewed and savoured at leisure. He was a lord at his repast, and the peculiar dignity with which he swallowed the abominable meal was almost worse than the sight of the blood itself. I say almost because when the meat was cleared, Vladimir lifted the plate into his hands, and never once breaking Edgar's stare, held it to his lips and poured the remnants into his mouth.

I followed the motion of his throat with my eyes. The ripples as he swallowed faded, and almost at once a touch of colour returned to his skin. He still hadn't broken Edgar's gaze, a silent contest playing out between them. My eyes trailed up, past the sinew of Vladimir's throat, over the hard ridge of his jaw, and settled on the pink of his lips – grotesque, inviting, and ringed by a circle of red.

"Magnificent," Edgar whispered.

I was frightened to admit that it was.

and the serpent has not the eyes of the mother or of the child but instead the eyes of the Professor and the doctor, of doctors and doctors and doctors and medicine, and it looks with the eyes of medicine and it sees with the eyes of medicine and outside of the eyes of medicine there is no truth other than that which the serpent can see, but it does not see Mother and it does not see the choking room and it does not see the gap that lets in the night and the cold, and it does not see how the people once struck sparks beneath their feet as they rushed from one place to another

OCTOBER

1ST OCTOBER

AND I BROUGHT YOU INTO A PLENTIFUL COUNTRY TO
EAT THE FRUIT THEREOF AND THE GOODNESS THEREOF
BUT WHEN YE ENTERED YE DEFILED MY LAND AND
MADE MINE HERITAGE AN ABOMINATION.

This was the last note the Anonymous Donor ever wrote.
In the cold light of day, we gathered at the open door to the
22nd Tower – and the 22nd Tower was empty.

There are few things eerier than a vacant room, much
less one that's been recently abandoned. I don't know if
I ever gave much thought to what his self-imposed prison
looked like. Sometimes I imagined that it was a little like
Rochester's attic, and that perhaps one day it too would
explode in flames, avenging. This is a quieter end, but I'm
more disturbed by it.

A sofa, a fireplace, armchairs and rugs, a desk, a violin,
a record player. At the very top of the room, a mezzanine
with a neatly made bed and a sleeping area, as though he'd
merely popped out and would be returning again soon.
I don't believe I'd taken in any of these details before the
stench hit me, something sweet and rotten that reminded
me of the bat enclosure in a zoo. I followed it across the

room, to the open stairwell below the balcony that led in a spiral to the bottom of the tower.

The stench of decay poured up from the mouth of the chute, and if there had ever been living quarters below, they didn't exist anymore. Instead there was a rotting pit, filled with refuse thrown down there endlessly from above. I wrapped my sleeve around my nose and mouth and squinted into the darkness. The windows downstairs had been blocked and all I could see were mounds of rubbish – old meals, empty packets, and even, I thought, human waste. Our Anonymous Donor had been living in here among an empire of shit.

"Do you think he went mad?"

Thane had followed me inside. His voice made me jump and I sucked in a mouthful of the stale air and gagged.

"Anyone would go mad like this. But what was he doing in here?"

Now able to take a step back and observe the room as a whole, there were other markers of madness among the obsessively neat space. The wall beneath the mezzanine was chipped, the plaster chiselled away to reveal the stone behind it and food smeared into the cracks. Fungus and mushrooms bloomed in strange patterns, as though the tower were being cultivated.

I imagined the Anonymous Donor alone in here, using his fingers to chip away the plaster and throwing it down the stairwell. I thought about him poised over the edge of the balcony or lying on his bed, flinging food down the stairs and creating this province of decay. The thought made me shudder, and my gaze caught on his violin, lying clean and well maintained on the coffee table. I was having trouble reconciling the silhouette of the man who'd played a serenade to the Tower with these after-images of a person so obviously unwell. Was it madness that had led him to abandon his refuge, or something else entirely?

"I suppose he really is gone?" I asked.

"The gates were open. Seems he walked straight outside."

"Without anyone seeing him?"

"We were watching for monsters trying to get in, not barring the way for people trying to get out."

I considered that to be true, but the thought that no one had seen him cross the courtyard still disturbed me.

"What shall I tell them?"

I realised then that only Thane and I were in the room. Alison was standing outside the door, keeping everyone else out, and the babble of their questions was rising. Hysteria. It needed only a single spark to begin an inferno. How were we to quench it?

THE JOURNALS OF THE ANONYMOUS DONOR

AND I SAY TO YOU THAT THERE IS A THREAD THROUGH EVERYTHING AND THAT THREAD IS STRONGER THAN TITANIUM AND WORTHIER THAN GOLD AND IT IS NOW SHATTERED IN THE LEVIATHAN'S JAWS, THE JAWS THAT EAT AND EAT AND GROW THE BEAST'S GREAT BULK, THE SERPENT AND THE WORM AND THE THREAD AND THE GLUTTONY AND THE CONSUMPTION THAT ROTS INSIDE EVERY MAN AND THE BEAST IS HERE AND IT IS NOW AND IT HAS TWO SHARP EYES AND A TEMPTING SMILE AND IT IS HERE TO PUNISH AND TO CONDEMN AND TO SAVE AND WE MUST GIVE OURSELVES UP TO THE LEVIATHAN BEFORE IT SWALLOWS US ALL FOR IT COILS AT THE BOTTOM OF THE TOWER AND IT IS EVER HUNGRY FOR MORE AND MORE AND IT WILL NEVER STOP BUT I DIDN'T KNOW IT WAS WAITING FOR ME UNTIL IT WAS TOO LATE

IT IS TOO LATE

CAN IT BE TOO LATE?

IT MUST NOT BE TOO LATE.

5TH OCTOBER

"Searching for monsters, Thea?"

I returned to the Donor's rooms this evening, and there I was met by Vladimir.

"Searching for reassurance, perhaps," I replied.

"Have you found it?"

"Would I know if I had?"

"That is a more interesting question, I agree. Does it disturb you that this is all his life amounted to? Possessions locked away, destroyed, and redistributed?"

I considered the question and moved towards him and away from the stink of rot drifting up from the stairway.

"Most people leave little behind," I said. "We're lucky if we make a mark."

"Do you think he was disappointed in how little a mark he made? In these few things becoming his legacy? In his monetary hoard becoming worthless?"

"I'm sure he was. But these things weren't the only marks he left."

"You speak of the Sleepless."

I nodded.

"Does it trouble you, then, to know that your work left the same marks as his money?"

"Yes."

"What would you have done differently, were you to have your time again?" There was real curiosity in his voice, and I wondered what he expected of me.

"I would have been less naive."

"In what way were you naive?"

The smell was beginning to overwhelm me, and I stepped past him and onto the stairs outside and felt him follow.

"I thought that all scientific discovery was useful," I told him. "I believed that we'd passed the point where Einstein could create the conditions for the atom bomb and the rest of humanity make him complicit in the slaughter of millions."

"You believed that humanity had reached a higher state of care?"

I scoffed. "No, far from it. But I thought that our societies, advanced as they were, had enough checks and balances in place for someone to realise the moment we over-reached ourselves, to draw us back from a path that science shouldn't go down."

Vladimir stood close at my back, and I resisted the urge to lean backwards and let his peculiar heat seep into me.

"Every society has thought the same," he said. "Every human yet born has believed they're living in the most advanced society in history, with access to more information than their predecessors. How could they then fail to be better than their forebears?"

It was a genuine question, and I thought about it for a long time.

"Because while technology and discovery might progress, humans are still humans," I said eventually. "Access to more information doesn't necessarily make us smarter. An easier life in some ways doesn't mean that we've become kinder or more aware."

"Humanity is still humanity," Vladimir agreed. "They err when they attempt to play God."

"I wasn't attempting to play God."

"What were you attempting to do?"

"I was trying to save my mother."

"And did you?"

I swallowed. "No."

Vladimir moved around me, his body compelling me to respond in such a way that I was forced to step back and angle myself towards him.

"You made exactly the same mistake that Einstein made," he said. "You became so focused on your own aims that you were blind to the society you lived in and the responsibility you had towards the people you experimented on."

"I didn't experiment on them." The denial came too quickly.

"Perhaps not. Perhaps you only created the conditions that allowed the experiments to take place. Does that make you feel better?"

"No."

"Good."

I turned away, my gaze returning to the Tower, to Troy. It felt possessed of a new mood today, its emotional landscape slipping over the borders of history and time. How viscerally wrong it feels for this place to be so silent and still when it was built to be the centre of all things – a tower and a palace, a prison and a symbol of power. I felt that it should be brimming with life, and I could almost taste its resentment at the feeble way we moved within it. A family of mice when we should have been lions, while the lions were outside the gates.

"Why did you come here, Vladimir?"

He shifted so that I was bracketed by his body, his arm leaning on the stone balustrade at my side. "I was curious. I wanted to meet the people who had stolen sleep from the world."

"And now that you have?"

"I will help you to return it."

My heart was pounding and I tilted my head up so that I could see the underside of his jaw. "How will you do that?"

A smile touched his lips. "Perhaps I will sleep on it."

A DREAM OF THE
IN-BETWEEN

When I opened my eyes, I was standing on a cold, arid land pockmarked by skeletal trees. The landscape, even the sky, was wreathed in a peculiar fog, and ahead of me was a wide black river flowing soundlessly to the west. At its side crouched Vladimir, dressed in a flowing dark robe that reminded me of nothing so much as the water. I wasn't surprised to find myself in dreams, nor that I felt so lucid. I sat beside him, and he tilted his head just enough to assure me that he knew I was there.

"Where are we?" I asked him.

"You are dreaming."

"I know that." In profile, I could see only one side of his face. "You're real, though, aren't you?"

"Reality exists only inside our own minds. We can trust only our thoughts to be true, and even then they may lead us astray."

I suspected that I'd get no more answer than that.

"Where are we?" I asked again.

"We are in a memory of mine, somewhere long ago."

I drew my attention away from him and forced myself to look. There was a lack of sound, not even wind or the noises of birds or animals. The word *becalmed* came to me, and I thought of us as two ships drifting on an ocean. Poppies wreathed the trees, growing like fungus into the bark. There was a mountain on the horizon, little more than a distant black smudge, and it was towards this that the water was flowing.

As my eyes grew accustomed to the murky light, I noticed other figures surrounding us, mere spectres standing and swaying as though caught in an absent breeze. I stared at the ethereal body of the one closest to us, naked, while the odd shifting light moved through him, sometimes rendering him invisible except for a shimmering in the air.

"What are they?" I asked.

"They're people."

"Like us?"

Vladimir turned towards me. "Would you say that we're the same, then?"

I shook my head.

"It doesn't bother you as much as it once did," he said. "The thought that I'm an aberration."

"I'm beginning to think we're all aberrations. Maybe that isn't such a terrible thing."

He turned back to the water. "If only you'd understood that before."

I didn't answer, instead rearranging myself so that I was sitting rather than crouching. I let my gaze drift up from the water, so black that I couldn't pick out a reflection in it, and watched instead the various shades milling around the banks. They didn't move, except I thought that perhaps they were crying.

"They are sleepers," Vladimir said at last. "Though not entirely."

I looked down at my hands, real and solid although I was undoubtedly asleep.

"They can't cross over fully."

"You trapped them," Vladimir said.

"Does that make you angry?"

"Yes."

He trailed his fingers over the surface of the water and a flower bloomed beneath them. A yellow chrysanthemum stark against the darkness.

"I'm sorry," I said.

"I know."

He scooped the flower out, water slipping through his fingers, and cradled it in the palm of his hand.

"What does it mean?"

He sighed. "It means death."

Perhaps it was where we were, or perhaps it was because a part of me believed that it was what I deserved, but the statement didn't shock me. I reached towards the bloom, damp and luscious in his palm, and he withdrew the hand that held it and caught my wrist sharply with the other. "Do not."

"Isn't that why you came to the Tower?" I asked. "To punish us?"

Everywhere his hand touched mine flared with heat. "Yes."

"Why haven't you, then?"

"I haven't given you a chance for redemption yet."

He crushed the petals in his fingers, and the image of the dream world, if that was what it was, dissolved like smoke and vanished.

10TH OCTOBER

Henrietta Lacks was a mother of five. She grew up picking tobacco and always kept her nails beautifully painted. A piece of her body was taken and it turned out to be a miracle, but although it was a miracle, like all bodies hers still died.

Henrietta Lacks has been dead now for over a century, but I can still touch her ancestral cells with my hands. I can still make them live.

The HeLa cells from Subject 001 rejuvenate in response to Vladimir's blood. The matrix not only holds but grows. I called the Professor into the lab to discuss the results, and I think in the hope that he would ease my fears.

"We still need to test the matrix on cells that haven't been exposed to the effects of the chip," I warned him.

"Yes, yes, that's obvious, but this is one of the last hurdles overcome. We are nearly there, Thea. So close that we might taste it." He was possessed by an energy that felt dangerous, and as he peered through the microscope something inside me curled up and hid.

"Tell me something first," I said. "Were you serious before, about keeping the chips operational?"

He sighed, his breath wheezing and his gaze growing distant, and under the laboratory lights he looked older than I'd ever known him.

"Perhaps it is a fool's hope," he said. "To you, young and hale as you are, no doubt it feels monstrous to extend life by these means." He shook his head, smiling, and I felt that same pull I'd always felt towards him, accompanied by a wave of sickness.

"I'm an old man, Thea. The majority of my life is behind me, and yet my mind feels as clear and productive as ever. Perhaps even more so, now that I begin to imagine the future tolling of the bell. I look at this world, broken and empty, and I think that I still want to be a part of it. I still believe in my ability to contribute to it as it is now, and in its restoration in the future. And then I think of losing dear Cassius so soon, and I wonder... Would things have been different, had he been able to stay?"

"Cassius was too far gone, Michael," I said. "Even for the neuralchips."

"Was he? Or could he have changed everything?" He sighed again, shoulders hunched over the table, staring down into the Petri dishes and the blood. "Death is such a final thing. Once we pass into it, we forsake our hold on this world absolutely. It's a failure of imagination, but I cannot conceive of a world in which I no longer influence anything, where my nonexistence allows it to continue, perhaps even further into destruction, just as dear Cassius's death did. Perhaps so much death, the world being so empty, prompts me to give us more importance than we'd otherwise have had?" He shook his head and looked away. "Our lives seem to matter so much more now that I realise so few of us are left. It was arrogance that led us to this place. We ought to have built an override into the chip, but now that we know that, can we abandon the work entirely? Is this not the point of science, to identify the flaws and fix them?"

I wasn't sure what to say, but I needn't have worried. Michael wasn't done.

"What is science, if not a journey from the imperfect towards the more perfect? We ride the stormy seas in the hope of producing calm. Is that not so?"

"That isn't where you're heading though," I said. "You're taking us somewhere beyond the boundaries of the map."

"We're already off the map, Thea. Perhaps in this instance, the only way out is through."

14TH OCTOBER

Why, at the onset of hope, do I feel so much fear? I have begun to ready myself and Mother for escape. This morning, before dawn, when the cold was as harsh as deep winter and the moon hidden behind the clouds, I crept from our home and made my way to the side of the engine room and the door at the base of the eastern wall. Under a pile of rocks arranged like a cairn, there was a key, and I used it to slip outside and prayed that Edgar's creatures were still under his control.

Thane had once taught us all to shoot, and I fingered the gun at my belt while in the other arm I carried a box and a rucksack on my back. From the Tower, there was a mud track down the hill towards the open concrete paths that were once the riverside thoroughfare. It was there I paused, aware that crossing into the open at night was perhaps the stupidest thing I'd done yet. But there was little choice – the boat needed to be supplied and I couldn't trust Alex any longer, he being as infected by hope as the rest of them. I stepped quickly, not trusting the sound of my running footsteps, the hairs on the back of my neck raised and my heart pounding with the awareness that each step might be my last.

Eventually I reached the shore, and took a moment to

marvel at the sight of the water so close, the sound and smell of it amplified by my long absence. For a second, I seriously contemplated continuing on, walking away from this place and into the open mouth of the city to see how far I could get. I didn't, of course, instead taking a set of stairs to the dock, where the moored boats bobbed at high tide.

The one I wanted was a sleek white motorboat, a pleasure cruiser for the rich. I suspected it had once belonged to the Anonymous Donor, due to how closely it resided and the surprisingly good condition it was in. As I eased myself onto the deck, I thought I might find him hiding here, eating the food Alex had stored for me, wrapped in one of the blankets I'd pilfered to keep Mother warm.

I froze in the darkness, one hand on the door, letting my rucksack and box slip to the wooden deck while I stood on the threshold, torn. I drew the key from around my neck, slipped it into the lock with barely a sound, and waited. I'm still not sure whether I'd hoped to find him or wished that he'd simply vanished, but when I opened the door only darkness and emptiness greeted me.

I didn't turn on the light for fear of the glow being seen. In the light of my torch, everything was as I'd specified: canned goods stacked on shelves, blankets arranged in piles, boxes of fuel and whatever else I thought we might need. The box I was carrying – I thought, perhaps, the last – contained medical supplies and clothes, and the rucksack held more of the same. I stored them carefully and sat down on the cot I'd procured for Mother. Opposite, there was a shelf of weaponry – guns and a knife – along with some bindings.

What a world we've made to live in.

I'm still unsure if this contingency is an act of hope or one of hopelessness, or whether or not I truly believe we could survive anywhere else. Still, sitting there in the dark, I almost wished to have an excuse to turn the ignition and sail away, heading for the distant horizon and the Eden Alex still believes exists. The sky was beginning to lighten in shades of grey and dreary gauze when I finally roused myself, locked the door behind me, and left.

In the blue-black gloom, I wasn't surprised to see a shadow waiting for me on the stretch of concrete between the river and the Tower. I think a part of me even hoped he'd be there.

"Abandoning ship, Doctor Chares?"

I walked towards him, no longer afraid. "You only call me Doctor when you're unhappy with me."

"Then it is a wonder I've ever called you anything else."

I came to a stop in front of Vladimir, craning my neck to look into his face, and saw only collections of shadows in the bones of his expression.

"You don't recoil from me as you ought to recoil from a monster," he said.

"You aren't dangerous to me."

"Is that all a monster is, an encounter with the dangerous? Are you not scared I might contaminate you?"

"How could you contaminate me?"

"With my strangeness," he murmured. "My aberration. My influence. Or, perhaps, my touch."

He raised his palm to my cheek, not touching, merely waiting for me to move. Around us, in the whispering dark, I thought I could feel eyes watching from the shadows. There was a magnetism in the air and it hummed through my body. I leant closer, so close that I could feel the movement of air between his hand and my skin, and all the while my eyes were locked on the darkness in his.

There is a yearning within me, to relinquish control and sink into oblivion. To cease. I felt that draw then, the need to give myself up to a force greater than myself and be subsumed. I closed the distance between us. His palm was hot against my skin, and I imagined I could feel my blood rising like steam to meet him.

"Do you trust me, Doctor Chares?"

"As much as I trust myself."

His fingers curled, slipping backwards, cradling my neck. I felt the scrape of his too-long nails pass over the tender skin beneath my ear and my pulse jumped. He leant closer, so close that we were sharing the same breath, and still neither of us blinked. Beneath his dark regard I was helpless.

"This is dangerous, Thea. You haven't made your choice."

I hadn't, and he was right, but also, wasn't this in itself a choice? Standing so close to oblivion with his claws at my neck? I pushed myself onto my toes, closing the distance between us, but something changed in him, the flicker of humanity turning hard and strangeness rising like a tide. His gaze snapped up, focused on a point behind my left shoulder, and the lines of his body turned rigid.

"Go back inside, Doctor Chares, and don't look back."

The quality of his tension terrified me, and I didn't even consider disobeying. Something was behind me, that much was clear, and the space between where I stood and safety seemed vast. The first step was almost impossible, but I felt that if Vladimir had it in his power he would protect me – and what a strange certainty to hold. The next few steps came more easily, and at the door I turned to see a creature standing across the way.

She was a child, and my first thought was that children were exempt from the chips. They hadn't been tested on bodies still growing, and for a moment I forgot my fear in a wave of incandescent anger. Then, though, her features resolved, and I realised that she was a teenager, perhaps only just eighteen when she'd had the machinery implanted. She was a slip of a thing, dirty matted hair in wild tangles around an emaciated face. Her clothes were stained and ragged, torn almost entirely from her body so that a single muddied breast spilled over the material. An almost maternal instinct overwhelmed me, and I wanted to cover her up, drape a blanket about her shoulders and hide her nakedness from the world.

"Go inside, Thea," Vladimir repeated. "You can do nothing here."

I couldn't deny him, and as I closed the door behind me a terrible scream split the air. I braced myself for Thane to begin firing from Lanthorn, but over agonising seconds nothing happened. As I stared around the compound and the sound of shrieking burnt adrenaline down my spine, I understood why.

The Tower was eerily quiet. No one stirred and the battlements were empty. The goats were deep in slumber and there were insects curled up in the flowers. They too slept, as did the ravens on the walls.

It was only I and the monsters awake in the whole of the desolate world.

20TH OCTOBER

"You were foolish to go out there alone."

"I wasn't alone."

"And if you had been?"

"I would have died."

Vladimir and I were sitting on the battlements, I in the last of the winter sun and he in a corner of shadow.

"Does your death mean so little to you, even now?"

I didn't answer.

"You've become too used to self-sacrifice, Doctor Chares. It has made you reckless."

"Surely self-sacrifice is a good thing."

"Not when it becomes selfish."

"Isn't that an oxymoron?"

"No."

I watched the ravens coast like dark shadows on the air, and I waited.

"Do you think that if you sacrifice enough you will find absolution?" he asked. "If you hurt yourself enough, deny yourself enough, you might be redeemed for the choices you've made?"

"Isn't that how it works? An apology isn't good enough for forgiveness. An apology without change is a lie. Restitution is the only path to absolution."

"Self-sacrifice isn't the same as restitution," he said. "What good is it to anyone that you suffer? What point would your death serve, except to leave this place at the mercy of those who would destroy it?"

"The people here aren't destructive."

"Edgar and your Professor are."

"Not the Professor," I said. "He wants to create."

"An act of creation in one area can destroy something in another. How often human creation has come at the expense of earthly destruction."

"By that logic, every invention is an act of destruction."

"And every attempt at redemption is not always selfless."

I sighed and turned to face him, although I could hardly make out his features in the shadows. "What is it you want to say, Vladimir? What should I see that I don't?"

"Restitution requires sacrifice for the good of someone else, not for the intent to self-harm, and even then it doesn't wipe the slate clean. Goodness is not a simple tally. You cannot commit great evil in one arena and have it washed away by an act of great goodness in another. No matter what you do here, the stain of your earlier actions will remain." He frowned and held my gaze. "There are no scales to be balanced, no input of good and bad that will return you to a neutral setting. You will not be made holier by whatever comes next. Your atonement cannot be for yourself but for the world. You will not be thanked, nor cleansed. Why, then, punish yourself when it only reveals that you haven't removed yourself from the central importance of the story?"

I could hear the rush of blood, loud in my ears, as though I were nothing more than a funnel for the ocean draining through me.

"You aren't important to what comes next, Doctor Chares. Only the world around you matters. So, you must ask yourself, are these actions you take a sacrifice for humanity or for yourself? Be honest about the choices you're making and why. Is your self-sacrifice for them, or is it a mistaken attempt to wipe yourself free of blame?"

He stood, and I leant heavily against the balustrade and sank against the stone. He hesitated and I closed my eyes, awaiting a final blow. Instead, his lips brushed against my hair, and I could have been no more devastated had he hit me.

"What do I do?" I asked. "What can one person do?"

I should have realised as I spoke that despair was a sin as well.

22ND OCTOBER

The Tower is changing, becoming smaller, more contained. It's almost a physical thing, this encroachment into our bodies and minds. Around our perimeter, the Sleepless are gathering, held under Edgar's control. They do nothing except watch, held in thrall, but the threat is within them all the same.

The ravens are leaving this place, and I cannot bear to be on the battlements. I cannot watch the farthest shore. I am compressed, brought down to the ground with everyone else while the walls rise higher around us. I have begun to look inwards instead, and here I find true cause to fear. In Dolly's obsession with the few birds that still remain, her screaming when they ignore her. In Miles picking heedlessly at his scars as though he might peel them away.

In Helen, who is beatific and vulnerable, abundant and ready to birth. In Alison's presence at her side, which has always been protective but now carries a shimmer of violence. In Maryam, because Maryam is afraid, I think, and I don't know what form that fear might take.

I believe that I'm afraid as well. Afraid and losing sleep.

The Tower is changing. It's beginning to hum like a generator, a vibration I can feel beneath the soles of my feet.

24TH OCTOBER

I found Michael in the lab, where he was peering through a microscope at my work on the subject's cells.

"The healing holds," I said, "but we don't have any unaltered samples to test."

"But it *is* holding. It's a shame. If only we could build this into a larger brain, we could see how the areas might talk to each other again."

"I have a question," I said haltingly. "You were talking before about a cure without turning the neuralchips off."

"And you thought it was a monstrous idea."

"I still think it could be monstrous. But what does it look like to you? What kind of society do you see if we manage to keep the chips on?"

He gave me his full attention. It had been such a long time since we'd talked together like this that I felt nostalgia while it was happening.

"I see a world in which we're free to nurture the mind, released from the trap of managing the body," he said eventually. "I see a society in which only the limits of our imagination prevent us from living and creating in the ways we see fit. I see the body relegated to its position as a servant of the will and not an enemy of it." He sighed. "I see freedom, Thea. Don't you?"

I raised my eyes heavenwards and tried to consider what he was envisioning free of all personal bias – which is, of course, impossible.

I've always had a complicated relationship with the body, which is to say I've never enjoyed living in one. A body is a tool, ignorable until it demands something, reliable up until the very moment it isn't. I've always been gently surprised when I recall that people don't see me as I see myself, because I simply don't see myself at all. My opinions, my desires, my strengths and weaknesses aren't filtered through the lens of my body. To myself I am but a mind in control of a vessel, but to everyone else I am Thea who lives in the body of Thea – woman treated as woman; odd communicator treated as odd.

My mother, too, I see as a part of her body as well as trapped within it. Before, when she was in control, she was a vibrant personality, as bright and persuasive as the moon. Afterwards, she was no longer vibrant, no longer persuasive, no longer self-assured. Yet who am I to say that of her? Inside her own mind, she may still be all of these things. But for the accident of her body, she would remain undimmed.

What, then, is the body but a vessel for the mind? Is it right that we should be limited by it? Is it not monstrous to constrain ourselves when there might be another way? I looked at the Professor, and the light in his eyes was as hypnotic and enticing as it had always been.

"You once told me that there was no such thing as the scientific mind, and nor was there a creative mind," I said.

"Indeed. There are only our personalities and the choices we make."

I nodded. "But some choices are made more freely than others. If you find a way to do this, to make humanity – the body of humanity – function like a vessel, then what about the people who don't want it?"

His brow furrowed and he regarded me with consideration. "Every new invention has created a group of haves and have-nots," he said.

It sounded weak to my ears.

"But has every advancement created an underclass?" I pressed. "Could you – could *I* – trust in these chips when they've malfunctioned so badly already? Would any of us here feel comfortable using one? If not, what happens then?"

"Isn't that what this research is for?" he replied. "To perfect the technology that will help humanity to progress?"

"Nothing is foolproof, Michael. Visions of utopia should always be taken with a pinch of salt."

"But utopia should always be striven for."

I swallowed and looked away. "But utopia for who? Have you thought about that?"

Later, I would ask this question of myself again, in private and without the need to consider his feelings. My opposing position had come naturally to me, but only because I was so used to being his sounding board; he has always wanted me to argue an opposing point. But did I actually believe in it, or was I simply falling into old patterns? Becoming the devil's advocate when none was needed? A barrier to progress?

The problem is that I'm tantalised by the idea of a society built around the mind. It suits my personality to believe that my body is not me, that my body is a container only, that whatever deficiencies I might have are perceived only in the eyes of beholders and not inherent within me. And, of course, a cure has always been my aim.

But a cure for what? A cure for Mother's illness, yes, but illness is not the same as divergence, is not the same as individuality. Suffering that comes from within should be alleviated, but does the body have to be broken to fit the world, or should the world bend to fit the body? Am I becoming Einstein and Oppenheimer again?

Before, there was an excuse, a naivety within myself that I hadn't excised. We were curing desperately ill people, and if the rich – at first – wanted to pay for the chips for themselves, surely that was their choice. But it didn't stop there. Michael is right that each new technology has created haves and have-nots – those with access to a phone and those without; those who had the internet and those who didn't.

The creation of a techno class had started long before the malfunction. Workers let go because they had to sleep, job adverts that specified that people without the chips need not apply. Protests about bodily autonomy, the Right to Rest, the overreach of the Orex Corp, whose technology was not only within homes but inside minds, a forcible melding of man and machine.

I must apply these principles now. We could rescue humanity and change them. Mandate, through their very existence, that we must all acquire the chips or else become an underclass within our own society. Would that be progress or subjugation? Can it not be both?

The Professor, I fear, has gone too far. *We* went too far, and took the manipulation of medicine to heights that ought not have been reached for. In this, Cassius saw through us, though I didn't recognise it then. I thought of Maryam and her wheelchair, and a conversation with her long ago in which she'd asked me to consider where the root of suffering lay.

"For your mother," she'd said, very kindly, "it came from within. Hers is a sickness that kept her from living, compounded by a medical system that didn't lift a finger to help her."

That sounded right to me.

"Mine though, beta, it comes primarily from outside. From a world of stairs and staring. Let the world bend just a little, let it believe in the truth that a human doesn't need two functioning legs to be human, and let it adapt accordingly. My suffering, such as it is, would be ended. Why, then, ought I to rage at my body when instead I could change the world?"

Maryam had given me a truth I hadn't yet seen – that the problem wasn't in the abnormal but in the distress.

Be wary, then, of the root of suffering. Seek it out, determine where the heart of it lies. That is what we should be doing. And I fear – no, I *know* – that in this the Professor is wrong. The chips are not a cure. No panacea comes from them. There will be no utopia forthcoming in the world he wants to create.

28TH OCTOBER

Night in the Tower, followed by nightmares of ravens and blue eyes and my Grey Lady and Mother dead in the bed. Then insomnia, and the sense again that I was being compressed inside a crucible, the walls around us a constriction on a boiling pot. I was unsettled, and left my room in search of the Professor, who was once more keeping odd hours now that his great cure was in sight.

There was a lamp lit at Lanthorn and Thane's silhouette looked over the walls. I thought that perhaps he should turn and look inwards instead, for the monsters were here after all.

The White Tower was dark and seemed deserted, but I felt that I wasn't the only one inside. I slipped up the stairs, creeping although I didn't know why. I walked across the ancient floorboards, between the imposing wooden beams, inside the stones of a Conqueror as though any of us could belong here. The laboratory door was open and nothing moved within, but some instinct I couldn't account for drew me inside, and there I found the darkness I'd sensed.

It's unsettling how repeat contact with a situation inoculates you against its strangeness. I've worked in this lab many times and it's always looked like a simple laboratory to me. Yet on seeing it with fresh eyes, it took on a grotesque horror. The sterile microscopes, machinery, and bright lights couldn't hide the gore. The walls were lined with jars of human remains – Subject 001 split into slices, packaged, and put on display.

Vladimir's blood was a stark point of red against the white, and the evidence of our vivisection couldn't be ignored. I stared at all of the labels – *001: nerve samples*, *001: brainstem*, *Vlad: haemoglobin* – and then a different set of handwriting caught my eye. Packed behind the others, on a shelf hidden at first glance, was a selection of specimens I'd never seen before.

AD: Glial cells.

My mind rebelled, even as the words condemned me with their silence.

AD. The Anonymous Donor.

The man in the 22nd Tower.

I reeled back, almost knocking a line of Petri dishes onto the floor in my effort to get away. The lights were too bright, their fluorescence providing nowhere for me to hide. Everywhere I looked there was the evidence of our depravity. Humanity split, spliced, piled into jars. Humanity dead, murdered, and done for. At the very edge of my perception I heard voices, and an almighty terror took me. It seemed obvious that if I were caught here, I wouldn't leave. I ran, stumbling out of the light and into the darkness. My eyes, no longer dark-adapted, struggled to make out the corridor, and I slipped behind a pillar and hid.

They came down the stairs, Edgar light-footed and the Professor stepping heavily, his breath wheezing gently in his chest. At first their voices were just a murmur, and then they gained sense.

"The problem is longevity," the Professor was saying. "The samples from AD prove that the usual degeneration of the cells doesn't occur, but how can we anticipate whether or not they'd retain rationality?"

They passed by me, hidden in the dark, and I thought, *There is no rationality here. We've passed the point of the rational and what's here is lunacy.*

At the door, Edgar turned back, and I thought for one wild second that he could see me, or perhaps even smell me – that after everything, he wasn't so human after all. Then he turned and closed the door behind him, leaving me in the dark.

My instinct was to run, but the darkness was impenetrable. I stepped slowly, my feet reaching into the void, somehow always grateful and surprised when I found the floor beneath me. I knew that at any moment I could be discovered. All it would take would be for the door to open and the light to flood in for me to be caught in its spotlight, and then... what? What did I fear would happen?

The corridor remained dark, and I crept down the stairs and out into the moonlight, into the rotten milk of midnight in the Tower, and I ran.

I ran to my home and locked the door behind me, chest heaving in the hallway – dry, empty, arid – and still I did not feel safe. As if in a dream, sleepwalking to my fate, I entered Mother's room and an overwhelming madness gripped me. Shame at my complicity, terror at my sameness – the recognition of my own evil, perhaps – brought me to what came next. I wanted to be purged, cleansed, distanced from the murder that had taken place here. Troy was falling. How long had it been falling for?

I tore open the curtains, spilling a curdled moonglow over

the inside of Mother's tomb, and she contorted – seeking to hide or be consumed, I didn't know. I flung the window open, my mind so far from peace I might have been a war within myself. I stood there, framed in the window, and I called softly for Vladimir, hoping he wouldn't hear but knowing that he would. Then I stumbled back, fell to the floor, and set my back against the wall to await him.

He didn't keep me waiting long. He appeared in the window, a silhouette against the falling moon, having leapt from the ground and perched there like a raven. A portent in the shape of a man.

"Will you invite me in?"

I nodded and he stepped elegantly inside. The room seemed small then, no longer the cavernous space holding a single secret within, but a cell too cramped and black for what I knew must come next.

"Have the scales fallen from your eyes? Do you see truth, or are you still cowering in the dark?"

I did not, could not, *would* not answer him. He turned from me and stood at the foot of Mother's bed. She raised her eyes towards him and became absolutely still. They held each other's attention, communication passing between them that was beyond my comprehension.

"So, this is where you keep your secret heart," he said softly. "The love that rots at the centre of everything you do." He tilted his head, still silhouetted in the pool of the moon. "Tell me, Thea, do you see her? Or have you blinded yourself to her state? In your mind's eye, is she the mother you knew or the person she is? When was the last time you looked?"

I had risen to my feet before I was conscious of having done so. He extended his hand to me, beckoning pale in the darkness.

"Come. Stand with me, and tell me what you see."

I could no more have refused him than I could have willed my heart to stop beating. I went, inexorably, pitiably, and I stood in his place and felt him press against my back.

"Look."

I did. I looked, first at her feet, pulsing with motion, the nails grown long and hard into black and sharpened points. I looked higher, at the thick rope and shining handcuffs that chained her ankles to the bed. My gaze traversed her thin and unblemished legs, to where her nightdress hid her body from sight. At her chest I paused and tried to turn away, but Vladimir's hands caught me from behind, cradling my head, holding it in place.

"No," I pleaded.

"*Look*."

His voice rang, polyphonic, a command impossible to ignore. I trailed my gaze up, passing over her head to where her wrists were bound and bloody above her. Then and only then did I gaze into her face. Sharp cheekbones when I'd known them to be soft. Teeth bared in an animal snarl between lips that should have been gentle with laughter. Teeth – too many, and too sharp. Until finally I came to her eyes. No longer hazel, no longer flecked with gold, but instead as blue as the sky, as cold as the ocean, as monstrous as the creature that hides beneath the bed. My mother, Sleepless and restrained.

Hot tears welled in my eyes and spilled down my cheeks and onto Vladimir's hands.

"Is she a monster, Thea?"

"I don't *know*." The words tore from me, an answer and a question in one.

"Is this how you imagined her? Is this what you envisaged when you placed yourself in the position of her saviour?"

I tried to shake my head, but he held me fast, and instead a horrible burbling sound escaped me, snot and tears bursting across my face.

"Tell me how she became this way," Vladimir said at my ear. "Tell me how you came to keep a monster in the bed."

My chest heaved with a dry rasping sound and I thought the word again: *Arid*. My insides a desert at last.

"It worked," I bit out. "She was well."

And I will say now that I was right. This was no lie. I moved her into the Tower when all of this began. She was not in the first round of fittings, nor even in the second. At the twentieth, when we'd seen the chip's effects on people with all manner of diseases, I'd come to her bedroom – to this very room, looking much as it does now – and I'd told her, *I think I can make you better.*

She was so far from the ability to communicate by then, tube-fed and bereft of language, but over the course of several weeks I asked her questions to which she returned yes or no answers with her eyes, and we agreed that it was time. On a cold bright Friday in September, almost a year after Cassius's passing, we wheeled her into surgery and the Professor conducted the operation himself. He was the only one I'd let touch her, while I paced in the courtyard and Maryam attempted to calm me with offers of gardening that I refused.

In the sixth hour, I left my post and stood on the battlements above Traitors' Gate, and I looked at the whole heaving city of London going about its business, heedless and unknowing of the importance of this day, and I thought, *This is what it's for. If she can walk out and join these people, all of this will have coalesced into its ultimate purpose.*

I was still standing there, watching tourists flock and flit and shivering in the chill, when the Professor came to find me.

"It was a success. Now all we must do is wait."

We didn't have to wait long. She slept intensely, one might even say greedily, even after the anaesthetic had worn off. For three days she was unconscious, and I would have been worried were it not for the vital signs that told me I'd won.

The thready pulse evened out. The erratic beat of her heart, which had oscillated through bradycardia and tachycardia for years, became regular. The tube feed was actually being absorbed and her breaths no longer rattled. The constant tremor in her limbs ceased. For the first time in years, she was still. On the third day, when she opened her eyes, the first thing she did was smile.

"It worked," I told Vladimir.

On the fourth day, she sat up. On the seventh, she stood. And on the ninth, I came downstairs to find her sitting at the kitchen table, staring down at the coffee in her hands and crying.

"I never thought I'd do this again," she told me. "And now I'm sitting here, crying over coffee."

I laughed, and I was crying too, and we clung to each other and wept and laughed and wept again until the coffee had grown cold. She held me, smelling as she always did – smelling, somehow, of the sea – and she thanked me, over and over again:

Thank you, sweetheart. Thank you, my brave, brilliant girl.

"How did you feel when she recovered?" Vladimir asked. "What happened to you then?"

I sobbed. "Weightless. Untethered. Like the world had opened up again."

"And now?"

I made an awful, animal sound, still struggling to turn my head away. Mother's jaws snapped. She snarled. Spittle flew from her mouth and all of her hatred was focused on me. What could I say to him? That I felt as brittle as a plaster cast and as weighted as a stone, or else she the millstone at my neck and I desperately struggling to keep my head above water. That every inch of me resented her and adored her while some part of me, locked away even from myself, wanted to peel off my skin, cut lines into my wrists, and condemn myself for everything that had brought us here.

How could I tell him that I was not a person – hadn't been a person for so long that I'd forgotten what it felt like to be one – but that instead I was an insect? A horrible, writhing grub, crushed beneath the weight of the cold and distant moon?

"I feel like a carapace," I whispered. "There's nothing left inside."

He sucked in a breath at my ear, and finally his hands relaxed their grip and I slumped forwards, drained.

"You are truthful at last."

He slipped from me like a shadow, crossing the room to stand at Mother's head, and I stared at my hands and wondered how they could appear so clean. When I looked up, he was unfastening the buttons at his sleeve, methodically rolling it up to reveal a pale expanse of skin.

"It's time for this to end."

He extended his arm to Mother and an electric terror lit up my bones. I screamed and launched myself between them, vision blurred with tears, pushing him as far back as I could and out of the reach of her snapping jaw. It was like trying to uproot a mountain.

"You must allow me to give her peace, Thea." He looked at me with pity. "To give it to both of you."

"I won't let you kill her."

He moved so quickly I hardly noticed it. In one fluid movement, I was turned away from the bed, his hands clamped at the top of my arms.

"Is death so much worse than the living hell you've confined her to?"

"It wasn't me who confined her!" I screamed back, my voice ragged, guttural. "Everyone abandoned her. The entire world. Doctors, friends, family. They left her in the dark. They didn't believe her. She suffered for decades and *still* no one would help!" I was breathing so heavily, tears choking me so thickly that I feared I would vomit or fall unconscious. "I was the only one left to care. The only one who thought she deserved to be cared for. The only one who tried to help."

"And is this still help, Doctor Chares? At what point did her saviour become her tormentor after all? At what point did you condemn her the same way everyone else did?"

I wheeled away from him, my hands planted flat on the wall, holding myself up while grief rocked through me.

"You still don't see, do you?" he asked. "You still don't see that the world altered your aims and you let it."

"What are you talking about?"

"You began this as a search for a treatment. A cure. And then Doctor Hope and Professor Galen changed your intent and led you into the realms of the monstrous, and you never thought to stop it."

My chest heaved. "I won't be like the rest of them. I won't abandon her like they did. They left her to *rot*."

When I turned back again, Vladimir was at my front, his hands once more holding me in place.

"It was wrong that she was abandoned," he said, very gently. "It was an injustice that she was left to suffer."

I closed my eyes, and his lips brushed my forehead and lingered there.

"It was wrong that you both were left without help."

I twined my fingers through his shirt and hung on, tears still dripping down my face.

"But this is no longer an act of care. Can you honestly say that it is?"

"If I can save her, if I can undo this–"

"And how do you propose to do that? If you turn off the chips, she may still die. If you let her drink from my body, a similar chance exists.'

My fingernails dug into his skin. I closed my eyes. I couldn't speak.

"When will you wake up from this delusion you've built for yourself? Would you remove her from the realm of the human to save her? Use my blood to make her Sleepless forever?"

"If she could live, if she could live…"

Vladimir made a disgusted sound and turned from me, pacing like an animal across the room. "And what kind of a life would you condemn her to?" he demanded. "After all of this time, you still have no idea what you did. You still don't comprehend what you stole from humanity."

I leant against the wall, my legs weak, trembling. Mother was growling, snapping up from the bed.

"So tell me," I whispered. "Tell me what I should know."

"You know the answer, Thea!" he shouted, and it was the first time I'd ever known him to raise his voice. "Not just sleep, but *rest*. Sleep. Rest. Freedom. They are the same things. Those who would steal your rest would steal the very soul from within you. The means by which you exist as an autonomous creature. The means by which you become more than a machine, more than a mere organism, but an individual capable of *life*."

He scoffed, running his hands through his hair as though he might pull it out at the root.

"Sleep, those little slices of death," he sneered. "No. Sleep, those little slices of *life*. Life that nourishes. Life that restores. Life that can be touched by no person other than the one at rest. You would take that from her, from all of them. And what then? You saw what the world did the first time. You cannot accumulate your waking hours with no regard for what you're losing. You would steal the very personhood from a person, and then deride them for becoming inhuman."

He fell still suddenly, his mouth snapping closed.

"You stole humanity from the world. You experiment on these people. You tear them apart to determine what they are, but you do not listen to what they *say*. Have you ever asked what they're screaming for?"

He was there again in front of me, so quickly that I hadn't seen him move.

"Would you like to know what they're screaming for, Doctor Chares? Shall I show you?"

I drew in a ragged breath. "Show me."

Quick as a snake, his hand shot out and pressed flat to the centre of my forehead. All I knew then was pain. The pain and the sound and the fury. And the despair.

It shot into me like a poison, a virus. Like air. It crackled along nerves I'd never known I had, tearing away the concept of blood and bone and skin. There was no end to me and no beginning. I was borderless. A Möbius strip. An ouroboros of matter, connected to everything yet lacking a body to connect with. It's impossible for a mind to contain so much and not to break. I felt my self – that is, my sense of self – break down and be obliterated. In its place, I saw out of a million, a hundred million eyes. I thought with a hundred million thoughts. Screamed with their mouths and writhed with their pains.

They were hopeless, bereft of hope, desiccated with its lack. They were themselves and they were also each other, and so they'd become nobody. They thought of rest yet they couldn't rest. Their bodies were strong and yet they spasmed in pain. They contained immense power but they were shut off from its control. They were starving and pitiable and monstrous. They screamed, and it was a cry of anger-revenge-desperation-despair-misery-REST. I thought that I must die. I, the thinking I, was subsumed.

We must die. We must rest. We must live. We help we help us we can't we must we should help us–

It ended suddenly. Vladimir's palm left my head, and I heard the echo of my own voice ricochet around the room. Mother was still screaming, and I realised that we had twin screams. I couldn't think. My throat was raw. I was on my knees, yet I could hardly conceive of myself as a person. I was crying, I think. I was still making noise. Mother's lament rang in my head. I could do nothing.

I must have fainted, for the next thing I knew I was lying in the corridor and Vladimir was closing the door behind us and shutting out her cries. I could barely lift my head and still less decipher the look on his face. His expression was closed to me and I fell into it.

"You have played at it for years," he said. "But now you know what it truly means to be a god."

I couldn't speak. Could hardly move. I thought that he might leave me there, piled in a heap on the floor. Instead, he bent and lifted me into his arms, then carried me down the stairs and into the living room, where he sat me in a corner of the sofa.

I felt as if I were in a dream. Still part of the chattering-yammering-screaming-pleading that would forever haunt my mind. Vladimir sat beside me, and I stared blankly at the wall while the strike of a match and the scent of burning filled the room. With great effort I turned my head. He'd taken his opium pipe out of his pocket and its smoke was curling into the air.

"Here. This will help."

The pipe hovered by my face. "That's a fire hazard," I said. "God forbid."

He held it to my lips, a match with its flame held steady in his other hand, and I sucked at the mouthpiece until my tongue was coated in a caustic, bitter taste and the world tilted sideways. I slipped down like a slug, vaguely aware that he'd rearranged my legs over his lap while my head lolled heavy on the arm of the sofa.

In the periphery of my vision, I saw the strike of a new flame, and the pungent smoke sailed in a veil around us as he drew more deeply and his head fell back against the cushion. My body grew heavy, and I sank further into my own bones, back into my skin, irrefutably mine. I thought that I could hear echoes of the Sleepless, but they were distant, like a memory of a song heard when you were young.

My vision blurred and a great upswell of horrendous euphoria lifted me like a cloud from within. I let out a strangled laugh, then another. Then I was laughing so hard my shoulders shook, my mouth and throat dry and raw, and the terrible hysteria echoing through the room. I couldn't move. I felt as though I were paralysed, and in the midst of my happiness I felt terror.

Vladimir anchored me, pressing his hand hard to the top of my leg, bearing me down, reminding me that I was solid. "Take another," he said, as if from a great distance.

The pipe was held to my lips again, and I sucked the noxious smoke into my lungs, and sank. Reality broke down around me, though I couldn't say how it happened. I thought I was awake; although my eyes had closed, I could still see the room. Vladimir's face loomed large at my side, and I saw in him time like a physical thing. A colour, a wave of colours without name. He was drenched in it. It filled him and moved through him. He was made of light.

I dragged my gaze away, and images rose before me as though my dreams were seeping into the material world. My Grey Lady rose first, though she was less a thing of fear now with my mind so fogged by the drug. She paced the room, drifting, and I felt that she wanted me to follow her.

Next came a parade of ghosts between the walls, conversing in a crowd, as though the room were a train station or meeting hall. Some were dressed in ancient clothes, others I vaguely recognised, as though I'd passed them on the street as a child and had never quite forgotten the angles of their face. They spoke to each other, and I was gripped by the horror of being overlooked. I tried to open my mouth and ask them to look at me, to acknowledge me, but I couldn't make a sound. I felt, then, that I was missing out on something vital, that if I could only hear them, I would have answers. It frustrated me to the point of torment, and tears trickled uselessly from my eyes.

Time passed interminably. I couldn't tell how long. A second. A minute. A lifetime.

Then the ghosts simply faded away. The room was quiet. I could see Vladimir sleeping at my side, his hands still holding my legs. Everything was silent, and I felt as though I were rising to lucidity again, though my body still refused to move. It was pleasant. Relaxing. I listened to Vladimir breathe and to the steady thrum of my own heartbeat. I heard the birds outside, the wind, and for a second the distant noise of music and cars, which I dismissed as hallucinatory.

In this state, I would have been quite content to drift forever, were it not for a persistent scratching from the walls. Though I couldn't move, I was able to direct my attention to the other side of the room, where the maddening sound was coming from. A bird trapped in the drywall, I thought, or else a family of mice in the gaps.

I wanted to get up and check, but couldn't. My eyes drifted, and the subtle patterns in the wallpaper began to make shapes, to mutate into peculiar fractals that were an unexpected pleasure to watch. They melted into each other, forming fabulous and eccentric patterns that I tried to follow with my eyes as they tracked up onto the ceiling, but inevitably I lost all sense of them and returned again to the centre. I was quite content to stay in this state. I felt, in fact, that this was a sort of pleasant purgatory. That I'd always been here, and whatever memories I had of my life before were a dream.

Eventually, though, the peace began to collapse. I tried to hold onto it, to rationalise around the sudden unease that warmed the base of my ribs. I focused harder on the wall, but the patterns that had seemed so beautiful now began to pulse with sinister energy. The scratching became louder, overlaid with a deep throbbing pulse. It seemed as though mine and Vladimir's breaths synchronised, and the walls breathed in and out in time with us. The pattern collapsed, gaining weight and depth, a beating shadow in the centre of the wall. I thought to myself, *The house has a heart, and if it has a heart then it has a stomach and if it has a stomach then it has a mouth and if it has a mouth then I have been swallowed.*

I wanted to scream, shout, take hold of Vladimir and run, but he was still immobile and my limbs wouldn't move. Instead, I watched the pattern become a shadow, become a heart, become a mouth, and then a silhouette in the shape of a person. The shape of the Grey Lady. The shape of my mother. She unfolded herself from her curled position, unfurling until she stood behind the wallpaper, and the scratching I knew was from her fingernails clawing inside the wall.

She pressed her palms flat, looking out at me, and then she began to creep. Slowly she walked, hunch-backed, suspicious, circling the room. I tried to follow her with my eyes, but she rounded the bend and disappeared behind me. I was taken by an astounding fear, certain that she would emerge into the room while my back was turned, but then she appeared again. Round and around she went, in and out the walls breathed, and it seemed as though this would go on forever. A frozen moment beyond the decay of time.

Gradually, I came to see that she'd left a scored line in her wake, splitting the wall into two halves. With each repetition the mark grew clearer, and I thought, *She is tearing the home's monstrous heart in two*. I tried again to move but couldn't. I tried again to scream but didn't make a sound.

Then, terror. She stopped, and in front of me she dug her claws into a weak point in the wall, pulling out chunks of plaster and stone that fell to the ground. She gripped at the masonry, snarling, snapping, and forced her head through. I was immobilised and could only watch in sublime horror as she emerged, head-first like a birth, her shoulders and body forming a sinuous, foetal mass as she dripped onto the ground. She raised her head. She looked directly at me, and I knew then that I would die.

and with each quickening step the fever grew in them and around them and through them, and how many of them there were, burning time burning rest burning bodies, burning their bodies and other people's bodies and the body of the earth as well, and maybe in the end we were not God-forsaken but self-forsaken, forsaken by ourselves and to ourselves and becoming liars knowing only of ourselves, and in my mind there are sparks falling from the sky and burning in the streets, and the fog is not a shroud but a final curtain that the will-o'-the-wisp at Lanthorn scatters to the winds with its eternal tempting fire

NOVEMBER

Death came for me and I resisted it, just as death had come for Mother and I'd resisted it for her too. But I am not unchanged by the experience. Their screaming persists in the back of my mind, like an echo rebounding against bone, and my body wants to move in new configurations. I find myself creeping, stooping my shoulders and bending towards the earth, my hands clenching and fingers twitching, wishing for claws with which to score a line around the Tower's walls. It frightens me that I might want to bring us to our knees.

In the deep dusk and the darkness before dawn, I believed I saw my Grey Lady poised like a statue in the landscape, ethereal and waterlogged. First she was on the far shore, little more than a watery silhouette whose features I knew intimately. Next she walked across the river, slipping and sliding and all of her limbs juddering, until she stood on the concrete path and waited to be let in.

During the day, I've seen her following at Thane's back, pawing at the weapons in his belt and whispering into his ear. I've watched his eyes glaze over and his hand twitch to his gun, and found Dolly and Miles staring blankly at the gates as though in some kind of trance. But her effects are more noticeable on the Professor and Edgar, who are growing larger and more substantial each day. They cornered me, came upon me in the night, and while they spoke of victory and new worlds I found myself tongueing the edge of my teeth.

"Are you all right, dear Thea? You seem a little out of sorts."

I smiled, just in case they could see the Lady in my eyes. "Oh, I'm fine. Better than fine. You don't need to worry about me."

I think that this is true. I'm no longer worried about myself. I'm even beginning to worry less about Mother, though I feel that Vladimir is waiting for my choice.

I see him almost as often as my Lady, but his attention is a deeper and darker thing. I am drawn to it, pulled like a feather into a black hole.

What will happen when I descend?

Today I met Maryam in the courtyard and there was nothing I could say. A group of us were there in the morning light, and I followed their gaze to the centre of the compound, between the greenhouses, beneath the White Tower's shadow, to Maryam.

"Did you know?" Miles screamed. "Did you know?"

I followed them to Maryam, who was standing out of her chair. To Maryam, who took three fluid steps into the weak sunlight. To Maryam, whose expression was a marble mask. To Maryam, whose head was shaved, a stark incision healing across her skull. To Maryam, whose eyes were a bright and Sleepless blue. To Maryam, who waited in the centre of the Tower of London, cured, whole, and unbroken.

Absolutely perfect.

* * *

Was I asleep? Was this creature sinking in the dark bathwater awake, alive, or dead? There were two bright strips of white meat bobbing beneath the water, two knees bent and jutting like icebergs. They were mine, I thought, but there was some distance between us that I couldn't breach. I was split off from myself, annexed and exiled, and the wiggling grubs that had been my toes bent and flexed at the porcelain.

What portion of time had I entered, anyway? What flow of cause-and-effect-and-cause was carrying me along? I tried to cast myself back to the moment of Maryam but found that the shape of the day was as malleable as clay. Let me tell you about horror, I said to myself, and my self refused to answer. Let me tell you about horror, because horror isn't a jump-scare or a step missed on the stairs. It isn't monsters howling through the night or the screams of someone you love heard through a locked door.

Horror is the loss of control, when the world exerts its power on us whether we want it to or not. Horror was seeing Maryam and knowing that she must have fought to avoid her fate and then been overpowered. Shame was knowing that I'd been complicit from the start.

So, what am I really telling you about horror? Horror is a revelation arrived at far too late.

I said her name. "Maryam?"

I said her name more than once, and only when I was screaming it did she deign to look into my face.

"*Maryam?*"

"No."

She leapt twenty feet to the top of the White Tower, and

she was a creature in grief. It's difficult to describe how it felt to watch her, the beauty and the horror of it. The grace and the monstrosity woven so closely together that they were inseparable from one another. She stalked across the balustrades, testing her body, examining what it could do. Then she took a running leap to the top of the Bell Tower and coiled there like a serpent. There she stayed, and there my Grey Lady joined her.

"Go away," I said. "I don't believe in you so go away."

My voice echoed off the tiles and the Lady didn't go away. I wiggled the grubs at the end of my feet and bobbed my icebergs up and down, and my fingers were fragrant tentacles floating in the void. I would not turn my head to look at her.

"You aren't real anyway, so I don't have to do what you say."

It's true that I haven't been sleeping. I can't remember the last time I laid me down to rest. But when I think about sleep, I think about the incision like a mouth on Maryam's head, and the smile like a surgical scar on the Professor's lips, and the red ring like a chain around Vladimir's teeth, and the bloodied chains like a judgement around Mother's wrists. I think about the laboratory and its clean white lights, and the bed where we cut up our subject and the bed where we drained Vladimir and the bed where they murdered the man in the Tower and the bed where they violated Maryam and the bed where what was once human was stripped for parts and unravelled.

I think of the bloody rags on the tiles on the day of Not-Maryam, and her hair – her grey, beautiful hair – scattered in strips on the floor in the nest of her discarded niqab. She never wanted this, but I knew who did want it, and I tried not to know it but couldn't, just as I tried to stop the panic spilling like oil between the Tower's breathing walls and couldn't. I saw Dolly only recently, I think, kneeling in the centre of the courtyard and wringing a raven's neck. She was gone, I realised. Gone somewhere beyond, to a place where the tearing of flesh beneath painted fingernails was a savage and brutal joy.

What came next? Images of fear seen through the shattered glass of a two-way mirror. The Professor under the microscope, dispensing words like scripture and creating damnation with each one.

"I need not die, Thea. This growth in my chest need not be the end of me, nor mortality the end of us all. Cassius couldn't see it, but I have always known. Life itself is a form of decay. It is what it has always been. We are born, and from the very moment we're born, we are dying. Until now. There is a cure, right here in the Tower. You need only implant it in me."

"You're placing me in the position of your executioner."

"I'm placing you in the position of my saviour. Isn't that what you've always wanted?"

The glass shattered and broken on the floor. The Professor mortal and dying. The whisper, the whisper of my Grey Lady into my ear, urging me to look back on the day Cassius died and tear the haze of love from my eyes.

"I won't."

How I have come to find comfort in the gentle sloshing of the water as the carapace forms around me and my skin takes on the quality of dead meat. I haven't closed my eyes in a long time, but I still find the capacity to dream. I dream about Helen of Troy and the men who fought to free her, and in my dreams they are all of them liars, because in the battle for Troy Helen need never have existed. She was nothing more than an extension of the men who desired her, a symbol of the things they aspired to but were not. They didn't fight for her love or her honour or her person; they waged war to retrieve a piece of themselves that had been stolen. There is no greater imperative than that.

Vladimir was dark and beautiful in my bed.

"Is that why you came here?" I asked him. "To retrieve a part of yourself?"

"Of course. Is that why you wanted to save your mother?"

Perhaps. But perhaps she had become Theseus's ship after all, and perhaps I should have let her sail on before I drowned us both in the tide. This tide that is all around me and softening me into meat.

Meat has no need for memory, but I must know whether or not he was in my bed or if I was merely dreaming. I seem to remember him waiting for me beneath the black poplar trees on a night when a child was born and the blood of birth was a siren song that called the monsters to our walls.

"You aren't celebrating, Doctor Chares."

"Are you?"

"All new life should be celebrated, just as all new life should be grieved."

"And what are you grieving for?"

"Disappointment," he murmured. "Dissatisfaction, disturbance, heartbreak. Suffering, pain, and helplessness and sorrow."

"Then what is there to celebrate?"

"Existence."

I remember the weight of a clawed hand on my jaw.

"We need more than to merely exist," I said.

"That's why we make space to dream."

I must have been dreaming, because I remember another who caught us there, bound to each other's mouths, and the glob of spit that arced from his lips and spattered across my cheek.

"He isn't even *human*."

I wanted to tell him that neither was I.

"I've waited for you. I've taken care of you. I've known you were weird and distant and aloof, and I've overlooked that because I thought there was someone good hiding behind it."

But I didn't want to be overlooked. I didn't want there to be pieces of me discarded just so that Alex could pretend I was someone else. I'm not good, not wholly, and I don't think I ever was.

I have always loved what I thought would make me better. What form this betterment might take, and who might be the judge of my improvement, I have never known. I don't know if this love has made me better, but it was real, I think. The slide of skin on skin. The heat of him and the terror and the bliss of being taken and becalmed.

I sank, shattered, gave up and gave in, and I thought that if this was what other people meant by desire then I didn't know how they could stand it.

Did I ever give Alison the key?

There is blood in the water in the dark but it doesn't belong to me. There is the sound of Edgar's army of Sleepless throwing themselves at the walls. There is a woman standing in the corner and a Leviathan in the tub, and Vladimir perched like a carrion crow with gore dripping from his mouth. Was it a punishment or an act of mercy to have me succumb to him?

I am dreaming, I said to him. I am dreaming of the beach back home, eerie with absence and silence. The sea is becalmed and the clouds are an endless grey as smooth as the water, the sand dark and damp with fresh rainfall. There's no pier, no walkway, no rows of beachfront houses, and no road. There's only the fog, thick as a mountain and rolling up to the summit, which is even more grey than the sky. My stomach is swollen.

Something is shifting beneath my clothes, and my skin is rippling and ripe enough to burst. You are standing, watching me, but you don't answer when I call your name. Pain is coming, pain the likes of which I've never felt before. It overwhelms me and I'm on my back, staring up at the sea-sky, my body a blinding point of bright white hurt, tugging up from my hips and roaring down my spine. I am as naked as a babe, and there are hands and claws tearing from between my legs, pulling me apart like a membrane. Obliterating me like sunlight on cloud.

I am screaming, and the creature hauls itself from inside me and writhes like an abortion on the sand. It is my mother, drenched in my blood, the placental sac tearing behind her and her eyes the blue of a newborn. My body is weak, torn apart, and when I try to crawl away the umbilical cord tightens and binds us together. Mother flies to me, her claws raking at my breasts and her teeth snapping wildly, needing – like all new births – to feed.

Then she is gone from me, and you are crouching between us. One of your hands is pressing Mother to the ground and the other is a caress upon my leg. You bend your head and place the cord between your teeth. I am staring into your eyes when you bare your fangs and bite.

* * *

"Thea," he said quite softly. "It's time for you to wake up."

I see her. I see her with her tentacle fingers and her
iceberg knees and her squirming grubs and her mouths-
mouths-mouths so many sucking mouths that I think she
must be a creature made of screams or else of hunger and
if she is that then she is a creature made of teeth and I am
afraid of her, afraid of the sharp bite of her many mouths
and her wide unblinking eyes that hold within them the
void and all of the light and the hope and the terror that
the world can't bear to feel.

Who is she? Who is this woman sleepwalking out of
the bath and into the dark, spilling shame like a brimming
chalice over the splintered tiles? She feels familiar, just
like the song she's humming

London's burning

so I watch her from the corner and I try to tell her

London's burning

that she needs to sleep but she says she doesn't believe
in me and so she doesn't need to do what I say, and there
is a man who is the beginning of life and the creation of
life and he has been denied life by her and by them and
by everyone else who doesn't understand that it's time to

fetch the engines

end the day at last, and I can't help but watch her even
as the ending now comes, slowly and then all at once.
She is drifting down the corridor leaving wet footprints
in her wake, and in their reflection there are two sharp
eyes that watch and see everything and are as irresistible

as gravity and the orbits of the planets around the sun. She is being followed.

fetch the engines

by a predator and a protector and a lover and the monster that hides in the comfort of the bed and whispers of peace and nightmares and an ever-circling song of mind and matter that breathes us all into sleep.

Fire!

She is leaving, and her skin is hard and splitting and the life inside her is roiling with maggots and decay and the febrile pulse of a mycelial system straining to be set free, set free like the monsters inside the walls

Fire!

as the kind woman with springs in her legs and machinery in her flesh draws open the gates and from the gullet of the braying horse the horde finally descends. The moon crashes out of a window on the first floor, bloody and screaming at the day, at this unnatural and terrible day that will not end even though it is night, and her pain is a burning spark of starlight

Fire!

but she is beyond the stars and the screaming, beyond the howls of the mantis-man whose flesh is being torn into shreds, whose blood is spilling control over the stone and into the earth and whose life is feeding the plants that drink him up and smack their petals in pleasure

Fire!

because she is no longer a rock in a stream around which the world bends and mutates, but an ice-floe woman hurtling into the ancient tower and down the hill of progress, and if she makes a choice here

pour on water

if she chooses to destroy it, tearing at metal and circuits and networks as the lights flicker out and the mushroom cloud is sucked back, back through time and space and into her lungs, smouldering,

pour on water

will she be redeemed?

If she chooses instead to keep it and birth something new, like the first creature taking the first breath and never knowing what kind of life will come next, will she be condemned? And if she believes that there's a chance they might do better after all, if she believes that mistakes are not a circle incapable of being broken but a sequence of branches growing from one eternal seed, then I hope it brings her peace when only one question remains:

What kind of a monster is she, this woman at the end?

so the world writhes and burns and it's no one's fault but our own, because we cannot outsource wickedness to the devil and goodness to a god when all actions are taken by us, and each spark that we struck was a choice and each body that was lit and changed and abandoned was a choice, and now we meet ourselves back where we are and have always been, standing inside the inferno of disaster and not knowing that we've already fallen into the fools' fire where we burn and burn and cry out for something better and something more, and our cries fall on ears that won't hear and our words are swallowed by mouths that won't speak and the gnawing fear rises that we've done harm after all, and that hope may be a burning and a scouring of the soul

ACKNOWLEDGEMENTS

Sitting down to write these a few months before publication feels both surreal and strange. Surreal, because a part of me can't quite believe that one day readers will be holding a book I haven't yet held myself, and strange, because no doubt by then there will be far more people to thank who simply missed the cut-off point for being included.

Knowing that I'll inevitably leave someone important out, then, extravagant thanks to my agent, Caro Clarke, who swept in to save me when I was floundering out of my depth. Also to the entire team at Angry Robot who've worked so hard on this book, and in particular to the marketing and publicity Dream Team that is Caroline Lambe and Amy Portsmouth, Sarah O'Flaherty for the most gorgeous cover, and to my editors Desola Coker and Simon Spanton.

Desola, for saving me from the Great Capital Letter Debacle of 2024, and Simon for falling for this story so quickly that he carried it off to an acquisition meeting before I was even certain it was worth a second glance. I'm not sure Awakened could have found a better champion, and I will be forever grateful!

Thanks, too, to my copy editor Alan Heal and proof reader Dan Hanks, who smoothed the edges of my words into something far shinier. And to Hayley Webster, my first reader and editor who took this book so quickly to her heart and made me brave enough to start sharing it.

As ever, there are too many people who deserve thanks merely for existing and allowing me to be their friend.

So, to Threadbear: Abbey Bursack, Anastasia Eulalia Campos, Alex Monks, Bethan Ratcliffe, Briony Anthony, Chloe Christian, Dan Turner, Jess Waller, Matt Till, Katy Robinson, Lewis and Lydia Dareheath, Liz Johnson, Nathan Spencer, and Waleed Arshad — thank you for being the best people in the world. Particular thanks go to Stuart Gresham, who read the opening section of Awakened almost as many times as me, and continued to care about it even when I was wailing like a banshee that it would never be right.

To Rebecca Menys, Joanna Joyce, Pippa Kelly, Lucy Stones, and Bekki Young, thank you for being here forever and hopefully for many years beyond.

To Ceriann Bailey-Rush and Rebecca Hughes for being here and understanding it all.

To Hattie Hofton and "Mr Bob" Heron, for always being around when I'm well enough to venture out — and to everyone at The Hallamshire House for making it the best place to venture out to.

To my dear Bumfriends: Kate Hargreaves, Misha Anker, and Melinda Salisbury, for being a constant source of fun and support, and with particular thanks to Gemma Varnon who read Awakened when it was still just a baby. You made sharing it much less terrifying.

To all of the authors and friends who've lent their quotes to this book. There will be more of you by the time anyone reads this, but for now: Amy Clarkin, Lucy Rose, Lucie

McKnight Hardy, Lyndsey Croal, Caroline Hardaker, MK Hardy, Cailean Steed, Verity Holloway, and anyone who just missed out on being included in the acknowledgements but has since said nice things: you've all been amazing!

To everyone at Queen of the Suburbs and Chapter One for keeping me well-caffeinated during the writing of this book, and to everyone at Novel Sheffield, both for the caffeine and the books.

To all of the many English teachers who encouraged me when I was far younger and much more precocious, but in particular to Sarah Jarvis and Louis Blois, who bear the dubious honour of getting me to university many years ago when it seemed very unlikely to me.

To my family: my mum Claire and step-dad Graham, for putting up with me and loving me as well. To my brother Michael, for always believing I would one day publish a book. In memory of my grandpa Alan Richards, who wrote one first, and to my grandma Evelyn Richards, who won't remember that I did but who always thought that I would.

And, of course, to my partner James. Thank you for being my favourite person in the world, and for loving me and taking care of me even when it's difficult.

Finally, with thanks to and deep admiration for the disabled and postviral communities, campaigners, and activists around the world, whether we know each other or not. The heart of *Awakened* belongs to you.

To anyone who feels that they deserve to be on this list but hasn't been included, my deepest apologies. Please feel free to add me to your secret list of enemies even though I'll never know.

ABOUT THE AUTHOR

Laura Elliott is a disabled writer and journalist, originally from Scunthorpe. Her work has been published by *The Guardian*, *ByLine Times*, *Boudicca Press*, *Monstrous Regiment*, Hachette Kids, and others. She lives in Sheffield with her partner, James, and their two feline overseers, Catticus Finch and Hercule Purrot.

~

Something solid drives through my gut, like a wall of water, and I'm a ghost. Split down the middle.

No... a human knot, plummeting down rocks and bony roots until I hit earth. My head cracks against something sharp and my skull splits, from my ear to the nape of my neck. Something like smoke pours out, but wet and warm. It curls up and around my face in a red veil. The earth licks and holds me still like a great wet tongue.

All is quiet. For a moment, all is quiet.

But from the silence, a shrill ringing builds in my ears. A scream, like an eagle testing the sky. Like I'm inside a brass bell. Trying to shift my joints is like bending the branches of a tree, so I push into the mud, sending feelers out to understand the state I'm in. Count my body parts, one, two, three. Grass tickles inside my left ear. My right palm rests on a rock, slippery and black. My jumper is twisted and pulls against my throat. Burnt orange knit, little brass sparrow button, splattered with black. My head throbs, and the hollow twists and weaves like the ocean.

There's no time.

Light flashes through my fringe. *Too long. Why didn't I shave it close, in case I had to run?* I brush it from my eyes and smear a clod of cold mud across my forehead. Behind and above, something delicate snaps and a shower of pebbles tumble down the crag face into the ditch.

They're here.

I turn my face into the earth and force every muscle to move. Every bone screams as I rise. Little details embedded in the earth are floating from side to side – pebbles, dangling bracken, my fingers in the soil, as if there's a lag behind my eyes. I cover my face with my hands, and when I pull them away, they're cupping blood. My palms are deeply lined, scored with pain. They look so old. When did I get so old? Why did I wait so long to run?

I retch into the ditch and my throat rips as easily as wet paper. All is red. This is worse than the ache; this is tissue tearing beyond repair. I grab my neck and make everything tight.

Pin it all closed, hold it together. I've made it this far. I can breathe. Move.

From my knees, I claw up the ladder of jutting roots. The black soil feels like clay. My legs drag uselessly behind, as if I'm a thick, sallow worm, heavy with water.

One, two, three more and I'm over the ledge. Rolling on my back, a lilac sky shifts behind swaying branches. *I can't lie here. I can't go back. It's too late. I've done too much.* And then, a whimper in the quietest part of me: *I never thought it'd be like this.*

I fight back a sob and push myself upright. Moving makes me gag, but I hold it down. Some long, deep breaths still the trembling forest. I scan the trees up by the cliff face for the two shadows, but whoever they've sent is either hiding or still too far up the mountain to see. I'd only caught a glimpse of them, dressed in faint grey, blending into the mist. Something was pinned to each of their chests, something that reminded me horribly of a timer.

Their eyes were black. Almost entirely black.

I must've fallen around thirty feet from the rocky ridge, but it's impossible to see the spot where I slipped. My stuff is gone – my yellow backpack, my kit, everything – either stuck up the crag or it's tumbled down further than me and out of sight. All is obscured by trees, standing so closely that their roots are in knots and their branches grapple for space between them.

Using a boulder as leverage, I scramble upright, but when I put my right foot down it won't take my weight. My ankle is hot and loose, as if all the bones are lost. Should it hurt? My trousers are heavy with mud, and a thick but uneven coat of moss has attached itself to the fabric. I try to knock it off, but it's stuck – as if I'm the stone each clump was born on. I prise the lumps off with my nails.

I need to get my foot going, so I test it on the ground again. It's then that I realise I'm wearing brown brogues, the type with serrated edges and little holes cut out from the leather. At least two sizes too large, the heel hangs away from my ankle, and the laces dangle undone, thick and slimy like wet black liquorice.

They aren't mine.

A second avalanche of stone comes rolling down the other side of the hollow, so I turn and lurch through the forest. The thin silver birches are densely packed, and I grasp them tightly to ease the weight on my leg. From there, I enter a crush of pines and my knitted jumper catches on the branches, but I press on, praying that I'm not leaving a hairy orange trail for them to follow. Here, the ground dips again, but this time I use my good leg to slide down the pass, using the roots to control my fall.

I must be sliding for miles. *How far down does the mountain slope?*

It's a long time before the ground starts to level out. Here the trees are plugged further apart, and through them I can make out a wide field of dry yellow grass, sticking up in short, round tufts like anemones. It's open ground and I might be seen, but I need to know where I am. I rub and squeeze my knees like my father used to do when he rose from his chair and needed to move quickly.

On my feet again, it takes a few tries before I find a branch long enough to hold me up, and I slowly creep out from the cover of leaves. I'm in a wide valley, split in half by a stream which froths white at the edges. At this side of the valley is the steep slope of white trees, and at the other is a range of tall brown crags, coated in dead brown grass like hair on a giant.

Being here is to shrink.

If I look along the valley, I can just about make out mounds of mauve veiled by mist. Hill and valley, repeated into the horizon.

Thank fuck. I've seen this before. The map Michael showed me, but never let me keep. Faded brown ley lines on a tea-stained sheet of paper, so old it felt like tissue. Like Bible pages in church, it had to be held with care and apprehension. Michael had let me touch it, even peer in close to memorize the route, but that was it. At the end of each lesson, he always rolled it back up in foam and locked it in the lowest drawer of his desk. It was too faint to even photocopy, but then something in Michael's eye told me that he wouldn't have allowed copies, even if I'd asked. He kept all the maps, the secrets, and the keys.

Michael had told me of the silence here in the valley. He said to me, "It's like the air is turned inside out." Already, I wish I could go back and tell him it's not like that at all. Write a research paper about it. Tease out the truth, that really, it's far more like being in an oil painting. The quiet comes from the absence of movement, of life. Each breath you take is the swill of a creaking ship, and you are electricity, bristling with noise. I clap softly, testing the sound.

Reassured for now that the two shadows must be still far above and seeking me in the trees, I step out into the open glen and dip my free hand into the water. It runs red, but soon it's glassy again. I plunge my other hand in and then lift the water to my face. Rubies drip from my chin. I wait for them to turn crystal before straightening up and searching left and right for my next steps. Michael's finger had traced a route along the valley with the crags on the right; I'm sure of that. Which would mean that here I should turn left.

I set off, trying to place a little more weight on my right ankle each time. It still feels strange and wet and hot, but I don't want to look at it. I have a feeling that if I inspect it, I might not want to hurry. If I tried to forget it, maybe I could move on quicker. Heal faster.

I carry on up the valley, careful to step in the brush and avoid the shining pebbles. My ears are open, listening for the slightest crack or creak from the white forest to my left, but Mothtown is silent, the breeze not even enough to rustle leaves. It's hard to believe it could ever have been a town, with its naked hills burning beneath the stars. It's wild twists of woodland. The loudest quiet. The only sounds are the light trickling of water on stone and the wet drag of denim on denim. The deep goose of the water is kind and easy on my eyes.

I had no idea the place would feel like this. Obviously I knew it was remote, but with that, I'd imagined the valley to be a host to wild things that loved the light of the sun but hid from people. But the sky was a wide grey blank, a dirty chalkboard with no clouds, no birds.

In one of our first lessons alone, I'd asked Michael if it was a town, as the name suggested. He sat back in his leather chair, brought his hands together in a steeple over his mop of gelled blonde curls and said, "No. If anyone ever lived there, they're long gone. No one's lived there for thousands of years. Anyone who did is now buried beneath a cairn. These days, Mothtown is home to a high population of native moths. Fluttering around in communities. Flutter… or flap – is that what moths do? These are rare ones, big and beautiful. The sort you don't see out in the open, or in places further south." Michael's eyes glared at the dirty cream lampshade on the ceiling. "I *believe* that's the reason."

The analytics in my mind clicked into gear. I wanted detail. "What sort of moths?"

"Why would that be important, Mr Porter?" Michael leaned forwards, his eyes small and squinting. "Besides, I've never been there. I haven't seen them myself. But no living man knows more about Mothtown than me, so my words are golden."

I imagine the crags to my right covered in sleeping grey moths, their markings blending with the cracks and crevices. But no – even I can see that it's bare, violent, dead rock, and little else. Not even a sprout or sprig of green. In fact, now that I'm here, there seems to be no life at all. Every time I take a breath, I'm stealing, and every time I release it, I'm polluting. The idea of being utterly alone had once invigorated me, but I'd never before imagined how it would feel to be completely surrounded by quiet. No, more than that. The complete absence of life. And in the stillness of the world, I bristled. Chaos.

Michael told me that nothing that stays here for long, survives. But that's OK, I don't plan to be here long. I can do this quickly. It's in my blood. My whole life has led to this moment.

Not too far ahead is a tall white stone, about twice my height. It's lodged in the middle of the stream so that the water runs around it in thin trickles. As I approach it, I realise that the lower third of the stone, so up to my stomach, is blotted with white paint. At first it looks like random streaks and splashes, but slowly the shapes become clear, and I see that the patterns aren't accidental at all. They're handprints. Hundreds of them, layers upon layers. I get close enough to reach across and press my trembling palm onto one. My metacarpals protrude through my skin. Did it always used to be so thin? The spread of my hand matches the upper levels of prints perfectly, but as I try the ones further down the stone, my hand covers two of the white shapes easily. They must be children.

How?

I close my eyes and see us as children, finger painting with mud, flicking little copper coins into a cup, and I struggle to catch my breath. My throat rubs raw with each gasp, so I try desperately to breathe slowly through my nose instead. This doesn't make sense. *Who were they?* This isn't a place for children. This is death's house. How would a child even get here? Michael wouldn't have sent children, no. That wouldn't be right. Someone that young – they could never make this choice. I trace one of the handprints with a stubby fingernail and discover that it's not actually paint. Whatever it is has permeated the stone over time. So perhaps they're from years ago, centuries perhaps, before Mothtown became what it is now? Yes. That would make sense. Maybe it was the native community here that originally found the door, and sent a message to the world that this was the way out?

Behind the standing stone, the stream forks to the left, back into the white forest, and to the right, slightly up and over a tight nest of stones. I force my mind back to Michael's map. On there, the stream was unbroken, and ran straight and true to the edge of the paper. It was as faint as everything else, but I'd traced it with a finger time and time again. The stream was the east to west compass. It didn't deviate.

Fuck.

Neither path seems right, but then again, I'm acutely aware that I'm standing in the open beside a focal point that could attract eyes from anywhere with an open view of the valley. I have to choose. I look up at the crags, jutting from the ground like teeth. The door is up there somewhere, and I'll be just as exposed on higher ground. If this is the quickest route up there, then it's the only way.

I limp across the narrow rivulets and squeeze through the stones, sometimes by sitting and swinging my legs over, and sometimes by sticking my branch in the gaps and pivoting over the most jagged. Luckily, the stones don't stretch far, and I can see the plateau where they break into a flatter stretch, where wild yellow grass with fluffy tops grows. It looks like it might reach past my shoulders.

Only a little bit further.

Michael had promised that once I reached Mothtown, it wouldn't take me long to navigate its hills and valleys to reach the door. The way out. Two days, at most. Perhaps I could even make it today, since I'd technically cut time by taking the faster, 'falling' route down through the woodland. My two shadows would have to turn back, return to their pale house with empty hands and dark eyes.

For the first time in as long as I can remember, my face breaks into a grin, before the ground falls away beneath me. I slide like a heavy stone into black water, and my head is sucked beneath the surface.